Midnight on Death Row

Mark Young

Funky Ink Press

ISBN: 978-0-9955676-8-9

CHAPTER ONE

The first time Jonas Calver had seen the girl she had been lying sprawled out in a shop doorway, and she had looked dead. It had been a freezing cold New York winters night with a light snow falling, shimmering in the car headlights, creating a kind of ethereal Christmas card look. He had approached the corpse like figure cautiously, rolling her onto her back, thinking it was going to be yet another derelict street drinker, but it hadn't been. It had been a young black girl barely out of her teens.

He had immediately been struck by her look. He could only describe it as angelic. And that impression had been accentuated by the light from the street lamp slanting across her face and hitting her dirty white headband, giving it the look of an improbable halo. As he'd studied her, wondering what to do, the corpses eyes had fluttered open.

'If you're tryin' to rob me or cop a feel, you're way too late,' she had said in a rasping whisper, her teeth chattering with cold, but her eyes had been bright.

Calver had wondered if she was faking it, just another clever way of begging. 'Hey, I thought you were dead. My mistake,' he had said, rising to his feet.

'Maybe I am.'

He looked at her again. 'Nah. You ain't dead,' he'd said. 'All you need is some hot coffee.'

'Make it whiskey?' she'd said, a question with an edge of desperation in it. He thought he recognized the yearning in her voice, but her words had been accompanied by such a beguiling smile that he had found himself nodding before he could stop himself. She caught it and managed a tired grin. 'Name's Anita. Anita Ritter,' she'd said, holding a frozen hand out.

Calver had looked at his watch. He'd had a really bad day in Manhattan criminal court. Mid-way through a hopeless trial with a crazy drug dealing client, a borderline psycho who refused to plead to anything even though he had no chance of getting a verdict, Calver had needed a drink. He had looked at the girl again. 'Why not,' he'd said.

He had lead her around the corner to a local Irish bar. Inside it had been Shamrock's, flags and Guinness, and nice and quiet and dark. She'd ordered a scotch straight up, no water, and then downed it like a sailor, then said, 'another, please.'

Calver had nodded at the barman. The guy had raised an enquiring eyebrow, then shrugged and poured a slug.

This time she had taken it more slowly, a sip at a time. When she'd finished, she had looked sated, like the drink had solved a shed-load of problems. Her eyes had been staring through him as she'd sipped away, her body trembling as the alcoholic glow spread, but then her eyes had come back into focus and she had seemed to see him for the first time.

'You shouldn't have woken me, you know, but thanks for the drink,' she said. 'I been thinking about Scott and Amundsen and the race for the South Pole. How you can just go to sleep in the snow and never wake up.'

'Why would you want to do that?'

'Well, if you lose the race, what's the point?'

'The race?'

She studied him. 'You look kind of slick. What d'you do? Real estate, Investment banking?'

'Lawyer.'

'Figures. God I hate lawyers.'

'Thanks.'

'Oh, not you,' she said. 'No, not you. You bought me whiskey.' She smiled, eyes dreamy as the drink kicked in. 'Mind you, back in the day, my family could have used a good lawyer.'

He realized it was a cliche as it passed through his mind, but when she smiled her whole face lit up like a glittering chandelier. 'How old are you?' he asked.

'Twenty two. You?'

'Hey, I bought the drink,' he said, signaling for another. 'So I don't have to answer. But tell me about this race and why you would want to go to sleep and not wake up?'

'You tell me something first,' she said when she had her drink. She looked pensive. 'You're a lawyer. How would you go about bringing down the biggest bank on Wall Street?'

'Legally?'

'We tried that. Didn't work.'

He looked contemplative for a moment, then said, 'Well, Nick Leeson did it in '95 when he took Barings down for a billion dollars in unauthorized trading.'

'Is that the only way?'

'I never really thought about it, but why would you want to?' he'd asked.

She had looked at him speculatively for a long moment, and then she said, 'because they destroyed my family, my parents. Just blew them away like they didn't exist; like they were nothing. They foreclosed on us, fucked us, took Dad's business as well. After the crash we sued, along with some other folks, and got fucked again. Oh, and along the way, they destroyed the world economy, then got rewarded and bailed out by their friends in Washington. That's why.' For a moment her eyes had burned with anger.

It was a common enough story, Calver knew. Millions of American lives ruined in the near apocalyptic financial crash of 2008, and no one held to account. And the consequences of that still rippled out in anger and resentment that never seemed to get a hearing, and the world now seemed to Calver like it was completely bat-shit crazy.

His face must have betrayed something of his feelings, because she said, 'you too, huh? It's history and done so lets move on, right?' She laughed bitterly. 'You know I did the occupy Wall Street gig in 2012. Didn't do nothing. Then I went out and bought a sandwich board and walked up and down front of the Bullshit bank with my sign saying they were all crooks, until New York's finest moved me on. I know, I'm crazy. We should just let it go, right?' she said. 'Well, that's just what I've done now. They beat us. We lost the race so why carry on?'

She sighed and looked at him obliquely. 'What's your name anyway?' she asked absently, like it was an afterthought.

'Jonas Calver.'

'Well, Jonas, cheers,' she said, finishing her drink and carefully placing the glass gently back on the table.

'Who are the Bullshit Bank?' he asked.

'Greenberg Metro,' she said. 'Corporate equivalent of Bernie Madoff.'

Calver nodded. 'GMB? CEO is—'

'Lloyd DeMasi,' she said. 'You know I once dreamed that terrorists would somehow target a missile on that annual economic forum at Davos when all those rich parasites are there. World would be a better place.'

'No doubt, but you can't go round killing everyone you don't like,' he'd said, looking at his watch again. 'One more for the road, then I got to go. You gonna be alright now? Can I get you a cab anywhere?'

'You get me another scotch and I'll be fine,' she said. 'Hey, you got a card or something? Case I need a lawyer sometime?'

'Sure,' he said reaching into his top pocket and handing her one.

She studied it carefully. 'Calver & Fedler. Who's Fedler, your girlfriend?' she'd asked, eying him up.

'Morganna's my law partner,' he said, a little stiffly. 'You got anyone I can call for you?'

'You could try my dad, but he's on death row.'

He'd glanced at her to check if she was joking, but all he could see was pain and sadness etched line by line into her face. She'd reached up and pulled the white halo headband off releasing a fountain of unruly tangled hair. 'Don't let me get maudlin,' she'd said.

Calver sighed, looked at his watch again - it was gone 11pm, but he had no one waiting up for him. He looked at the girl. She was hunched over now, looking down into her empty glass, her hair like a birds nest. He wanted to ask about her father, but if the guy was on death row, getting into that in her current state was only going to make her even more depressed. 'Look, you got anywhere to go to tonight?' he'd asked, coming to a quick decision. Then seeing her look, he quickly added, 'hey, I got a spare room. Just thought you could use a bed for the night.'

'As it happens, I could,' she'd said. 'Got chucked out my squat couple of days ago, and been on the street since. But I couldn't impose on you. Don't sweat it. I'm sure I'll find somewhere.'

'I insist,' Calver had said. 'Come on, lets go.'

She'd looked at him for a long moment, eyes indecisive. It had looked like she was ready to go with him, but then the moment seemed to pass and she'd smiled sadly and shook her head. 'Thank you, but no. I gotta go. And don't worry, I'll be alright now. It was good to talk to you,' she'd said, getting to her feet. She turned to go, but then hesitated, and turned back. 'Say, its nearly Christmas, and you've been real kind. I want you to take a picture of me, to remember me by.'

Calver smiled. 'Sure. Why not,' he'd said, eager to humor her and not break the mood. He'd taken his phone out and snapped a quick picture, and then he'd watched her leave, an irrational pang of regret gnawing away at him.

CHAPTER TWO

Five months later she called him out of the blue and he only took the call by chance. It was gone 10 pm and he was on his way out of the empty office. He'd stood for a moment, wavering, then sighed, dropped his bulging attache case on the floor and grabbed up the phone.

'Yeah,' he said abruptly.

There was silence for a couple of beats and he was about to hang up when a soft tentative voice enquired, 'is that Jonas? Jonas Calver? I know its kinda late….'

'Yeah. Who is it?' he asked.

'You probably wont remember me,' she said. 'The girl in the snow who you rescued and bought a couple of drinks for?'

'Anita?' he said, not sure of the voice at first as it sounded odd, disembodied. 'The girl who wants to kill all the bankers?'

'You remembered,' she chuckled. 'Look, I'm sorry to bother you but I'm in a bit of tight spot and I didn't know who else to turn to.'

'What is it?' he asked.

'I can't really talk on the phone,' she said, her voice sounding breathless. 'I've got something, and I know it sounds corny, but its big, and…..and I'm scared.'

Calver stood looking out of the window of his darkened office, the headlights from the cars on the street arcing like tracer beams across the darkness of the silent room, his mind floating, remembering the girl with the halo. 'What are you scared of, Anita? Is it about your father? You said he was on death row?' he asked, his mind parsing possibilities.

'No. Well, maybe,' she said. 'No, its to do with the bank.'

In the background, behind her voice, Calver heard a faint scraping sound like a door or a chair. She said hurriedly, 'look, I got to go. Meet me in the Irish bar in one hour.'

'I'll be there,' he said to a phone that was already dead.

Calver entered the bar sideways, holding his case against his thighs and squeezing past a tall statuesque blonde on high heels who tottered past him out onto the street. Inside it was dark, busy and noisy. There was a ball-game showing on a couple of big screens. Calver looked around and couldn't see Anita. He ordered a scotch and took a seat in a corner booth from where he could watch the door.

After an hour and three more drinks she still hadn't shown. He dug his cell-phone out and then realized he didn't know her number. He looked at his watch and ordered another scotch and went back to the booth and sat down. The crowd was starting to thin out now, the ball-game over. He re-ran the conversation with Anita, trying to analyze her words. She'd said she was in a tight spot, didn't know who to turn to, couldn't talk on the phone; she had something big, and she was scared. The big thing she had wasn't directly related to her father's case, it was about the bank.

The only thing he really knew about her was that she hated the banks and she had a father on death row, or said she did. So the quickest way of tracking her down might be through the law firm representing her father. He googled the name Ritter for inmates on Death row and found Floyd Ritter who was currently incarcerated in Tennessee, awaiting execution. He was represented by Minter, Rafflin and Coughlan, based in Nashville. He checked his watch. Too late to call them tonight. If she didn't turn up, he'd try them in the morning.

Next morning at one minute past nine Calver called the death row appellate lawyers. They were less than helpful but did reveal their client had a son and the best they could do would be to pass a message on to him.

The call came in at ten minutes past eleven just as Calver was sipping from a cup of scalding hot coffee, just the way he liked it. He leaned back in his chair. 'Put him through please, Hettie.'

'Mr. Calver, I'm Joel Ritter. My father's attorneys say you wish to speak with me urgently about my sister, Anita?' he said. The voice was quiet and Calver sensed a certain guardedness in the tone. Not unreasonable; having a father on death row tended to bring out all the crazies, so being cautious with an unknown caller was probably smart.

'That's right, Joel. I spoke to her last night, and she seemed scared about something. We agreed to meet an hour later, but she never showed. I don't have a number for her or an address and I'd just like to check that she's okay?'

'Well, if you know my sister at all well, Mr Calver, you'll know that that kind of behavior - disappearing and being uncontactable - is far from unusual,' he said.

Calver thought he could detect a slight hint of disapproval in the tone, but maybe he was imagining it. Phones did strange things to voice and nuance.

'I'm sure she'll turn up in due course,' he added. 'Now, if there's nothing else?'

'Okay, Joel,' Calver said quickly, anxious not to lose him. 'I understand you're not bothered, and you know her far better than I do, but I am a little worried. I know she was living in a squat somewhere at one time, but I don't have an address or phone number. If you can give me that, at least I can go and check she's alright? Otherwise I'd be thinking of lodging a missing persons report'

Calver held the phone, his grip tightening with tension as the silence on the other end lengthened.

'Bear with me,' Joel finally replied. Moments later, he said, 'phone number I had for her is dead. She left the squat but apparently she's still living on the Lower East Side.' He gave Calver the address, and then said, shortly, 'thank you for your concern Mr Calver. I'm sure its misplaced. Good day.'

Calver held the phone away, looking at it. 'Families, eh,' he muttered to himself. 'Who'd have them?'

Two hours later he stood outside a rather unprepossessing building. The place didn't seem to fit the street. It had an incongruous look, like a ghetto block from the 1970's, transposed to the modern day.

He pressed the big brass buzzer. A moment later a large woman opened the door. She had dark smudges under her over made up eyes and she carried a whiff of sour wine about her. She regarded Calver suspiciously. 'Yeah? What d'you want?' she said.

'I'm sorry to bother you madam,' he said, 'but I'm looking for a friend of mine and I'm told she lives here?'

She frowned. 'I ain't no madam, and this ain't that kind of place. Now beat it.'

She started to close the door, but Calver was too quick with his foot, shoving it into the closing gap. 'Look lady,' he said. 'A good friend of mine is missing, and before I call NYPD down on this shit-hole to search for her, I would like to know whether she's here. If she is, that's an end to the matter, and I can leave you in peace. So what d'you say?'

The woman hesitated, doubt and suspicion in her eyes.

Calver pulled a silver hip-flask out of his pocket and took a shot of vodka. 'You look like a woman who might enjoy a drink now and again. Maybe you'd care for one now?' he said, offering her the flask.

'Now you're talking,' the woman said, her face lighting up with a covetous smile as she grabbed the flask whilst letting the door swing open. She stood out on the front stoop and took a long pull, leaning her head back then wiping her lips. 'So who's this girl you're chasing? She in trouble?' she asked, raising the flask for another shot.

'No,' Calver said. 'No trouble. Her name's Anita Ritter.'

The woman shook her head. 'Don't know anyone of that name.'

'You own this place? Calver asked.

'Are you kidding me,' she laughed. 'I'm the janitor. Boss lets out a few roach infested apartments to poor Wall Street interns and charges them sky high rents.'

Calver watched her knock back another shot. He ruminated. He didn't think the woman was lying. He dug his cell phone out and scrolled through some images until he found the picture he was looking for. It was the one she'd asked him to take before she'd walked out the Irish bar. He held the phone out. 'That's her,' he said.

'That's not, what you say her name was?' she said, studying the image closely. 'No, that's Annie Rainer. Apartment 3, but she ain't here.'

'So where is she?'

'Its strange,' the woman said. 'The boss said she's gone away for six months but she's paid the rent up front. That's real odd. So her apartment's locked up waiting for her to come back.'

'When she go?'

'I dunno, I never saw much of her. She was out all the time working, I think.'

'Where?'

'I dunno that either, mister. Say, you ask an awful lot of questions about somebody you say was a close friend,' she said, suspicion starting to cloud her eyes again.

He held his hand out for the flask which she returned, empty. 'Well, I hadn't seen her in a while. Any chance I could take a look at her room?' he asked hopefully.

She shook her head. 'None. We don't allow that.'

Calver nodded, disappointed. 'I thought not. Well, thank you for your help,' he said.

The woman nodded before slamming the door.

As Calver walked away he had a bad feeling.

Back in his office he asked his secretary, Hettie to download and fill out a visitation form for Riverbend Max Security prison in Tennessee. The prisoner he wanted to see was death row inmate Floyd Ritter. Then he called Courtney Pascal, his investigator.

They met for a late lunch in the Irish bar around the corner from his office. He was already seated in his preferred corner booth when she arrived. He watched her approach across the bar. He never knew what to expect with Pascal, but the feline movement was still there, a kind of street grace. It was almost as if she displaced no air as she moved, like a shadow. She was slim and toned although you had to look to see the muscle, and she never seemed to age. She still looked like a young punk rocker; short spiky hair, pale almost translucently white face with large dark eyes. Today she wore a short cropped black leather biker jacket over a purple teeshirt, black jeans and soft mauve moccasin pumps.

'Calver,' she nodded as she slid into the seat. 'How you bin?'

'Still defending the bad guys,' he said. 'You look good.'

She nodded, ignoring the compliment. They ordered chili and a bottle of house red.

'So why we here?' she asked.

He told her about Anita Ritter. As he talked she ate, looking almost as if she wasn't listening. When she finished her chili, as he talked on, she played with some garlic bread, crunching the hard baked crust with her fingers until it eventually shattered and flew over the table in a thousand pieces.

'Jesus,' Calver said, pausing in his story. 'Why d'you always make such a mess? Its like taking a toddler out to lunch.'

She flicked a red chili bean at him. 'Lighten up, Calver. And carry on. I'm starting to get intrigued, always a good sign.'

He quickly told her about his visit to the dingy apartment block on the Lower East Side. Then they sat for a while without talking.

'What's with the brother?' she asked.

'Dunno. I haven't done any digging yet, but you know families. Always difficult to judge relations between siblings, 'cause there's always baggage going back years.'

'So what d'you want from me, Calver?'

'A favor.'

'I figured. What kind of favor?'

'I just want you to check out her apartment, and the fake name, Annie Rainer.'

'So, home invasion and B & E. Anything else?'

'Funny, hah hah,' Calver said. 'And I can't pay you either, that's why its a favor.'

'So you're not taking a fee, and you have no client? So why you doing it? And why should I put my ass on the line for a chick I don't even know?'

'You owe me,' he said quietly. 'Look,' he added quickly as he saw her eyes clouding with anger. 'This girl is special. I don't know why but she is. She touched something in me, and I think she's in trouble. She said as much on the phone. I just want to find out what's happened to her. And I shouldn't have said you owe me because you don't. You've repaid that debt many times over.'

She sat watching him, expressionless. 'So just what is this "debt" I owed you? I'd really like to know,' she said, voice low, which Calver knew was not a good sign. 'You represented me back in the day, in London, when I was barely out of my teens, on a murder charge. You were my lawyer and you were paid for what you did by the government under legal aid. So how is it that you think that that job you did for me created any kind of a debt to you?'

'It doesn't. I misspoke and I'm sorry,' he said. 'Look, Pascal, I'm asking for your help with this.'

The fire in Pascal's smoldering eyes began to fade. She sipped some wine. 'The father, on death row,' she said. 'What's that all about?'

Calver sighed. 'I don't know that either. I had a cursory look at the old news reports. Looks like it was a slam dunk murder case. Black guy gets convicted in Tennessee. Myriad incompetent lawyers hustling for a pay check whilst selling him down the river, and now he's on death row. The American dream. But I'm hoping to go down there so maybe I'll find out.'

'Your partner, Morganna, she cool with that?'

He didn't answer. She got up. 'Okay, Calver,' she said. 'I'll take a look, but I don't want to hear anymore of this, I owe you. Clear?'

'Crystal. And Pascal…'

'I know, "thanks".'

'No. Be careful.'

'Always.'

She left, as she came, like a shadow, and now he couldn't really tell if she had been there at all. He shook his head. He needed to cut down on the booze. He smiled to himself, thinking about Pascal and her selective memory. She had been in her early twenties and working as a stringer for British intelligence, MI5 when she had been charged with murdering her step-father. He had defended her at the Old Bailey and got the charges reduced to manslaughter; she'd got 6 years, out in 4. Okay, he had been paid by the government for defending her, but he had also given her a job when she got out, when no one else would. MI5 had dropped her like a hot stone when she was convicted. So maybe she had owed him, but he wasn't going to push it. In fact if you weighed it all up, since coming out to the States, given what she had done for him, it might be argued that it was him who owed her.

He got up, paid the tab and made for the door.

CHAPTER THREE

Pascal stopped and stood on the street corner watching the apartment block. The moon was full, bolstered by the neon signs and street lights, giving the grimy brown and gray urban landscape a kind of ghostly glow. There was still plenty of noise, cars chugging in the street, scraps of music, laughter, all shimmering through the still night air.

She glanced again at the alley to the side of the block. She had walked by three times in the last two hours, slowly focusing in on that aspect of the building. She hitched the small black rucksack up on her shoulder and moved off towards the dark opening.

From the front the building looked shabby, but down the side it was worse. The pointing on the brickwork was flaking and coming away and there were a couple of broken windows at street level but they were protected by iron bars inside. She moved further down the alley, the lights from the street starting to fade into the background. Looking up, studying the wall, there was another window there, this time unbroken, slightly ajar, with no bars inside. A drainpipe ran to the roof, but the pipe was about three meters from the window. Her eyes crawled over the wall. There was a ledge running under the window, around the building.

She moved to the drainpipe and tested it. It was old, cracked and moved slightly in its brackets when pulled. Looking around towards the lighted mouth of the alley, there were still people passing by intermittently, as the night wore down. She waited, stood against the wall, in the shadow, watching. As a last straggler walked across the mouth of the alley, she swung around onto the drainpipe, gripping it firmly with both hands and began to climb.

Her light weight made it easy to move fast. As her fingers grasped the ledge two things happened. There was a cracking sound as a bracket came away, the drainpipe swinging out from the wall; at the same time a window opened in the building opposite and light splayed out all around her. She froze, praying the pipe would hold. A man leaned out of the window and flicked a cigarette stub. Time stood still. Then the window slammed shut and the light extinguished, but as this happened the pipe made another cracking sound and dropped her a foot further down the wall, the whole thing straining against its moorings, about to collapse. She desperately stretched her fingers out towards the ledge, to her right, but couldn't reach it. Her fingers scrabbled at a crevice in the brickwork where the pointing had come out, and as her fingers closed around the edge of the brick, the pipe collapsed away from her with a crash. With the last of her strength, she lunged with her left hand for the ledge, and got her fingers onto it.

For a moment she clung to the wall waiting to be discovered, but nothing happened. With both hands gripping the ledge, it was possible to cautiously edge along it towards the window, with her body hanging down over the alleyway. At the window, she pulled herself up onto the sill and looked in.

There was a short corridor with numbered doors off it, a

threadbare carpet and a couple of old fire extinguishers affixed to the wall. The space was empty and quiet, dimly lit by a halogen bulb. She silently pushed the window open and clambered over the sill onto the floor and padded across the coarse stubble of the carpet to the room numbered 3. Ear against the door, listening intently - nothing.

Digging out her ring of picks and leaning down to study the lock, it was old and a cinch, open in less than 30 seconds. Slipping into the silent darkness and closing the door, she stood for a while acclimatising herself to the quiet night sounds. The room faced the street and a neon sign filtered a dim light through a scrappy curtain hanging in the window, illuminating the interior. The room was small and sparsely furnished. A sofa bed positioned against the wall, a freestanding wardrobe with mirror on the front, small chest of drawers and a table with a desktop computer on it. There was a small kitchenette leading off the room. Pascal guessed the girl shared a bathroom with others on the floor.

She moved into the room and opened the wardrobe. It was empty. In the chest of drawers she found some underwear and an old pair of jeans, looking like left-overs. In the kitchenette the fridge was switched off and empty. On a wall shelf there were a few cans as well as jars of coffee, sugar, tea, flour and then some smaller jars of spices. There was also a half empty bottle of scotch. She uncapped it and took a shot, running the liquid around her mouth and savoring its harsh bite.

Back into the room and over to the desktop computer. The table on which it sat had two drawers both of which were empty. She sat down in the desk chair and took another swig from the bottle. The computer was a pretty ancient Dell. Flicking it on, it buzzed and whirred into life and slowly booted-up.

When the screen settled down there were only two icons showing, one titled "Greenberg Metro Bank Employee Handbook", and the other, "Journal". Clicking on the journal icon, it wouldn't open and merely prompted her to enter a password. Clicking on the other icon, it did open. It contained a number of documents including a contract of employment that suggested that Annie Rainer had joined the Greenberg Metro Bank 5 months previously as a junior market trader.

Speed reading the document, it was mostly standard boilerplate text. Her eyes returned to the Journal icon. No time to try and crack the password, but she did have an old flash drive in her rucksack. Digging it out and plugging it into the back of the computer, when prompted she pressed the copy command. A dialog box opened showing progress. As it reached 98%, suddenly there were muffled voices outside, drawing closer to the door. As the copying hit 100%, she scrambled, hitting close, grabbing the drive and diving for the wardrobe, opening it and climbing in just as a key turned in the lock.

A male voice coming in said, 'here's twenty bucks for your trouble, lady. Now scram.' The voice was quiet, but with a harsh edge.

'If my boss finds out I let you in, he'll skin me alive,' the woman wailed.

'Lady, you want a demonstration of what I'll do if you don't leave, huh?'

The woman let out a gasp of fright and there was the sound of her quick footsteps retreating. The guy laughed, but it wasn't just a chuckle, it was a deep-throated belly-laugh that didn't stop when it should have done. It went on and on. Then it seemed to morph into something else, the guy hyperventilating and almost crying at the same time, and then it suddenly stopped. Pascal strained her ears but all she could hear was his breathing, coming slowly back under control.

She heard a light scraping sound and gently eased the wardrobe door open a crack; the man was kneeling down with his back to her. He was working with a screwdriver on the computer. He abruptly stood up and approached the wardrobe mirror, holding in his hand the computers hard drive. It was too late to pull the wardrobe door closed. She held her breath as the guy examined himself in the mirror, but she couldn't see his face.

Finally he moved away, then the sound of the door opening and closing. She remained frozen, listening for at least a minute before letting out a long exhalation of breath, pushing the wardrobe door open and raising the scotch bottle to her lips.

After a last look around, the severely depleted scotch bottle was replaced on the shelf from which it came. With the drainpipe collapsed, the front door was the only way out. Padding down the hall to the top of the stairs, the sound of a TV on very high volume drifted up from the ground floor. Looking down, an open doorway could be seen, probably the janitors room.

Creeping down the stairway, eyes on the open doorway, then peeping around it, the back of a woman's head could be seen over the edge of a settee. Pascal crept past to the front door, slipping silently through it. Outside, cellphone in hand, she texted an old MI5 colleague, Christoff Wisliceny.

A moment later, walking, her phone vibrated with a response. He was in a bar in the East Village. She hailed a cab.

Twenty five minutes later she sat across from Christoff in a booth drinking Gin and Tonic. The tiny place was packed, the music incredibly loud, the handkerchief sized dance floor roiling with squirming, vibrating bodies. She watched for a moment, feeling the tremors of the bass and drum ripple through her body making her want to get up and abandon herself to the groove. Instead she turned to look at Christoff.

Back in the day he had been her original mentor at MI5 in London. Then he'd followed her across the Atlantic to help on a case for Jonas Calver, and just like her he had stayed on. He was now semi-retired, but again, like her he still occasionally got called on by MI6 for low level work.

She estimated he must be in his mid-fifties now, but he still looked pretty good with his short-cropped curly graying hair and keen green eyes, tonight shielded by blue-tinted pebble glasses perched on the end of his nose. Slim and fit he was also ostentatiously gay, as was the bar they were in.

Pascal flicked the flash drive across the table and he grabbed it out of the air. She said, almost having to shout over the music:

'Its got the contents of an old desk top on it but its password protected. Can you crack it and let me know what's on there, with particular reference to the Journal file?'

'Surely,' he said. 'Anything else, my sweet?'

'Yeah. See what you can find out about an Anita Ritter, using the alias, Annie Rainer. Its her computer. Also any scuttlebutt you got on Greenberg Metro Bank. I know, I know,' she said, holding her hand up. 'They're a top five investment bank on Wall Street, world famous, etcetera etcetera, but do we know anything else about them that the rest of the world doesn't know?'

He leaned back and shouted over the music, 'I'll get on it. Give me a couple of days. Now I've business to attend to,' he said, rising and moving towards the dance floor.

She watched him for a minute, surprised at how lissome he was. She smiled, knocked back her drink and left.

A few days later she sat in Calver's Brooklyn office, drinking coffee.

'So, she was working undercover there, with a false name?' Calver said.

'Yep. Looks like it.' Pascal replied. 'I called them, the bank, on the off chance. Said I was a family member. Tight as a drum. We can't reveal confidential data…blah blah blah.'

'And this Journal from the desk top?'

'Hmmm. Not helpful,' she murmured. 'Its very brief and kind of elliptical, written almost as if she was afraid of it being discovered and read by the wrong people. There'll be a couple of weeks with no entries and then there'll be a single cryptic comment like, "I think the Bogey Man is suspicious. Better watch out."'

'And what's the last entry?'

'Its from about six weeks ago. It just says, "this is big."'

Calver looked out of his window at the Brownstones across the street, thinking about the angelic girl with the halo who'd said she wanted to bring down the biggest bank on Wall Street. Pascal watched him, waiting.

'And this guy who was in her room, the one who took the hard-drive?' he said.

'I didn't see his face. I didn't need to. One bad motherfucker, I'd say.'

Calver nodded. 'The police for the moment are out. We're not family, and her brother doesn't appear to be worried. We need more before we could go to them.'

'So what d'you suggest? We can't leave it here.'

'No, we can't. I was thinking maybe another crack at the brother, but with her rent paid up for 6 months, that just fits his theory. She's gone gone off joy-riding somewhere, acting true to form. '

Pascal got up and went to stand at the window. Calver took a sip of coffee and watched her. She turned back to face him and said, 'but he doesn't know she's joined the bank using an alias and had some guy break into her apartment and steal her hard-drive?'

'Yeah, but if we tell him that he's going to want to know how we know. So, until we know a bit more about him, we'll just keep that to ourselves.'

'So what do you want to do?' she asked.

'Well, I got a telephone message this morning from Riverbend Maximum Security Prison. Floyd Ritter's got my letter and he wants to see me, so my visit's been green-lighted.'

'You think he's going to know anything, stuck in a prison cell in Tennessee?'

'I don't know, Courtney,' he said. 'But its all we got. Can't hurt to talk to him. I'm going down tonight, and I'll see him tomorrow morning.'

She got up and grabbed her jacket. 'Call me when you know anything,' she said, grim faced, 'cause I've got a bad feeling about this case.'

CHAPTER FOUR

Riverbend Maximum Security Institution sits just outside Nashville, on Cockrill Bend Boulevard in Davidson County. From a distance you might mistake it for a modern day funeral parlor. The entrance comprises a low single storey gray building with raised brown lettering on it that tells you what it is. It is also fronted by some rather attractive trees that Calver guessed had seen some expert pruning in their time.

He left his car in the parking lot and navigated his way through the elaborate security regime. He had visited a number of max security facilities in his time, but Riverbend seemed to have an unusual vibe. It felt relaxed; he couldn't think of a better word to describe it, which was odd bearing in mind that it housed some of the most dangerous felons in the country. Most of the guards he interacted with on the way in seemed human, lacking that overt aggression he had found in so many other institutions.

When he arrived in the death row visiting area he sat down at a table to wait for Floyd Ritter. He had no idea what to expect or what he was going to say to the guy. Out of the window he could see a small structure that the guard had cheerfully assured him was the execution chamber. He looked away and studied the small visiting area; it was just a few tables and a drink and snacks vending machine against a wall.

The place was plastered with notices that seemed to prohibit every activity known to man. Calver was the only visitor that day. A minute or so later the door opened and a large black man entered, accompanied by a warder.

Calver stood to greet him, holding his hand out before noticing the mans wrists were shackled. Calver hurriedly dropped his hand, covering his embarrassment by saying loudly, 'hello, Mr Ritter. I'm Jonas Calver.'

'I know who you are,' the man replied. His voice was deep and gravelly, seeming to come from the depths of his chest. His brown eyes were limpid and soft and seemed almost impossibly placid. They were neither friendly nor unfriendly.

The guard who had brought him faded back to stand by the door.

'How do you know my daughter, Anita, mister Calver,' he rumbled slowly. His eyes remained passive but there was a slight edge to his voice. Maybe it was that age old fathers sensitivity to any potential suitor.

'I didn't really know her at all,' Calver said, feeling his way in whilst trying to take the measure of the man. 'I met her just once, but she made that big an impression on me that I didn't forget her. So when she called me and said she was in trouble, I believed her, and here I am,' Calver said, keeping his look neutral.

Ritter watched him for a moment, his eyes like dark pools. 'Mister Calver, tell me how you came to meet my girl, then I'll know whether you're a straight talker, or just another hustler come to shake me down. See, Anita sometimes flew a little too close to the sun and kind of burned folks off. Only a few could stay the course.'

Calver's mind drifted back to that night. 'It was just before Christmas,' he said, his voice low but strengthening as the memory firmed up. 'I'd spent a grueling day in Manhattan criminal court, then gone to my office and had a few drinks. Hadn't been in the States long and was feeling lonely, missing my ex-wife. I went out to walk in the snow to clear my head and that's when I saw her. You know, to be honest I thought she was dead. She was lying in a shop doorway with the snow drifting down, some settling on her.

'You know it was funny, when I rolled her over the street light caught the head band she wore, made it look like a halo and like she was some kind of angel, her face looking so peaceful and all. I know that sounds crazy.'

'Ain't crazy at all,' Ritter whispered, his voice choked and his eyes moist.

'Anyway, I got her up and offered to take her for a hot coffee, but she wanted whiskey. So we went to my local bar, and she told me a little bit about herself,' Calver said. He paused there, wondering just how much to tell the guy.

'Don't you hold nothing back, mister,' Ritter said watching him closely, his eyes bright and piercing.

Calver inclined his head a fraction and continued. 'She said the banks ruined you and your family, tore you apart, and she wanted to do something about it. Maybe get revenge, but she'd discovered it was hopeless, and I think that had kind of put her in a real low mood she was finding difficult to shake…' Calver said, his voice tailing off.

'So, what? Ritter said, leaving a big pause between the two words.

Calver looked out of the window at the execution chamber standing not far away. Ritter followed his gaze. He smiled. 'We all gotta die sometime,' he said. 'Tell me what she was doing that night?'

'She said she wanted to go to sleep in the snow and not wake up, like the Polar explorers, and she mentioned Scott and Amundsen.'

Ritter laughed. 'You know, that little girl, ever since she was knee high to a grass-hopper, she just never could stop reading. Me and Mary, we thought she was gonna turn into a talking encyclopedia,' he said, and now his passive eyes were full of merriment which then turned slowly to sorrow again. 'You. You saved her, then?'

'I don't know about that,' Calver said, uncomfortably. 'I talked to her, sympathetically, and bought her a couple of drinks, and maybe that's all she needed that night.'

'So what did she tell you about me?' he asked, a slight accusatory edge coming into his voice.

'Very little. She talked mostly about the Greenberg Metro Bank. Like she was maybe obsessed, wanted to know how to bring them down and nail their CEO, Lloyd DeMasi.'

'You tell her that's a fool's errand? That it can't be done?'

'Not exactly.'

'What d'you mean?'

'Look, mister Ritter, your daughter needed something to believe in, a purpose. Someone's got a self-destructive urge, you have to try and address the underlying causes, not crack jokes. I was trying to do that, suggesting maybe she could do something if she stuck with it, hoping that'd give her a more positive look on life as time passed.'

'So she didn't say nothing about me, huh?' he said, returning again to the same issue. He raised his manacled hands to rub his chin.

'When we got to the bar,' Calver said tentatively. 'I asked her if there was anyone I could call, and she said I could try you, but that you were on death row. And, and I could tell it made her real sad, and that she didn't really want to talk about it. Just the bank and that you'd done all the right things, set up a business and worked 24/7, but then they took it all away.'

'You know, mister Calver, I can see why she might have liked you. You talk straight and you listen. But I don't know if I like you.'

'You don't have to. I'm not here about you or your case. I'm here because I'm worried about your daughter, and I want to know if you might be able to shed any light on where she might be.'

Ritter sat for a moment looking down in his lap. He raised his head. 'Would you mind getting me a can of coke and snicker bar?' he said, nodding his head at the vending machine against the wall.

'Sure,' Calver said, getting to his feet. 'I could use a bite myself.'

When Calver was seated again, munching on a candy bar, Ritter said, 'you said in your letter you were worried about her. Why?'

Calver told him about the frantic sudden phone call when she'd said that she had something big on the bank, and then how she'd failed to show at their meet. He told him about the vacant apartment with 6 months rent paid up front, but for some reason he didn't tell him she had been working for the bank under an alias.

When he finished, Ritter said, 'you know what I got, a few days after your letter?'

'Uh-huh,'

'A postcard from Anita,' he said. There was no triumphalism in his voice.

'So why d'you invite me here?'

'I don't know, really,' he said. 'I guess I wanted to see you. Don't get many genuine visitors, and your letter interested me.'

Calver held his eyes. 'Its more than that, isn't it? D'you have the postcard? Where's it from and what does it say? Is it her handwriting, her tone?'

'Whoa there, slow down, counselor,' Ritter said. 'It was from Cuba, but in her whole life she never sent no postcard before. Why didn't she just call me? Don't make no sense, but she always was a headstrong girl.'

'Was it her handwriting?' Calver asked.

'Yes. No doubt about that. I'd recognize her scrawl anywhere.'

'What did it say?'

Ritter leaned back and closed his eyes. 'It said, "Having a great time drinking mojito in the sun. Daddy, please stay strong and I will talk to you soon. All love Anita".'

Calver watched a single tear squeeze out of Ritter's closed left eye and run down his cheek. He angrily wiped it away. 'When I got your letter I called my son, Joel. He said she'll turn up like she always does, but why no phone or messaging? Its dead. He says, and he's right, she often went away, and she's dumped phones before because she wanted to avoid certain people, but my gut's telling me something ain't right, and I trust my gut.

'You seem like a genuine guy, Mr. Calver, a straight-talker, and I ain't never met a lawyer yet who was one of them. You know, I'd like you to put my mind at rest about Anita. I mean, its probably nothing so wont amount to a pile a beans to check it out, but it might be something, and,' he said, fixing Calver with a hard stare. 'I'll pay you to do it.'

Calver sighed. 'Getting paid was never my motivation in this, but it would sure help placate my law partner,' he said.

'But,' Ritter said, eyes no longer placid. 'A little subterfuge may be required.'

'I don't follow you?'

'The money I have is from insurance, and its basically a fund to pay my legal fees. My son Joel is running things and paying the lawyers and such like, and I don't want to upset that particular apple-cart,' he said.

'I'm still not following you?' Calver said.

'Well, you're a lawyer, ain't you?' he said, as if that were an explanation

'I am, but I still don't follow.'

'I'd want you to join my legal team. That way I won't get any blow-back from Joel,' he said. 'He'll get you a copy of all my case files. You don't even have to look at them, but bill him as if you have. Easy,' he said with a smile. 'By the time any questions get asked, you'll have found Anita safe and sound.'

'I don't know, mister Ritter,' Calver said doubtfully. ' I don't think your current lawyers would be too crazy about me poking around in their case.'

'It's my case and they don't seem to be doing very much poking around at all. I'll just say I want a second opinion. What do they call it? Outside counsel?'

Calver nodded, still dubious about the prospect. The guy had already had a slew of attorneys working on it years and they surely wouldn't welcome another lawyer sticking his nose in - but then if he wanted information about Anita - if she wasn't just out joy-riding somewhere - he'd need to stay on side with Floyd Ritter. And what would it hurt to play along.

He nodded reluctantly. 'Alright. I read a bit about your case, but if I'm coming on board, even if it's a snow job, I'll need to know the details. So tell me, briefly,' he said, looking at his watch, 'in your own words what happened?'

Ritter nodded, smiling. 'I stand convicted of killing a low-life Nashville hoodlum for hire called Vincent Fachetti. See I was born here, in Tennessee, but we lived in Baltimore. Mary and me had just come down here for a couple of weeks break to stay with her parents. First day we got here, this guy Fachetti turns up and asks to talk to me. He takes me aside in the garden and says we need to drop our lawsuit against the bank, or else. I told him to go fuck himself. He smiled and said, 'so be it,' and left.

'You see we were suing, along with some other folks, Greenberg Metro Bank over mortgage foreclosures on our properties. Mary was the prime mover. All the others agreed a settlement, but not Mary. We'd been threatened before in Baltimore, anonymous phone calls, saying settle or else - could a been the other litigants, who wanted us on board, I suppose. I don't know, but anyway, Mary just laughed it off. A week after Fachetti had threatened me when we were still down in Tennessee, Mary was driving on her own. Big truck was pulling out of a junction and she rode straight into it at 60 mph. Mary was the most careful driver you could ever meet. Catastrophic injuries, airlifted to hospital, ICU and into a coma.

'I stayed on here whilst she was in hospital, and when I'd got my grief under control I went looking for Fachetti. Found him in a Nashville bar. I asked him how he rigged the car. He laughed and said he should a lynched her instead. I saw red and went for him but he had a knife. I took it away from him. There were only two witnesses from the bar, and both lied on oath. Said it was my knife and Fachetti was unarmed and I'd gone looking for him and threatened him before killing him. The all white jury took 40 minutes to convict me of first degree murder, and here I am. Thing is, I didn't kill him. He was alive when I left the bar.'

Calver nodded, thinking hard. There were a thousand questions he could ask, but they would have to wait, and anyway, it wasn't his case. 'What happened to Mary, and the law-suit?' he asked.

'Mary never came out the coma. Had to turn the machine off. That's where the insurance money comes from, but boy did they wrangle forever, but its here now. Don't know what's happened about the lawsuit; Joel can tell you. I felt they might go after my kids if we carried on so I left it,' he said.

'Last thing, mister Ritter. Where d'you think Anita is?'

'If you're coming on board, you better start calling me Floyd. As for Anita, I don't know,' he said. 'I been in here so long I wouldn't know where to start.' He paused, smiling, a questioning look in his eyes. 'You know, mister Calver, you're the only one to ever visit and not ask?'

'I already know,' Calver said. 'Baring a last minute appeal to the supreme court or clemency from the Governor, you're due for execution in just under three months.'

Ritter rolled his head back on his neck and laughed uproariously. 'Hot-damn, boy,' he gasped, 'but you is one cool lizard.'

Calver stood up and nodded. 'Thanks for your time, Floyd,' he said. 'I'll be in touch.'

The guard led Ritter out, and Calver followed another guard back through the labyrinthine corridors and out to the parking lot, the blazing hot sun and his baking car.

CHAPTER FIVE

Calver was sitting on the bed in his hotel room scrolling messages on his phone when reception called up to say a mister Joel Ritter was downstairs asking to see him. Calver looked at his watch and told them he'd meet him in the bar in ten minutes. He showered and put on black jeans and his only clean shirt, grabbed his wallet and phone and took the lift down to the ground floor.

The place was small and anonymous, a place to get a last minute drink in on the way to somewhere else - somewhere better. It was early evening with a smattering of guests. The decor was light brown and cream with a few potted plants dotted around and light schmaltzy lift-music playing in the background. There was only one black guy in the bar; Calver approached him.

The guy spoke first. 'Mister Calver, Joel Ritter,' he said, shaking Calver's hand with a firm grip. 'We spoke before, and maybe I was a little short with you.....'

'Forget it,' Calver said. 'You wanted to make sure I wasn't some crazy red neck out to hustle your father. Don't sweat it.'

'Well, its good of you to say so. I gather you met with my father this morning. He called me and said you were coming on board and that I should meet with you to talk.'

'And how d'you feel about that?' Calver asked, watching him carefully.

A quick fleeting smile. 'I know my father, Mr Calver,' he said cryptically. 'Look, lets get a drink and sit. What are you having?'

'Scotch.'

They got their drinks and moved to a booth. Calver took a shot of scotch whilst studying the other man.

'You don't look much like your sister,' Calver said.

'Sorry.'

Calver smiled. 'You sounded pretty blasé first time around when I called you about Anita. You still feel that way?'

'Not exactly.'

'So?'

'As you rightly surmised, I was being cautious when we first spoke, but I am worried,' he said. 'You see, we had a rule. We always kept in touch because of what had gone down with our father and because of her thing with the bank,' he said. 'If no call, she'd text.'

'How long's it been?' Calver asked.

'A month. Longest time before that was two weeks. I mean, she's never been what you'd call reliable, but this was something she took pretty seriously, so I'm guessing something is wrong,' he said, lifting his gaze and fixing it on Calver. 'When did you last see her, and how was she?' he asked.

Calver noticed the slight accusatory tone in his voice, which he ignored. 'Like I told you on the phone. I met her just once, months ago and then she calls me, just like I said, out the blue. Said she was scared, wanted to meet, but she never showed. Thats when I got the lawyers to get you to call me.'

Joel nodded, his eyes turning inward. 'What else she say on the phone?' he asked.

'Not much. She seemed excited. Said she'd got something big, but didn't say what it was, and that was it. You check her apartment?'

Joel took a shot of his drink and grimaced as if he wasn't used to scotch. 'No,' he said, eyes watering. 'Dragon lady who runs it wouldn't let me in and threatened to call the cops if I didn't leave. And her phone is dead,' he added, after a moment. 'I mean why would she call you and not me?' he said, his face twisted with anger and confusion. 'See, the whole point about keeping in touch was to stay safe.'

'What about the cops?' Calver said.

Joel just looked at him. Then a gleam of suspicion. 'Hey, I gave you her new address, didn't I? You went there as well? What you find?' he asked.

Calver smiled. 'I didn't have much luck with the dragon lady either, until I gave her a shot of vodka. Rents paid up for six months and she's gone away somewhere. There was some stuff in there that suggested she had got a job with the bank?' he said.

'I knew it,' he whispered angrily. 'I knew she'd go and do something stupid like that.'

Calver sipped his whiskey. 'Why stupid? Risky, and possibly dangerous, yes. See, I believe Anita had worked out that going after the banks the legitimate way through the courts doesn't work, not least because the big banks own Washington and are protected, so the only way left to her was to get inside.'

Joel leaned back in his chair and ran a hand through his black curls, his face troubled. 'You know, Anita had many faults, but one thing she was good at was judging character. And she was hard to impress too, but for some reason she took to you. She never said your name, just referred to a lawyer she'd met, which I guess could only be you. But from what you just said, you're even crazier than she is. How's some little black gal from Baltimore going to take down one of the biggest banks on Wall Street, even from the inside? I mean, are you serious?'

'I don't know, Joel, but at least she's got the guts to try, which is more than I can say for virtually everyone else on the planet,' Calver said, getting heated.

He sighed. 'Sorry, forgive the sermon,' he said. 'I didn't used to care much, but I did some reading after I met your sister, and it kind of opened my eyes a little to what went on, so forgive me for getting carried away.'

'No, you go right ahead,' Joel said. 'But it isn't going to help us find Anita.'

'If she's missing,' Calver said. He knocked his scotch back, thinking. 'You know we phoned the bank asking about Anita, and of course they stonewalled us - data protection, confidential information they were not at liberty to divulge. But you are next of kin, so if you phone, they're going to have to talk to you,' Calver said.

'That's right,' Joel said, looking at his watch. 'I'll call them first thing.'

'Good. You do that and get back to me,' Calver said. 'Meantime, if you want to copy your fathers case files and get them sent over to my New York office, we can meet up there.'

'You really want them, huh?' Joel said, a knowing smile on his face.

'Why wouldn't I?' Calver replied, innocent.

Joel held his eyes for a long moment. He nodded. 'Okay, counselor, have it your way.'

Calver wasn't about to divulge legally privileged information to Joel without pop's consent although it seemed pretty clear Joel had worked out he was really on board to get a line on Anita. Still, Calver needed to get paid to placate his law partner, Morganna, so best to keep up the fiction he was on board for Floyd's case.

'So, Joel, what d'you do for a living?'

'Journalist,' he said quickly. 'And I give myself the tag, "investigative" when the mood strikes me. And based in New York City, just like you. Its mostly on-line freelance stuff at the moment, digging and working 24/7, waiting for that career defining story.'

'Can be a noble calling, even in the fake news era,' Calver said. 'What drew you to it?'

'You know, it was just one story,' he said, enthusiasm lighting up his eyes. 'When I was fifteen, and just starting to write, when our family was already going down the pan courtesy of the banks, I read an article in Rolling Stone Magazine that just about blew me away. It was called "The Great American Bubble Machine" by a guy called Matt Taibbi. It basically defenestrated the Wall Street Banks, in particular Goldman Sachs. He essentially nailed them - and by the way, nothings changed. It made me want to write like that, with that kind of power and coruscating anger.'

Joel relaxed back in his seat, the tension in his body created by the passion he felt, slowly dissipating. 'Long way to go though,' he added self consciously.

Calver watched him for a moment, reflecting on the fact that the guy had the same kind of intensity that Anita had, although distinctly his own brand. Calver looked around the sparsely populated bar that was beginning to remind him of Edward Hopper's "Nighthawks". Joel caught his look and smiled. 'Cool bar, counselor,' he quipped. Then serious again. 'Thanks for talking to me. Hope we can work together on this and find her. You never know though, she might just pop up smiling and make us all look stupid. She's probably on the beach in Cuba. That's what Pop wants to believe. I'll phone the bank in the morning,' he said, rising to his feet. 'I'll call you tomorrow.'

'A Sabbatical?' Calver repeated, holding the phone to his ear. He was sitting at his desk, running an electric razor over his chin.

'That's what they said,' Joel replied. 'Just got off the phone to them. Took 20 minutes of persistent questioning before they could put someone up who knew something.'

'How you get them to talk?'

'Said I was a journalist, as well as being her brother, and unless I got some answers I was going to come down there personally,' he said.

'What did they tell you?'

'Virtually nothing,' he said. 'She's on a 6 month sabbatical - period. That's it. Then she hung up on me. How d'you like that? I know stonewalling when I hear it. Think I should go down there anyway?'

'No,' Calver said. 'They're not going to tell you anything. We need to take five. Look, I've received your father's case files this morning. Why don't you come round to my office this evening. My investigator will be there as well, and we can see where we go?'

'Sounds like a plan,' Joel said. 'I'll be there.'

The three of them sat around Calver's spare office that doubled as a conference room. It was L shaped and the walls were lined with law books and down the middle of the main part ran a long table with chairs either side. From the ceiling hung a cheap chandelier that Calver had got knock-off; he believed it gave the room class although the jury was still out on that. He sat looking up at it now, wondering if he should go for an upgrade. Joel took one of the cups of coffee off the tray Hettie had just brought in, and took a sip. Pascal sat to the side talking quietly into her cell-phone in muffled tones that the others couldn't hear.

Calver said to Joel: 'While she's on the phone I'd like to ask you something about your father. When I visited with him, he mentioned your mothers car crash as being the motivation for him to go looking for this Fachetti guy, the vic?'

Joel nodded. 'That's right.'

'So, what happened to your mothers car after the crash?' Calver asked. 'See, I've had a skim through your father's case files and I can't find a mention of any follow up. Maybe I've missed something?'

'No, you ain't missed nothing,' Joel said. 'Car was scrapped and crushed within 48 hours of the crash.'

Calver shook his head. 'How the hell does that happen with what was essentially a fatac? I mean, not just the cops but the insurers would have wanted access to that vehicle, surely?'

'Hey, you don't know Tennessee.'

'What d'you mean?'

'Jim Crow is alive and well. The truck driver was white and completely uninjured in the crash. And the cops were white trash rednecks. If the medics hadn't got there as quick as they did, those cops would a stood there and let her die.'

'I'm sorry, Joel, but I don't buy that,' Calver said. 'Not in these days where everybody films absolutely everything with their cell phones. There would have to have been an investigation of the crash, period.'

'There was, but the cops said the report is missing.'

'You're kidding me?' Calver said. 'These reports are digital, saved on-line or whatever, so that's got to be bullshit. I mean you say you're an investigative journalist, and you don't look into this a little bit deeper, when its your own mother?'

'I *did* look into it,' Joel snapped back, stung. 'They stonewalled me, okay? But so what, it changes nothing. Even if mum's car was rigged, so what? Prosecution proved my dad went looking for Fachetti with a knife, and killed him. That's first degree murder in any state, and any motivation he may have had is completely irrelevant to that guilt. I mean, for Christs sakes, you're the lawyer. You should know that.'

'Hey, you guys need to calm down,' Pascal said coming back and joining them.

Calver looked a little shamefaced. 'Yeah, sorry, Joel,' he said. 'You're right, but I'd still like to know about that report.'

'No, I'm glad someone with fresh eyes is taking a look. Maybe it needs that, but dad's clock is running down fast now,' Joel said, a hunted look in his eyes.

Calver and Pascal's eyes met, a brief look of compassion for the man, passing between them. They all knew the new execution date was just over two months away. 'Lets talk about Anita, shall we?' Calver said, deftly changing the subject to try and takes some of the strain off Joel. 'We've got an idea.'

Joel's face immediately looked less stressed, a little brighter. Calver nodded at Pascal.

'We've hit a dead end so far,' she said. 'So let's just take five and have a look at what we've got here. Anita joined the bank because we think she wanted to try and do some damage from the inside. She'd tried from the outside, but got nowhere. She used an alias, Annie Rainer, to go in, undoubtedly because she thought they'd pick up the fact your family had litigated against the bank if she used her real name. But also because she'd personally been a thorn in their side, parading outside their Wall Street office with a sandwich board, and she'd posted unpleasant pieces about them on-line, so she needed a disguise to get in. To support her cover she got a flea-pit apartment on the Lower East Side, something that prospective interns to the wall Street banks often do. So she gets in, and then she phones Calver saying she's got something big on the bank. She asks to meet, but fails to show. The rent on her apartment is paid up for six months and her employers, the bank, say she has gone on a sabbatical but they wont give out any further information. Then your father gets a postcard from her, from Cuba. Its written by her and says she's on vacation having a good time. All phones and numbers we have for her are dead.'

'I wouldn't argue with a single word of that,' Joel said. 'Although I still can't figure out why she phoned Jonas instead of me,' he added, shaking his head. 'So what's your idea?'

'I follow her in,' Pascal replied, taking a sip of her coffee. 'To the bank.'

'You're crazy,' Joel said.

'Why crazy?' Calver said. 'Tell me another way of finding out what's happened to Anita. She says she's got something on the bank and she's scared; she disappears and the bank says she's on sabbatical.'

'So the bank's the key,' Pascal said. 'So we gotta start there.'

'I don't know,' Joel said.

Another look passed between Calver and Pascal. He nodded. 'And there's something else we haven't told you,' Pascal said.

'What?'

'We just wanted to be sure about you first,' Calver said. 'Before saying anything.' He paused, then continued. 'Pascal gained entry to Anita's apartment. You don't need to know how. But inside there's an old desktop computer, and she managed to copy the contents - they don't help us much. But while she was there, another guy turned up.'

'Yeah, a real badass,' Pascal said, taking up the re-telling. 'Didn't see his face but he sounded like psycho. Scared the shit out of the janitor and she's no shrinking violet. But the important point is, he was there to remove the hard-drive from the computer, which he did.'

Joel looked from Calver to Pascal and back. 'Why would he do that? You said it doesn't help, what's on there.'

'That's what we need to find out, and fast,' Calver said. 'Cops wont want to know, and the bank wont give us squat, voluntarily, so I figure we've got to go in and find what we need inside.'

Joel sat mute, thinking. 'Why don't I go in?' he muttered.

'I don't think so,' Pascal said. 'From what I've heard, Anita was very far from being a fool, and it sounds like they may have rumbled her. No offense, Joel, but I don't think you're likely to do any better than she has, but worse, there's no way you're going to be able to disguise who you are.'

He nodded reluctantly. 'How will you get in to the bank?' he asked.

'Same way Anita did.'

Calver looked across the table at Joel. 'You told me you're a journalist, investigative journalist?'

'That's right.'

'Well have you looked at the bank, I mean professionally?'

Joel smiled. 'You know, I held off for a long time, because of what happened to us. It cut so deep and hurt so bad that I had to leave it alone. It made me so angry and it was so corrosive to keep on looking at it, thinking about it, that I needed to bury it in order to move on, so that's what I did. But lately, with what's been happening, I decided it was time dig it up and face it.'

'So you been digging?' Pascal asked.'

'Yeah. A little,' he said. 'So far I'm just been doing some basic research.'

Calver reached over to the jug and poured some more coffee into each of their mugs. 'Why don't you give us a little bit of that background now?' he said.

'Why not,' Joel replied. He raised the replenished mug to his lips and took a sip whilst he ordered his thoughts.

'As I say, I'm just scratching the surface, and I guess you know most of it anyway. Greenberg Metro Bank, or "GMB" as its called on the street is now one of the top three investment houses on Wall Street. It grew out of the 2008 crash when M J Greenberg merged with Metro Bank. It's got 32,000 employees world wide and clients that range from foreign governments, to oligarchs to some of the biggest names on the S & P 500. Its fans say it's a capitalist force for good, that it facilitates the free flow of money to risk takers who build businesses and create prosperity and employment.'

'And what do its critics say?' Pascal asked.

'How long have you got?' Joel replied, deadpan. 'Its been buffeted by scandal after scandal, whistle-blowers coming out of its ears, writing books, secret recordings from the New York Fed and the SEC, and yet nothing ever seems to stick; its like Teflon. It frequently has to pay regulatory fines and penalties and some of its low level ex-employees have been indicted and imprisoned, but it just endures, seemingly getting stronger and stronger and even more influential, especially of course in politics. And the revolving door in Washington of course helps immensely. That's where the banks senior officers are either destined for or coming from, top posts in Washington. The regulatory rules are changed in the banks favor on a nod and a wink, and it just goes on.'

'So what about Anita's particular beef with the bank?' Calver said. 'And yours, of course,' he added.

'Sub-prime mortgages, essentially,' he said. 'I think we all know the basics of the story. The banks were looking for a new group to scalp and they lit upon selling mortgages to people who would never be able to pay them back.'

'I don't quite understand that,' Pascal said. 'Why would you lend money to someone who you knew would not be able to pay it back? And also, without wishing to be disrespectful to your parents, Joel, would they not have carefully examined what they were being offered before signing anything? And they don't sound like the kind of people who would default on a financial obligation without good cause?'

'Its a fair point,' Joel conceded. 'My parents were hard-working people, church-going folk, but not sophisticated. They trusted the broker who sold them the deal, and in fact my parents could probably have made their payments if the market hadn't crashed, but you have to remember that the market did crash as a direct result of the banks selling these products. What happened was that the competition for mortgage brokerage fees got fiercer and fiercer with guys chasing lower and lower grade risk, even canvassing trailer parks and offering deals to people who had no credit history. In fact in some cases the brokers forged credit histories to get the deals, all for the brokerage fees and commissions. My parents weren't in this group.'

Pascal still looked puzzled. 'You'll have to help me out here, Joel,' she said. 'Finance was never one of my strong points.'

'Except when you ask me for money,' Calver quipped.

'No, that's okay,' Joel said, ignoring Calver. 'These brokers offered what's called "teaser" initial rates on the mortgages. So, first 2 years you pay a reduced interest rate thats rolled up. So you start out paying $250 a month that jumps to $750 a month after 2 years. Course they didn't emphasize the increase that would come, and their unsophisticated marks jumped at the deals. But it gets worse, much worse,' Joel said, his eyes darkening. 'We now know that in places like Chicago, and Baltimore, where we lived, there was essentially a racial bias in play where brokers actually targeted black and Hispanic families. A lot of them they got through the black churches, where they figured they could encourage church leaders to influence congregants to take the sub-prime loans. They called it "reverse redlining". That is they specifically targeted the most expensive and onerous loans at black customers. Some good journalism was done in exposing it. One piece they showed how a black household earning $68,000 a year was five times more likely to hold a high-interest sub-prime mortgage as whites of similar or even lower incomes. They called them "ghetto loans" and the loan officers were given huge cash incentives to refer borrowers who should have qualified for a prime loan to the sub-prime division. There were all sorts of tricks employed; the loan officer would say the client had no income documentation, when they did have it, so the loan would flip to sub-prime. Or they'd simply cut and paste one customers bad credit record onto a customer with a good record. One broker boasted she made $700,000 one year from these type of scams. So a homeowner taking out a $165,000 mortgage could expect to pay perhaps three percentage points more than a prime mortgage holder for the same amount which could add $100,000 in interest payments over the term of the loan.'

'Jesus,' Pascal said. 'How the fuck did they get away with it?'

'Welcome to America,' Joel said. 'To be fair, they didn't all get away with it. There's been some federal suits on violations of fair lending and civil rights laws, but my parents missed out on that. But that's not the end of the story. What I've told you so far is just the first layer if you like, where these loans started out, but then it gets complicated. You see, all these low grade mortgages were then mixed in with some better grade mortgages into funds or pools, like fund A and fund B. And this was done by?' he asked, like a school master, looking at Pascal and Calver, who looked back, blank-faced.

'That's right. Our friend the bank,' Joel replied. 'The bank then sold these repackaged funds, say fund A, or parts of the fund, often to their own clients, telling them they were grade A investments when they clearly weren't. This is where we get into all those exotically named vehicles they used like credit default swop's and collateralized debt obligations that we heard so much about in the press when this whole stinking mess exploded. Once they'd sold these tranches of toxic loan funds, they then arranged insurance against the mortgage funds going bad, so they got fees coming in from every which way, and from every part of the process, and they had skin in the game as well. Talk about insider trading and conflict? In this case the fox had complete control of the hen-house.'

'Then the shit hit the fan with Lehman Brothers and the rest is history,' Calver said.

'That's right,' Joel nodded in agreement. 'The sub-prime underlying mortgages went bad quick and when that started filtering through and the true scope of the liabilities started to become known, panic set in. The housing market and the banks collapsed and we got the great bail out.'

Pascal got up and stretched. 'So Anita blames the bank, because of all this, which ultimately resulted in foreclosure, your family losing their home to repossession and all that followed?' she said

'Essentially, yes,' Joel said. 'The bank created this monster, based on greed and fraud, and they fed it, whilst squeezing out every last drop of blood, until it popped. Then they got bailed out, no criminal charges. In fact the opposite, huge bonuses derived from public bail-out money, and now they've moved on to the next scalping opportunity. You can draw a direct line from the greedy mortgage brokers they turbo-charged with sky-high commissions, right up to the CEO of the bank, Lloyd DeMasi, who ran M J Greenberg at the height of the sales frenzy. And that seems to be just what Anita has done; drawn that direct line from the bottom right up through GMB to Lloyd DeMasi at the pinnacle.'

Calver shook his head and said. 'Okay, Joel, but what about your parents civil suit against the bank. Your father mentioned it when I visited him. He even said you were threatened to drop it, and that this Fachetti guy, the guy he's accused of killing, was all part of that?'

'My father says a lot of things,' Joel said cryptically. 'And maybe there's an air of wishful thinking, clutching at straws, the closer he gets to the death house at Riverbend. I'm not so sure about what he says about these threats, maybe they're just in his mind.'

'Okay,' Calver said, 'we can come back to that when I have a look at your father's case papers in detail, but as far as Anita is concerned, what happened to the civil suit against the bank? Is it still pending?'

'He let it go when Mum had the accident. She was always the prime mover. It was like a class action I think, but she refused to settle for what was offered, wanted to go it alone, and there was some bad feeling with the other folks who were suing with us. One of the reasons that Anita got estranged from our father was that he would not pursue the claim, and with mum in a coma he was the only one who could, and he flatly refused and would never give a reason why. I think that's what may have pushed Anita into going after the bank in the way she has. I don't know about the claim. It may have lapsed or even be statute barred.'

Calver looked at his watch. 'I think we've done enough for now, Joel. Can you get me whatever papers you have on the civil suit, who the attorneys were, and I'll have a look at it. May give us another angle.'

'No problem. I'll get on it,' Joel said. 'But what about your idea of getting into the bank?' he added, turning to Pascal. 'How are we going to work that?'

'Nothing to work,' she said. 'Because I'm in.'

'What the hell are you talking about?' Calver said. 'In where?'

'The bank,' Pascal said. 'Well, I'm not exactly in, but I've got an interview for a secretarial job there tomorrow.'

CHAPTER SIX

Courtney Pascal looked at her watch again. Boy was time dragging. Being an administrative assistant in the securities department of GMB was not exactly the most interesting work she'd ever done, and three weeks of it - a necessary period to establish her cover before she could start digging - was starting to try even her legendary levels of patience. A cobbled together and largely fictional resume, backed up by some impeccable references - a result of some called in favors - had got her an interview from where she had done her usual superlative job of winging it. After some minimal checks they'd offered her the post; her chosen alias: Carrie Potter.

After the usual induction and meet the team merry-go-round she had dug in and worked her butt off. Keeping her head down, she'd eased her way in, acquiring a rep as the go to girl who would volunteer for anything and everything - covering for co-workers whenever asked, getting the coffee - and it was beginning to pay off. A level of trust with the other two girls in her pod was developing where they were starting to take her into their confidence, giving her warts and all character sketches of the major players in their team.

The floor they were on was open plan but Pascal and her two colleagues were in an alcove with a screen boxing them in and giving them a bit of cover from the prying eyes of the office manager. To Pascal's right sat Mercy Mercedes, second generation Puerto Rican, sassy and sharp as a knife, 32 years old. Across from her sat Patty Hendrix, black, a bit quieter, perhaps more reflective, but also watchful.

Pascal had been assigned to work for an asshole trader called Bud Allan. He barely acknowledged her existence and mercifully kept personal contact to a minimum, preferring emails and texts to one-on-one's, which suited Pascal. Her task that morning was to bring order and legitimacy to one of his fantastical expense claims which was now displayed on the screen in front of her. It covered six weeks, including foreign travel all around the world, but had virtually no supporting evidence by way of chits or receipts. Most of the claim was clearly bogus, but it was her job to sanitize it so it would pass muster, something she was superbly qualified to do. She willed her eyes back to her screen and the claim; she had worked on it deep into the night, roughing up legitimate looking evidence to support it, which she now attached. Done, she pressed send and off it went for checking. Next she had to work on her bosses calender and organize upcoming meetings. She checked what was already in place. In two days time she noticed an entry, "departmental quarterly meeting with CEO, Lloyd DeMasi."

She turned to Mercy. 'So, big pow-wow Thursday, then?' she said

The girl smiled. 'Freak show, you mean. All those psycho's in one room? Man, I figure you could collect enough testosterone there to supply an IVF clinic for a year.'

Pascal laughed. 'Yeah, but who'd want it?' she said. 'Where's the meeting take place?'

'Top floor conference room,' Patty chimed in, looking up from her screen. ' And we don't even get an invite - so sad,' she added, miming a tearful face.

Pascal relaxed back in her chair. So far she had held off doing any surreptitious digging or asking any questions about Annie Ranier because she felt she needed to be a trusted part of the team first, but now it was time to start earning her keep.

Later in the day, in a brief moment of calm when Patty was away from her desk, Pascal casually turned to Mercy and said, 'I met an old school friend last night from upstate. Here for a couple of days, and she was asking about a friend who works here, or used to work here, but she can't get hold of her? I said I'd ask around?'

'I been here 6 years and I couldn't give you the names of more than a handful of people here,' Mercy said. 'But try me. What's the girls name?'

'Annie Rainer,' Pascal said, just as Patsy arrived back at her desk.

'Don't know her,' Mercy said. 'Which department?'

'All she said was she was a junior market trader. But hey, don't worry about it.'

Mercy nodded and said she was going to the john. As she left, Patsy said, 'you should be careful about asking questions around here. They don't like it.'

'Who doesn't? Why not?' Pascal said. 'Its a simple enough question?'

Patsy's eyes narrowed but her expression remained casual.

'You'll learn,' she said, turning back to her screen.

Pascal shrugged and got up to stretch her legs.

A day later she was called into the floor managers office. Bob Heidegger was a frenetic type, thin and athletic with a face like a rectangular dinner plate and hair like fine electric wires. He seemed to smile surface deep, which he did now, before looking down and continuing the pretense of writing on a pad whilst Pascal stood fidgeting in front of his desk. She endured this for around 25 seconds before tiring of the amateur power-play. Uninvited, she slid into the chair opposite and kept her eyes ice cold as he raised his. A fleeting look of indignation passed over his face, quickly replaced by a pained smile. 'Carrie, I called you in to give you some feedback on how you're doing here, and also, just as important, to let you come back at me with any issues you may have,' he said, syrupy as hell.

She adopted a similar mien and simpering tone she had seen other lower tier employees use when dealing with Heidegger. 'Why, Bob, how nice,' she said. 'Its such a great opportunity you've given me here at the bank.'

'Cool,' he said. 'Look, you're doing great, but there's always room for improvement, right, Carrie?'

'Absolutely.'

He looked down at his pad for a second, then leveled his gaze on her. 'I hear you've been asking about another employee, an Annie Rainer? Is that right?' he asked, his voice no longer syrupy, in fact it had no inflection at all.

'That's right,' she said. 'Friend asked me to look her up as she couldn't get hold of her. I mean, why? Is there a problem?'

'Well, we don't encourage prying here,' he said, softly. 'Respecting the data and information of individual employees is a cornerstone in our employee relationships. When you join the bank, your personal data is safe with us. Now, you wouldn't want us to compromise that, would you?'

'No, of course not. Forgive me, I didn't think,' she said.

He kept watching her; she kept her expression neutral.

'If friends and family are reluctant or reticent about broadcasting personal information about a close member, that tends to suggest it may reflect a wish for privacy on that persons part, no?' he said

Pascal itched to scream the answer 'no', to his condescending face, but had to settle for a meek, 'I understand. It won't happen again, sir.'

'Good,' he said, smile back in place. 'Okay, Carrie, you can go back to work now.'

She got up and left. As the door closed behind her, Heidegger raised a cellphone on speed-dial.

An emotionless voice answered with a clipped, 'yes?'

'She's been told,' Heidegger said.

'She's on a months probation, right?' the voice asked.

'That's right. Expires end of this week.'

'Terminate her then,' the voice said and the phone went dead.

On Thursday Brad Allan called Pascal over to his desk, the first time he had done so. The guy reminded Pascal of a Whippet; he had a kind of skinny, bony, prominent frame that seemed to bow outward. And she was sure he had had work done on his face - his mouth, nose and teeth just didn't look right. She reckoned the guy who had done the work should have been disbarred or whatever they did to cosmetic surgeons who fucked up. Another first though - he smiled at her. 'Carrie! Hey, babe, how you doing?' he said, ignoring the company's policy on sexist modes of address.

'Good. What can I do for you, boss?' she said, wondering where this was going.

'Look, I just wanted to say thanks for doing the expenses. You know that's the first time they've ever, *ever*, passed my claim without a peep. No reductions - awesome,' he said, beaming.

She might have known that the one thing that would give her some traction with the guy would be an ability to gain him a monetary advantage. She heard activity and looked over towards the lifts where a couple of guys were snooping around, looking like maintenance workers, but they weren't dressed for it. More like security; both in shades, one with an ear bud. 'What's going on?' she muttered, before remembering who she was talking to.

He didn't seem to notice. 'Big cheese is in town,' he said. 'Lloyd DeMasi will be in later for the quarterly meeting, and that's the advance team,' he added.

Pascal wandered back to her desk, wondering how she could get a look at DeMasi. Looking at her watch, then at Mercy. 'Okay if I take an early lunch?' she asked.

'No problem,' Mercy said without looking up, her fingers skittering across the keyboard like demented spiders.

Pascal made her way down to the grand ground floor atrium, all soaring glass, marble and gold rising up through the center of the building. She moved over to stand near a mini art exhibition situated near the entrance way and the lifts, mingling with others, always watching the entrance. After a few minutes she watched through the doors as a convoy of large black limousines drew up outside. She recognized DeMasi immediately by his completely bald head. Pascal began moving, plotting a course towards the lifts so she would arrive at the same time.

DeMasi was accompanied by three others; two men who looked honed and slick, obvious security, and a young woman speaking into a phone and holding a tablet in her other hand that she was studying as she walked and talked. DeMasi, in the middle of the group, was tall, around 6'3", and solid built wearing a black suit with a yellow silk scarf around his neck, his gleaming bald head and substantial frame marking him out from the crowd.

As one of the three lifts arrived and the doors opened, Pascal darted into it before the two guys could stop her. One of them studied her intensely, the other looked pointedly at her crotch and licked his lips. The woman briefly and dismissively scanned her eyes over Pascal and imperceptibly nodded her head, and the group entered the lift barely having broken step. Inside, the guy who had eyed up Pascal's crotch slid in behind her, the other three in front, and the lift began moving, no one asking which floor she wanted, so she blurted out, 'fifteen, please.'

DeMasi turned and smiled at her and pressed fifteen. As the lift gathered speed the man behind her slid his hand up her skirt between her legs, squeezing and goosing her butt. He said, 'whew, hot in here,' to cover his movement. Pascal remained motionless, not reacting at all. As the lift arrived and the doors opened, the three in front moved aside to let her out. At the same time the man behind slid his hand down her leg and out from under her skirt, but as he raised his hand back up, Pascal grabbed it in a vice-like grip. As she moved out of the lift she swung the guy out also, by his arm, around in a short arc, so that he slammed up against the wall next to the lift doorway. As he bounced off the wall she hit him square on the jaw. It cracked with a sickening sound and he collapsed like a bag of bricks dropping into the hold of a ship. 'Next time you try feeling someone up in a lift, make sure you know who your dealing with,' she said.

It had happened so fast, the other guy had not had time to react, but now he did so, clumsily pulling a gun from an underarm holster and waving it at her, saying, 'step away and put your hands—'

'Fuck you,' Pascal said turning to face the guy.

'Hey, relax everybody,' DeMasi said in a deep drawl. He turned to Pascal, looking her over. 'I can't believe this lady would react so dramatically without some cause,' he said, turning to look at his female assistant.

She lent into DeMasi and whispered, 'boss, we can do without sexual assault lawsuits.'

But Pascal heard her. 'Hey, lady, that fucking ape stuck his hand up my skirt, and I've dealt with it. So you can forget about lawsuits,' she said, starting to move away.

The injured guy struggled up, holding his jaw and groaning

'Wait a minute,' DeMasi said. 'What's your name?'

'Carrie Potter.'

'Well, Carrie. I like your style,' he said. He turned to the woman and added. 'I don't want this guy on my security detail. Get rid of him.'

The woman nodded. 'I'll deal with it immediately, Mr DeMasi.' She said.

He turned back to Pascal but she was already out of earshot. He said to the woman, 'make a note of her name.'

The woman grimaced but made an entry on her tablet, then the group got back into the left and carried on to the top floor.

The next day, Friday, Heidegger invited her into his office again. This time he had moved the chair so she had nowhere to sit. He kept her standing again as he went through the same routine of pretending to write on a pad. After a suitable interval, he spoke without looking up. 'Carrie, we've decided not to offer you a permanent position here, so five o clock you're done. Sorry it didn't work out for—'

'Bob,' his secretary interrupted, head around the door. 'Sorry, I've got Lloyd DeMasi's office, on line 1.'

He nodded. 'I'll take it,' he said.

Pascal watched the guy. He mostly listened, nodding and saying, 'yes,' and 'I understand,' his face growing darker as the conversation proceeded. He put the phone down, and looked up. 'It seems you're not finished here after all,' he said, a speculative look in his eyes. 'You're to report to the top floor tomorrow morning at 9 am.'

'What for? Its Saturday.'

'Search me. Don't matter what day it is, cause somebody up there likes you.'

CHAPTER SEVEN

The top floor was quiet; it had the rarefied atmosphere of a monastery, a financial monastery, but underneath that quietness Pascal could sense the rich hum of power. It was reflected in the original art work on the walls and the quadrillion dollar interior design that was projected out all over the floor. The place was virtually empty, a few people moving around speaking in muffled tones going into offices and closing doors. Earlier Pascal had been escorted up by a security guard who had gruffly told her to wait.

Some aeronautically designed uncomfortable looking chairs were placed around a sleek low white table covered with newspapers; FT, Wall Street Journal and Economist. She picked one up and idly leafed through it. She checked her watch - gone half nine. She took a water bottle off the table and tried it; tasted like shit, surprisingly. She grimaced and put the bottle down just as one of the two doors across from her opened. It was the woman from the lift who had accompanied DeMasi. 'Good morning, Miss Potter. I'm Joyce Van Zim, one of Mr DeMasi's personal assistants,' she said, making a play of not offering her hand.

This time Pascal took a good look. Early thirties, square face with short swept across auburn hair and green eyes that seemed to oscillate between calculating and slightly mocking. She had a masculine look about her, her chunky body encased in a rather old fashioned, but obviously expensive beige trouser suit. All in all a rather unappetizing dish, Pascal thought as she rose to her feet and mumbled a subdued, 'good morning.'

'Follow me,' the woman said peremptorily. She led the way back into the room she had just come out of, and waved Pascal into a chair.

It was a corner office with an extraordinary panoramic view of the city, but the room itself was small and unwelcoming with an austere feel. It had a desk and two chairs, the only personal touch being a portrait photo of a rather attractive blonde woman of a similar age, probably a partner, Pascal guessed.

'I imagine you're wondering why you're here?' the woman said.

Pascal decided to fuck with her. 'Nope,' she replied, looking at her watch. 'You just kept me waiting half an hour an its Saturday. You got something to say, make it snappy, cause I got things to do.'

The woman smiled. 'You like to subvert, don't you, Carrie?' she said. 'Or perhaps disrupt is the better word, all the rage now of course.'

'Get to the point.'

'You know what we do here, Carrie?' she asked.

'Make billions ripping off ordinary folk?'

'Some would say that, but not the clever people,' she said. 'The clever people would say that we're disruptor's; disruptor's of the old order, and that's how we profit. So we're looking for special people who excel at that; people who can take that vision forward. We of course have our normal intake of Ivy League graduates from the right families with the right resumes. Same as the other investment banks, but we also have another intake that's certainly not publicized. You getting my drift, Carrie?'

'Spell it out for me?'

'Mr DeMasi was impressed with the way you dealt with his security operative,' she said. 'You see, the special people we're looking for don't come through normal channels. So we have to use different techniques to identify them. One such way is simply to observe how someone behaves in a challenging and highly stressful situation. I have to say,' she said, her voice slowing and turning slightly dreamy. 'I thought the way you dealt with that guy, that ape, in the lift, when he tried to hit on you, it was…..I've never seen anything quite like it.' Her eyes were shining and her lips moist as if she were caught in the grip of some minor passion. 'It was decisive, explosive even, and shockingly effective - quite extraordinary.'

'Glad you liked it,' Pascal muttered, wondering at the woman's words and body language.

But Pascal's tone and expression were lost on the woman who was now back in business like mode. 'I was impressed, but more importantly, so was Mr. DeMasi - very,' she said.

'Okay, I think I get that, so I'm listening,' Pascal said.

'Good. So we have a special program for such people, but before we consider whether someone meets our very strict criterion we carry out an in depth investigation of that person,' she said. She lifted a couple of sheets of paper from the desk and Pascal realized it was a print-out of her resume. Van Zim's smile was wintry and her eyes turned calculating as she regarded Pascal. 'This resume is a little bit threadbare, don't you think, Carrie?'

'What d'you mean?' Pascal asked, summoning up a look of self-righteousness.

The woman ignored her comment. She opened a drawer in the desk and took out a thick sheaf of papers. 'If you're interested in being considered for this program, I'll need you to fill this form out covering your history since birth. That is, with some detail, rather than….this,' she said, nodding at the old printed resume

Pascal reached her hand across the desk and took the forms, her face impassive.

'And just a word to the wise, Carrie,' the woman said, rising to her feet. 'Anything you put in this form will be checked, so be careful with your answers. And one last thing: assuming your background is acceptable to us, this is not something to be embarked upon lightly. To some extent, once you are committed, and you start, there is no going back.'

Pascal stood up, feeling the need to leave the woman with some needle. 'Sounds like a portentous load of horse-shit to me,' Pascal said. 'But I'll have a gander at the forms and get back to you if I'm interested.'

For the merest fraction of a second there was blazing rage in the womans eyes, then it was gone, covered by a bland smile. 'Subvert and disrupt, Carrie. That's the spirit. I have a feeling we'll be seeing you again very soon,' she said.

The young man bounded out of the bedroom pulling up his jockey shorts with one hand, piece of toast in the other. 'Sorry, I'll be out of your hair soon,' he said breathlessly, running for the bathroom.

'Oh, don't mind me,' Pascal said leaning up against the kitchen door, bemused expression on her face.

A moment later Christoff emerged from the same bedroom, doing up a ratty bathrobe. 'You know I'd forgotten I'd given you a key,' he said.

'Yeah, look, sorry to intrude,' she said. 'I need a favor, fast. That Mickey Mouse resume of mine doesn't pass muster and I need something kosher, like with a full checkable background. And specifically a connection with an old schoolfriend of Annie Rainier, who as we know, doesn't actually exist in real life.'

Christoff sighed. 'How solid has it got to be?'

'It'll be checked, properly this time, and I get the impression these people don't fuck around. It'll have to hold.'

'I can but try,' he said.

'Good.' She handed him the forms. 'This is what Cruella de Vil asked me to fill out.'

Christoff regarded the papers with distaste. 'All right,' he sighed. 'Leave it with me and let me have a think. What are you going to do?'

'Sleep,' she said. 'Call me later.'

Jonas Calver and Joel Ritter stood outside the breakers yard on the outskirts of Nashville. 'This is it, is it?' Calver said

'Supposedly,' Joel answered, peering dubiously at the piles of rusting vehicles - trucks, cars, burnt out hulks. The compound seemed to stretch away a football pitch in length. At the front, tall iron gates were attached to a lean-to with a big gaudy red sign on it, "Nashville Central Auto-Recycling"

As they approached the office, Joel said, 'can't believe they'll have any records going back 6 years, place like this?'

'We'll never know unless we ask,' Calver said. 'Besides IRS say 7 years records, if you've claimed loss for business bad debts deductions.'

'These guys?' Joel said. 'Tax records? Are you kidding me?'

'Lets find out,' Calver said opening the door and going through.

Inside it was cool and dim, a small claustrophobic room with a counter behind which stood a large man in biker dress; black jeans caked in grease, boots, dirty indeterminate colored shirt, leather waistcoat and red checkered bandanna tied around his forehead. A cigarette dangled from the side of his mouth.

'Can I help you gentlemen?' he said in a raspy tone. 'Saw you draw up in that big Lincoln outside, and I thought, that looks official to me? Am I right?'

'No you ain't right,' Joel said. It's a hire car.'

The man ignored Joel, keeping his eyes on Calver.

Calver said. 'It's not official, but I am an attorney, and I'm looking for some information.'

'What kind of information?' he said, and now the lazy look that had been in his eyes was gone.

'About 6 years ago,' Joel said. 'My mother's car was brought in here following a road traffic accident.'

The man laughed, still watching Calver. 'That's before my time, boy,' he said, finally turning to look at Joel. 'I bought this place 3 year ago, so I can't help you none.'

'You remember the Floyd Ritter murder case?' Calver said, playing a hunch.

The man spat. There was a metallic thud near his boot where Calver guessed there was a spittoon. 'Yep,' he said. 'Hope he's gonna fry soon. Hear he's got a date from the Governor.'

'You'd like for an innocent man to die?' Calver asked.

'Hell yes. If it's a nigger,' he said, and threw his head back and laughed. When he'd got himself under control, he added, 'funny how they is always innocent, or they find Jesus.'

Calver felt Joel tensing next to him, ready to spring at the man. He put his hand on his arm, restraining him. 'That car, that was bought in here, we have reason to believe it may have been tampered with. It's alleged Ritter killed the man he thought responsible for fixing the brakes on that car in which his wife suffered fatal injuries.'

'Sweet. Two birds with one stone,' the man muttered, his eyes fixed on Joel.

As Joel launched himself across the counter, Calver was ready, throwing an arm around his shoulders and pulling him back. 'Hey, hey,' Calver said. 'He ain't worth it.'

Joel struggled for an instant before letting Calver pull him back. 'I know,' he muttered.

'You better get that boy outta here before I have to give him a whipping,' the man said, his eyes hard. 'I told you anyway, I purchased this place 3 years ago. Anything happened before that ain't my concern. Now git, or I'll be calling the law, and I don't think they'll cotton too much to you folks round here.'

Calver held the man's eyes for a moment, weighing his look and stance, wondering if he could take it any further. He nodded. 'Good day,' he said, and half pulled, half led Joel out and back to the car.

As they pulled away, the man in the office put a cellphone to his ear. 'Pete? Its Randy,' he said. They spoke for 30 seconds.

In the car Joel said, 'you should have let me at him.' His hands gripped the steering wheel tightly, his foot pressed hard to the floor, the big car rearing away down the freeway.

'Take it easy,' Calver said, looking around at him. 'What good would it have done?'

'It would have made me feel a whole lot better, that's what good it would have done,' Joel said, almost spitting the words out.

Calver nodded. Better to let the guy stew; he'd get over it in his own way.

And he was right, because after a couple of minutes Joel said, 'sorry. I'd forgotten what it was like down here.'

'Hey, don't worry. I felt like punching him out myself,' Calver said.

'Fuck him,' Joel said. Then reflective, 'you know, I been thinking about Pops case,' he said, turning to look at Calver. 'See, I been going on with it because it gave him something to believe in. Some hope, if you like. Like, these appeal lawyers he's got, they only involved because he knew one of them from when they were kids. To be honest I always thought the appeal stuff was a waste of time, but it made him feel good, like there was some hope.'

'And now?' Calver prompted him.

'And now you turn up and start questioning everything.'

'You know, for a budding investigative journalist, you really don't seem to be curious about anything, I mean even the most basic curiosity,' Calver said, eying Joel up. 'I mean, a case involving your own father? Who's facing the death penalty? No offense intended, but you want to make it in the fourth estate, you gotta question everything. I mean everything.'

'I know,' Joel said softly, almost to himself, eyes focused on the road.

Calver glanced at him again, noticing the almost tortured visage. 'What gives, Joel?' he said. 'What's burning you, man?'

'D'you have that thing in your profession,' Joel said. 'Where you're your own worst lawyer, like when you try and act for yourself?'

Calver nodded. 'Sure, I know what you mean. It's an old saw, and it can be true, because you're emotionally involved and it clouds your judgment.'

'Well, there's something of that with all of this, and its also because I'm a coward. I got a strip of yellow down my back a mile wide. I couldn't face it, wading through it all again.'

For a moment Joel's face brightened. 'You know we had a great childhood,' he said. 'But then it turned into a nightmare. The house, then pop's business, then the car crash, mum's death and now Pop's going to die as well. I guess I copped out. The lawyers were the professionals. Let them get on with it, and if it helps Pop, gives him some hope, well, I'll go along with that.'

'And now?' Calver asked.

'And now, I don't know,' he said, his voice tailing off into uncertainty. He turned to look at Calver again. 'You've been through his case papers, and you haven't really said anything, but you obviously have some reservations about something, or why else would we be here?'

'Yeah. But don't read too much into that,' Calver said. 'After all, your father asked me to look at the papers, so a bit of basic fact checking doesn't signify I've discovered anything his lawyers don't know about.'

Joel smiled for the first time, his lips compressed together in a thin line. 'You don't give a whole lot away, do you, Jonas?'

'What d'you want me to say? You've already pointed out that even if we could show the brakes in your mother's car had been tampered with, it wouldn't do us much good. As well as that, I'm sure you're aware how extraordinarily difficult it can be to overturn a murder conviction in a state like Tennessee, even if you turn up gold-plated exculpatory evidence of innocence.'

Joel drove on, silent, deep in thought as the suburban sprawl started to build up around them as they entered the outskirts of Nashville. 'You know, me and Anita are twins, but we're so different,' he said, quietly. 'She's the brave one, always. But maybe its time I got on board. Try and be a bit more like her. You don't have to tell me nothing, Jonas, but if you think its worth going over daddy's papers again, having a harder look, I'm going to be with you hundred and twenty per cent. In fact, maybe I can do a bit more than that,' he said, his eyes brightening again.

'What you thinking?' Calver asked, catching his excitement.

'There's a girl from here, from way back. She worked on the Nashville paper. I spoke to her couple of times in the past when I was looking for contacts in the business, and she helped me out. If there's stuff we want to get a lead on, maybe she can help?'

'Now you're talking,' Calver said. 'Let's freshen up at the hotel and I'll tell you what we need. Maybe she can get a line on who owned the scrap yard before our racist friend bought it? Save us hiking around. And there's a couple of other things I'd like to get a line on. Maybe we can visit the bar where Fachetti was killed.'

'Sounds good,' Joel said. 'What about pop's lawyers, Jonas? You want to talk to them before we go asking questions?'

'Not yet. They'll have very set views they've formed over the long haul, and I doubt they'll be particularly anxious to listen to the likes of me,' he said. 'Lets us just have a fresh look at what we've got, then I'll go talk to them.'

CHAPTER EIGHT

Pascal stood at the window looking out over the city, enjoying the spectacular view from the top floor corner office. She turned around at the sound of the door opening behind her.

'So, Carrie,' Joyce Van Zim said, coming into the room, walking over and taking her seat behind the desk. 'I'm glad you seem to have overcome your reluctance to consider our special program.'

'There was no reluctance. I was busy Saturday,' Pascal said.

'Fine,' Van Zim said, airily. 'Lets move on shall we. You're new resume certainly makes for interesting reading, but how on earth does someone like you end up slumming it as an administrative assistant?'

Pascal shrugged. 'Maybe I just fancied something mindless and unchallenging for a change.'

'Carrie, you're going to have to give me a bit more than that. Mind you,' she said, looking reflective for a moment, 'it does perhaps explain how you were able to come up with that wonderfully creative expenses claim for your boss.'

'Thank you,' Pascal said. She continued to watch Van Zim, wondering what was going on in her head. She still hadn't quite distilled the essence of the woman; what you saw, clearly wasn't what you got, but what did you get? There was a a kind of self-contained air about her, overlaid with a superficial layer of charm where nothing was given away in terms of body language, expression, or her eyes - that cliched window on the soul. The only chink in her armor Pascal had seen was in that last meeting. The womans barely concealed rage, evident for a second, when Pascal had needled her about her offer of the special program. It was a safe bet Van Zim knew about the questions she had been asking about Annie Rainier. Should she volunteer something or wait and be asked? Surely the latter - better to wait and be asked. To do otherwise would be to suggest the questions were important, and not just a casual enquiry on behalf of an old school friend. It wasn't long before Pascal's assessment was proved correct.

'So, Carrie. Why were you asking questions about Annie Rainier?'

'Annie Rainer?' Pascal said, feigning ignorance for a second. 'Oh, yeah. Old school friend Martha asked me to look her up'

'That's it, is it?' Van Zim said.

'Yeah, look,' Pascal said, impatience in her voice. 'I'm starting to get just a little bit freaked about this. I was asked by a mutual friend to ask about Annie because she worked here and no one had seen or heard from her in a while. So I asked and its like I'd asked someone to help me rob the place. I mean, for Christ sakes what is so sensitive or important about Annie Rainier?'

Van Zim got up abruptly and went to stand at the window, looking out. 'You know how much trouble we get with fake whistle-blowers, Carrie?' she asked, back to the room. 'People who try and get in here, and then secretly record stuff, film and audio, and then try and blackmail us or flog it as a book or TV exposé?'

'I guess you get your share,' Pascal said. 'Not without reason.'

'Annie Rainier was one of those. We caught her trying to access confidential information with password details she bought from a hacker. So we did what we almost always do in such cases; we offered her a deal; she could sign a non-disclosure agreement, resign and walk away, but she disappeared. To maintain our position and keep our options open, we told any interested parties she's on a sabbatical. So maybe you can see why we got a little excited when you started asking questions. That's why it was originally decided to let you go after your probation period expired, but then with your performance in the lift in front of Mr DeMasi, that all changed. So, I just wanted to ask you directly to see your response. '

Pascal nodded as if she understood. 'And?' she said.

Van Zim turned back from the window, half smile on her face. 'Welcome aboard,' she said.

Van Zim walked back to her chair and sat down. She pressed something on the underside of the desk and there was a clicking sound followed by silence. The quiet hum outside was gone. 'We're now secure and your cellphone won't work in here,' she said. She opened a drawer in her desk and took out a pack of cheroots and shook one loose. 'Care for a smoke, Carrie?' she asked, placing one to her lips. She lifted a lighter from the desk that Pascal hadn't noticed before. It was in the shape of a little figure with a large face made out like Edvard Munch's the Scream. Van Zim lit the tip of the cheroot and drew hungrily on the smoke. 'Made by the best Rohingya slaves in Myanmar,' she said with a giggle, holding up the cheroot and looking at it.

'So, seems like you get to do just about anything you please here?' Pascal said, eyebrow raised. 'New York City no smoking ordinances don't stretch to the big bad bank, apparently, just the little people?'

'Oh, Carrie, didn't you ever grab a smoke when you shouldn't have? I bet you've done some real dark things in your time, which is good, because you need some of that if you want to make real money in the real world,' she said. She leaned back in her recliner chair and regarded Pascal. 'And that, after all, is what we here at the bank are all about. That's our primary purpose. So I, and others, are going to tell you how we do it and how you can help us do it, but first, I need you to sign a non disclosure form,' she said, sliding a document across the desk.

Pascal speed read the boilerplate. 'Got a pen,' she asked.

Van Zim slid one across the desk and Pascal signed and slid the form back.

'D'you know how real power works in the US, Carrie?' she asked.

'Yeah, I think I do,' Pascal replied. 'But you tell me your version.'

Van Zim puffed on the cheroot. 'Power in America doesn't reside in Washington, in the Senate or the House, or even the Oval office. Power resides in Wall Street. You know, they say a US senator can be had for as little as $100,000, sometimes less. But who needs a pissant senator, right? Not if you've got say the Secretary to the Treasury, or the chairman of the Federal Reserve on board, or moving further afield, say the chairman of the World Bank, or even the

European Central Bank. Because these people control the levers that open and close the money sluices, and thats where we have to be. That's where the power is, Carrie. Real power in the real world, and that's the key to untold riches.'

'Sounds like you're talking, in a round about way, about good old fashioned corruption,' Pascal said. 'I suppose little details like your RICO statutes are just an inconvenience?'

'Are you really that naive, Carrie, or are you just playing dumb to ride me?' Van Zim said, but she was still smiling, enjoying the back and forth. 'The chumps think that places like Nigeria and the Philippines are the hot spots for corruption, but those places have got nothing on the good old US of A. Corruption is just human nature, Carrie, and its everywhere. I mean, I know you're actually British, and we've all heard their shtick about fair play, and that's the biggest crock of all, because the Brits probably invented corruption and are the worst.'

Pascal said: 'There's nothing new in what you say; there's always been a nod and a wink. Everyone knows it goes on everywhere. So what? Unless you're saying something else is in play here, that's related to this special program of yours?' Pascal said.

'Maybe I am,' Vin Zim said. 'But elaborating on that will have to wait. At least until we've got to know you a little better.'

Van Zim stood up and went to stand behind Pascal's chair. She felt Van Zim's hands lightly touching her bare shoulders, gently kneading the muscle there. Pascal managed to stop herself from tensing even though she found Van Zim's touch distasteful. It wasn't as bad as the guy in the lift she told herself, but there wasn't much in it.

'You like that, Carrie?' Van Zim asked, voice dreamy.

'I can take it or leave it, but I wonder what your friend in the picture would think?' she said, nodding her head at the portrait on the desk.

Van Zim giggled. 'What my little wifey doesn't know can't hurt her, right, Carrie?' she said.

'Wrong,' Pascal said, standing up so that Van Zim's hands slid off her shoulders. 'I don't like to mix business with pleasure.'

Van Zim reached over and slowly traced Pascal's mouth with her fingers. 'You'll keep,' she said. Then serious once more, she added, 'you have no close friends or colleagues, do you, Carrie? Another box ticked for us, so if you were suddenly to have to go away, you have no one to tell or to worry about, yes?'

'That's right,' Pascal said, glad to get back onto more conventional territory. 'Why, am I going away?'

'Yes, tonight, but I can't tell you where. We'll provide everything you need, just turn up here at midnight ready to go,' she said.

'I have no problem with that, but I do need to know how long I will be away, ball-park, otherwise I'll have to say no,' Pascal said, calculating that if she volunteered too readily it would create suspicion.

'It will be two weeks absolute tops, Carrie, and then you'll be brought back here' she said. 'Its by way of an induction course. And don't worry, having seen you in action, it'll be nothing you can't handle, believe me.'

Pascal focused on Van Zim's eyes for tells, but they looked guileless. But then they would, wouldn't they, because the woman was a professional dissembler. But if Pascal wanted to track down Anita, there was only one way to go. She nodded. 'Bring on the magical mystery tour,' she said.

CHAPTER NINE

As Joel drove across the Cumberland river into the Buena Vista area of the city Calver looked around dubiously. 'I hate to say it, Joel,' he said, 'but I gotta say I'm disappointed. Where's the Grand Ole Opry and all those country singers I heard so much about?'

'Man you is way off base,' Joel said. 'You think a hoodlum like Fachetti was going to hang out in a tourist bar? Come on.'

Joel pulled the hire car into the curb a few vehicles down from a dive called, "Harry's". 'This is it,' he said.

Both men looked around. First the road; it was run-down as hell, under a kind of gray pall of early evening gloom, the streets off it windswept and empty, a few darkened buildings, a liquor store and a fast food joint on the corner. The place itself was just a non-descript bar; two large windows next to a doorway, with no other signs offering insight into what went on inside other than the blaring red name-plate hung over the door. It looked decidedly unwelcoming, certainly to strangers.

The two men hesitantly decamped from the car and approached the door. 'You first,' quipped Calver.

Joel grabbed his shoulder and stopped him. 'Why don't we split up? Go in separately,' he said. 'See how we do individually, then join up and get talking by accident? Might get more that way.'

Calver nodded. 'Its a plan. I need a drink so I'll go first,' he said. He pushed through the swing doors expecting more of the same, but inside, although the lights were dimmed, it seemed warm and welcoming. There was a long bar at which a few people sat on high stools, four booths down one wall and a handful of tables and chairs splayed out across the interior.

Calver took one of the high stools at the bar and waited as the barman served another customer. He looked back over his shoulder to the far corner where the doors to the toilets were situated and where he knew the killing had taken place. If there had been no changes to the building he knew there should be a corridor the other side of the door that led to male and female toilets and a fire door to the street. The killing was said to have occurred in that corridor. He looked back to find the barman standing in front of him.

'What'll you have mister?' he enquired.

'Scotch and water,' Calver said. He studied the man. As Pascal had told him so many times, bar people were almost always repositories of extraordinary troves of information about all manner of things. The key of course, as she was so fond of smugly telling him, was how you went about getting into that repository of knowledge. She said you had to examine your prospect as if you were Sherlock Holmes. What can you deduce? What can you intuit about the mark standing in front of you? Every little detail counts. Then you have to put it all together and develop a line, a commonality of interest between you and the mark that will get you in. To hell with that, Calver thought. Anyway, guy looked like an aging sourpuss; mid-forties, receding greasy black going gray hair, dandruff on the shoulders of his black waistcoat. Where d'you start with a guy like that, Calver wondered. He wished Pascal was there. She'd just start talking, but he was no good at that.

He turned his head to watch Joel enter the bar and stroll over to stand a few feet away. He ordered his drink, studiously avoiding eye contact with Calver. He collected the drink and strolled over to take a seat in the far booth right next to the doors to the corridor and toilets.

Subterfuge or straight up Calver wondered. Subterfuge never worked very well for him, so straight up it would have to be. The barman was now standing a couple of paces away polishing a glass with a white cloth. Calver was about to open the conversation with some lame line that might get him in, when the barman preempted him. 'You British?' he asked. 'I caught your accent.' His voice was soft.

'Yeah,' Calver said. 'Sorry for burning the White House down, but it was a long time ago.'

The guy didn't smile, just carried on polishing. He looked up. 'Strange kind of place to come to if you're a tourist, although we're not complaining. We welcome all sorts in here, even niggers,' he said casually, nodding over at Joel in the corner booth.

Calver tried to keep the shock out of his eyes. The guy watched him. And now he could see that the guy had been carefully observing him, and probably Joel too, all the time.

'It takes all sorts,' was the best Calver could come up with. He smiled. It wasn't going well, so go for broke. 'To tell you the truth I'm a bit of a true crime freak, and I came in here for a reason.'

'And what would be?' the guy said, although Calver guessed by now he knew very well. Calver felt a distinct urge to get up and go sit with Joel, but the guy was waiting for an answer. 'You had a murder in here 6 years or so back. Vincent Fachetti. Killed in here, out there I believe,' Calver said, pointing back to the doors to the toilet. 'Floyd Ritter's currently on death row for it, and about to take that long black ride to hell.'

The man nodded. 'Can't be too soon for me,' he said. 'You talk like a lawyer, even though you're a limey, and I know who the jungle bunny over in the corner there is. We don't like folks like you coming in here and asking questions. So I'd like for you both to finish your drinks and get the hell out of my bar?'

Calver watched the guy wondering whether to come back at him. But he was outgunned and on foreign territory. He finished his drink and put his glass carefully back on the bar. 'Thanks for the drink and your hospitality,' he said. 'I'll get my friend.'

He walked over and found Joel had been joined by a young woman. Calver said, 'covers blown right to hell. We need to leave now, or I think there'll be trouble.'

Joel looked surprised and disappointed. 'Man, I knew I shouldn't of let you come in here alone,' he said, forgetting it was his idea. He climbed to his feet, nodding at the girl. 'It was nice talking to you, even if it was only for a second.'

She looked disappointed as she watched them leave. As their car pulled away from the curb, back inside, the barman motioned her over, a cellphone clamped to his ear.

'What the fuck happened in there, man?' Joel asked as the big hire car picked up speed. 'I mean we hardly get our feet under the table and you get us kicked out.'

'He knew who we were,' Calver said, patiently. 'Or, he knew who you were. And he sounded like a member of the Ku Klux Klan.'

'What did he say?' Joel said, anger spilling out of him as he began to slow the car. 'I'm going back, see him try and say it to my face, fucker.'

'Forget going back, we're a busted flush,' Calver said. 'Come on, keep driving. Tell me about this journalist on the local paper you mentioned earlier?'

Joel looked around at him. 'Man, I should be used to it by now,' he said. After a moment he smiled, perhaps to himself. 'Fuck it. Shouldn't let it get to me. We'll go see Kelly Phillips,' he said.

'Kelly Phillips?' Calver said.

'Yeah, the cub reporter on the Tennessean, time of the murder,' he said.

Calver nodded. 'Who was the girl you were speaking to just now, in the bar?' he asked.

'Know what she told me?'

'How would I?' Calver said.

'She told me her momma used to work the joint time of the murder.'

They rode on in silence for a few beats, Calver waiting for Joel to elaborate. When he stayed silent, Calver said, 'you're kidding me, right?'

'No,' he said seriously. 'Told her who I was, but I think she was trying to hustle me. Soon as I'm hooked, she'd set up a phony meeting with her momma, then ask for money.'

'How do you know that, Einstein?' Calver said. 'And, what if you're wrong? What if she actually does know something? Can you afford to take a chance when your pop's life is hanging in the balance?'

'Hey, don't try and tell me about my father's life hanging in the balance,' he said, blazing anger flaring up again. 'I've lived with it for years, so I don't need some half-assed lawyer trying to tell me about it.'

'Sorry,' Calver said gently. 'Look ,lets both calm down and go see your friend, Kelly Phillips.'

After a beat, Calver added, 'but it wouldn't hurt?'

'Wouldn't hurt what?'

'Wouldn't hurt if in the next couple of days you went down to Harry's bar and watch until she comes out, and then talk to her, find out what she's knows. If its nothing, we lose nothing. If its something……'

Joel drove on in silence, brooding. 'There's something in what you say,' he muttered grudgingly. 'Okay, I'll go down there tomorrow and check it out.'

Calver didn't say anything, anxious not to provoke another outburst. A short time later they pulled into a small brightly lit parking lot. 'Welcome to Nashville's online news hub,' Joel said, anger gone and a smile back on his face. 'This is where we'll likely find Kelly this time of night,' he said, glancing at his watch.

The brightly lit motif carried on into the bustling interior of the hub; it was like an internet cafe, but with no pattern to the layout, just a few tables where little groups sat drinking various beverages, chatting or working on screens amid a lot of boisterous chatter. Joel made for a small table in the corner where just two were sitting, a man in his sixties and a girl, mid-twenties. When the girl saw Joel approaching she said something to the guy. He nodded, rose and left the table.

She got up and hugged Joel. 'Great to see you, Joel. How you been?' she asked, pushing him away and looking him up and down. She had a sweet pale face with freckles, topped off with curly brown hair.

'Good. How about you, Kelly?' he said. 'You're looking great.' He gestured at Calver. 'And this is my friend, Jonas Calver. He's an attorney from New York, here helping me with Dad's case.'

They took seats around the table. 'How is your father, Joel? I hear you got a date. Sorry,' she said. 'How is he taking it?'

Joel said, 'he's okay. Well as can be expected.' He moved in his chair, restless. ' Look, Kelly, we're here for one last maybe desperate trawl through his case, and with Jonas I got a fresh pair of eyes. So we're going through it all again, see if there's anything we missed. Me and you talked at the time before and at the trial, but can you just take us through it again. Like what you saw and found out. Tell it to Jonas afresh, like I'm not here.'

A pained expression crossed her face. 'I wish I had a lot to tell you, Jonas, but I don't. I had no direct involvement in the murder investigation or trial, I was just a very junior reporter on the Tennessean at the time,' she said, looking apologetically at Joel.

'No problem,' Calver said. 'But I think you may be downplaying your involvement. Isn't it true that you reported on the auto crash that ultimately killed Floyd's wife - Joel's mother? As I understand it, it was a biggish local story because the auto accident blocked the freeway and there was a helicopter brought in to get her to hospital?'

'Is that right?' Joel muttered.

'Yeah,' Calver said. 'Google's not quite as good as everyone seems to assume. I had to dig the old fashioned way, in the archives at the library. There were a couple of small pieces there, one under your bye-line,' he said.

'Yeah, I remember it,' she said, puzzled. 'I did cover it, and I know it came up in the trial as motive, from both sides, but then Floyd admitted the fight with Fachetti, but denied killing him, so the car crash went out the window, because it was irrelevant.'

She paused as she thought back, digging down into her memory. She started again, tentatively. 'Prosecution said there was no evidence that the auto crash was anything other than a tragic accident. But crucially, Floyd believed Fachetti had set it up, and that's why he went looking for him with a knife, and that's why he killed him. Premeditated murder.

'I remember they were real careful about the crash evidence and were anxious to keep it to a minimum. I guess they felt if they played on it too much, juries are fickle, and they might think Fachetti deserved to die for setting it up. The only other thing I'd say,' she added, looking at Joel. 'Is I never thought Floyd's then lawyers were going to set the world alight, and in the end, I don't know how much investigation the police did on a white on black killing. And just remember, this was no big murder case, even around here, just another unfortunate killing in a bar, so there was no great interest in the story. Obviously, because of my connection to Joel, I followed it closely.'

Phillips looked at Calver expectantly, but when he didn't respond, she continued. 'Surely the issue is did Floyd kill Fachetti or not, and can you prove he didn't, not the motive. Why start digging into that, the crash, especially this late in the day?'

'That's right,' Joel said. 'That's what I said.'

Calver sighed. 'I'm a pretty unusual lawyer, folks, because I'm a truth seeker,' he said. 'I want to know what happened, even if at trial I'm going to flat-out deny it, if that's what it takes to get my client off. Most lawyers will tell you that's unethical, since you're an officer of the court and mustn't knowingly run a defense you know to be untrue, but I say, fuck that. Disbar me, or stick me in jail if you want to, if that's your way, but the client's king, and we only get one life, right? So here, I want to know what happened first, not even whether what my client is saying is true or not. I want the truth. Then I can do something with it.'

'Wow!' Phillips said. 'I like this guy. You want the truth, Jonas? You should have been a journalist.'

They all sat for a moment without speaking. Kelly Phillips was first to break silence. 'Okay,' she said slowly. 'I'm guessing you want to know what happened at the crash? Was there any evidence that the car had been tampered with? What did the cops do at the site, witnesses?'

'You got it, Kelly,' Calver said. He raised his eyes and met Joel's steely glare.

She ran a hand through her curly brown hair, looking serious as she thought back to the crash call out.

CHAPTER TEN

'It was my first solo gig,' Kelly Phillips said, smiling to herself as she remembered the callow professional pride she had felt at the time. 'It was 2 am in the morning and they hauled me out of bed because no one else would go and it didn't sound serious. So I scooted down there determined to do the best job ever. Boy was I green. TV were already there and police chief Rawlins was doing his usual PR bullshit, while his point man, officer Gillespie was manhandling onlookers and press away from the scene. When I got close to the vehicle I couldn't believe anyone could have survived. It looked like the car front had been concertinaed right into the front seats, but the twelve wheeler road hog it had hit was virtually undamaged. I mean, the driver was walking around cracking jokes, probably in shock.'

Calver grimaced. 'Is that all?' he said rather abruptly, disappointed, cutting in on her.

'No, that's not all,' she said, throwing a look at him. She reached down to a string bag under the table. 'In them days I still used a notebook,' she said, removing a tablet and switching it on. 'I know I'm a nerd but I couldn't resist transposing them all onto the tablet. People might be interested when I win a Pulitzer Prize,' she said with a wink at Calver. 'Here it is,' she added, running her eye over a scanned image of her scribbled notes.

'It was an auto crash right?' Joel said. 'So you'll have just taken the basics for a factual news story? But was there anything else that struck you?'

Kelly closed her eyes and rubbed her face. 'I remember there was a guy there. I think he was in the vehicle behind your mother's car, and he looked like he was in shock too. He was walking around mumbling "the red lights were on but nothing was happening?". Kind of muttering to himself, and he said it a couple of times. But there were no traffic lights there, so I thought he was just gone crazy, and then the uniformed cop, Gillespie grabbed a hold of him and herded him away. Told me they would take a statement from him, so he couldn't talk to me, so I didn't pursue it.'

'That was your first mistake,' Calver said softly.

'What do you mean?' Kelly said.

'I don't think the guy was talking about traffic lights,' Calver said, watching her face.

Joel nodded, his expression bitter. 'He's talking about mum's brake lights, isn't he? They were on, but the car's not slowing down.'

'Shit!' Kelly said, slow realization crawling across her face. She sat for a moment shell-shocked, then looked down at her notebook. 'I got the guy's name and car registration, if its any use now,' she added forlornly. She gave the details to Joel.

Calver smiled grimly. 'We all make mistakes when we start out, Kelly. Its the only way to learn. You should see some of cock-ups I made when I was a young lawyer.'

'Yeah, but did they result in someone getting away with cold blooded murder, and another man, for all we know, quite possibly going to be executed for a crime he didn't commit? she said.

'Hey,' Joel said. 'You can't put that all on yourself. Sounds like the fix was in from the start.'

'I agree,' Calver said. 'But maybe you can redeem yourself by helping us out as much as you can now? Could be there'll be a story in it for you at the end of it all.'

'I don't care about a story,' she said. 'What do you need?'

'"Nashville Central Auto-Recycling",' Calver said. 'We think the car was taken there after the crash, but current owner says the business was sold to him a few years ago. Can you track the seller down for us?'

'No problem,' she said. 'But I can remember this much, their truck was at the scene when I got there. I remember it cause its got their signs plastered all over it.'

Calver nodded. 'And what about this cop, Gillespie, who was at the scene? Sounds like he made an impression on you? You remembered his name without looking at your notes?'

'Who could forget him. A racist redneck of the worst kind,' she said. She looked at Joel, gauging his mood. She said, tentatively, 'he made some disgusting comments about your mum as they were cutting her out, that I wont repeat.'

She added as an afterthought, 'of course, I didn't now it was your mother at the time, I only learned that later.'

'What do you know about Gillespie?' Calver asked.

'Nothing really other than what I've told you,' she said. 'Haven't run across him again since then. But I still know the guy on the crime beat at the paper. He'll know if there is anything. I'll give him a call.'

Calver and Joel looked at each other, wondering if there was anything else to ask. Kelly said, 'look, guys I've got to go.'

'We do too,' Calver said, getting up from the table.

'I'll run this stuff down and give you a call tomorrow,' she said. She hugged Joel and nodded at Calver, and then she was gone, moving between the tables and out the door.

Pascal rolled out of bed wondering where she was. A loud klaxon horn was sounding like an air raid siren, blaring out in the semi-darkness. She rubbed her face remembering the journey from the night before. First a private jet from JFK to Havana, Cuba then a helicopter ride to God knows where. It had been dark and they had refused to tell her where they were going, but after leaving Havana they traveled over large tracts of the sea so she guessed it was to one of the small islands. She knew there were many dotted around, inhabited and uninhabited. They had landed in the middle of what looked like a modern prison complex - high wire fences, powerful lights and array of bunker warehouse type buildings - and from there she had been escorted to a small cell with a bed. She was told to sleep. The guy, or maybe guard, had said goodnight and then locked the door. Bushed, she'd slept.

She checked her watch; it was 5.30 am. She went to a small sink in the corner and splashed water on her face. As she dried her hands on a rough towel she heard steps outside then the lock being turned. It was the same guy. He gestured for her to follow.

As they went along a corridor, she said, 'any chance of getting breakfast round here?'

'Later,' he grunted. He pushed open a door. 'Go in,' he said.

She heard the door close behind her. She was in a small lecture theater, twenty or so benches running down to a stage with lectern and screen. The place was empty. As she looked around a door at the side of the stage opened and a man came bustling in. 'Good morning, good morning,' he called up to her. 'Class of one today I'm told, so you can be assured of my full attention.' He clapped his hands. 'Come on down to the front, so I can see you.'

'Any chance of getting some breakfast round here?' she asked as she made her way down.

'You'll be having breakfast with Ms Van Zim at 9 am, but for now you need to concentrate,' he said. He had a head that jutted forward on a thick neck, giving an impression of restrained aggression, and his black eyes were intense. Worse still, he had one of those goatee beards that seemed way too tidy, almost sculpted, like a fastidiously manicured lawn. It spoke of a terrible vanity.

He smiled thinly and continued. 'My name is professor Paul Zimmerman and I'm here to give you a personal lecture on real world economics, not the crap they teach you at Harvard and MIT, because that's strictly for the birds. No, this is a crash course in real finance if you will. Economics based on what really happens out there, not on what some outdated model says should happen, because, let me tell you: the world has moved on and those monkeys still ain't worked out how to peel a banana.' His words were delivered in a kind of rapid staccato, rat-a-tat- tat, like a machine gun.

Pascal bit back a smart retort. 'Look, professor,' she said, her tummy rumbling with discontent. 'I hate to disappoint you, but I know nothing about economics. I flunked it at school, and it really doesn't float my boat. So maybe we could just move right along to breakfast. What d'you say?'

He smiled again, his thin lips compressed into a humorless line. 'Miss Potter, I am not here to give you a lecture on classic economics,' he said, carefully enunciating each word. 'As you rightly surmise, that would be a waste of my precious time. No, I'm here to teach you about the exercise of financial power, and that, my dear, is based upon gaining control of the rules of the game.'

Pascal sighed. If she wanted breakfast, she guessed she was going to have to sit and listen. 'Okay, professor, I'm all ears. Go for it.'

And that's what he did, non stop for the next three hours. In the end, Pascal had to admit, it actually was a fascinating lecture, supported by newsreel footage, charts and talking heads. He sketched out an unorthodox and honest, if completely immoral, authoritarian world view of economics and finance. And as he had alluded to in the preface to the lecture, the key really was in seizing control of the rule making and enforcement apparatus, and using it for exclusively your own enrichment. In the middle section of the lecture he did a kind of workshop tutorial on the 2008 crash and the bail out, and Pascal had found herself both fascinated and horrified at the details he casually imparted to her.

But first he'd given her a brief explanation of the main players and institutions. The two most important in America were the Federal Reserve Bank (known as the Fed) and the Secretary to the Treasury, the top financial adviser to the president. 'So, the Fed, Carrie, that's the mother of all banks, the big Kahuna. Biggest central bank in the world, and it regulates all dollar activities. Of course its run by a guy, the chairman. Underneath, it has a load of state Federal Reserve banks as well, like the New York Fed that all oil settlements in the world go through. Then we have a guy possibly equally as important as chairman of the Fed, thats the Secretary to The Treasury, the President's most important financial adviser. And he wields enormous power, and as we'll see, often for his own benefit rather than that of the country. Underneath these two titans we have some bit players like the SEC, thats the Securities and Exchange Commission that's there to protect investors, and boy, that's a joke, as you'll see. Then we have the CFCT, Commodity Futures Trading Commission, its brief, to prohibit fraudulent conduct in the trading of futures contracts. Its about as effective as the SEC but serves the same purpose of window dressing.

'Okay, Carrie, lets take a look at some of the guys who've held these roles and turned them to the benefit of themselves and their friends at the expense of the people they're there to protect.

'At the top of the pyramid was Ben Bernanke, head of the Federal Reserve at the time of the crash. This guy, essentially, secretly handed over $29 trillion in loans to the criminal banks, hedge funds and billionaires who had caused the crisis. This was in addition to the billions paid out under the very public TARP program we all know about.

'So as an example of how things worked in the nexus between Wall Street and Washington,' Zimmerman said, 'lets take a look at Citigroup, one of the mega banks at the center of the crisis. Citigroup was insolvent during the crisis and yet the fed gave them $2.5 trillion even though the Fed is not allowed to loan money to insolvent institutions. Remember, Carrie,' Zimmerman emphasized, 'this is trillions, not billions.'

Pascal had nodded, numbly, already seeing zeros stretching away to infinity.

Zimmerman had then relentlessly moved on to glory in what the chairman of the New York Fed had done at the time. He was meant to be acting as a tough regulator but instead took 29 lunches, dinners and breakfasts with Citigroup, before they offered him a job, which he declined when he got a better offer as Treasury Secretary from the Obama administration. There, he did what he was programmed to do, he kept the insolvent bank, Citigroup afloat despite its wrongdoing. Sweet, huh?' Zimmerman said aglow with admiration. He continued, 'and this was the guy who later admitted that the Home Affordable Modification Program, or HAMP, was not in fact there to help struggling families with children keep a roof over their heads in the face of foreclosure proceedings, it was actually there to "foam the runway for" the crooked banks. That's right, Carrie. You heard that right. That's what he said.

'The last one of our culprits for study today, Carrie, is George W Bush's Treasury Secretary. He was there when the shit hit the fan, but it didn't harm him one little bit. Used to work at Goldman Sachs in the run up to the crash, thats when they were selling those toxic CDO's to their own unsuspecting and trusting sheep-like investors. Get this Carrie, they reckon Goldman's packaged $73 billion in synthetic CDO's between 2004 and the crash. On one of these deals that we know about, Goldman's were betting the investments would lose value. In street parlance, Carrie, they shorted their own deals they'd sold their own clients, by a factor of 10 - 1. Know how much they made out of scalping their own investors, Carrie?'

Here she had shaken her head numbly.

'Oh, only about $930 million.' Here he laughed so uproariously he could barely get his final words out. 'Goldman's investors who went long lost almost all their money. Way to go, eh, Carrie?

'These guys are beautiful, aren't they? They are our model. During that period, 10 million Americans lost their homes to foreclosure, while these guys were minting it. Charged with overseeing and protecting the ordinary folk, they skinned them alive instead, and made billions.

'And d'you know what they're up to right now, Carrie? I bet you'll never guess?'

'Go on, surprise me, professor,' she said, beyond shocked, her rumbling stomach long forgotten.

'They're only trying to get congress to repeal even more of the Dodd-Frank financial legislation, so when the next crisis hits they'll be free to chuck another $29 trillion to their friends on Wall Street.'

She thought he was going to swoon at the audacity and shamelessness of it all, his eyes shining with fervor and passion. Then he seemed to come down off his cloud. 'Now, Carrie,' he said, finally looking at his watch - it was 8.45 am. 'I guess you're wondering what all this has to do with you, right?'

'Well, that question did kind of skip across my mind about two hours ago,' she said. But she was interested now, because so far she couldn't see a link between herself and what Zimmerman had been talking about for the last three hours.

He nodded, calm now, after the storm. 'You and your ilk, Carrie, are not the king pins, like the guys we have been discussing. You're the infantry, the place-men, or woman,' he said, brief smile. 'You can be one of our cohorts of people we are putting in place in all the major financial and legal institutions, at all levels. Some of you are finance people, warrior traders, others, where it turns out they perhaps don't have a flair for finance, they can become real warriors, in our protection squad.'

'A Financial Mujahideen, waging a capitalist Jihad?' Pascal said, half smile, but she wasn't laughing

'I'm sure it does sound fantastical to you, Carrie, but I can assure you it is real. Over breakfast Ms Van Zim can fill in the gaps and answer your questions.' He nodded. 'Thank you for your time.'

With that he turned and left as he had arrived, through a door at the side of the stage.

CHAPTER ELEVEN

Eggs, bacon, sausages, tomatoes, mushrooms, fried bread and beans. As the plate was brought over the juices in Pascal's mouth began to work. Back home they would have called it a full English. As the waiter, clad in black and white livery, placed the plate down before her, Pascal fell on it. Joyce Van Zim sat across from her, smoke rising from a cheroot dangling from her lip, an amused expression on her face.

They were sat in a big canteen adjoining the kitchen, all zinc and stainless steel surfaces, with one long service hatch. It was the kind of place you might expect to find on a military base, only this one was empty apart from Pascal and Van Zim, and the waiter hovering just out of earshot.

After about five minutes of Pascal's concentrated munching, she looked up and nodded at the waiter. 'Man, that was something else,' she said. 'Anymore coffee in the pot?'

The waiter flashed a gleaming smile and hustled over, grinning as he poured.

Pascal turned back to Van Zim. 'Thanks for smoking whilst I ate. Really helps the flavor,' she said.

'Oh I didn't think you'd notice, Carrie,' Van Zim replied. 'You know, gluttony can be kinda sexy, in a funny kind of way,' she added, her eyes dreamy.

Pascal let that pass. 'Where are we anyway?' she asked.

'Our island, 27 nautical miles from Cuba. How do you like it?' she asked.

'Reminds me of Guantanamo,' Pascal said. She sipped her coffee, ruminating on the elephant in the room. 'So, okay, Joyce. I've had the lecture, and I'll admit, it was an eye opener, even for a cynic like me. And obviously I listened with interest to professor Zimmerman's rather fanatical rant about creating an army of financial zealots, but he didn't really expand on their purpose. So putting two and two together, I assume they are placed in say the regulatory and enforcement bodies, to be used when the time is right. Kind of like sleeper cells. Oh, and with a private army to protect them of the ones who can't cut it as financial geniuses?'

Van Zim sat silent, a slight smile on her lips, waiting to see if Pascal would develop her analysis further.

'So trouble is, Joyce,' she continued. 'It doesn't stack up. There have been a thousand exposés written about the 2008 crash and the wrongdoing and corruption of officials and bankers. And yeah, they all got away with it. So what, that's the American way. Why d'you need a private army. When the shit hits the fan again, just rinse and repeat the same old process. Too big to fail, and you can't cure stupid, so they get bailed out again. So why would you need a load of little people to help you.'

'You're wrong, Carrie,' Joyce said, serious. 'Nothing is ever a perfect repetition of what went before, and we think it will be very different this time, when the coming crash hits. We have employed some of the best minds on the planet to try and work out and model what's coming this time, and let me tell you; one thing we know for sure: it won't be the same. Its partly because the financial tools to fight the last crash are now played out and used up. There's nothing left in the toolbox. They've printed trillions and trillions of dollars out of thin air, and they had interest rates around the world at the lowest levels ever seen, in some cases they've even been negative, and in the real world it hasn't worked. In politics too, the discourse is not too far away from actual physical violence between the two sides. How long before a US president decides he doesn't actually want to leave office, and decides to stick around? Fuck the constitution? And there's more, Carrie. Okay its anecdotal stuff, but that's often where you get the first inklings of a new order. The very rich, the billionaires, and relatively and historically speaking, there are now a lot of them about, what are they doing?'

Pascal shrugged. 'Jerking off over their loot?'

Van Zim ignored the quip, completely engrossed in her soliloquy. 'They're beefing up their security for the long haul. Private armies abound. Gated communities with razor wire, dogs and moats. The physical distance between them and the mob gets wider every day, so that now it apes the gap of financial inequality between them as it yaws to levels unseen at any time in history. As we all know, there comes a tipping point, and we calculate, when it comes this time it will be truly apocalyptic, and we think maybe some of these billionaires have sensed this - they are by definition not usually stupid people. Pitchforks on the street won't get close, but perhaps the Chinese and Russian revolutions give us a clue. What did the people do? They rose up and killed all the landlords, or, now, in our modern parlance, it will be the rentiers. The people who've managed to purloin all of the wealth that a community has to offer, at the expense of that community.'

Pascal, eyes narrowed, watched Van Zim. The woman sounded even madder than Zimmerman, although there was a clear logic to what she was saying.

'So, Carrie,' Van Zim said, then paused dramatically before delivering the punchline: 'would you like to join us?'

Instead of saying what she wanted to say - you must be fucking crazy - Pascal said: 'who is us? And, forgive my ignorance, but I am still completely mystified as to what your master plan actually is? I mean, like how many of these little financial worker bees have you got buzzing around inside these institutions, just ready to start stinging when the pheromones come a calling? '

'All will be revealed, when we know you can be trusted,' she said.

'I thought I was trusted? That's why I'm here'

'Come, Carrie, you don't expect us to tell you all our secrets in one go, do you?' she said, playful again.

'Fine, so what's the next step? How do I gain that trust?'

'A test,' she said.

As the words left Van Zim's mouth her cellphone lit up on the table. She checked the screen, stiffened and grabbed it up, her whole body coming to attention. She got up from the table and moved away, listening, then beginning to reply in muffled tones that Pascal could not hear.

Pascal beckoned the waiter over. 'How you doing, buddy?' she asked him.

He was a young Hispanic man with friendly eyes but he seemed nervous. He nodded. 'Good, si', he said, beginning to move away. She noticed his eyes kept darting over towards the corner of the vast eating area, and now she could see there was a man sitting there that she hadn't noticed when she had come in. She couldn't really make out his features from that distance, but he was leaning back in his chair so that the upper part of his body was in shadow, and all she could see was a cup of coffee held in front of his face.

Pascal looked up as Van Zim came back, her phone call finished. Her smile seemed brittle. She said, 'someone up there seems to like you. No two week sojourn for you.'

'What d'you mean?' Pascal asked.

'You're going straight back. We've provisionally tagged you as a soldier rather than a trader but that may change, if you satisfactorily complete the test,' she said. 'Normally you'd stay here two weeks, but not you.'

'And this test is what? Find the golden fleece?' Pascal said. She'd been an ardent fan of the Jason and the Argonaut movie franchise as a child. Not happy memories, as her stepfather used to leave them on a loop when he would lock the lonely child in her punishment cupboard when he went out.

'Not quite, my dear,' Van Zim said, looking up as the man who had been sitting in the corner approached. 'This, my dear, is, Cimino,' she said nodding at the man as he came to a stop.

'Cimino what?' Pascal said, eying up the stranger.

'You know, I don't know?' Van Zim said. 'That's all anyone has ever called him, right, Cimino?'

He nodded without speaking, his eyes never leaving Pascal's face.

'Cimino is head of security for all our operations, and you will be working with him during your test. I'm sure you'll have a whale of a time, right, Cimino?' she said with a laugh.

He laughed as well, briefly, but it was enough. A visceral shiver passed through Pascal as she remembered the last time she had heard that same laugh when she had hid in the wardrobe in Anita's apartment. This time his mirth didn't quite degenerate into paroxysms of hysteria like the last time, but it was enough.

His eyes were still on her, and Pascal kept her face blank. He was about 5' 10" and powerfully built with dark greased over hair and sunken black eyes in a marble face. Pascal guessed he was early forties. He had a slight paunch but she doubted it would slow him down any. He was dressed in a smart and expensive dark blue suit with an white open-neck shirt undone rather too far for Pascal's taste. Nestling amongst the rather disgusting tight black curls on his chest was a gold medallion on a chain.

Pascal nodded up at him, not rising or offering her hand. Start the psychological tricks early was always her way. 'Cimino's a bit hard on the tongue, so I'll just call you medallion man,' she said. 'Its got some dodgy connotations where I come from, but its fine over here,' she added with an innocent smile.

Cimino didn't smile back, he just kept on watching her, unblinking and relaxed. Pascal did the same, holding his eyes as well, waiting to see who would blink first.

Van Zim broke the battle of wills, unaware it was taking place.

'Sir, or Mr Cimino, will be fine I think, Carrie. Now, as to the test, since you expressed interest in Annie Rainier, your test will be to find her. Its that simple,' she said with a quick smile. 'Cimino has all the information you should need and you will report to him. When you have successfully located her, you will have passed the test, but there is of course a time limit - you have one month.'

'I take it you've already tried to find her?' Pascal said. 'So how d'you think I'm going to do it if you can't?'

'That, Carrie dear, is why its called a test,' Van Zim said, picking up her bag. 'I have to go now, so I will leave you in the capable hands of Cimino.' She nodded, and walked away towards the exit.

It was gone 8 pm when Calver got to the offices of Ritter's lawyers, Minter, Rafflin and Coughlan. They occupied a swish place in the commercial district of Nashville, all glass and chrome, and Calver was surprised. He had expected a country hick outfit, rustic and quaint, but this was the opposite. His shoes sunk into the thick pile carpet as he approached the lone girl on reception, surprised there was any support staff still there at that time. She was blonde with great teeth. He told her he was there to see Mike Shapiro. She smiled again and Calver felt a fleeting erotic frisson, a fantasy of being eaten alive by the big bad wolf.

She said Mike was waiting for him and led him down a short corridor to a door where she knocked quietly and ushered him in. Calver turned to watch her go, a pang of regret rippling through him.

'Look but don't touch, especially with the "me too" thought police out there watching you,' the guy behind the desk said. He got up to shake Calver's hand. He looked a trim mid-forties with an easy smile.

'Mike Shapiro,' he said. Firm grip with no power posturing. 'Sit down,' he said, gesturing at a chair.

When they were both seated he steepled his fingers and regarded Calver over them. 'We're both lawyers, Mr Calver, so perhaps we can cut through the bullshit. What exactly is your angle? Or, perhaps angle is the wrong word. How about, hustle?'

Calver smiled. 'Relax counselor. I'm not here to get my snout in the trough. I'm just a fresh pair of eyes. Let me look, then I'm gone. I'm sure there's nothing to see. Then state can nix him in less than two months and you can pocket a big slice of that insurance money.'

Shapiro shrugged. 'That's not what this is about, and frankly, do we look like we need the money?' he said, gesturing around his sumptuously furnished office.

'Maybe not. But then again, you don't strike me as the crusading type, all fired up with righteous justice,' Calver said. 'But, of course your motives are none of my business, and you have already graciously provided me with a copy of all the case papers, which I've been through.'

'And?'

'And nothing,' Calver said. 'Can't fault the logic or the moves, given the information I've seen so far.'

'So why are you here?'

'Just to ask a few questions, then I'm gone.'

'Fair enough,' he said. 'Shoot.'

'I'll start with the easy stuff first. Are you making a plea for clemency to the governor?'

'Of course. Its standard procedure. Floyd didn't want us to, but Joel persuaded him,' Shapiro said.

Calver nodded. 'I assume it will be full of the usual bullshit about his tough childhood, blah, blah, blah, and that you already know its a waste of time?'

'Hey, you've done this stuff before,' he said with an empty laugh.

Calver ignored it. 'Can I suggest a revolutionary concept for the clemency plea?' he said.

'I'm listening?' Shapiro said, glancing at his watch.

'Tell the story of the banks.'

He shook his head slowly. 'I'm not following you.'

'I think you are,' Calver said. 'You know the family's history, or should do. Bank wiped them out. Hard working American family who did all the right things, trying to better themselves and got crucified by the greed of the banks, along with millions of others. That was the start of Floyd's descent into a place where the killing took place. You need to start there'

'You're kidding me, right?' Shapiro said. But there was a hint of something in the back of his eyes. 'That's crazy. Governor would laugh his ass off, and it'd make the firm look stupid. But anyway, Floyd still denies the killing, so how could we run it anyway? No way.'

'I hear what you're saying,' Calver said. 'So I got a proposition for you?'

Shapiro's expression didn't change. 'You don't give up do you, Calver?'

'Let me do a draft clemency plea of my own. Then we can ask

Floyd which one he likes best?' Calver said.

'I can't stop you drafting something up,' Shapiro said. 'But you'll be wasting your time, and I will argue in the strongest possible terms that Floyd should leave that stuff out.'

'Fair enough,' Calver said.

'Anything else, Calver, because I have a dinner date?'

'Couple of things. I think you were not his original attorney, is that right?'

'Yeah. He had some ambulance chasing drunk first time around. Part of his appeals were based on incompetent counsel. What's your point?'

'Nothing. Just wanted confirmation. What was his name, the attorney? Ned Peters, wasn't it?'

'You know it was, its in the papers.'

'He still around?'

'I believe so. Check the drunk tanks,' Shapiro said. 'Its a bit late in the day to go down that road, but its your time, counselor. Look, I have to go now.'

'No problem,' Calver said. ' I won't keep you, but just two last things? First the story, or the allegation, that Fachetti was responsible for rigging the brakes on Floyd's wifes car. Was that ever pursued?'

'Not really. Ned Peters was apparently interested initially but with Floyd denying the killing, it didn't go anywhere, and I think he got stonewalled.'

'Yeah. Thats what I heard,' Calver said, a questioning look on his face. 'The police accident report's gone missing and her car was scrapped and crushed within 48 hours of the smash?'

Shapiro's expression didn't change. He said, 'its what I heard as well, but as I'm sure you've already worked out, who cares about a motive for a killing he denies? Now I really have to go. So what's you're last question, Calver?' he said, rising to his feet.

'There were two witnesses in the bar that night swore blind it was all down to Floyd. Anyone ever go back and talk to them?'

'No. Why would they? Both guys were unshakable on the stand. Their stories corroborated each other. One of them is dead anyway, I believe, but he said he didn't see the actual killing because it took place in the corridor outside the toilet. And the other was Frank Ross, who says he went into the corridor and did see it.'

'Isn't it true his original birth name was Rossi, before he anglicized it? So I guess he's Italian extraction, just like Fachetti?' Calver said. 'How about that?'

'Word of warning, Calver. Don't go interfering with witnesses, or you'll have the district attorney and Nashville PD down our throats, just when we don't need it.'

'Yeah, well, I'd hate to spoil the execution party,' Calver said, getting up and holding out his hand. 'Thanks for you time.'

'No problem,' Shapiro said. As he watched Calver walk out the door he reached in his jacket, took out a cell-phone and hit a speed-dial number. 'We need to talk,' he said, voice clipped and tight.

CHAPTER TWELVE

Pascal sat on the plane looking at the single sheet of paper Cimino had given her. It contained two bits of information she already knew - Annie Rainier's name and her last address - and that was it. Other than handing her the useless piece of of paper and an economy ticket to New York, thats all Cimino had done. They had spent roughly ten minutes together during which he had barely said more than two words, before she had been bundled back onto a helicopter for the trip back to Havana. Pascal was puzzled by the fact that they didn't seem worried by not being able to find Rainier, which perhaps suggested that she and Calver might have misunderstood what was going on.

Pascal looked out of the cabin window at the bank of brooding blue-gray clouds below. In her mind she reviewed what she thought she knew. It was clear Van Zim and Cimino didn't know that Annie Rainier was in fact Anita Ritter, which in turn suggested that they were probably telling the truth, that they had discovered her snooping, believed she was the usual run of the mill whistle-blower, and offered her a deal to walk away in exchange for silence? That was their usual procedure in cases where they thought a mole might have dug up some dirt. And they had her hard drive, and that had no dirt on it, so that supported the view they didn't really consider her any kind of serious threat. So it might be logical for them to want to find her just to close the deal and tie up the loose ends. That would fit in with making finding the girl part of Pascal's test. They probably thought Pascal was well capable of doing that, passing the test and coming on board. That in turn suggested they probably hadn't expended much effort in finding Anita, which was borne out by Cimino's casual attitude. So maybe it wouldn't be so hard to find her. But then why would Anita disappear and not contact her father or brother? And why phone Calver and then fail to turn up for the meet? That made no sense; or the 6 months rent paid up on her apartment or the postcard from Cuba?

What about Cuba? Maybe she should have stopped off there and had a look around? But from what Calver had told her, Anita was a New Yorker who knew how to live on the street. So thats where she would start. Find the girl, then they'd know what the hell was going on. Satisfied on a plan she lay her head back on the rest and slept.

Calver pulled the hire car up around fifty meters away from the property. He turned the engine off and sat back deep in the seat. He ran a hand through the stubble on his chin. He needed a shave and a bath, but first he would see whether the guy was going to talk to him. Kelly Phillips had come through with the name - Pete Atkins - the guy who owned the auto wrecker yard at the time the car was taken there. And this was the current address for the guy.

Calver studied the property. It was on a landscaped plot and Calver reckoned, having done some online price comparisons, you wouldn't get much change out of $2 million if you wanted to buy the place. Not bad for a guy whose last business accounts for the firm showed a big loss. But Kelly had told him, scrap car businesses were often cash only and sometimes fronts for criminal activity. No kidding, Calver had thought, but hadn't said. The business losses were probably fictional, set up as tax losses to run against whatever income he was pulling down now.

Calver got out the car and walked down the street and up the path to the door. The house was a modern one storey affair, lots of wood and long vistas of glass. Calver pressed the ornate bell and heard a pleasant tinkling sound reverberating around inside. He turned and studied the garden as it flowed away down to the road. It was mostly verdant green lawn interspersed here and there with some well-tended beds, and there was a large pond with a water feature gurgling away amongst some frolicking marble nymphs.

Calver turned back as the door opened. The guy standing there looked sixty plus. Short and wiry, gray hair in a ponytail, and a beard and mustache combo lightly stained with orange yellow nicotine.

'Yeah? What d'you want?' the guy asked, his eyes briefly studying Calver then rising over his shoulder to study the street behind him. The voice was reedy and thin with a hint of irritation at being disturbed from whatever he had been doing. 'Whatever you're selling, Bud, I ain't interested.'

'That's good, Mr Atkins, because I'm not selling anything,' Calver said, too tired to dissemble. 'I'm an attorney and I just want some information about Mary Ritter's car you recovered from an auto smash 6 years ago? Maybe I could come in and talk. Its a little public out here,' Calver said, gesturing across the way at the house opposite.

The mans eyes seemed to flicker, darting around in their sockets.

They fastened on Calver. He seemed to be trying to make his mind up about something. He shrugged. 'I'll give you five minutes, Bud,' he said, letting the door swing open.

Calver followed him down a short corridor to a large airy room with a huge window running down one side showing the rear garden stretching away. The floor of the room was comprised of large flagstones covered by rugs and there was a long settee and some chairs around a coffee table. The place had a kind of empty look about it and Calver got the impression the guy lived alone.

'So what's this about, mister?' he said

'Name's Calver, Jonas Calver.'

The guy nodded and they stood looking at each other. 'You didn't seem particularly surprised by my request?' Calver said.

'I been expecting you. Guy bought my business told me. He called me after you'd been there,' he said. 'You know I been expecting something for a while.'

'What d'you mean?'

The guy sighed and plumped himself down on the settee. He seemed pre-occupied. 'Its been tough,' he said, almost to himself.

Calver moved to one of the chairs and sat down, staying quiet, waiting. He sensed, for whatever reason, the guy wanted to talk.

'Joan, my wife, died last year, and we got no kids,' he said. 'So I been kind of knocking around in here on my own, and you get to thinking.'

'I understand,' Calver said, although he didn't. 'I'm sorry for your loss,' he added, quickly.

'Are you a religious man, Mr Calver? D'you believe in divine retribution?' he asked, his face sad, his eyes boring into Calver's as if he expected some kind of answer there.

'No, I don't, but I do believe in redemption.'

'Redemption, huh?' he said, his mouth twisting. 'Redemption didn't help my Joany when the cancer was eating her brain, making her whimper like a whipped dog.' He drew in a deep breath and looked down at his hands. 'A life for a life, right? An eye for an eye? Ain't that what the bible tells us, Mr Calver?'

Calver sat silent, letting it play out.

'That nigger woman, out on the freeway. I knew it was wrong what they wanted, but I was weak, and I wanted the money. Well I got my thirty pieces of silver, but I lost my Joany.'

Calver nodded, waiting, watching the guy, trying to work out a play. He hesitated. 'That woman's husband,' he finally said, tentatively. 'He's on death row, about to die, and maybe you can do something about that. Put things right.'

The words didn't seem to register, but then the guy nodded. 'Well I didn't do anything so wrong. I didn't kill her. I just got rid of a car real quick, but its played on my mind, and as Joan got worse, with the cancer, it like came back and haunted me, and its still haunting me.'

'I understand, Mr Atkins,' Calver said. 'Maybe it would help if you told me what happened that night?'

'I guess,' he said, tiredly. 'What does it matter now, right?'

Calver nodded, staying silent.

The guy looked out of the long side window at the greenery out there. He sighed. 'It was after two when Officer Gillespie called me that night,' he said. 'I grumbled a good bit, said, why couldn't it wait, but he he was pretty full on, said there'd be something in it for me. We'd done bits and pieces together before and he'd always looked after me. So I got the truck and headed out there.'

'What did you find?'

'Chaos. Road was blocked, but they gave me an escort through, and I must have been one of the first there, other than the emergency guys. They were cutting that poor gal out and Gillespie was real pushy, he wanted the vehicle pulled away before the TV cameras got there, and he wouldn't let up. I didn't argue with him when he was in that kind of mood. So when they'd got that gal out, I hitched on the haulage lines and tugged it out and onto the back of the truck, no problem.'

'You said earlier you knew it was wrong, what they wanted,' Calver said. 'What did you mean by that?'

'An accident like that? They should a been all over it, photo's, measurements, skid marks. There's was none of that. At the time it didn't really strike me as strange. I knew what Gillespie was like and that they needed to clear that freeway and get it running again. I knew there'd be lots of political pressure coming down from the top.'

'But afterwards?'

'Yeah. I mean even driving the truck back to the yard I wondered. I mean accident like that, there had to be an official report, by law. Insurance guys and law enforcement crawling up each others assholes, digging in to the causes, and liability, who's to blame, but I didn't see any of that.'

'What else made you suspicious?' Calver asked.

'Gillespie wanted it crushed that night, and he wanted a call when it was done. He called me as I was driving the truck back and insisted I confirm when it was done,' he said. 'That's when it started filtering through that this wasn't just any old job. I knew Gillespie cut corners and I heard rumors about other stuff, and I didn't want to get caught up in anything, where I'm left holding the baby, if you know what I mean.'

'So what did you do?'

'Well, when he called as I was driving I asked him what all the fuss was about. Said I was worried about getting into something.'

'What did he say?'

'He got real mean and heavy, but then he smoothed it over by saying there were some real important people wanted this done and there would be something sweet in it for the guys who'd come in on the first floor without too many questions.'

'And that satisfied you?'

Atkins looked up at Calver as some of the shame he felt started to seep through into his psyche. 'Look mister—'

'Hey,' Calver said. 'I'm not judging you. We all do what we have to do. What did you do?'

Atkins rubbed his face. 'When I got back to the yard, I had a real good look at that wreck. Put her up on the lift and looked underneath as well.'

'You find anything?'

'Yeah. Plenty. The brake lines had been cut. No doubt about it,' he said. 'There were fresh marks there, gouges in the metal, looked real amateur and like they didn't care much about being found out.'

'What did you do?'

'I crushed that car down to a lump of metal the size of a shoe box. That's what I did.'

Calver got up and went over to the long window where he stood looking out at the garden. 'If it came to it, would you be prepared to testify to any of what you've just said?' he asked, turning to look back at Atkins

'You're an attorney,' he replied. 'You know that would be a plum waste of time, trying to go up against them. And,' he added, 'not that I care now, but they'd come after me and I doubt I'd get anywhere near testifying.'

Calver nodded because he guessed that was pretty much a fair assessment. Atkins shuffled to his feet and stooped down to the coffee table and picked up a large portrait photograph of a woman. 'You know,' he said. 'Joany never knew about any of the bad stuff I did. She wouldn't have approved, because she was good through and through. And she's the one gets taken while I just carry on going bad.' He studied the photograph intensely.

'If Joany was here, Pete. What would she tell you to do?' Calver asked, moving to stand behind Atkins and look down over his shoulder at the photo of a pleasant faced woman.

Atkins stayed motionless for a few moments looking down at the picture of his wife, then he carefully placed it back on the table. He sat down again, rubbing a hand over his face.

'That night,' he said. 'Before we crushed it down, I had my man, Jethro, come in to help me. I didn't tell him nothing, and he wasn't too bright even at the best of times. You know, I use a cellphone for calls and nothing else, but Jethro, he used his to take photographs all the time. Well, I figured if I ever needed a little insurance, if Gillespie's deal turned sour, some pictures might help,' he said, looking up again and meeting Calver's eyes.

'You got photo's?' Calver said, excitement rising up in his voice.

'I didn't say that. He took some, 6 years ago, and I have no idea what happened to them,' he said.

'Where is he now, this Jethro?'

'I have no idea. I think he moved on when I sold up,' Atkins said. 'And, as I said, he was kinda slow. Big as an ox, so he was handy to have around for hauling stuff, but he sure wasn't clever. I think maybe it was a mental thing, like his momma dropped him when he was a baby.'

'Any idea where I could get a line on him. What was his full name?'

'His name was Jethro Tucker, and I guess he'd be mid twenties now. I have no idea where he is.'

Calver held his hand out. Atkins studied him, trying to discern whether the gesture was genuine. He saw understanding in Calver's eyes. He grasped the hand and they shook. 'Thank you for your time,' Calver said.

As Calver made his way down the path to the road, Atkins stood at the open door watching him, then he slowly turned and walked back into the house, closing the door behind him. A hundred or so meters down the road, on a bend, a dark SUV stood with blacked out windows. Inside a man watched the door close and Calver climb into his car. The man held a cellphone to his ear as he quietly described the scene playing out in front of him.

Pascal held the phone to her ear listening to the purring ring tone. She'd decided to ring Joel rather than Calver. He picked up third ring. He said he was on his way to meet Calver. She said she'd like to meet with them too, soon, but for now she was in a hurry, back on the street in New York City looking for Anita. She told him it was possible Anita was not really missing in the sense that they had assumed, and she was trying to run that down now. Could he tell her anything about personal contacts Anita may have had over the last 4 or 5 years? Boyfriends, girlfriends, anyone special?

'Shit! She didn't tell me nothing about stuff like that,' Joel said. 'But let me think.'

Pascal could hear the car engine in the background as he drove. She looked out of the window of the Brooklyn bar she was in. He came back on. 'Only one guy I knew about, couple of years ago. He's the one dragged her even deeper into all that protest shit, street demo's and causing mayhem. He was quite a bit older than her. From what I heard he was a real control freak and she had some trouble when she split from him. Wouldn't let go.'

'Name?' Pascal said.

'I'm trying to remember,' he said. 'But I doubt she'd go anywhere near the guy. He had a street name I think, something from Star Trek or shit like that. Loki! That was it. But his real name. I can't remember. It was something kind of English upper class, like Benedict. Can you believe that?' he said, memory returning. 'Sorry, I can't remember the real name right now, but what I can tell you is he was very involved in the Occupy Wall Street thing, back end of 2011.'

'Thanks Joel,' she said and hung up quick before he could ask any questions. There would be time for that later, she hoped, and anyway her guest had just arrived. Christoff slid into the seat opposite her. He was having a hands-free conversation with someone on his phone through ear-buds, and it sounded like a lovers tiff. She watched him twist and turn in the wind as his current squeeze put him through the mill. As his conversation petered out Pascal sent a question in: 'Do MI6 do any monitoring of the demonstration crowd here, Occupy, Extinction and the like?'

He nodded, still pre-occupied with emotional fall-out. 'They do, on a limited scale,' he said, absently, eyes turned inward. He glanced up at her as the question filtered through and began to engage his professional antenna. 'In fact, strangely there is quite a lot of back and forth of these people over the Atlantic. You wouldn't think they'd have the money but they do, so they pop up all over, New York, London and Paris, so we do keep a weather eye on them. Especially the ones who are not exactly in it for the professed ideals of the group. The ones in it for something else, chaos and anarchy. And we think there's some foreign government involvement as well.'

'So what, you got a database?' she asked.

'Maybe,' he said.

'I'm looking for a guy, street name, Loki,' she said. 'Apparently it was something to do with Star Trek,' she added, raising a questioning eyebrow.

Christoff smiled. 'I remember the very episode,' he said. 'Its the one where the man has a half black half—'

'Hey, I was never a fan,' she said, holding her hand up, warning look in her eyes. 'This guy's real name may be Benedict or something similar.'

'I'll see what I can do,' he said. 'Provided of course you let me tell you all about that episode, because it was a classic, even to us Trekkie aficionados.'

She watched him, realizing he meant it. She was going to have to listen to him droning on about Star Trek, if she wanted to get anything out of him. She sighed. 'If you insist,' she muttered through gritted teeth. She sank back in her seat, ready to be bored out of her skull.

<h1 style="text-align:center">CHAPTER THIRTEEN</h1>

Calver said, 'Your mother's car was rigged.'

'I guess I knew all along but didn't want to admit it,' Joel said. 'But where does it take us? Don't help my dad much.'

'No, it doesn't, but I needed to know. And there may be pictures of the cut brake pipes out there, and maybe we can use them to go after the people who did it. I called Kelly and asked her if she could get a line on this guy Jethro Tucker, and she's gonna get back to me. But for now we need to concentrate on your dad's case.'

They were sat outside Harry's bar again, the big red sign flickering across the windscreen of the car. Calver was studying transcripts of Floyd Ritter's murder trial. 'There were two witnesses to what went on in the bar, but only one actual eye witness to the killing. Frank Ross, and he essentially says there was an altercation, or he calls it a bust-up, in the bar,' Calver said, his eyes tracking the testimony as he paraphrased it for Joel. 'He says he heard Fachetti call the guy a nigger, there was an argument that developed into a fight. Ritter chased Fachetti into the corridor leading to the toilets. Ross followed them and was the only one there when Floyd allegedly drew the knife. Fachetti held his hands up and said he was only funning. But Ritter plunged the knife into his neck and then again through the heart. Forensics back up and support that on the knife wounds. They suggest the neck wound came first and wasn't fatal, but the heart stab was, right through the middle. That's it.'

Joel nodded. 'My dad said it was Fachetti's knife. He took it away from him and knocked him down. Says he dropped the knife there and Fachetti was alive when he left.'

'So, classic he said, she said,' Calver muttered. 'But then prosecution said forensics supported Ross's testimony.'

'Yeah, but my dad's black, so that's corroboration enough to an all white jury,' Joel said.

'But,' Calver said, ignoring him. 'Prosecution couldn't link the knife to Floyd. They couldn't show that he acquired it from anywhere or provide any evidence of him possessing it previously. Obviously it had his fingerprints on it, but he didn't deny handling it.'

'So it's another dead end,' Joel said.

Calver shrugged. He folded the trial transcript up and slipped it back into his pocket. 'So, Joel, why we here? What did the girl say? She hustle you for money?'

'No way, man. She still sweet on me,' he said, smiling. 'She told me her momma did work here and was here the night it happened. Says it went down how Ross said, and since she didn't follow them into the corridor, she didn't see the killing. She disappeared long before the police arrived and they never knew about her or questioned her, but then they already had their two witnesses, so why would they?'

Calver studied the outside of the bar, thinking. 'No point in running at Ross now. We got nothing to play against him, and I'm not exactly sure where he is, but what about the girls mother? Can we meet her? Will she talk to us?'

'That's why we're here,' Joel said. 'Cindy's in there now. I'll text her.'

As they waited, Joel told Calver about the call he had received from Pascal.

'Why didn't you tell me? She's undercover and we don't hear nothing, seems like forever, and then she phones you?'

'I am telling you,' he said. 'Nothing to tell, anyway. She's back on the street, looking for Anita. Wanted to know about any old contacts. Told her what I knew. She was in a rush and gave the impression she's onto something. Didn't say anything at all about the bank. So who knows? Said she'll meet with us real soon. Here she comes,' he said. 'Let me do the talking.'

They both looked up together to watch as the girl exited the bar. As she walked towards them she was making a surreptitious shooing motion with her hand.

'What the fuck?' Joel said.

'She wants you to move the car round the corner, lunk head,' Calver said. 'So guys in the bar don't see her get in.'

'Oh, right,' Joel said. He started the car and pulled away from the curb.

Once in the car the girl aimlessly chattered away, and all the while she held her smart phone, simultaneously scrolling and sending messages. Her mother lived ten minutes away in a trailer park, and they had to knock loudly to get her to open the door. She looked out at them, face puffy and garish, moonlight glinting off her glassy eyes. Calver didn't think the prospects looked good.

Cindy had asked Joel for 10 bucks for drink, which he gave her, and then they sat in her mother's tiny kitchen, around a white plastic table drinking straight vodka out of wine glasses. The mother looked like an older version of her daughter, but worn right out. Her name was Velda.

'So what you got for us, Velda?' Calver asked.

'What d'you mean?' she answered, her voice querulous. 'Cindy told you what I saw, mister, and that's a fact.'

'So why we here then?' he repeated

Her eyes took on a cunning look. 'Maybe I know something, and maybe I don't,' she said, eyes turning coquettish.

'You better be careful what you say, ma,' Cyndy said. 'Harry don't want no one talking about nothing, you know that.'

'Harry?' Joel said.

'The bar owner,' she said. 'Guy kicked you out the other day.'

'Harry's a nobody,' Velda said. 'He can't tell me what to do,' she added, belligerent. 'But I don't talk for free.'

Calver took his wallet out, thick with notes. 'Tell us what you got. See if its worth anything'

'Money first,' she said.

Calver studied her. She didn't look quite as drunk as he had first assumed. He counted out five 10 dollar bills and laid them on the table.

'Make it a straight 100 dollars, mister. I'll tell you what I know.'

Calver nodded. He slid the five notes over. 'Talk,' he said. 'You get 50 more when you finish.'

She held his eyes as she picked up the notes and tucked them in her blouse. She nodded. 'I still can't tell you what happened in the corridor, because I didn't see it. But I can tell you there was another guy there that night. He was—'

'Who?' Joel blurted out excitedly.

Calver put his hand on Joel's arm. 'Let her tell it.' He nodded at Velda. 'Tell us what you saw?'

'It was quiet, a weekday, I can't remember, maybe a Tuesday,' she said. 'Vincent Fachetti was a regular when he was around. Flashy, mouthy guy, kinda low rent hoodlum, talked big, and maybe was big from what I heard afterwords. Anyways, he was there that night; he used the land line phone end of the bar a lot. I think he thought it was safer than a cell phone. Anyway he was sat there half an hour making calls. I never spoke to him. I was with a guy I know having a drink.

'Frank Ross was also there that night. I recognized him later from the TV coverage of the trial. He wasn't a regular but I'd seen him a few times. He was quiet, sitting at the bar talking to Harry. Anyway, when Vincent finished his calls, another guy arrived, and they spoke. I never seen this guy before or since. They sat at the bar and did some business, fifteen, twenty minutes, talking in low voices, so I didn't hear nothing, but I wasn't paying attention to them or listening. So they finish their business, bar's virtually empty. The guy with Fachetti moves away to the corner and he's making a call on his cellphone, and thats when this big black guy, Ritter comes in the bar, and makes straight for Fachetti.

'They was shouting at each other, Ritter talking about his wife Mary and her car and I didn't understand any of it. Then they were grappling with each other, but Ritter was bigger, and Fachetti was getting the worst of it, backing off. And then he turned and ran back into the corridor that led to the toilets with Ritter right behind, chasing him. Frank Ross followed them into the corridor. Next thing Ritter comes charging out, doesn't stop. Leaves the bar. Ross came back out and called to this guy who'd been with Fachetti. Guy was still on his cell phone but went out into the corridor to look. That's when I decided to leave. Next day I saw it on the news. Vincent murdered, stabbed to death.'

Calver took a sip of the cheap vodka, grimaced and put his mug back on the table.

'Hey, if you don't want it, mister?' Velda said.

Calver slid the mug across to her. 'We know about Ross because he testified at the trial, but tell us about this stranger, Velda? What did he look like? Did you hear a name?'

'Say, you want a lot for a hundred bucks, mister,' she said. She rubbed her eyes. 'He was another wop, I'd guess. Greasy black hair, little bit of gray. Lower key than Fachetti, but I wouldn't have wanted to mess with him. Looked like trouble, and believe me, buster, I've learned how to spot that a mile away. But he was smartly dressed.'

'Anything else you remember?' Calver asked, counting out another five tens.

'Yeah. He had this real crazy laugh, sent shivers down my back.'

'What d'you mean?' Joel asked.

'Well, Harry used to have a TV over the bar, and while Fachetti and this guy were talking, the TV showed a clip of a police shooting. Its the one where the unarmed black guy is running away with his hands up and the cop shoots him in the back and then sets up the scene, but its all caught on the dumb-ass's dash-cam. Anyway, when that clip came on,

Fachetti and the guy watched it, and this guy almost fell off his chair laughing. It was almost like he couldn't stop, tears running down his face. I'll tell you, I almost felt like leaving the bar then,' she said.

Calver pulled out the trial transcript and scanned through it, looking for something. 'Ross testified that he didn't know Fachetti personally, although he had seen him around. That right?'

'I don't think so,' Velda said.

'Why d'you say that?' Joel asked.

'Because this Ross guy drove Fachetti to Harry's bar. Saw them get out the car together. I thought Ross was some kind of bodyguard to be honest,' she replied. 'I mean he just sat at the bar talking to Harry while Fachetti did his business. You know, like he was the hired help.'

'Shit,' Calver said wryly. 'Guy swore blind he didn't know Fachetti.' Calver slid some more notes over the table. 'Thanks, Velda,' he said, getting up out of his chair. 'If you remember anything else, give me a call.' He handed her a card.

Velda looked up at him speculatively. 'Say, maybe you guys would like to party some?'

'Maybe some other time,' Calver said quickly, holding his hand out.

She shook limply. 'Well, if you change your mind, you know where we are,' she said hopefully.

As they left, Cyndy tagged along out to the car, still fixated on her smart-phone that had been on all through the conversation in the trailer. She and Joel moved away a few paces and spoke quietly, then he was coming back. They got in the car and left, Calver glad to get away from the place.

Pascal sat in her apartment, telephone to her ear, waiting for the guy to come back on the line; she'd been on it all morning, chasing down leads on Anita. Firstly Christoff had come back with bad news on the mysterious Loki; the guy was dead, lying in the morgue. It had been some kind of drugs bust gone wrong; seems the guy had been a low-level drug dealer as well as an eco warrior. When she had complained she was getting nowhere trying to track down Anita, with one dead end after another, Christoff had suggested she reach out to her friend on NYPD, detective Daly. So now she sat waiting for him to come back on the line, after an earlier briefer call.

She had met Daly couple of years back when Calver had been facing murder charges, and she had come out to the US to help him. Daly had been the lead detective and had initially tried to nail Calver for the murder, but had gradually come round to the fact that it was a frame. They had got to know each other pretty well during that period. Later he had helped her with a kidnap case when she had had to go down to Mexico and he had given her a DEA contact, who had turned out to be dirty, but she wasn't going to hold that against him. He was a tough, hard-nosed detective; quick and clever, but he also had a softer side. She knew he was attracted to her but it had never really gone anywhere, and she used the mystery of why, as a kind of come-on; useful when she needed information, as now.

She heard rustling and then Daly was back on the line. 'Got something for you, hot-shot,' he said in his clipped hard-ass voice.

'You still mad at me, Daly?' she said. 'I'm looking for someone and you give me a dead body?'

'Quit bitching, Pascal. I'm going out on a limb for you here, so save the smart comments.'

'Hey, cool down,' she said. 'We're all on the same team here. What, you get out the wrong side of bed this morning, Daly? Look, when I've tracked this lady down, what say you and me get together and paint the town red?'

'I'll hold you to that,' he said, his voice a few degrees warmer.

'Deal. So what we got?'

'Okay, I checked with vice and when they took this guy down he had a collection of burners for drug deals. So they went through the numbers, seeing if they could snag a big fish, but nothing doing. However,' he said, and let it hang.

'Come on, Daly, quit fucking around.'

He laughed. 'So, one of the numbers takes you to a homeless shelter on Bowery smack in the middle of Chinatown. So, seems this monkey was dealing to people actually in this place. How do you like that?'

'Get to the point, Daly.'

'Well, they got a copy of a kind of roster they have there of transients, and guess who's on it? And using her real name? Yeah, that's right: Anita Ritter.'

'You're shitting me?'

'No. She's right there. Hiding in plain sight. How d'you miss that, hot-shot?'

Pascal frowned, wondering about Van Zim and Camino, and

whether they'd missed it as well. Still she'd yet to find the girl.

'So how d'you like that?' Daly prompted her.

'I like it fine, Daly. Thanks. But tell me something. This guy was meant to be some kind of eco warrior demo freak, but are you saying he was actually a drug dealer?'

'Seems so. But I'm told this guy was low-level, and he just got caught up in a sweep. My guess is it was a sideline.'

He gave her the details of the shelter.

'Daly, I owe you, man. Dinners on me. I'll call you,' she said.

'Yeah, well, you better.'

CHAPTER FOURTEEN

Calver looked around wondering if it was the right place. He was outside a rustic country cottage. He had come off the highway down a rutted lane thinking he was lost and then suddenly it had been there, opening out in front of him like something from an old fairy tale. The house was shrouded by trees, and in the garden there were car tires and old rusting garden implements strewn about in the wildly growing grass, and at the side of the house stood an old Buick Riviera, a relic from a bygone age.

Calver stepped up to the door, lifted the ornate looking knocker and banged it hard. He was met with an eerie silence. He turned and surveyed the gently swaying trees. Looking back, he noticed the door was slightly ajar, wedged against something. He pushed it and shouted in, 'hello? Mr Peters. Mr Ned Peters?' He was met with more eerie silence.

He pushed the door open over a rucked-up door mat and entered, immediately seeing a man lying prone in the entrance to the next room. He moved quickly and rolled him onto his back. There was an overpowering smell of alcohol in the air. The man coughed and his eyes fluttered open. They were bloodshot and looked blank of intelligence. There was a slight cut to his head but it didn't look serious. Calver lifted the guy up and half carried him into the next room and laid him down on the settee. The man let out a muffled moan and subsided back into sleep.

Calver looked around. The room was sizable with almost all the wall space covered by book shelves, and dominated by a huge antique desk littered with papers, with an old style desk lamp training a flickering light on them. There were also innumerable empty Wild Turkey whiskey bottles lying around. Calver turned to look at the guy, who was now lightly snoring. He was mid-sixties, on the short side with white hair and a beard.

Calver went through to a small equally chaotic kitchen; piles of unwashed dishes and crockery. He found and filled a kettle with water and set it to boil, uncovered a large blackened coffee pot, then some coffee and some sugar. The milk in the fridge had solidified into a smelly block. Coffee would have to be black, no bad thing. When he was done he found a tray and took the coffee back into the room.

Now the guy was sitting up rubbing his eyes. 'And just who might you be, stranger?' he asked, his voice gruff but seemingly devoid of interest or anger.

'Names Jonas Calver. I'm an attorney interested in the Floyd Ritter case. Thought you might talk to me about it?'

The guy sat silent, so Calver moved to pour the coffee. 'I'm assuming you are in fact Ned Peters, his original attorney?' he said. 'Sorry its gotta be black. You don't seem to have any milk.' He handed the guy a cup which he took absently.

'Yeah, I'm Ned Peters alright,' he said softly. 'But I don't think I'm gonna be a able to help you a whole lot, do you?'

'I don't know. Why don't we see,' Calver said amiably. He was trying to gauge the guys state and the best approach to adopt. 'You know, I've been there - where I guess you are right now. Runs in my family like a river. Old Irish stock on my grandmothers side, I reckon. No disrespect to the Irish. Funny how people don't seem to appreciate how many high functioning alcoholic lawyers, doctors, even airline pilots, there are out there.'

Peters stared back at him. 'What d'you say your name was? Calver?'

'Yeah, and you don't sound drunk to me. You sound like you're in the zone.'

They looked at each other for a long moment and maybe there was an understanding that passed between them that only a hard drinking attorney would ever be able to understand. Peters said, 'so why don't we have a real drink, counselor? In the kitchen under the sink you'll find a fresh bottle of Wild Turkey. Why don't you bring it out here and maybe we'll have ourselves a real drink, and maybe we'll talk a little, too?'

'Sounds like a plan,' Calver said. He got up and moved back out to the kitchen to get the whiskey.

'So what's your interest, Mr Calver? I thought Mike Shapiro was Floyd's attorney,' Peters said.

They were now sat at the large desk, Peters occupying a recliner chair and Calver sat across from him. The whiskey bottle stood between them, about a third full. Peters' face was shiny with sweat, but his eyes were clear.

'Well it's a rather long and convoluted story,' Calver said.

'And I got time to hear it.'

Calver nodded. He decided he liked the guy even on such a short acquaintance. 'It all started when I met Floyd's daughter, Anita, sometime back, and now she seems to have gone missing.'

Peters nodded. 'So you're not on the case at all, really?'

The guy was quick and the alcohol didn't seem to slow him down much, Calver thought. 'I am, and I'm not, I suppose,' he said. 'I visited Floyd in Riverbend and he wants me to find his daughter, so he's put me on the case, as a ruse so he can pay me, but it also helpfully placates my law partner, who's not happy about me gallivanting around Tennessee without getting paid. But it means I got access to the case papers and so I went through them. Have to say, even as a seasoned seen it all attorney, what I saw intrigued me.'

Peters nodded again, gently rocking the half-full tumbler in his hand. 'What about the little girl, Anita?'

'I got a colleague working on that up in New York. I came down here initially to see if I could get a lead on her whereabouts from Floyd.'

'But you're still here?

'And I'm still here.'

'You think Floyd's case is linked to her going missing?'

'Yes and no. Or perhaps, maybe.'

'If they ever start giving out prizes for prevarication, I guess I'll know where to come,' Peters said. 'Mind you, its the stock in trade of any good attorney. So, tell me how you think they're linked?'

Calver stood up to stretch his legs. He moved over to the

bookshelves to have a look at the titles. It was an eclectic range; classic literature interspersed with law books, cookery books, books on wine and antiques. Calver gently removed a well thumbed hardback from the shelf. It was Dostoevsky's Crime and Punishment.

'You a reader, Mr Calver?' Peters asked him.

'Not so much, but only because I don't get the time.'

'Well, if you're ever looking for some inspiration for doing some detective work, you should read that book in your hands. Dostoevsky's, Porphyry Petrovitch would be my go to guy. Forget Sherlock Holmes.'

'I could do with someone like that right now,' Calver murmured, moving back to his seat. 'But to answer your question about linkage. I believe that the thing that connects them is—'

'The bank.'

Again, they sat looking at each other in the silence, the whiskey bottle standing between them like a mute umpire. It was now dark, the branches from the trees outside throwing shadows across the windows, adding to the gloom.

'Mr Calver, why don't you tell me what you think you know, and I'll just have a look see; see if I want to talk to you about anything pertaining to my erstwhile client. Course, clocks all but run down for Floyd now, so anything anybody might have a mind to do, they better do it pretty damn quick.'

'Amen,' Calver muttered. 'I got no problem telling you what I know, because I know very little, but what do I think I know? Not much. But here's the thing: the girl, Anita, went into the bank undercover, and now she's disappeared. The girl, rightly or wrongly, blamed the bank for the ruination of her family, her parents. And you got this civil lawsuit against the bank, where I can't get any information, but it seems, understandably, back in the day the bank weren't keen on it, and it seems likely some pressure was put onto Floyd's wife to drop it, before she died. Again, was that pressure legal? Floyd obviously believed this Fachetti guy fixed the brakes on his wife's car. He says Fachetti threatened him that if his wife didn't drop the lawsuit there would be trouble. Who wanted the lawsuit dropped? The Bank. You join up the dots, where does it take you?'

Peters rose unsteadily from the recliner, walked over and switched the overhead light on, then went and drew heavy drapes across the window. As he sat down, he said, 'not far without proof, counselor. And even if you develop your line of reasoning, how does it help Floyd?'

As Peters finished speaking they heard the door knocker banging loudly. He looked at his watch, his face screwed up. 'Who the hells gonna call on me this time of night?'

Calver got up. 'I'll find out.'

As he pushed the door open the porch light was on, and further back there was a white vehicle with a rack on top with blue lights intermittently flashing, and in front of him stood a police officer. The guy was medium height and wearing a black uniform, a peaked cap and shades. The blue on white circular cloth badge on his tunic said he was Metro Nashville Police. His forearms were bare and he wore tight black gloves. But what really struck Calver was the guys shoulders and upper arms. They seemed grotesquely over developed, straining out of his black uniform. Calver couldn't help smiling as an image of Popeye the sailer man popped into his head, and then he wished he hadn't. The guys thin lips pursed in a prim frown.

'Good evening officer,' Calver said. 'How can I help you?'

'You can step away from the building and put your hands up, boy,' he said casually.

Calver heard Peters approaching and then his voice behind him, saying, 'what is all this? Gillespie? Is that you?'

'Sure is, Ned,' the cop said. 'Thought this stranger here might have been on some business, out to do you harm.'

'Not at all. This here is Jonas Calver down visiting from New York.'

The cop sniffed the air suspiciously. 'You boys been drinking some?'

'That we have,' Peters said. 'And I'm not aware that that's a crime, even in Tennessee.'

Gillespie took his cap off and pushed the shades up on top of his head. Calver tried to age the guy, but it was impossible. His hair was dirty blonde, looked dyed, short and the face looked sort of young old, preserved. The eyes, gray, seemed full of a weird kind of mirth, but restrained, as if he could see something funny that no one else could. 'Well, I'll tell you,' he said, turning to look at Calver. 'If that's your vehicle over there, Mr Calver, and you was intending to drive tonight, that might not be such a good idea.'

Calver nodded. 'I'll bear that in mind, officer. Wouldn't want to get stopped for DUI.'

'Why you here, Silas?' Peters asked.

'Well, I'll tell you, Ned. I heard some big flashy lawyer from up north had come down here to stir stuff up that don't need stirring up. Come done here to show us country cousins how they reckon things should be done. But we don't need no kikes or niggers from the city of Sodom coming down here all high and mighty, trying to tell us how to run things.'

'I'm actually English Irish extraction, officer,' Calver said mildly.

Gillespie ignored him as if he hadn't spoken. 'So I'm here, Ned, to deliver a message. You know, I thought you got the last message loud and clear, but maybe this, this pinko nigger lover,' he said, turning to look at Calver. 'Maybe he's somehow given you some backbone. Made you think you ain't just a broken down drunk. You know, Ned, if'n it weren't for your dear departed momma leaving you this place, you'd be on the street, with all the other crooks, hustlers and scum we have to police down here.'

'We don't want no trouble, Silas,' Peters said quietly, his eyes downcast

Calver was surprised at the tone of acquiescence. 'What is this?' he said, indignation starting to sound in his voice. 'You gonna let this two-bit—'

'Leave it!' Peters said, a bit of steel in his voice. He put his hand out, restraining Calver. 'You've delivered your message, Silas, and now I'd like you to leave,' he said.

'No problem,' Gillespie said. He pulled his shades down and put his cap back on. 'I'm sure looking forward to Floyd Ritter facing justice, and I'm sure you folks wouldn't want to interfere none with that. Hell, you can come and join the celebrations. And that's a fact.' He looked at Calver. 'You be mighty careful out there, Mr Calver. You're a long way from home.' He nodded, 'Ned.' Turned and ambled off the porch back to his car.

They stood, neither speaking, watching the cars back lights disappear up the rutted country track, into the night.

'We need to talk,' Calver said softly.

Peters nodded tiredly. 'Yeah, I guess maybe we do.'

As they moved back into the house, Peters said, 'you better bed down here tonight because I wouldn't bet against Gillespie staking out the end of the road for a traffic stop.'

'You're kidding me?'

'No, I'm not.'

Calver looked at his watch. It was gone 1 pm. 'Okay, thanks. But if I'm staying, lets finish talking.'

They retook their seats at the desk. Peters opened a drawer and took out a fresh bottle of Wild Turkey. 'Hidden reserves,' he said, tapping the side of his nose.

'Tell me about Floyd Ritter?' Calver said, settling back in his chair.

'Floyd, Floyd, Floyd…' Peters said softly, his eyes taking on a far away look. 'Hard as it may seem, Mr Calver, at one time I was a pretty good lawyer. Conscientious, and I didn't cut corners.'

'I can well believe it,' Calver said. 'And less of the mister. 'Call me Jonas.'

'Long as you call me Ned,' he nodded. 'I got Floyd because judge Hukabee gave him to me. I didn't want it because I was too busy with other stuff, but I took it on as a favor to the judge. In this town you can't afford to go round antagonizing judges. Case seemed like a slam dunk anyway. So I met with Floyd, and funny thing is, we really seemed to hit it off. I liked the guy, and I believed him. I know, I know,' Peters said, waving a hand. 'You don't need to believe your client, or believe he's innocent, to represent him, but as you'll know, it sure as hell helps.'

'Amen to that brother,' Calver said raising his glass in a toast.

'Funny thing with Floyd though,' Peters continued. 'I always believed he was holding back on me. Not telling me everything. It was just a feeling.'

Calver nodded. 'I read the trial transcripts. You did a pretty good job with what you had. Floyd admitted the fight in the bar, and that he went looking for Fachetti. Prosecution put up one unshakable witness who testified it was Floyd's knife and that he used it to kill Fachetti. Your guy says it wasn't his knife and that he didn't kill Fachetti, but you got no evidence to support that. Did the DA ever offer manslaughter?'

'They might have done, but Floyd was never ever going to admit to the killing, even though I told him he'd lose and likely get the death penalty. At the time, he didn't seem to care. He just told me to roll the dice. So we did.'

'D'you think the eye witness was lying?' Calver asked.

'Oh, he was there all right, in the bar when the confrontation took place, I have no doubt about that, but as to what he saw? I'll tell you, I think he was lying through his teeth, but I couldn't shake him on my cross. I had nothing to put to him.'

'Lets go back,' Calver said. 'Tell me about Mary Ritter and the car crash, and this whole Fachetti set-up? How d'you think that played out?'

'Fachetti was a hoodlum, a punk,' Peters said. 'I have no doubt pressure, even threats were made by him, probably at the behest of the bank, although I doubt you'd ever be able to prove it.'

'Did Fachetti fix the brakes on Mary Ritter's car?' Calver asked.

'I don't know,' Peters said. 'I have no proof of it, but then again, I didn't investigate it. Didn't have the time, or the resources, and it wouldn't have helped us anyway, 'cept perhaps in the penalty phase of the trial. Floyd had a reason to go looking for Fachetti, and its immaterial whether that reason was based on fact or whether it was just something he believed. Its his belief in it that matters, not whether it was true or not.'

'Tell me about Gillespie, then?' Calver said. 'What's this message he's giving you? I mean, you no longer act for Floyd anyway?'

'Its a message, as he said, not to stir things up so close to Floyd's execution, and spoil the death party,' Peters said with a dry laugh. 'You can't keep nothing secret around here. Silas Gillespie will have seen you coming before you even knew you was coming yourself. Course, the guy's a certifiable psychopath. It still amazes me he keeps the job, but I guess he's got so much stuff on so many people, he's near untouchable. And the guy loves money. Anything, anything, you want done. You got the money, he can do it.'

'How old is the guy?' Calver asked. 'I couldn't work it out, even guess at it.'

Peters chuckled. 'He's mid-sixties if he's a day.'

Calver looked doubtful.

'Really. Guy is a fitness fanatic, but also into cosmetic surgery in a big way, mixed in with a cocktail, or so I heard from some of my old clients, of hormone replacement drugs, Viagra and steroids.'

Calver studied the bottom of his empty glass his sluggish alcohol imbued brain slowly processing Peters' information. 'Why d'you drop Floyd?'

'I didn't. We kind of mutually agreed. I'm no appellate lawyer anyways, and we'd come to the end of the line. It was all nice and amicable and I believe Floyd or his son, Joel, knew Mike Shapiro, went to school with the guy or something.'

'What?' Calver said, intuiting something in Peters' voice.

'I dunno. Something about the son, Joel, I didn't take to,' he said. 'Guy was pretty rude and brusque with me, but I guess with his daddy about to die, maybe he blamed me for it all. And of course they wanted to run an incompetent counsel appeal brief as well.'

'Did Gillespie suppress or lose the auto-crash accident report?' Calver asked.

'Hell, yes,' Peters said with a sudden laugh, leaning back to slap his thigh. 'I've no doubt about that.'

'The brake lines on the car were cut,' Calver said emphatically, looking up to meet Peters' eyes. 'And there may be photographic proof out there and a witness.'

Peters held his gaze. 'My, you have been busy,' he said quietly. 'Doesn't help Floyd avoid the death house though, does it? Whichever way you cut it.'

Calver sighed, frustrated. He looked up. 'Getting philosophical, Ned,' he said with a thin smile, breaking their sombre mood. 'And changing the subject slightly: d'you believe in the death penalty?'

'Yes and no,' he replied, evenly. 'I like to prevaricate, same as you, Jonas, sometimes. I believe in retribution, an eye for an eye, if we could be sure of guilt, but we can't. You know, when the DNA thing blossomed and became mainstream, I couldn't quite believe how many they exonerated post execution. The system gets it wrong so many times, and of course penalizes low income, poverty and race. It's not fit for purpose and probably never will be. But there are some crimes make your blood boil. Crimes that are so bad. I mean Ted Bundy admitted to killing 30 women for christsakes. What do you do with a guy like that, who's pure evil? Well I say you light 'em up and watch 'em burn.'

Calver nodded. 'What about Floyd's case? Say he did kill Fachetti?'

Peters grinned. 'I'd give the guy a medal.'

Calver laughed, then said, 'I suggested to Shapiro a novel approach for the clemency plea to the Governor?'

'And what might that be?' Peters replied, thinking a joke was coming.

'We base it on the wrongdoing of the bank; we put the bank in the dock. We lay the blame for Floyd's behavior at the door of the bank, and we lay it on with a trowel via the media. What d'you think?' Calver said. 'Needless to say, Shapiro wasn't keen - he blew me out.'

Peters got up and moved unsteadily to the window, pulling the heavy drapes aside and peering out into the blackness. 'Boy, you got some nerve, I'll give you that. But…' he said, his voice tailing off.

'But?' Calver prompted him.

'You know, you might just have an angle there that's worth

playing. To the public, over the head of the Governor. There's so much mistrust out there, what with what the bankers got away with. Time could be ripe.'

'How about you help me?' Calver said.

Peters came back and sat down. He held his tumbler across the table and they clinked glasses. 'Maybe I will at that. Let me think on it, boy. Now,' he said, brightly. 'I better find you a spare bed and some blankets.'

CHAPTER FIFTEEN

Pascal sat in a window seat, steaming bowl of chicken chow mien in front of her, but she wasn't hungry. She'd come in off the street from watching the shelter for the last couple of hours. It had been closed most of the day. Then a guy had opened it up but had been in no mood to talk; told her to go away and come back at sun down. It was now way past that. She'd watched stragglers slowly turning up. A small army of destitute and troubled people, barely noticed by those around them. The majority so far had been men, with only a couple of women.

She looked down the street. She was in Chinatown, off Bowery, in a little Dim-Sum joint, across the road from the shelter. The place she was watching didn't advertise itself, it was just a small doorway away from the main entrance to the building which seemed to house offices and some retail along the ground floor. She guessed the shelter extended back into the building, but you couldn't tell which floor the main bulk was on. If Anita was there, Pascal worried how she was going to get the girl to speak to her, a complete stranger. She'd cross that bridge when she got to it; if she got to it. She suddenly felt hungry. She dipped her chopsticks into a mound of aromatic noodles and hoisted it towards her mouth. As her eyes rose at the same time, across the street a figure approaching the doorway caught her eye. There was something furtive about the gait that struck. Her chopsticks stopped mid-flight as she watched the figure. It was a girl, no question; slim and slight, in black with a woolly hat pulled down and carrying just a small canvas sports bag.

Pascal on instinct lurched out of her seat and out the door into the street, horns blaring as she made her way across, her eyes tracking the slight figure as she reached the doorway. Forgetting subtlety, she blurted out, '*Anita?*'

The girl turned and looked at her, perhaps startled, although her eyes were in shadow so you couldn't tell.

As the street light fell across her eyes Pascal knew it was her; Calver's weird comment about her looking like an angel struck her immediately. Working a hunch Pascal held Calver's card out to her, and said, 'he's worried about you. Just asked me to make sure you're all right.'

'Leave me alone,' the girl said quickly. 'You're putting my life in danger.'

As the girl turned to go, Pascal said, quietly,' I'm in you know? The bank.'

The girl hesitated, half turning.

'I know you tried, but I'm in. I mean really in, with Joyce and laughing boy Cimino. I'm good at it; its what I do. You're not. Talk to me, Anita.'

'I can't. Now I have to go.' But she didn't move.

Pascal spoke softly, urgently. 'Calver's in Tennessee right now, with your brother, Joel, trying to help your father. Why don't you help us. We can nail these fuckers.'

The girls eyes looked flat for a moment, then she half smiled, wearily. 'Who the fuck are you, anyway?'

Twenty minutes later they sat in Pascal's Brooklyn apartment. It was her real apartment, not the short let cover dump she'd taken on to get into the bank. Her place was minimalist, small, done out in dark colors with not a single photograph or personal touch. They were in the living room, Pascal on the antique couch and Anita in the arm chair. There were two cans of beer on the coffee table between them, illuminated by a sole lamp at the side of the room that gave a out a weak glow; in the background an old Van Morrison tape was playing on a loop. They had spoken very little. Pascal giving her time to analyze things and get comfortable.

After a while Pascal said, 'what I don't get, Anita, is why you're hiding?'

'Because, believe it or not I don't want to die, and I'm an addict,' she said. 'How's that for a conundrum?'

Looking closely at the girl, Pascal could see she was stick thin, with a ghostly whitish look about her. 'You're not making sense,' she said, softly. 'Loki's dead. So I guess I understand the addict bit, but what are you scared of?'

'So that's why I can't get a hold of him?' she said wonderingly. She looked up at Pascal. 'They killed the last whistle blower, you know?'

'What are you talking about?'

'I can't prove it, but when they came to me, to offer me the walk-away deal, I knew they knew,' she said.

Pascal got up to stretch her legs. 'I don't want to shock you,' she said. 'But I don't think they know shit about you. They think you're just another kiss and tell irritation who's going to sell a story about double-dealing in the financial world. Par for the course for them. That's why they offered you the deal. Shit. I mean, they don't even know you're Floyd Ritter's daughter. If they did, it'd be a different ball game. And remember, I do this stuff for a living, and I'm not often wrong. That Cimino. He searched your apartment, got your hard-drive, but there's nothing on it. That journal of yours doesn't say shit. So why would they worry about you?'

'How the fuck do you know these things,' she said with a flash of anger

'I told you. I do this for a living.'

'Can you get me some heroin?' she asked, her eyes steady but full of yearning.

'I will get you something, I promise, if you work with me. Tell me what you know.'

Anita nodded tiredly. 'Long as its not methadone,' she said.

Pascal disappeared into her bedroom and came back with a small tin and bag. 'All I got for now is some very strong cannabis,' she said, opening the tin and taking out some papers and some weed.

'Are you fucking with me?' the girl said, an edge of hysteria in her voice. 'I got a monkey on my back and you're offering me that shit? Won't even make a dent.'

'Take some now, relax and talk. Later I'll go out on the street and get you something. I promise,' Pascal said, handing her a large joint.

'You're pretty smart aren't you?' Anita said, bitterly. 'You's all sweetness and light, but you ain't gonna get me nothing, less I talk to you, right?'

Pascal didn't say anything. The girl took the joint and drew in a huge lungful of smoke, holding it in, then gradually letting it out. She sighed. 'Lets get on with it then, cause I'm going to die, less I get something.'

Pascal grabbed her can of beer off the table, took a drag on it and sat back down on the couch. She knew she needed to get as much as possible from the girl before she went cold turkey. 'You went in the bank, because you wanted to bring them down, right? Did you actually find anything?'

'They thought I did, but I don't know what I found?'

Pascal mulled that, but it didn't take her anywhere. 'Did they invite you on this special program of theirs? To be one of their financial worker bees?

'Phoenix, you mean?'

'Is that what they call it?'

'Yeah. Its after the old 'Nam black-ops thing back in the day. And yeah, they kind of invited me on it, but I bugged out before we got anywhere and before they did any due diligence on me. Just as well I guess.'

Pascal got up and began pacing. 'Why did they offer you a walk-away deal? What made them suspicious? And you said, earlier, they killed a whistle-blower?'

'Maybe I exaggerated?'

'Maybe you saw something, you don't know you saw?' Pascal

said. 'Tell me about the whistle-blower?'

'Melissa McCarthy was an intern, bright as hell. She was at the bank when I joined. I got friendly with her. She overdosed three months ago, but I don't think it was self-inflicted. That's why I got scared; thought they'd come for me as well. It's why I cut and run, went to Cuba and hid out. I got sad about a lot of things, Daddy, Melissa. So, what do I do? I start using. Used to be booze, but drugs are better. I guess I always had an addictive personality.'

'Tell me what happened to make you scared, enough to cut and run?'

'They have these get togethers every so often. The chosen few for this phoenix thing go out to DeMasi's place in the Hampton's for a long weekend. Melissa got invited. She was pretty excited about it. But when she got back afterwords she'd changed.'

'How?'

'She seemed sad, and kind of tired. A spark had gone, and she was using a lot more than before. She'd been a recreational user, usually when she was run down and needed a pick me up, but now she was taking more. I asked her what was wrong a couple of times, but she blew me out. Then she called me one night, late. Asked me to come around because she needed some one to confide in, and it was about the bank. When I arrived at her apartment she was dead. And Cimino was there. He'd called emergency services by then. Guy freaked me out so much I kept my mouth shut, but he kept asking me what we had talked about. Had she given me anything as they were missing some important records from the bank. He asked me why I had come around and I said I was just passing and thought I'd drop in.'

'So it went down as suicide?'

'Yep. But it was crack Cocaine, which I never knew her to take. Coroner said given the amount and purity it was highly doubtful it was a mistake, had to be deliberate, and that was that.'

'So what happened after that to spook you?'

'Little things. Cimino started popping up outside of work, turning up if I went to a bar or restaurant, like he was checking up on me. I think they may have put something on my phone. Tracking or listening, and that got me more paranoid and using more. The night I called Calver, I'd had enough. So I was going to go and meet him and tell him my suspicions about Melissa and everything else, and maybe ask him about my fathers case which was starting to freak me out.'

'What happened?'

'Well, stupidly I phoned Calver from the bank. Ten minutes later Cimino was there. Says they're concerned about my association with Melissa and possible reputational damage. I wasn't being straight with them. Melissa must have talked to me about the meetings at DeMasi's residence. They would offer me a walk-away non-disclosure severance package and I should attend a meeting the next morning at 9.30. In the meantime, if I chose to speak openly to anyone there would be consequences. Thats when he scared me. The way he spoke.'

'And that's when you up and ran?

'Yeah.'

Pascal rubbed her face. 'My guess is they're satisfied that you don't know anything damaging about them, because they checked your apartment and got your hard drive and there's nothing on it. That's why they never really came after you.'

'So where does that leave us?'

'Sitting pretty, I'd say. Van Zim set me a test, for coming on board, to find you. So I am going to give them the good news, then I'm in. They will want to verify it. Will you be cool with that?'

'I'll be cool, if you go out and get me some smack.'

Pascal nodded. 'You know I have an idea that might fit in with our cover. As part of the deal, we get them to fund you going into re-hab. You want to be clean so you can help your father don't you?'

'Pascal. Just get me some stuff. I'll agree to anything you want. Just get me something.'

An hour later they sat in Pascal's other apartment which was lower rent but more comfortable, with even a few fake photos scattered about the place. On the way over Pascal had stopped off and got some heroin, after phoning detective Daly and getting a run-down on where to buy unadulterated product without risk. He had been on an arrest and had no time to question her. Back at the apartment Anita had immediately retired to the bathroom for fifteen minutes and now she sat on the couch, a serene smile on her face.

While Anita had been in the bathroom Pascal phoned Van Zim to give her the news. Van Zim seemed ecstatic and was now en-route to the apartment to verify completion of the test. As the buzzer sounded, Pascal told Anita to leave all the talking to her, and keep her mouth shut. She was pretty sure Anita would comply because she had kept back some of the heroin.

Van Zim breezed into the apartment, eyes flicking around, taking in the threadbare but cosy surroundings. She was wearing another rather severe trouser suit, hair pulled back into a pony-tail. 'My, my,' she exclaimed. 'You two are like two peas in a pod. How are you my dear?' she added, leaning down to kiss Anita on the cheek.

Pascal held a hand out, to avoid a clinch. 'Joyce,' she nodded. 'Take a seat. Drink?'

'No, thank you my dear. In a bit of a rush, so lets keep this short.' She took some papers out of her bag. 'I have our non-disclosure agreement here for Annie to sign and go on her merry way and then you and I,' she said nodding at Pascal, 'can firm up our relationship.'

Pascal took the papers, skim reading. She took a seat. 'This looks okay, but we want something more.'

Van Zim raised an eyebrow. 'And what might that be?'

'Annie Rainer is not in a very good way at the moment, as you'll see if you look at her closely,' Pascal said. 'In fact she's in the grip of heroin addiction. And I could argue you, the bank and our friend Cimino are partly responsible for that, but I don't think I'll need to. I'd like you to add to the agreement that you will fund three months for Annie in a drug re-rehabilitation program?'

'Oh I'm sure we can spring to that, and it will keep her out of mischief. Let me make a phone call first though?' Van Zim said.

Pascal nodded and showed her into the bedroom.

'And what if I don't want to go?' Anita said, defiant, the heroin giving her self-confidence.

'You want to help your father, don't you? Be strong for him?'

'Hey. Never trust a junkie, right? Maybe I'll say I'll go for now, but how d'you know I won't just skip out?'

'I don't,' Pascal said. 'I think your father needs you, and I believe that'll be enough, but we'll see.'

'Trusting aren't you? now you have what you want,' she said as Van Zim returned.

'That's agreed,' she said, her expression beaming. 'In fact I've spoke to Mr DeMasi himself and he is most pleased at our progress. As a result, you, Carrie, my dear, are cordially invited to Mr DeMasi's residence in the Hampton's this weekend. It will be a small gathering, social in nature, but we shall also discuss other things as well.'

Anita smiled as her eyes locked onto Pascal's.

Pascal said, 'do I wear the little black cocktail dress?'

'Ummh, that's something I'd like to see,' Grace said.

Anita rolled her eyes at Pascal who pretended not to notice

CHAPTER SIXTEEN

Calver woke to the sound of a cock crowing. His head ached and he couldn't remember where he was - then it all came rushing back. He was in a small box room lying on an old Japanese futon, surrounded by piles of dog-eared files. Looked like Ned's filing system. He scrambled out of bed, found a threadbare bathrobe and went looking for the bathroom. As he went through he could smell bacon cooking and hear Ella Fitzgerald singing the radio.

Half an hour later, scrubbed up and shaved, he sat at the kitchen table eating eggs and bacon, marveling at how bright and alert Peters looked after their nights drinking. 'Ned, you sure got some constitution,' he said.

'I can thank my mama for that,' he replied. 'Scottish stock that hailed from Glasgow, Scotland. Woman could drink a river, still be thirsty. Never got a sore head.'

As Calver speared some of the thick cut bacon, he watched his cellphone trill on the table as a text came in. He leaned over to read. It was from Kelly Phillips, a lead on auto repair guy, Jethro Tucker. He moved the phone across the table to Peters. 'You know where that is, Ned? Cause that might just be proof that Mary Ritter's brake lines were cut?'

He studied the text. 'Sure, that's way up out in the sticks.'

'Fancy a trip?'

'Why not,' he said. 'I got nothing better to do. By the way, where's Floyd's son, Joel? Thought he was chaperoning you around down here?'

'He was, but he had to go back to New York for work, so you can take over for now.'

Their destination was a small farm, apparently owned by Jethro Tucker's mother, where he was supposed to be living. It took them 45 minutes to get there, Calver driving the hire car. As they trundled up a graveled lane, fields of green growing crops either side, they could see a rough wooden frame house up ahead. It was small but with a big open porch on the front. As they moved around a slight bend in the single track lane, they both saw the police vehicle at the same time, coming into view as some trees moved out of their sight line. It sat parked outside the house, blue light flickering dimly in the late morning sunshine.

'Too late to turn back,' Peters said under his breath.

As they pulled into the rough hard-packed earth area to the front of the house, they could see another white vehicle that looked official, parked next to the police car. As they sat watching, a small group of people came out of the house with a tall guy at the front in hand cuffs.

'Shit!' Peters said. 'That's Gillespie in back. Beat us to the draw.'

'It's a free country,' Calver said as he climbed out the car.

Peters sat for a moment longer, shaking his head. 'Which

country you talking about, boy? Not in Tennessee it ain't,' he murmured softly. He slowly climbed out the car and moved around to stand with Calver as the group approached them. 'Be careful what you say,' he whispered.

'You boys a bit late for the show,' Gillespie said as they approached. 'Excitements all over.' There was still that strange kind of merry mirth dancing in his eyes as he looked on.

Calver studied the group. It comprised four people; Gillespie, the big guy in cuffs and two others; guy in a white coat and a young woman. The big guy was about 6' 5", looked kinda vacuous and slow. Curly black hair and empty looking eyes. He had a big bleeding gash on his forehead. Back on the porch, at the door of the house stood an elderly, fearful looking women.

'This big boy was maybe looking to hurt hisself, and maybe others too,' Gillespie said. 'So we got doc Halloran here,' he added, nodding at the white coated figure. 'To come out and certify things good and proper. So what's your business here folks?'

'I've been retained by Floyd Ritter as outside counsel on his case,' Calver said. 'And I've come out here to talk to Jethro Tucker about that.'

Gillespie looked at Peters. 'You party to this, Ned? Cause this guy, far as I'm aware, he ain't even certified to practice in this state.'

'I'm just a driver, Silas, showing my legal friend around Tennessee,' Peters said.

Gillespie spat in the mud. 'You don't listen too good, do you, Ned? I told you and your friend last night what's what, and you turn up here. What am I gonna do with you guys?'

The girl spoke up then. 'We need to get Jethro into a facility officer, quickly, if we could move along, so we can screen him to see if its right to hold him.'

For a second Gillespie's eyes went flat, and the smile dropped. 'Why that's right, Miss Roberts,' he said, mock serious. His sly smile reappeared. 'This little lady's from the Mental Health Cooperative, helping us out here. But don't worry, Doc Halloran will certify the hold. Gives us another 14 days I believe, Doc?' he said. 'Now, when is it Floyd's due to fry?'

'Gentlemen,' he nodded. He prodded Tucker in the back and began moving him off towards the police vehicle.

Peters and Calver stood and watched the vehicles leave. They both then turned and looked up at the house where the elderly lady still stood, warily watching them. 'Come on,' Peters said. 'And this time, let me do the talking.'

They moved up to the house, Peters shouting a greeting. The lady didn't answer, just watched them approach. Twenty feet away Peters tried again. 'We are attorneys, Mrs Tucker, and we wanted to speak to Jethro. Maybe we can help him?'

She spat off the edge of the porch into the hard packed earth. 'What you want with my boy?' she asked. 'Heard you talkin' with that crazy policeman and you didn't cut no ice with him. State your business or get off my land.'

'It's a mighty fine spread you got here, ma'am,' Calver said. 'What are those green crops you got growing so well we drove through coming up?'

She smiled. 'This here's a small spread, come down from my

grandaddy, but we grow all sorts. Soy, cotton, corn and tobacco,' she said. Her face dropped. 'Don't know how's I'm gonna cope without Jethro though?'

'Well, maybe we can help you with that,' Peters said smoothly. 'We are attorneys after all, and we ain't looking to get paid here, just help you and Jethro out and see if he will talk to us.'

She studied them some more, nodded, and said, 'come on in then. I got some coffee on the stove.'

Ten minutes later they sat out on the porch as she poured from a big old black pot. 'What happened this morning, with Jethro?' Calver asked her.

She looked up, her bright bird-like eyes shining with native intelligence. 'That crazy cop showed up, took Jethro out to the barn,' she said. 'He said he needed to talk to him. Twenty minutes later the other two showed up. Think they were waiting just down the road. Cop said Jethro went crazy, talking all sorts about killing himself and *me*, his own mother. Cop said he had to quieten Jethro down, hit him with his billy-club. Said they were taking Jethro in for his own safety before he hurt anyone,' she said, her eyes turning anxious. 'Jethro never hurt a fly his entire life. He hasn't got it in him. He's a simple soul, and a gentle giant.'

Calver turned to Peters. 'So this is what, Ned? They committing him to a mental institution? Can they do that, just like that?'

'Simple answer is yes,' Peters said. 'State's commitment law says law enforcement, doctors and mental health crisis responders can detain an individual if he suffers a serious emotional disturbance, is likely to do serious harm, needs care and there is no suitable alternatives. So looks like Gillespie set it up with the mental health folks on hand to certify. They take Jethro in and then do a second screening, approve the holding and he'll go to a psychiatric hospital if they got a bed for him. My recollection of the law is a bit fuzzy but I think they have to have some type of probable cause hearing and can hold for 15 days.'

Calver looked out across the green fields of ordered crops, his mind working the angles.

'What do you men want with Jethro anyway?' the old lady asked. 'That crazy cop mentioned that Ritter guy on death row? What's that got to do with my boy?'

The two men's eyes met. Calver said, 'Jethro worked for an auto place that handled a car from a crash Ritter's wife was involved in. We think Jethro may have taken some pictures of the damaged vehicle, and we wanted to see if he might have them.'

Calver sensed a knowledge of something in the old lady's eyes. She said, 'can you help my boy? Get him back to me?'

Calver imperceptibly nodded at Peters.

'I could be his and your attorney, as he is entitled to counsel,' Peters said. 'So I can protect his position, challenge the detention.'

The old lady quickly reached across the table and grabbed Peters' hands. 'Thank you, thank you,' she said.

Peters shuffled his feet uncomfortably under the table, his face reddening at her show of gratitude. 'Although what Gillespie will do about it, I don't want to think about right now,' he said, a worried frown crossing his face.

The old lady stood up. 'You fellas mentioned pictures, right?'

Calver nodded.

'Well the one thing my boy does have, is pictures. Thousands and thousands of them,' she said smiling.

'What do you mean?' Calver asked.

'Come this way,' she said. She lead them back into the house to a door set under the staircase. She pulled it open, leaned in and pressed a light switch. 'The basement is Jethro's and he didn't like me going down there so I didn't. Its his secret world away from all the nasty folks out there who make fun of him, so I didn't complain. You can go down and take a look, long as you help my boy like you said, and get him back here.'

'We'll do our best,' Calver said.

'Can't ask for more than that,' she said, stepping aside.

Calver went first, moving slowly down the stairway with Peters following. As they descended they could see photographs all around, pinned to the walls, many of them old-style Polaroid's and Kodaks, some of them yellowed with age.

'What the hell have we got here?' Peters said, awe in his voice.

'Let's find out,' Calver said, quickening his step.

As the big black limo purred through sumptuous extended green lawns and water fountains, Pascal studied the imposing building as it emerged from the mist. Lloyd DeMasi's Hampton's mansion looked as if it had been modeled on French Chateaux of the 16th century, all yellowy brick with spires and turrets everywhere. It really did look like a fairytale castle that might hold a princess. It was situated in the exclusive Sagaponack village area of the Hampton's about 80 miles from

Manhattan.

After settling Anita into a drug rehabilitation facility for an assessment, Pascal had caught a plane down to the Hampton's. Leaving the girl had been hard but it was clear she was in safe hands. The doctor had seemed quite hard in his questioning of Anita but Pascal knew that was all part of how they worked, and what made the process effective. Most junkies Pascal knew were endlessly untruthful, mostly too themselves, as well as being manipulative and dishonest, especially when it came to getting their next fix. But she had a feeling about Anita; the girl was not a veteran long term user, she was a newby, her preferred poison, until recently had been booze, so there was some hope for her. Also it was clear her father's situation and possible imminent execution was playing heavily on her thoughts. It was clear she wanted to get clean, get out and join the effort to save him. The girl was safe for now, and Pascal would check straight back in with her after the weekend's activities. She wondered idly what Calver was up to; she'd left a string of messages, but so far he was not responding.

She was broken from her reverie as the car came to a halt. As she got out a doorman in black and white livery greeted her with a 'good afternoon, madam. May I take your bags?' But as usual she had none, other than a small canvas sports bag which she retained. The guy led her inside, then up a sweeping staircase under a million dollar looking chandelier to a sumptuous bedroom with a balcony that looked out across the estate. She was told dinner was at seven and formal attire was desirable. She bit back a smart retort, wondering whether she was meant to tip the guy, but as he didn't linger suggestively, she kept her hand in her pocket.

As the door closed, she looked longingly at the four-poster bed; she hadn't slept in an age, and needed to re-charge her batteries because she would need to be hyper alert from now on. She moved to the bed, flopped down, curled up into a ball and instantly fell asleep.

She woke at 2 minutes past six and went and showered in the en-suite bathroom. Coming out, hair turbaned in a white towel, she opened the canvas bag and took out a lap-top and the black cocktail dress. Later she studied herself in the mirror, her lip curling slightly; still, acting was all part of the game. Her watch said it was 7 pm - time to go.

The waiter guy met her at the bottom of the staircase and escorted her down a corridor to some ornately patterned doors which he opened, and gestured for her to go in. She immediately spotted DeMasi's gleaming bald head towering over the group around him which comprised 4 other people including Joyce Van Zim. 'Welcome Carrie,' his voice boomed over. 'Come and join our merry group.'

The room was large with huge windows down one wall looking out on green lawns and water features. The walls were a kind of dark red canvas on which hung many large old master style paintings. There were also books and some antique furniture.

DeMasi smiled and kissed her hand. 'You look wonderful, Carrie. A Cinderella style metamorphosis, if I may say so. You've met Joyce, but meet our other guests.'

First names only; they were Boyd, a supercilious preppy guy, thin and smiling; Jenny, black and butch looking with calculation in her eyes, and Joan, sweet and blonde. They greeted Pascal with ill disguised looks of suspicion; an impostor come to steal their spot. There was some small-talk before they repaired to a dining table set at the side of the room where a procession of waiters proceeded to lay out their meal.

Pascal contemplated the plate in front of her on which sat a small piece of bread with some pate and a piece of orange.

DeMasi said from the top of the table. 'Starter not to your liking, Carrie?'

'What is it?'

'It's seared Foie Gras on toasted brioche with caramelized orange. Food of the God's.'

Pascal pushed her plate away. 'I don't eat food that involves torture of animals,' she said. 'A bloody, well-done steak will do me, with French fries, if you have such a thing?'

Van Zim laughed. 'Carrie has moral scruples about eating pate that involves some mild discomfort to a stupid animal, but she doesn't mind breaking the jaw of Mr DeMasi's bodyguard, or indeed, eating meat from a slaughterhouse where it's common knowledge the animals are mistreated.'

'How do they make the Foie Gras?' sweet blonde Joan asked.

'They put a tube down the ducks throat and pump grain down it until the liver bursts,' Pascal said.

'Wow,' Boyd said. 'Give me some of that.'

'And Joyce,' Pascal added. 'Mr DeMasi's bodyguard was worse than a stupid animal. He attempted to sexually assault me, so I meted out my own form of justice. As for your comment about my beefsteak, if you can't tell the difference between how each is produced, I would seriously question whether you should be occupying such a senior position in the bank.'

DeMasi leaned back, clapped his hands and laughed, but the laughter didn't seem to reach his eyes. Van Zim struggled to hold a weak smile on her face.

'Mr DeMasi,' Pascal said. 'Tell me a little bit about the history of the bank and how you got here?'

'Good question,' he said, turning around in his chair and addressing a waitress: 'bring Carrie a well done steak with French fries.' He turned back to Pascal. 'I joined M J Greenberg way back in the 90's as a young punk trader. Worked my way up from there, to the very top. Not bad for a boy from the Bronx.'

'Yeah, but you got some help along the way, I hear.'

'Hows that?'

'Well, as I heard it, you got bailed out. Metro Bank owed M J Greenberg, what was it, $12 billion, just before the crash? As I heard it, you got your friends in Washington to bail out Metro with government money, simply so they could pay M J Greenberg the $12 billion owed, which they duly did, before collapsing. So you were then able to buy the corpse of Metro for $1. Ergo we now have Greenberg Metro Bank. The moral of the story,' Pascal said, looking up from her steak. 'Its great to have friends.'

'Bravo, Carrie,' DeMasi said. 'What are you, a socialist? Don't believe in capitalism?'

'I don't believe in feudalism or crony capitalism? But tell me about Phoenix,' she asked lightly.

The chatter around the table stopped, at the same time the large doors opened and Cimino, in a tuxedo, entered.

'Just in time, Cimino,' DeMasi said. 'Carrie was asking about Phoenix.'

Cimino smiled thinly and took a seat. 'She got all the gen she needs on the island. What more is there to tell?'

'C'mon,' she said in a joshing way. 'We're all friends here, aren't we? All been vetted, tested and sized up and found acceptable. No more secrets, huh?'

'You're right, Carrie,' DeMasi said. 'You're all in the family. No going back now folks.'

'What is it, like Scientology, you're not allowed to leave once you join?'

'You know that's quite a good analogy, Carrie,' Van Zim said. 'Did you notice the security we have around here?'

'Hard to miss it. Armed guards and dogs on the gates, razor wired walls, cameras everywhere, and I'm sure I saw at least two drones flying over as I came up in the limo.'

Cimino watched her, bored expression. 'Smart chick, huh? Keeps her eyes open?'

'No cameras inside the building though?' she replied, wanting to check something she'd noticed.

'Maybe,' Cimino said cryptically, no doubt wanting to leave her guessing.

'You know, Cimino,' DeMasi said. 'I Might just like Carrie as my personal bodyguard.'

Pascal smiled. 'One question though? What's all the security for? I mean, you're, if a may say so, only a banker.'

'Wrong,' he said. 'I'm a billionaire, and as such, I believe part of a group who are going to face the wrath of the dispossessed, when they finally catch on to what has been done to them. I am perhaps the first one of this group to start taking action to protect myself from what is to come?'

'You mean when the proletariat rises up and goes for the pitchforks?' Boyd the supercilious guy said.

'It's coming,' DeMasi said.

'So, that's where the bank's private army comes in, right?' Pascal said. 'The financial wizards do the clever stuff and the sharp and violent ones do the combat. So which group are we in?' she said, gesturing at her three associates.

'These three are definitely bankers, but you, Carrie, are a conundrum, because you would clearly be at home in either role,' DeMasi said.

'You've got quite a burn-out rate if I may say so,' Pascal said. 'What happened to Melissa McCarthy?'

'She wasn't strong enough,' Cimino said. 'It may sound brutal, but there is something to natural selection. She committed suicide because she couldn't handle the pressure.'

'And on that rather sad note,' DeMasi said, glancing around at the mostly emptied plates on the table, 'I have business to attend to. Feel free to linger or retire to your bedrooms. I will see you all tomorrow.' He rose and moved away.

Pascal also got up from the table. 'I will take an early night as well,' she said, knowing it was going to be anything but for her because she had work to do. As she left the table, she noticed Cimino's reptilian eyes following her, full of interest and a kind of question mark. Van Zim also watched her, but her look was more difficult to discern, although there was a fair element of desire in it. Maybe she'd have to use that at some stage. She shivered at the thought.

CHAPTER SEVENTEEN

As Pascal exited the large room, she made for an alcove she had seen that lay in shadow, under the wide sweeping staircase. She stood there for around three minutes, only seeing a waiter or two passing intermittently. A moment later Van Zim and Cimino came out, heads together talking quietly. Pascal let them pass, her eyes following them as they proceeded down a passage by the side of the staircase. As they went through some double doors, she moved out and followed, peeking through. She watched them walk up the corridor, still deep in conversation, and then stop outside a door.

Pascal watched them, heads together, and she was sure she saw something, a crawling kind of intimacy, that made no sense. It was just a feeling watching the body language, of something hidden between them. Van Zim turned and entered the room, as she did so, Cimino turned as well, as if alerted by some sixth sense, to look back a microsecond after Pascal had slipped back into shadow. She cautiously leaned around the door and watched him move off down the corridor to another door, near the end. So she'd ascertained their respective rooms; now what? She made her way back to her room.

Inside she got out of the hated cocktail dress and donned running gear; track suit, bobble hat and ear-buds for music. No one could complain about her going for a late night training run. She opened out her fake MP3 music player and checked the contents; assorted lock-picks and a remote audio camera. She reckoned Van Zim was the most sociable, and therefore probably the best room to place a bug, if she could get in. Cimino was too much of a cold fish, and close-mouthed to boot, unlikely to say anything, unless he had to. She moved out of her room, her step jaunty.

Down the sweeping staircase and into the corridor, there was no one about. Stepping up to Van Zim's door and listening - silence. Taking a chance, pressing the buzzer and hoping she wouldn't have to come out with a lame excuse and then get drawn into a clinch. Silence again. Pascal looked about; no one.

She studied the door and the lock; it was original, probably antique. Inserting her pick, the door was open in thirty seconds and she was inside in the darkness, heart beating loud in her ears. Standing for a few moments listening, her eyes slowly acclimatized to the light coming from the moon filtering in through the window. No point searching for anything; quick in and out. Up on the wall was an air condition grille similar to the one in her room. With her penknife it was easy to ease it away from the wall, and place the tiny audio camera in the empty vent. She tested the view and sound by tapping it and watching and listening to the results on her smart phone. Slotting the grille back into the wall she heard the door handle moving and looked wildly about for somewhere to hide. The space under the bed seemed the only viable place, but scrabbling for it her foot caught in a rug, bringing her crashing down, but as the door opened and light spilled in she carried on rolling until covered by the bed frame. Her breath came fast and her ankle throbbed with pain.

Grace came into the room giggling, 'I won't be a moment, Jenny, just got to take a leak.'

Pascal could see their feet as Grace went for the bathroom. So it was Jenny, the black butch looking intern who was with her. The girl stood near the door and waited and then Grace was back, Pascal desperately hoping they were not going to try and get it on there, so she'd have to stay and listen, but luck was with her. Grace led the girl out and the door closed behind them enveloping Pascal in the moonlit darkness again. She let out a sigh and felt down around her ankle. It felt okay now.

She made her way back to her room without incident and set up the feed on her smart phone, propping it up by the side of her bed. The camera was activated by sound, or light or movement. Pascal lay back on the bed and flicked the TV on with the remote, but soon fell asleep.

She came awake with a start. Something had woken her. The TV had gone into black sleep mode, but her smart phone screen was alight with images: Grace Van Zim wearing a nightgown, ushering Cimino into her room. Pascal rolled her feet off the bed, and into a sitting position, phone in her hand as she watched the images.

'What's so urgent you gotta drag me outta bed at 2 am in the morning, Cimino?' she asked drowsily. 'This better be good.'

'Oh it is,' he said, coolly. He was wearing tan chino's, open neck shirt and sports jacket, like he'd just been to a game.

'Well?'

'Annie Ranier.'

'What about her? dumb junkie who couldn't make the cut. If

Carrie doesn't pan out we can drop them both together,' Van Zim said.

'Wrong. Annie Rainer is not her real name.'

'Really?' Van Zim said, starting to get interested.

'Really. Her real name is actually Anita Ritter. Ring any bells?' Cimino said, voice like velvet.

Van Zim's face lost the humor. 'That's not possible,' she said quietly. 'I mean we did a deep dig into her, or, to be clear. You, Cimino, did. And you searched her apartment and digital devices and found nothing. So what gives, and are you sure?'

'She radically changed her appearance, and I'd almost think she had professional help, her cover story and back-up was so effective. But anyway, that's the past. We need to concentrate on the now and what we do. First thing, what about the boss?'

'No,' Van Zim said emphatically. 'No need to take this to him. At least not yet. In the past we've cleared these kinds of messes up without involving him.'

Cimino nodded. 'What about this Carrie? I don't like her. There's something there I can't put my finger on, and this chick is slick. Are they linked, working together?'

'I like Carrie, and so does the boss. She could have a great future with us, so lets not be hasty. So, first thing, we go back and take a very good look at Carrie's credentials and background, and this time we do it properly.'

'Check,' Cimino said. 'What about Ritter? Father's due to be executed shortly. You think they've uncovered anything?'

'No. How could they?' she said. 'How d'you find out about the Ritter girl?'

'I got a mole in NYPD, checked her prints from when we first looked at her, and he's only just got back to me,' Cimino said. 'Maybe we should just OD her, like the Melissa McCarthy chick,' he added with a reptilian smile and a chuckle. 'Easy to set up, given where she is. Piece of cake, just like the other one.'

'Maybe later,' Van Zim said. 'But for now, we know where she is - in the re-hab clinic - so she's not going anywhere soon. No, first we check on Carrie, then we act. But we need to do it right now, so get on it,' Van Zim, said, getting up and walking over to Cimino. She placed her hand on his crotch and began to rub it, holding his eyes. He remained motionless for a moment, then his hand lashed out taking Van Zim across the face. It was clear she was expecting the blow and took it, staggering back, wiping her mouth, eyes on fire with passion. 'Yes' she whispered, quietly. 'That's what I want.'

As Cimino began to move towards her, her phone began to ring. She glanced at the screen. 'Shit,' she said. 'Its the boss. I gotta take this. Come back later,' she added, passion gone, replaced by total focus.

Saved by the bell Pascal thought, rubbing her face, wondering what the hell she was going to do now.

'Looks like the kid dreamed about living in a zoo,' Peters said, looking around at the many pictures of animals adorning the walls of the basement.

They had been down there for twenty minutes. It was hot and Calver felt claustrophobic in the windowless space. 'These photos all look old, like from when he was a kid,' Calver said. 'I mean who still takes these kind of pictures anyway, when everybody and his dog has got a smart phone?'

'Well this kid, obviously.'

'Yeah, well you saw him, and he sure ain't a kid now,' Calver said looking around. Other than the pictures on the walls the only other things in the space were a long bench and a couple of chairs. 'Come on, let's go talk to his mother.'

When they first re-emerged up top they couldn't see Ma Tucker, but could hear the rattle of a keyboard which led them to a small office space off the main living room, where they found her sitting at a desk with a computer screen. She looked up from a thick bundle of papers she was working on, pebble glasses perched on the end of her nose. 'Come right in boys,' she said. 'I could do with a break. Farming used to be fun, but now its all paperwork. Husband used to do it, but he's been gone more'n two years now. Did you find what you were looking for?'

'Not exactly,' Peters said. 'But we sure liked the animals.'

She smiled. 'Jethro was always happier with them, than with humans.'

'Mrs Tucker,' Calver said. 'The photos in the basement are all pretty old. I was told he had a phone that he used to take photos on more recently?'

'Yeah that's right,' she said. 'Trouble is he's always misplacing it and losing it.'

'So what happened to his phone and the photos he took on it?' Peters asked.

'Well his daddy used to transfer them from the phone onto the computer screen, and then they'd look at them, and mess about, changing them, but with him gone….. I think Jethro just looks at them on his phone now, cause I didn't have the time. And I ain't no good at computers. I just type and print stuff.'

'You're like me,' Peters said. 'Use 'em when I have to.'

'The pictures we're looking for, if they exist, date from around six years ago,' Calver said. 'So, from what you say, it's possible they might have been transferred by your husband onto computer. Is this the machine he would have used?' Calver asked, gesturing at the desktop.

'We've never had any other,' she said.

'Mind if I have a look?'

'Sure,' she said. 'Let me close what I'm working on so I don't lose it.' She clicked a couple of times on screen, then stood up. 'I'll get us some coffee and biscuits,' she said. A frown crossed her face. 'You are going to help get my boy back, aren't you?'

'Absolutely,' Calver said. 'Soon as I've had a look on here, we'll get back to Nashville and Ned will go on the record for you and Jethro.'

Mrs Tucker nodded, placated for now. Calver took her seat, worrying briefly about just what Gillespie might do, when he found out they were really going to go head to head, but that would have to wait. He studied the screen in front of him. It was covered in icons, many of them clearly old. Down the left side of the screen were some titled: "Jethro Picture Album", then numbered, 1 up to 8. Calver clicked on the first one. The pictures were dated from about 8 years previously, mostly stills, but there were also some brief video clips with audio. It was mainly pictures of farm workers, crop picking, driving tractors, and occasional pictures of Jethro and his mother, and another guy Calver guessed was the father. It appeared to be in chronological order and carried captions, sometimes humorous, explaining what it depicted and the date.

Calver clicked on album 5. He asked Peters the date of the auto crash, which he gave him. Calver scrolled, saying, 'this is a year before.' And now the pictures of farming were interspersed with others that were clearly from the auto yard and included film of the then owner, Pete Atkins and Jethro working on car bodies and horsing around. Calver slowly continued to scroll.

Mrs Tucker returned with a tray, cups and biscuits. Calver said, 'some of these pictures look like the people don't know they're being filmed?'

She sighed. 'Jethro had some trouble, way back, when he was a teenager. He was taking some pictures of some school kids. It was completely innocent, but a cop stopped him, and he was arrested, taken to the precinct. Took his camera away and roughed him up, before his daddy got there. He sorted it out but it left Jethro real scared. So from then on he was careful, and he found the pictures were often better if people didn't know. So, specially with the phone camera, he could virtually hide it in his hand, and people would never know he was filming.'

Calver reached the date of the accident. First up was 4 stark pictures of the underside of a clearly mangled vehicle hoisted up on a lift. Peters leaned down over his shoulder. 'There,' he said pointing. 'It's been cut, looks like four places, but not all the way through, so it would drip out and not fail straightaway.'

Calver scrolled on. Next was a video clip of Pete Atkins talking to Gillespie and another guy, who was indistinct as he was standing in shadow, and there was no audio. They were stood around the vehicle which was now lowered down to ground level, and they were pointing at it. Peters whistled, looking at the concertinaed front end, which was still soaked in blood.

As the next clip started there was audio, laughter, loud and unrestrained as the camera panned up to the face of the guy who had now come out of the shadows. He was standing with Gillespie, and Atkins was no longer there. 'Hey, dummy,' he said. 'What you waiting for? Your boss told you to scrap it, now. So get to it.'

'Yes sir,' a faint voice in the background said.

'Kid's a retard,' Gillespie said, and they both laughed again. 'But, you may have a problem,' Gillespie continued. 'Because that's one tough nigger bitch. They haul her out, she still ain't dead. I held off calling the medics long as I could but with the fucking media coming, what could I do? Had to cover my back.'

'She was a mess though, right?' Cimino said.

'Oh yeah. She won't be causing Mr DeMasi and the bank any more problems, trust me. And if that ain't right, I'm sure you can finish the job.'

As both men laughed some more, Calver looked up at Peters and their eyes met. Calver picked up one of the biscuits and took a bite, cocked his head to one side. He said to Mrs Tucker, 'these are damn good biscuits, Mrs Tucker. Mind if I email this clip to a friend?'

'Not at all,' she said. 'Go ahead. Will it help Jethro?'

'Ultimately, yes,' Calver replied. He dug his phone out and

checked it. Many miscalls from Pascal - Calver rarely checked his phone these days - and an old text from her he hadn't seen or read, saying, "found AR. We need talk f2f." Calver, full of relief, searched for her email address, then turned back to the computer. He typed his message, attached the stills and video clip, and pressed 'send'.

Calver stood up. 'Like to thank you, ma'am,' he said to Mrs Tucker. 'For your time and your help. Now, me and Ned will go see if we can help your boy.'

CHAPTER EIGHTEEN

As Pascal re-watched the clip of Van Zim and Cimino she noticed she had received an email from Calver with an attachment. Just as she moved to open it her door buzzer went. She checked the time; it was 3.10 a m. She threw a robe on and went to the door, opening it a crack. It was Lloyd DeMasi.

'Carrie. I was hoping you'd be awake,' he said, eyes bright. 'I wondered if you'd fancy a stroll up to my sanctum sanctorum. The nerve center, where lesser mortals dare not tread?'

She wondered if he was high; even better if he was. He was dressed casually in jeans and open-necked shirt. He stood waiting, arms crossed, relaxed. She said, 'sure. Love to. Give me a moment.'

She moved back into the room, donned baggy pants and teeshirt. As she went back to join DeMasi she stopped, head cocked to one side. She moved back and got her cellphone, took it into the bathroom and placed it in the toilet cistern, then went back out to join him. He lead her back down the corridor and up the sweeping staircase. He didn't speak, he hummed to himself. There was no one else around. They turned into an alcove where lift doors stood open, as if awaiting their arrival. They entered and DeMasi tapped in a code and the lift began to move upwards.

It slowed, came to a halt, the doors opened and she moved out into a large room. She had expected space-age decor festooned with tech stuff, but it was actually a comfortable space; to the side a couch, chairs and a table, in the middle of the room a large antique desk with a couple of monitors on it and some papers, and down the other side there was an exercise bike and a basketball hoop high on the wall. Three large Georgian-style windows looked out on the greenery and water features outside, in darkness now.

'Come and sit,' DeMasi said, gesturing at the couch. 'Drink?'

'Thanks. Scotch,' she said. She went and sat astride the exercise bike, looking around as DeMasi mixed two large scotches.

He handed her one, studying her. 'You're a strange one, Carrie,' he said. 'You asked earlier about my history and the bank, but I didn't feel like sharing reality with your colleagues, because I doubt they're ready to hear it, or ever will be, still less, understand it. But I believe you would.'

'Try me.'

He put his drink down and walked over to the wall, picked a ball up and began to bounce it whilst moving around the floor. He feinted to turn, went the other way, reared up and launched the ball skyward. It arced over into the hoop. 'You've been to the island and Grace has talked to you, so you've got a pretty good idea about who we are,' he said, coming back and sipping his drink.

'I heard the spiel,' she said. 'Forgive me though. Its not exactly earthshaking, so all this cloak and dagger kind of double talk is getting tedious. My take, you've built up like a sort of secret army of loyal folk who are getting into positions throughout the financial world and maybe politics who will do the banks bidding when the time comes. Big deal. I call it networking. Okay, you've got a second cohort who I suppose could develop into some type of para-military protection squad but for now they're just muscle, who you might call upon when the masses rise up to kill the few - the new rentier class who own everything.'

She sipped her drink and put it down. She began to peddle the exercise bike, slowly, then building up speed until her feet were just a blur. After a minute of sustained pedaling, she began to slow, her breathing barely disturbed. As the pedals came to stop, she reached for her drink. 'Trouble is,' she said. 'I think you may have gone rogue. What happened to Melissa McCarthy?'

'Does it matter, in the great scheme of things? Do the little people really matter, Carrie?' he asked, smiling.

'Well, if you need to ask, I'd suggest you've got a problem.'

He laughed. 'Expressing concern for others has always been an attractive character trait, which is why so many people feign it, and it's such a ludicrous affectation. From politicians to celebrities, they all love the little people. They all want to help them, but in reality, when push comes to shove, how real is it? Its a jungle out their; dog eat dog; every man for himself, and it always has been. Wake up, Carrie.'

'And smell the napalm, right?'

He laughed again. 'When I started out as a trader at Greenberg's we scalped everybody. The eighties traders used to say: "Shear, don't kill". I mean everybody; from little old ladies to pension funds to cancer charities. We rigged the rates, we lied about prospects. We sold pigs painted up as renaissance old masters. And we ran our own book, using client's money to move prices to our own benefit and their detriment.

But it didn't matter. And now it's even better - its virtually paradise. After the bail outs, moral hazard's gone. You can do literally anything now, and you get bailed out come what may. The banks and their trading floors have always been criminal enterprises, and at the end of the day it used to boil down to matters of degree, but now, not even that matters. Because now anything, literally, anything, goes.'

'Including murder?'

'You know, Carrie, I think I can tell you my deepest thoughts, my story, everything I've done, in here,' he said, gesturing around the room. 'Because you'll understand, and anyway, our conversation is privileged, confidential and deniable.'

'Go for it,' she said.

'McCarthy was weak. We invited her in, but her work was sloppy, and she threatened us and our vision of the world.'

'So you got Cimino to top her. Nice and subtle.'

DeMasi frowned. 'As the official record shows, Melissa McCarthy suffered an unfortunate overdose, she having become heavily dependent on narcotics.'

'So, what?' Pascal said, leaving the question hanging in the air. 'Anything doesn't go? Murder's too great a stretch?' She got the impression he felt he had gone too far, told her too much and now was reining himself in.

'Back in the day,' he continued. 'We did a lot of stuff that we don't do now. That was before the merger with Metro, before we became top three in the world. Coming up with Greenberg, wanting to match the big-boys, we had to fire fight along the way. Stopping bullshit, speculative lawsuits, that could have stopped us in our tracks, and sent some of the guys to jail. We did some things, with the genesis of what is now the protective force, lead by Cimino, that we wouldn't do now.'

She knew he was getting close to talking about Ritter, but he was also starting to water down his telling of what happened. She was about to prompt him when the lift doors opened and Cimino entered.

He was smiling grimly, walking quick into the middle of the room. 'Sorry to interrupt, boss, but we got a problem with our friend here,' he said, gesturing at Pascal.

DeMasi looked startled, like he was coming out of a dream. 'Well?' he said.

'She ain't quite who she says she is,' Cimino said. 'Real name's Courtney Pascal. She's ex-British intelligence, currently working for a New York attorney, Jonas Calver. He in turn has joined Floyd Ritter's legal team as outside counsel.'

DeMasi frowned. 'I'm disappointed, Carrie,' he said. 'Or should I call you, Courtney?'

'And that's not all, boss,' Cimino added. 'Annie Rainer is Ritter's daughter.'

'You're kidding me' DeMasi said. 'How about that? We need to beef up our security checks, don't you think, Cimino?'

'I agree, boss, but the girl, Ritter, went to great lengths to disguise herself and her background, and this one,' he said, nodding at Pascal. 'Had some help, and given her background, it's not so hard.'

'Can we contain it?' DeMasi asked.

'Absolutely,' Cimino said. 'Let's put her in cold storage for now, get Grace up here, and work up a plan. The Ritter girl is safe, stuck in the rehab joint, for now.'

'Good. Lock her down,' he said nodding at Pascal. 'And get Grace.'

'I'm on it,' he said, taking Pascal's arm and pulling her toward the lift.

'Calver knows I'm here,' Pascal said. 'I don't call in, you'll have cops crawling up your ass before sunrise.'

'She's bluffing, boss,' Cimino said, casually. 'And even if she's not, we can handle the cops.'

'I agree,' DeMasi said. 'Lock her down. We may need to question her some more later.'

Cimino shoved her into the lift and followed, the doors closing behind him.

Calver wandered around the house exploring its nooks and crannies. He had dropped Ned off in Nashville, so he could go see about challenging Jethro Tucker's incarceration. Peters had seemed fired up and had admitted as much, saying he hadn't felt this good for years. He had offered, and Calver had accepted, Peters' invitation to stay at the house, so they could work better together, look at the evidence again and put together a clemency plea. When Calver had mentioned Gillespie and his threats, Peters had said that when he was on his own he had been scared, but if Calver was with him, it gave him the strength to face Gillespie off.

Calver wandered into the main living room and took a seat at the desk, thinking about Pascal's cryptic text that she'd found Anita. He'd tried to phone earlier, but got no answer, straight to voice-mail. He tried again - nothing. Next he tried Joel who was back in New York on an assignment he'd said he couldn't get out of. Joel picked up straight away.

'Man, I got the news from Courtney,' he said, excitement in his voice. 'But I been tied up, still am in fact. She's found Anita.'

'You spoke to her?' Calver asked.

'I spoke to Courtney, but she was on the run and couldn't really talk. Said she was out at DeMasi's joint in the Hampton's,' he said, breathless. 'Said Anita is fine, but there were issues she couldn't go into on the phone. When I started to ask questions, she just said, "gotta go," and hung up. Since then I haven't been able to get hold of her. But man, that's good news sis is safe.'

'I agree its great news, but I'd like to get hold of Pascal because we need to talk, with you also, because I've found some stuff about your dad's case.'

'What you got?' Joel asked.

'I met with your father's old attorney, Ned Peters and he's been very helpful so far. What I've got I don't want to talk about over the phone,' Calver said. 'Maybe I should go and see your father, tell him what we got so far and of course about Anita, although it would be nice to know what these "issues" Pascal mentioned are. Can you get down here anytime soon?'

There was a brief silence, before Joel said, 'unfortunately not. In fact I'm currently in San Francisco on a story, and can't get back before the weekend. Two things though; don't talk to Pop yet, until we know more; don't want to falsely get his hopes up. Second, be careful of Peters. Guy's a drunk and I don't trust him.'

This time Calver was silent for a couple of beats, surprised at the anger he detected in Joel's voice. 'I like what I've seen so far,' Calver said, ' but I hear what you're saying. In fact, he's invited me to stay with him while I'm down here, and I have agreed. At least I'll have quick access to him and his papers when I need answers.'

'Be careful of the guy,' Joel said. 'Look, I gotta go, man. Deadline won't wait,' he added, clicking off the phone.

Calver looked at the handset. He pressed redial for Pascal - still dead. What the hell was she up to, he wondered?

He turned to the desktop computer, tapped it awake and opened a new word document; his fingers began to move: "Application to the Tennessee Governor and Board of Pardons and Paroles on behalf of Floyd Ritter." He stopped and leaned back in his chair, eyes closed. Two minutes later he opened them again and began typing, his fingers moving slowly at first, then speeding up.

It was pitch dark in the room. No windows and no light. Cimino, after hand cuffing her, had thrust her into the room an hour or so ago, banging the door shut behind her and noisily locking it. She had made one round of the space with her hands on the wall, then crawled around the floor. It seemed to be a medium sized rather spartan bedroom with just one bed in the middle of the room, which she was now sitting on.

The darkness seemed to help her thought processes. They knew who she was, and they knew who Anita was, and they had linked it all to back to Calver and Floyd Ritter. So what would they do? They hadn't hesitated to dispose of Melissa McCarthy and probably Mary Ritter as well, and she had seen Cimino in action and at close quarters.

They would come for her and then go after Anita. As those thoughts tumbled through her mind she heard the door lock turning and at the same time an overhead strip light, clearly controlled from outside the room, buzzed and stutteringly came to life.

Grace Van Zim stood in the doorway, smiling. 'Carrie, or is it, Courtney?' she said with an affected simper. 'My, you look delectable, dear. All trussed up for me like a rather wonderful Thanksgiving Turkey.'

Pascal watched her warily, a rather unpleasant feeling of dread starting to crawl through her insides. She had always found men exceptionally easy to decipher and anticipate, could see there moves coming a mile away, but women? As she pondered that, another figure appeared at Van Zim's shoulder. It was Jenny, the black intern she had met earlier at the dinner.

'This is my playroom, Carrie,' Van Zim said, gesturing around the room. 'This is where I bring my playmates. A place where we can let our hair down. Let ourselves go with no silly limits, or moral boundaries of what is right and wrong. And I've brought along a new friend, Jenny. She is with us now, part of the family if you like.'

'That would be the Adams family, would it?' Pascal said.

'Mr DeMasi has outlined your fate,' she continued as if she hadn't heard Pascal, her eyes looking as if she were in a trance. 'He occasionally indulges my particular peccadillo's; a reward for my service to the cause. So, my dear, since your fate is now sealed, there is no reason why I shouldn't enjoy some quality time with you. Yes?'

'If you're expecting an answer to that, Grace, you'll have a long wait,' Pascal said. 'What about, Anita? She due for the same treatment?'

'Of course,' Van Zim said. She turned to Jenny who had been standing just inside the door holding a tray with a bottle of vodka and three full glasses. Why don't you have a drink with us Carrie, so we can all get comfortable.

'Sounds good. Since we're getting so friendly, how about taking the cuffs off? Some of my female lovers tell me I have fingers like a concert pianist. You wouldn't want to miss out on that would you, Grace?' Pascal said, her eyes placid and unreadable.

Jenny giggled whilst Van Zim's smile froze for a second, before melting back in place. 'Maybe you won't find it as much fun as you think, Carrie. You see, my kick is the infliction of pain. Maybe we'll take the cuffs off later, when I've broken you. We'll see.'

'If you're trying to shock or scare me, Grace, you're wasting your time,' Pascal said. 'You'd have to live a thousand years to see the things I've seen and done. So your little S & M ménage à trois, apart from being quaint, sad and bourgeois, is not remotely scary to me.'

Van Zim smiled. 'Good,' she replied. 'So drink up, then. Perhaps a toast?' Jenny held the vodka glass to Pascal's mouth, and began to tilt it. Pascal swallowed instinctively, finishing it, her eyes watering as it went down her throat.

Grace smiled again. 'You like that, Carrie? The Rohypnol gives it a special kind of flavor, don't you think?'

Pascal started. 'Date rape drug,' she whispered, her insides going cold. 'Gamma Hydroxybutyric acid. Even with cuffs on you need to drug me, Grace?' It was if she could already feel her eyes getting heavy and drowsy even though the drug couldn't yet have had time to enter her system. In the background, sounds of Van Zim asking Jenny to go and get something, and the door closing. Pascal lurched forward, grabbing the vodka bottle with her cuffed together hands, swinging it up and around to hit Van Zim in the side of the head. She went down like a skittle and lay silent, out cold. Pascal, her brain sluggish, already beginning to slow, riffled through Van Zim's pockets and got the handcuff keys and opened them. Moving to the door, using everything she had to stop her eyes from closing, waiting and listening, and then the door was opening again and Jenny was coming through. Pascal couldn't risk subtlety, desperately afraid she would pass out before she could get free, so she used the bottle again, swinging it into Jenny's head and knocking her down.

Studying the two prone figures and trying to get her brain to work, the thought ran through her head that running on the spot might be good. Dragging up every last reserve of strength, her feet began to pump. Moments later she was dragging Jenny over to Grace and handcuffing them together through a stanchion of the bed. Taking Jenny's socks off, she stuffed one in each of their mouths, then tore strips off the bed sheet to fashion crude tie-arounds to keep the gags in place. Then through their pockets taking their wallets, ID's and phones, and from Grace a set of car keys. Pascal's breathing was haggard now and sweat ran down her forehead. The two cuffed women began to moan and regain consciousness. If she hit them again, they might die.

Best to keep moving while she still could. Hoisting herself up and dragging all the blankets and pillows off the bed, she spread them over the two figures, still lying prone, then the mattress. Moving to the door, it was still ajar. Not having seen any keys, it surely must self-lock, and could only be opened from the outside. Pushing it open a crack and looking out, it was an empty corridor that looked like maybe for services. Sliding out, closing the door behind her and hitting the light switch on the wall, it was time to go.

Her still sluggish brain reckoned it was about 5 a m, a good time to be creeping around, but she needed to get out fast before the domestic staff rolled into action. Most of all she needed to get her phone. Coming to a fire door and moving through into a service staircase, on autopilot, her feet took her upwards. They must have been down in the basement and now it was the ground floor. It brought her out near the sweeping staircase. A quick check for all clear, then running stooped over, silent, to her room and in, moving straight into the bathroom and grabbing her phone from the cistern.

Cold water splashed on her face felt good, and slapping herself and screaming inside helped some more. Then she was retracing her steps to the service entrance in the basement and looking out on the parking area. Stealthy movement, slipping out, pressing the toggle switch on Grace's keyring and hearing a blip and seeing lights flash on a big blue BMW, then she was inside and driving. Should be easy to get out, unless the protection goons had been alerted. Approaching the security gate and lowering her window as a man approached, she said, 'I'm just popping out for Miss Van Zim, to the village. Its urgent and I'll be back in fifteen minutes.' She held the mans eyes. Luckily he looked half asleep, then he was waving her through and she was out.

Speeding down the winding lane to the main drag, she had her phone to her ear listening to the ring tone, then Joel was picking up. Cutting him short, her words forced out, telling him, as next of kin he needed to get Anita out of the rehab clinic immediately, because she was in danger. Couldn't explain it all now and they would all need to meet up later, preferably in Tennessee. He needed to do it right now. Her last resources of energy were almost expired now and she could barely hold the phone, but could just make out him saying he was at La Guardia, just got in and would go straight to the clinic. She smiled weakly, knowing he would do what was necessary.

She was done and had to stop. The copse of trees about 300 meters from the road caught her eye, and then the wheel was turning instinctively and the vehicle veering across the field and into the trees. When she was deep inside and no longer visible from the road she switched the engine off and collapsed into a deep sleep.

She woke with a start, eyes springing open. A single beam of sunshine came down at an angle through the trees that surrounded her. Her head ached terribly, but her mind had cleared. Memories of the night before came tumbling back. Then she remembered Calver's email with attachment that had come in just before DeMasi had come calling, and which she hadn't had time to look at. She dug her phone out, switched it on and viewed the clip. After the last 24 hours at DeMasi's place, the contents of the clip were not really a surprise. The footage drew a direct evidential line between DeMasi, Cimino and the setting up of the auto crash that had ultimately killed Mary Ritter.

As she re-watched the clip an incoming text from Joel appeared. It read: "Got Anita out safe. What now? We need talk urgent."

She texted back, "Tennessee".

She turned her phone off and started the engine.

193

CHAPTER NINETEEN

It was 5 days later and Lloyd DeMasi sat in his cavernous and spectacular Wall Street office. One whole wall comprised strengthened glass, giving a panoramic view of New York's skyline. To the side of his desk stood a bank of 12 brightly colored screens showing feeds of stock prices, foreign exchange and other financial data. But today he wasn't interested in any of that. Today he was focused on Grace Van Zim and Cimino, who sat across from him in straight-backed, hard chairs. DeMasi's chair, by way of contrast, was state-of-the-art and ergonomically designed, positioned on a raised dais, allowing him to look down on those who sat across from him.

'So what did you find out, Cimino?' he asked, his voice understated and quiet.

Cimino looked at Van Zim, but she kept her face expressionless. He shrugged. 'I been down Tennessee for 3 days, boss. I believe the woman, Pascal, and Anita Ritter are down there, but I can't find them. I got people out looking, along with the cop, Gillespie. So we'll find them.'

'Sure, sure, we'll find them,' DeMasi said, waving his hand expansively. 'But that ain't exactly what I was asking. What I want to know is: what have they got? What have they found out? You see, its come to my attention that you,' and here he looked at both of them. 'Have been keeping stuff from me.'

'Only because we thought we could sort it without troubling you,' Van Zim said quickly.

'And look where that got us.'

Cimino took something out of his pocket and slid it across the desk. 'I found this. Its a camera, audio bug. It was in the air vent in Grace's room.'

Van Zim turned to look at Cimino, anger spreading across her face. 'Why didn't you—'

'So, to repeat,' DeMasi broke in patiently. 'What do they have?'

'Not much, from the bug,' Cimino said. 'But the lawyer may have turned up some stuff in Nashville.'

'We'll get to that,' DeMasi said. 'What will the girl have seen and heard on the bug, Grace?'

She rubbed her face, her mind winding back to the weekend. 'Not much. Cimino told me in my room that he'd made Anita Ritter, so she knew that early on.'

'What else?'

'I think Cimino here may have blabbed something about how we should OD the Ritter girl, like we did Melissa McCarthy,' Van Zim said with a vindictive smile.

Cimino sat silent, unconcerned, like a lizard sunning himself on a rock.

DeMasi turned and looked out of the window. He knew the girl knew, because she'd said so when he'd spoken to her in his inner sanctum.

Cimino said, 'I'm not bothered about that, and nor should you be, boss. That case is dead and closed and NYPD ain't gonna re-open it on tittle tattle. But what we ought to worry about is the lawyer, Calver.'

'How so?' DeMasi asked.

'He's digging into the Mary Ritter auto-crash. He's teemed up with Floyd Ritter's original lawyer. They've already been to the breakers yard, and tracked down the original owner. I paid the guy a visit,' Cimino said, his thin lips forming into a wintry smile. 'After a little bit of persuasion, he couldn't stop talking.'

'And?'

'He says a guy at the yard may have taken pictures of me there, and the vehicle, including the cut brake lines. I can't remember but there was talk between me and Gillespie there at the time that may have referenced the bank. May even have mentioned you too, boss.'

'So who's this guy from the yard, and what did he get?' DeMasi asked.

'Gillespie has got that covered. Guy's name is Jethro Tucker. A retard; real slow and stupid. Anyway chief Gillespie acted quick and has got him committed to a mental institution. No access to him except family, and easy to get him declared unfit to testify in a court about anything. But.'

'But?'

'I paid the guys mother a visit, and she talked. Calver had been there already, and they copied pictures from her computer.' Cimino removed a smartphone from his jacket, tapped the screen a couple of times and slid it across the desk to DeMasi.

Voices could clearly be heard emanating from the phone as

DeMasi watched the screen. His expression didn't change. When the clip finished he slid the phone across to Van Zim.

As she watched the tape, DeMasi said, 'When's Floyd Ritter due to fry?'

'21 days from today,' Van Zim said. 'Barring a reprieve, which I'm told, from an impeccable source, is not gonna happen.'

DeMasi turned to her. 'What will the lawyer and the Pascal woman do, Grace?'

'I'd guess they'll put what they've got to the DA, but I don't see it changing anything, because what they've dug up it has no bearing on Floyd Ritter's conviction or sentence. And even if Tennessee law enforcement were interested in taking a closer look at the auto-crash, they won't, because we own the state.'

'I agree,' DeMasi said. 'But I want you, Cimino, to go down there and stay until the execution, so you can ride shotgun for Gillespie. And Grace can be available 24/7 for consultation, and she can go down there as and when required.'

'Why don't we just whack 'em, boss?' Cimino said

'Because I don't think we need to,' he replied. 'As Grace said, we own the state. Bought and paid for, all the levers of power greased. But, you will be there to monitor things, and if you take a view we or the bank are at risk, we can review the situation and act. By the way, where do you believe the woman Pascal, and Anita Ritter are?'

'They're down there, hiding out, but as you say, boss, maybe we don't even need to find them for now.' He smiled to himself, then added softly, 'but Gillespie will go on looking anyway, and if he finds them…..well, you know. Maybe we won't have to lift a finger.'

Mercy Reeder woke with a start, heart beating wildly, damp-with-sweat bed sheets wrapped around her so tight she could hardly breathe. It was still dark. The green LED of her bedside clock read 2.37 a m. What had woken her? Maybe another nightmare? She started to untangle the sheets, and then she heard the sound. Her breath caught in her throat. It was movement downstairs; somebody was there, in her house. Her phone was down there. She rolled out of bed in just her shorty night-shirt, went to the door and opened it ajar and looked out onto the landing. A dim glow of light that shouldn't have been there rose up from below. She moved to the rail and looked down.

He was sat back in her favorite armchair, the one she sat in to watch TV when she wasn't on Facebook, and he was looking up at her, a smile on his face and a can of beer in his hand. He looked more than well-oiled, canned most likely, and that made him even more dangerous. As he looked up at her she realized he could see right up between her legs. She stepped back abruptly. He laughed and got up out of the chair and walked towards the stairs.

'What do you want, Scooter?' she said, backing away towards her bedroom door. 'I told you, we're through.'

'You know that ain't true, Mercy,' he said. 'I mean, why would you give me a key, if that was the case.'

She watched him as he reached the top of the stairs, knowing she'd never given him a key. He stood there, intimidating and nasty as a cop with a night stick, but way worse. At over 6' 2", he was muscled like a weight-lifter, with curly brown hair, tanned face and those dark eyes that at first she had thought soulful, but which she now saw were just mean and empty, like sunken piss holes in the snow.

'Baby, don't fight me,' he said. 'You know I don't like to hurt you, but you make me.' He lent back against the rail that ran across the top of the stairs, watching her.

She knew it was pointless to argue. Maybe this time he wouldn't beat the shit out of her, 'cause if she missed another shift at Riverbend, the job would be gone. She gently leaned her back against the bedroom door, realizing that this was the way it was always going to be. There was no way out for her, because he was never going to let her go. He would kill her before letting that happen. Maybe it was better to accept the way things were.

'I don't come to you,' he said. 'You come to me, but this time you crawl on your hands and knees, and you beg me to stay.'

She started to cry softly. Glancing down at her hands, they were red and raw from hand washing clothes the night before. It made her think of her mom, long gone, killed by a violent husband, her father. Maybe it was like they said, it ran in families, you were marked by it, and you perpetuated it in your own life. She would be just like her momma, just another victim, like she had a big sign on her head. You couldn't break the mold.

She slowly began to lower herself to the floor, and now her crying was louder. Scooter smiled and began to unbuckle his belt. He'd give her a whipping anyway, just to keep her in line. A woman needed discipline, needed to know who was boss.

The Happy Eater Breakfast joint wasn't exactly buzzing, but the food was good and cheap. Pascal sat at a table toward the rear tucking into a plate of scrambled eggs on rye. There were only a few customers today, couple of old guys sat at the counter chewing away, a morbidly obese lady sitting in the corner, and a spotty kid wearing a red bandanna around his head, a few tables away. There was a little TV over the counter that Pascal was pretending to watch, but her eyes were actually trained on the street outside that she could see through the restaurant door and frontage. She checked her watch again. Maybe her mark wasn't going to show this morning. She'd been watching the woman for a couple of days now, and she seemed to be a creature of habit, but today she was on the drag.

As Pascal watched the street outside - it was just off the main drag and not very busy - her mind drifted back over the last few days. They had seemed to pass each other like ships in the night; Calver and Joel had returned to New York for work commitments but Calver would be back at the weekend, and they would meet up then. They had face-timed a spell, so they were up to speed, as well as you ever could be without a proper face-to-face. Ned Peters, Floyd's old lawyer, had opened up for Pascal an old country shack he had inherited from his mother, that hadn't been used in years. It was still held in his mother's maiden name so would not show up as being in Ned's ownership. It was a couple of miles from his place, deep in Hicksville, surrounded by trees and well overgrown. Pascal loved it, and so did Anita, when she was awake, which wasn't often. She was on prescription medication to help with withdrawal and seemed to sleep forever, which maybe wasn't such a bad thing, what with her father's execution date coming screaming down the line at them, with little chance, according to Calver, of arresting it.

Pascal looked up as the mark entered the cafe. She hadn't seen the car arrive. She immediately noticed the woman seemed to have acquired a very slight limp and she was wearing dark glasses. Other than that, she wore her usual wind-sheeter over her uniform top, and a baseball cap. This morning she just ordered coffee. The waitress said, 'no toast today, Mercy?'

'Not today,' she answered abruptly. She came toward Pascal and took a seat two tables away. She usually chatted with the waitress, but not today. Pascal could sense something was wrong; something had changed.

They both looked up as a big, heavily muscled traffic cop entered the joint. Pascal could almost feel the girl flinch, seeming to sink lower in her chair, like she wanted to disappear. This was interesting. Pascal watched the guy saunter over toward Mercy Reeder - a wannabe alpha male intoxicated by his own testosterone.

'Mercy, baby, why you light out so quick this morning?' he said, possessive whine in his voice. 'You know I like my breakfast in bed.'

'I'm sorry, Scooter,' she said quickly, her eyes nervously darting around. 'I, I had to clean myself up for work.'

'Well, next time you ask good old Scooter before you go running off,' he said, making a clucking sound in the back of his throat. As he spoke his eyes slid onto Pascal's. His smile widened and he tipped his cap at her. 'You know, Mercy,' he continued, chuckling, eyes still on Pascal, 'if you weren't such a hog for the rough stuff in the bedroom, you wouldn't need to clean yourself up.'

For a second the girl looked frozen, staring down at the tabletop, trapped, a red blush of shame rising up her neck. The man leaned down and lifted her chin up so she was looking up at him. 'You know, Mercy, we—'

'Scooter, we gotta go,' a traffic cop shouted from the door. 'Pile up on the highway.'

Anger flashed his face. 'We'll talk later,' he said tightly. He turned quickly and strutted away.

Pascal watched him go, hungering to wipe the smile off his face, but she needed to keep a low profile and not draw attention to herself, especially with the cops. She looked at Mercy Reeder. The woman was sat hunched over, wetness on her cheek. She began to rock in her chair, short gasps of breath stuttering from her mouth as hopelessness devoured her. Pascal and the spotty kid at the other table both moved at the same time, the kid unwinding the red bandanna from around his head and handing it to Mercy, saying, 'Here, for the tears.'

Pascal sat down at the table and put an arm around her. 'Hey, hey, its okay,' she said. 'Its okay to cry. Let it out.'

The waitress, having watched from the counter, came over and put another coffee down on the table. 'That's on the house, Mercy,' she said. 'Child, you should stay away from that mean sonofabitch,'

'Who is he?' Pascal asked

'Buck McConnell. Scooter to his good ole boys,' the waitress said. 'You know, I'd guess most of the unsolved rapes in this county are down to that guy, only don't quote me. I like my job,' she added, before wandering back to the counter.

Mercy wiped her face. She hadn't looked at either Pascal or the kid yet. He was now sat at their table as well, typing on a tablet that was wired up to his smartphone and an ear-bud. Mercy raised her head and looked at Pascal. Her eyes seemed desolate. She tried a smile. 'He's okay, really. It's not like it looks, and I'm fine,' she said.

'I don't think so,' the kid said, without looking up from his tablet. 'It's called coercive control, if you didn't know. Oh, and it grows, takes over, unless you stop it.'

'How do—' she started, then stopped, familiar hopelessness seeping back into her eyes.

'He stalk you?' Pascal asked quietly.

She laughed with a bitter edge. 'Are you kidding me? He just about owns me. Got in the house last night. Raped me, over and over.'

'You report it?' Pascal said.

She looked at Pascal as if she were stupid. 'You're not from round here, are you?'

'Doesn't matter,' Pascal said. 'You should still get it on the record.'

'Honey, you don't know shit,' she said, a bit of fire in her voice. 'Scooter's the police. Okay, he's only a traffic cop, but that don't matter. If I reported him, he would kill me. It's that simple. That's the way it is in this state.'

'It doesn't have to be,' Pascal said

'Oh, I think you'll find it does,' the kid said. He reached over and took Mercy's fresh untouched coffee and took a sip.

Mercy looked at her watch. 'I gotta go, or I'll be late,' she said, rising to her feet.

'Where d'you work?' Pascal asked, knowing the answer.

'Riverbend Max. Look. Thanks for….you know,' she said, turning quickly to go.

'Mercy,' Pascal called out, stopping her. 'I can help you stop him, for good.'

'No,' she said. 'Nobody can. I just got to carry on best I can until he kills me.'

Pascal scribbled her number on a scrap of paper and held it out to her. 'If you change your mind, call me. I promise I can help you.'

She hesitated, then took the paper, turned and walked away. When she was sat in her car, she looked at the number on the scrap of paper for a long time, then shook her head, sighing, crunched it into a ball and chucked it in the well of the car with all the other junk.

Back in the cafe, the kid said, 'Shit, she took my bandanna.'

'Don't worry, kid, you'll still look like a badass,' Pascal said.

He smiled and held his hand out. 'Dalton McHenry. Fingers to my friends,' he said.

She shook across the table. 'Courtney Pascal. Fingers?'

'Yeah. I hacked the Pentagon. So that's what they called me in Juvy,' he said matter-of-factly.

She smiled naturally, an unusual event in itself. 'I'm impressed, if its true. What you doing in here?' she asked, leaning over and glancing at his tablet screen.

'Trading crypto. Mostly with Venezuelans or Iranians.'

'How d'you do that with all the US sanctions, and whatever?'

'Shit,' he said smiling. 'I'm a libertarian, and the state haven't yet worked out how to regulate digital currencies. It's a free for all. Modern version of the wild west. Any restrictions there are, I'm the king of the work-around.'

'What you into at the moment?' she asked, getting interested in the nerdy looking kid.

'Well I'm heavily weighted in Bitcoin, of course, but I'm also into Ethereum and Tether.'

'Tether's linked to the greenback, right?'

'That's right,' he said, looking up and seeming to see her for the first time. 'What's that accent?'

'British,' she said. 'I'm a writer doing some research over here.'

'Uh huh,' he murmured, tapping something on his keypad and smiling. 'I just made 700 bucks.' He looked up at her. 'What kind of research?'

'Its a thriller. Say, maybe you can help me,' she said innocently. 'How difficult would it be to hack into the Tennessee Department of Corrections mainframe?'

'Walk in the park,' he scoffed, full of the cocky bravado of youth. 'Wait a minute,' he said. 'That lady with the knuckle-dragging boyfriend? She had a corrections officers uniform on under her coat, and she said she works up the road at Riverbend. You were watching her. What's the deal?'

Pascal just smiled.

CHAPTER TWENTY

District Attorney Bill Monroe leaned back in his well worn leather recliner, a kindly expression on his face as he listened to Mike Shapiro, lead counsel for death row inmate Floyd Ritter.

'I know it's bullshit, Bill,' Shapiro continued. 'But we got this meddling limey lawyer, Jonas Calver, out of New York City, brought in by Floyd. So we got no choice. We gotta go through the motions.'

'I hear you, Mike,' Monroe nodded, sagely. 'And there's nothing wrong with going through the motions, especially in a case like this. But you know, I'm charged by the state to look solely at Floyd Ritter's trial, conviction and sentencing. Nothing else. What you've sketched out for me here has no relevance to those issues. I mean, what kind of a lawyer is this Calver, if he can't see that?'

'Well, he ain't gonna set the world alight, that's for sure. Word is, he rides on the coattails of his partner, Morganna Fedler. She's pulled down a couple of big civil settlements over the last few years.'

'Freeloader, huh?' Monroe said. 'Look, Mike, can I suggest you just carry on with whatever mix of last minute appeals remain open to you and stick in a clemency plea to the Governor in the normal way, and forget this Calver guy. As regards the stuff about Mary Ritter's auto crash, take it to the state police. I'm sure you'll get a fair hearing.'

Shapiro stood up. 'Thanks for your time, Bill,' he said, extending his hand. 'I'll go tell my client.'

'Appreciate it, Mike,' he replied. 'Say, we got a fund raiser coming up at the weekend over at the house. I'd be honored if you and your lovely wife would come out and bless us with your company?'

'Shit, really, Bill?' Shapiro said, smile widening. 'We'd be right honoured.'

Sunday morning dawned bright and pristine. Pascal sat out on the rickety wooden stoop - veranda was too grand a word for it. It was peaceful out there, just the sound of birdsong and the slight rustling of leaves in the breeze. She sipped sugary tea as she looked around at the towering greenery that surrounded the place. A flight of birds suddenly took to the sky as she heard the unmistakable sound of an approaching vehicle. She checked her watch. One thing about Calver, he was always on time. She watched the car approach, bumping over the uneven track, clouds of dust whirling up around the wheels. It drew to a stop and he climbed out. Pascal got up to meet him, surprised he was on his own.

They embraced. 'You want some breakfast, Calver?'

'Coffee would be good.'

'I got that,' Anita said, pushing through the swing door behind them, carrying a blackened coffee pot and a couple of mugs.

They both looked at her, Calver's face dropping as he took in her spindly frame, dark sunken eyes and deathly pale face.

She laughed lightly. 'Hey, Calver. Its not as bad as it looks. I'm getting better every day.'

He stepped forward and clumsily embraced her, kissing her cheek. 'Sure. You look fine,' he said.

Later they sat around the table on the stoop as Pascal explained Anita's methadone treatment and the fact she had put on half a stone in weight over the last week.

'Can't be down to your cooking,' Calver said.

Anita laughed. 'Boy, you're right there.'

Calver smiled. She looked okay, after all - maybe. He could still just about discern a shadow of that angelic smile he had been struck by when he'd first met her, and he hoped it would come back.

'Nothing wrong with my cooking,' Pascal said.

'Yeah, if you like beans on toast,' Calver said.

'Fuck you, Calver,' she replied. 'Where's Joel and Ned Peter's, anyway? Thought they'd be with you.'

'Joel had to stay in New York, working. And Ned's trying to get access to Jethro Tucker, guy I told you about.'

Pascal nodded. Anita looked out across the overgrown front area with its tall grass and rusting farm implements, her eyes going flat. 'Lets talk about my daddy and the bank,' she said.

Calver and Pascal exchanged glances. 'Yes,' Calver nodded. 'It's gone time. He poured some more coffee into his mug, leaned back in his wooden chair, getting comfortable. 'Have you showed Anita the clip?' he asked Pascal.

'No. Nor discussed any of it. Didn't think she was ready, but I think she is now.'

Calver rummaged in his shoulder bag, pulled out a laptop and powered it up. 'This is a video clip, filmed by Jethro Tucker at the breakers yard your mothers car was taken to after the crash,' he said to Anita. 'I'll warn you, stuff they say is disgusting and upsetting. Sure you want to see it?'

'Jonas, I grew up black in America,' she said, as if that should be explanation enough. 'Play the tape. My daddy's got less than 3 weeks to live.'

They watched the blurry images firm up, Tucker's hidden camera somehow getting the players dead center. Calver said, 'the cop in uniform is Gillespie, and the other guy you'll both instantly recognize as Cimino.'

They watched the screen as the audio kicked in:

'Yes sir,' a faint voice in the background said. 'That's Tucker,' Calver said in voice over.

'Kid's a retard,' Gillespie said, and they both laughed. 'But, you may have a problem,' Gillespie continued. 'Because that's one tough nigger bitch. They haul her out, she still ain't dead. I held off calling the medics long as I could but with the fucking media coming, what could I do? Had to cover my back.'

'She was a mess though, right?' Cimino said.

'Oh yeah. She won't be causing Mr DeMasi and the bank any more problems, trust me. And if that ain't right, I'm sure you can finish the job.'

Both men laughed some more as the clip ended. Calver moved to another clip, glancing over at Anita

She was gently wiping her eyes. He looked at Pascal and she gestured he should get on with it. He nodded, still unsure. He pressed play and the screen showed the underside of the car as the camera panned across it. 'You can clearly see the brake lines have been cut,' he said. 'Before we talk about that though, I just want to play you something else; audio of a lady called Velda who was in Harry's bar the night Vincent Fachetti died.' He pressed play again, and Velda's loud, boozy voice filled the air:

"And then he turned and ran back to the toilets and Ritter followed him. The guy I was with left quick, but Frank Ross followed them into the corridor. Next thing Ritter comes charging out, doesn't stop. Leaves the bar. Ross came back out and called to this guy who'd been with Fachetti. Guy was still on his cell phone but went out into the corridor to look. That's when I decided to leave. Next day I saw it on the news. Vincent murdered, stabbed to death."

After the clip finished they sat silent for a while. Anita looked out at the trees, her eyes far away. Calver sipped coffee. Pascal got up and walked to the rotted wooden rail that ran along the edge of the stoop. She came and sat down again. She said: 'I think the bank murdered Melissa McCarthy, the original whistle blower, as well. Cimino made it look like a suicide. DeMasi didn't deny it, but he didn't admit it either.'

'But none of this helps my daddy,' Anita said.

'Unfortunately, that's right,' Calver said. 'The key is—'

'Frank Ross,' Pascal interjected.

'Right again,' Calver said. 'We now know he witnessed whatever happened in that corridor. He's the only living eye witness, apart from Cimino.'

'So what do we do?' Anita said.

Calver rubbed his face. 'Well, first I need to tell you something.

I've already given a heavily edited run-down of some of this stuff to Floyd's lead attorney, Mike Shapiro, and he's spoken with the attorney General.'

'He blew him out,' Anita said.

'That's right,' Calver replied. 'Expected him to really, but at least we know which way the wind is blowing. He said take the auto crash stuff to the state police.'

'Waste of time,' Anita said. 'And we just about run out of that.'

'So we need to track down Frank Ross and talk to him, right?' Pascal said.

'That's about the size of it,' Calver said.

'Okay. I'm on it,' she said.

'What if he won't talk to you?' Anita said. 'And even if he does, surely all he'll do is repeat what he said on the stand.' She rubbed what looked like tears from her face. 'Let's face it. It's fucking hopeless. They're going to kill my daddy, finish the job. And there's nothing we can do about it.'

'You're wrong, Anita,' Pascal said. 'I don't operate in the official world like Calver, where you're hemmed in every way you turn. I'm in the shadows. That's my world. And in my world, there's nothing that can't be done. Just remember that, and try and keep the faith.'

'Amen,' Calver said.

Anita studied them both. After a moment she nodded. 'Let's do it.'

'Good,' Calver said. He turned to Pascal. 'You might want to talk to a local journalist, Kelly Phillips, who's helped us. Here's her number.' He slid his phone across to her. 'I'm working on a clemency plea to the Governor with Ned Peter's right now, and Shapiro is filing the usual appeals across the appellate courts. But I think its time I had another visit with Floyd. You be up for that, Anita?'

She looked apprehensive for a second, afraid even, then the old smile Calver remembered ignited across her face and it was like the sun coming out. 'You bet,' she said.

Pascal held the phone tightly to her ear, listening to Kelly Phillips as she gave her a run down on what she had discovered about Frank Ross.

'His father is Gino Rossi, second generation Italian. And Frank was christened Franco, but changed the whole caboodle to a nice and simple, Frank Ross. Got a nice ring to it, don't you think?'

'Sounds Scots-Irish to me,' Pascal said. 'What else you got, Kelly?'

'Well, Gino runs a kinda pseudo Italian restaurant. And its not too far from Harry's bar. Its really a glorified Pizza joint, maybe with delusions of grandeur. Anyway, they operate out of there.'

'Operate?'

'Yeah. Guy on the crime beat tells me Gino and Fachetti were a crew, believed to have been behind some robberies, extortion, that kind of thing, but nothing ever stuck. Guess the restaurant was a kind of front or base. Its where Frank apparently hangs out. Not quite sure what he does, but I bet he ain't cooking linguine, if you catch my drift.'

'I do, and its a far cry from the poor boy made good horse shit he gave the court. You got a picture of him?'

'Sure. He was all over the paper, time of the trial. I'll send it soon as we finish talking.'

'Appreciate it. He got family, wife, kids?'

Married with one daughter. She'd be about 8 or 9 now.'

Pascal nodded to herself. 'I need to meet this guy.'

'When?'

'Today. Floyd Ritter's clock is ticking and it ain't gonna stop.' She looked at her watch. 'Its just gone noon. Maybe its time for a Pizza.'

'Mind if I tag along?'

Pascal thought for a moment. 'Better not. It may get hairy, but I'll give you a call after and maybe we can meet up. What's this joint called?'

'"Gino's Ristorante", out in Germantown. You want directions?'

'I'll find it. Ciao.'

Pascal sat in the hire-car outside Gino's, other side of the street, pretending to talk on her cell phone whilst scanning the joint. It had an unassuming exterior; white lettering across four large street windows behind which hung brown colored venetian blinds, half open, allowing her to see inside; there were only a few customers. Still, it was lunchtime, which maybe was not so busy in that neighborhood. She put on shades, grabbed her bag, climbed out the car and mad her way to the door, pushing through inside.

The place had a nice, open welcoming feel about it and stretched back quite some way to the rear. The floor was faded black and red diamond tiles on which sat rustic wooden tables and chairs. Along one wall ran a bar at which a couple of guys sat on stools talking desultorily.

Only two other tables were occupied; one by a couple of stiffs in suits - office types grabbing a bite - the other by a couple, looking like skittish secret lovers.

Pascal took a table at the back, away from the other punters, near to what she assumed was the kitchen. Studying the menu, the Pizzas looked good, "Rabe, Sock Sausage, Mozzarella, Parm, Garlic and Chilies" perhaps worth a try

'Help you, ma'am?'

It was the waiter who had been standing behind the bar when she had come in, a young blonde corn-fed guy, definitely not Frank Ross. She ordered the Pizza and a glass of house red and watched as he walked away with her order, her mind parsing possible approaches. Fact is, as Anita had said, there was no reason for Ross to speak to her, and even if he did, he was only going to repeat his court testimony; why wouldn't he? Also, as Calver had told her over the phone, Ross could go crying to the police in the form of chief Gillespie, although, given Ross's background that might not be so likely. But she kept coming coming back to the clock. They didn't do something soon; make something happen, Floyd was going to die.

As the waiter returned with a large glass of red, which he carefully placed down in front of her, she said, casually, 'Frank around today?'

The guy had seemed to be on auto-pilot, doing his job like most folks do, almost reflexively, but now he straightened up, his eyes flicking over her, assessing and categorizing, a half-smile edging into a smirk. He lowered his voice. 'If you're one of his lady friends, let me tell you something: its a real bad idea to turn up here uninvited.'

Pascal leaned back in her chair, pushing the shades back up on her head, fixing the guy with a cold stare.

The half-smile hovered, then faltered, doubt clouding his face. 'I'll go see,' he finally said. 'Who should I say is calling?'

'Just tell him Cimino sent me.'

'Cimino, huh?' he said, trying the obviously unfamiliar name on his tongue. 'I'll go see.'

'You do that, boy, and don't forget my Pizza.'

Fifteen minutes later a door to her right swung open and a girl in kitchen whites came through with a Pizza on a large earthenware plate that she placed carefully down on the table. 'Enjoy,' she murmured, before floating away.

Pascal studied the Pizza and smelt the juicy, herby aroma. A large triangular piece had been cut for her. Taking a bite, slowly chewing, it was good. As she took a sip of wine the waiter re-appeared, this time with another man in tow. He looked over and said something.

As he approached her first thought was "Goodfella's", the movie. The guy really did look like Joe Pesci, even down to his size, and not so much the photo Kelly had texted her. He flashed a thin smile devoid of humor or warmth, his brown eyes running over her.

'Cimino sent you, huh?' he said. The name clearly meant something to him. 'Prove it. What does he want?' he added, confusingly.

'Sit down, why don't you,' she said. 'Have a slice Pizza. Listen, I don't have to prove anything to you. If you don't think I'm from Cimino, guess he'll have to come down here and straighten you out.'

His eyes held hers. 'Say your piece, and then I'll check you out.'

He slid into the seat opposite.

'Fine, no problem,' she replied. 'It wont have escaped your attention that Floyd Ritter, baring some unfortunate hold up, is shortly due to fry. We want to make sure your solid down here, because the family are digging and making noises. They've been out to Harry's bar, talking to people, stirring up trouble. We want to know you haven't talked and that you're solid.' She watched him as her words sunk in. She had played a hunch that the guy was essentially bonehead muscle; not very bright. May even have been in Harry's bar that night by coincidence and the thing was purely opportunistic, as how could they have known Ritter would turn up there when he did. They couldn't have.

'I don't know what you're talking about, lady. Who are you anyway?' he said. 'It's no secret I testified at the trial, but I've never met anyone from Ritter's family, and would have nothing to say to them if I did.' He stood up.

Maybe he wasn't as stupid as he looked, Pascal thought. This was going to be harder than she thought. As the guy looked down at her, a young child ran out from the back, shouting, 'daddy'.

She was small, blonde, about 8 years old. She stopped in her tracks when she saw Pascal. She moved up behind Ross's legs and peeped out at Pascal, who smiled back at her.

'Go back to Mama, Carmen,' he said, tussling her golden locks. She peeped out at Pascal again.

Pascal said, 'pleased to meet you, Carmen.'

The girl smiled, giggled, then skipped away back the way she had come.

Pascal stood up. Took her wallet out.

He said, 'its on the house, lady, but don't come back, yeah?' He turned on his heel and walked away.

She got some napkins and wrapped up the large remaining slice of Pizza and took it with her, dropping a five buck tip on the bar as she passed, her mind already working on what she had witnessed, the very faint outlines of a plan shimmering and firming up as she exited the joint.

Back inside, as Ross watched her leave, his cell phone began trilling. He slipped it out of his pocket. No caller ID. He connected, putting it to his ear. 'Yes?'

The thick guttural voice was unmistakable. 'Cimino,' it said. 'That you, Franco?'

'Hey, Cimino, I got the message,' he replied, caught off balance. 'She just left. You could have just called me. I'm solid, man.'

The phone was silent for a beat, then Cimino, almost whispering, so Ross had to strain to hear, said, 'what message is that, Franco? Who is it that's just left?'

Ross licked his lips. 'The girl,' he stammered. He switched to speaking Italian. 'The girl who was just here. Said she was from you, warning me the family's digging, and to keep my mouth shut. For Christ sakes why wouldn't I?'

Cimino answered in Italian, icy calm. 'What was this girls name? Describe her?' he asked.

'You know what?' he said in wonder. 'I never asked her. She said she was from you. I mean just knowing your name....'

'Describe her?'

Ross did so. He could hear Cimino breathing over the phone.

'Her name is Pascal, Franco. She acts for an attorney who now represents Floyd Ritter.'

Ross rubbed his face, staying silent.

Cimino continued. 'Did you say anything to her?'

'No, no. Absolutely not,' he said. 'I told her I was going to check her out, call New York first. In fact I was just about to do that when you called. Lucky, right?'

Cimino weighed what he had heard. On balance he believed Rossi. 'I'm on my way down to your shit hole of a state,' he said. 'I'll be staying for a while, until they fry the nigger. Meantime, you don't say a fucking word to anyone, less you want to end up in the Cumberland River wearing concrete boots. You got that, soldier?'

Ross started to reply, but realized the phone was dead.

CHAPTER TWENTY-ONE

It was early evening when Pascal got back to the shack. Nothing stirred, only the faint creak of wooden boards as she stepped onto the porch disturbed the stillness. Inside she found Anita dead to the world, gently snoring away on the broken down settee in the living room. Pascal moved to the open fire-place, glancing at the small pile of newly cut wood in the grate, pleased to see that Anita had been busy. She got some newspaper, stuck it in the wood and lit it. The fire slowly took hold and began to crackle. From the tiny kitchen a couple of plates and a long fork were taken through and the half-eaten Pizza from the restaurant was affixed to the fork and held to the fire.

'Something smells good,' came muffled sleepy words from the settee. Anita's hair was a tussled mass, her eyes fuzzy with sleep; she rubbed them and rolled her feet onto the floor so she could move up into a sitting position.

'You chop the wood?' Pascal asked her.

'Yep,' she said. 'Used to be a country girl, back in the day. Felt good to get some exercise and swing that axe.'

Later they sat chewing pizza and drinking cola. 'What's up?' Anita said, after a while.

'What d'you mean,' Pascal asked absently.

'I've known you long enough to know when you're thinking hard about something. You're tuned out, somewhere else.'

Pascal smiled grimly, acquiescing. 'How well are you, Anita?' she asked, studying the girl carefully.

'Pretty good,' she replied. 'I was a light smack user and it wasn't for long enough to take hold. The worst is past.'

'Good. Its what I thought.'

'So?'

Pascal pursed her lips. 'I don't need to tell you how little time we have left to save your Daddy.'

'You know, you don't need to keep this up for me, 'Anita said, gently shaking her head. 'Its too late now, and we have no time left. Maybe I should just try and make his last days as good as they can be.'

'You're wrong, Anita,' Pascal said. 'But let me ask you something. Just how far are you prepared to go, to save him?'

Anita raised her eyes and fastened them on Pascal. 'What are you asking?'

'I'm not sure yet, but there's something you need to understand. Jonas Calver and Ned Peters are attorneys and they have to operate within the law. That's what they're doing. With Shapiro, they're canvassing the appellate courts, and Calver is working up a clemency plea. That's the official position. It might work.'

'But you don't think so?'

'I don't know, but history is not on our side. Guy in Arkansas, executed couple of years ago, has just been exonerated with DNA. Happens all the time, and they don't seem to give a shit.'

'Hey, I know the history,' Anita said, eyes flashing. 'Stop

skirting around. As my momma used to say, throw it out on the ground where the goats can get at it.'

Pascal smiled. 'Okay. I took a run at Frank Ross today. He's the eye witness. He's never going to tell us what happened.'

'Unless?'

'Unless we bend the law, in order to encourage him to speak freely.'

Anita grinned. 'Are you kidding me? I'm in,' she said. 'What's your plan?'

'Whoa there. Slow down,' she replied. 'First, if things go catastrophically wrong you could end up sharing a cell with your pop. Second, even if we got something, it might not be enough. As I said, history's against us. Lastly, the point about the attorneys. We can't tell them what we're doing because it will pull them in and make them culpable, prejudice what they're trying to do for your pop. Also it will put them in danger. And that is something you need to be aware of - danger. These people are killers.'

'I'm not scared,' she said solemnly. She kept watching Pascal, a small smile starting on her mouth. 'If none of this works, what then?'

Pascal returned her look, deadpan, but she was unnerved by the girls intuitive quickness. 'Nothing,' she said. 'We take one step at a time. Now go to bed. I'll wash up.'

Pascal basked in the early morning sunshine, watching through the patchy screen of trees as a delivery truck bumped along the rutted track, rounded the bend and came fully into view before pulling to a stop in front of the stoop. Guy climbed out with a handheld, looked up and said, 'delivery for Courtney Pascal?'

'That's me,' she said, jumping down off the stoop.

The guy opened up the back and removed a large cardboard box which he placed on the ground. Pascal signed his handheld and watched the truck leave, before carrying the box into the house. The return address said it was from Christoff Wisliceny, New York. The tape which was thickly bound around it was removed and a flap lifted revealing the inside. As she reached in, there was a noise behind her, causing her to grab and swing round, leveling her arm in one smooth motion.

'What the—' Anita said, frozen in the doorway.

Pascal relaxed, hefting the menacing looking hand gun. 'This,' she said, 'is an FBI standard issue 9 mil, Glock 17.'

Anita, still wide eyed, wandered over and peered down into the box. She reached in and pulled out a black jacket with FBI stenciled on the back. She shrugged into it and followed it up with a black baseball cap, first bunching her hair up, then pulling the cap on. 'I always wanted to be a Fed,' she said.

Later they sat at the kitchen table looking at the other items whilst they talked. They would need to alter their appearances and then get photos for the ID cards.

Calver cradled the phone receiver against his neck as he studied the monitor screen in front of him. He raised his hand and nodded as Joel entered the room, looking like he was fresh off the plane. Calver continued his conversation. 'Floyd, that's what I said.'

Joel looked up quickly, realizing Calver was speaking to his father.

The conversation continued. 'That's right. Seems that the civil claim has been discontinued. Looks like it went down about two years ago, so the claims dead.' Calver said. Cocking his head, listening. 'So you didn't instruct Shapiro to pull the plug on it?'

Pause, then, 'Are you sure, Floyd?'

Calver listened some more, nodding. 'That's right. Anita and me are coming to see you Friday. Want to talk to you about the clemency plea, but meantime, you should think hard about sacking Shapiro, and re-instating Ned Peters. Well, just think about it. You too,' Calver said, signing off and replacing the receiver in its cradle.

He looked up at Joel whose expression was not friendly. 'What?' Calver said. 'I didn't expect you so soon, but its good to see you, man.'

'Yeah, I'll bet,' Joel muttered. 'Looks like you don't need me anyway. You got it all figured out, trying to get my daddy to sack Mike in favor of that broken down drunk. Mike's the one been trying to clear up the mess created by Peters.'

'Did you know about the discontinuance of the civil claim against the bank?' Calver asked softly, watching him.

Joel's eyes went flat and he looked away. 'Mike may have mentioned it. I don't recall,' he said angrily. 'We're trying to save my daddy and all you're interested in is getting Mike off the case, and hassling me about some old cockamamie claim that caused all this shit in the first place. Maybe its you and Ned Peters who need to take a hike, because I don't think you're doing my Daddy any good, only yourselves.'

Calver nodded, his face calm. Outside they heard a car arrive and a door slamming, then Ned Peters was ambling in, wearing a suit and tie and carrying an old light brown leather attache case. He nodded at Joel, sighed and dropped into a chair, not appearing to notice the tension in the room. 'Jethro Tucker's puckered up tighter than a bull's backside in fly season,' he said wearily. 'No way we get access to him in the short term, but I'm working on it.'

'That's good, Ned,' Calver said

Peters nodded, starting to feel the atmosphere. 'You boys been scrapping, maybe on account of me?'

'No, man—' Joel started to say.

'Yes,' Calver said firmly. 'And we need to clear the air, because if we're fighting between ourselves, then Floyd's going to die.'

'Jonas says my Daddy should sack Mike Shapiro,' Joel said. 'And you should take his place,' he added, nodding at Peters. 'Even though, for good reasons, my Daddy lost confidence in you, and sacked you. What's changed?'

'Hey, I had nothing to do with this,' Peters said. 'I didn't suggest it. Didn't even know about it.'

'Yeah, well Calver here, did,' Joel said, resentful. 'Seems like he's determined to take over. Well I don't agree. I want Mike to stay in charge.' He looked around at both men. 'In fact, I don't even feel welcome here anymore.'

'Hey, Joel,' Calver began, placatory.

'No!' he said, turning and going to the door. 'I'll find a hotel. And tomorrow I'll go visit my Daddy. I'll tell him I don't think you guys are the answer, and he should stick with Mike.' He turned and walked out. They heard a car engine, rising and then fading into silence.

'Well that went well,' Peters said, getting up slowly and walking to the sideboard where he lifted down a half-full bottle of Wild Turkey. 'Don't worry,' he said. 'I'm not going to get drunk. We'll just have a couple, while you tell me where the hell you think we're going with this.'

'As if I know,' Calver said, accepting the tumbler and taking a shot. 'But I'm going to see Floyd Friday, and hopefully, Anita's coming with me. We'll see what he says.'

Peters reached over and clinked his glass against Calver's. 'Good luck with that.'

They sat in the new, larger official looking hire car, parked up around the corner from Frank Ross's apartment building. Pascal flicked on the cars internal light and studied Anita, who in turn studied her back. Pascal was in plainclothes, dark-cut official looking suit, black long hair wig and eye obscuring glasses. Anita was in black tunic with small FBI logo, black baseball cap over blonde tinted wig and reflective shades. They both also carried firearms and fake ID.

'Are you sure he'll come?' Anita muttered, watching the darkening street, tension in her voice.

'Positive. I set up a mini-camera in the tree opposite the block. This guy is like a German train; he's always on time, trust me.'

They were parked facing down the street towards the junction he should walk up from. It was a quiet street with lamp posts set far apart, a perfect take-down spot. Pascal checked her watch. 'Okay, get the coffee,' she said.

Anita nodded, got out the car and made off towards the junction where there was a take-out coffee joint. Pascal moved into the passenger seat, rummaged in the pigeonhole and removed a container of tablets marked "Thiopental Sodium"; holding them up to the light and then placing them back on the car seat. She scrolled her phone looking for the text from Christoff covering optimum doses. Couple of minutes passed and then Anita was walking back up the street carrying three take-out coffees, passing two into Pascal and then climbing into the driving seat.

'Remember what we discussed,' Pascal said. 'Let me do all the talking. You're a grunt, muscle, so act like it. Chew gum. Look disinterested, and do exactly as I say.'

'Yes boss,' Anita said, smiling despite her fear. She looked up and froze. 'I think it's him.'

'Choo, choo, right on time,' Pascal quipped. 'Stay loose and follow my lead.' She looked around at the barren street. No one around as Ross crossed the junction and began walking up the street towards them. 'As he approaches, I'll get out and accost him, then you get out and walk around behind him.'

When Ross was around two meters away from the car, Pascal opened the door and stepped out in front of him, holding out her FBI ID. 'Mr Ross, FBI agent Carrie Madison. We need to talk to you urgently, sir.'

'What, what is this?' he said, stopping and looking at her, then turning as Anita moved in behind him.

'D'you have a daughter called Carmine? Sir?' Pascal asked.

'Sure I do,' he said, confusedly, rubbing his face. 'What is this?'

'Please get in the car, sir,' Pascal said, urgency in her voice. 'We have reason to believe your daughter is about to be kidnapped, and we need to take you to the scene, now.'

Anita took his arm, and started guiding him into the car. He hesitated and then grabbed for his phone. Pascal grabbed his arm. 'No phones,' she said. 'We believe your cell maybe tracked and bugged.'

He looked at her, still trying to take it in, but allowing himself to be seated in the rear of the car.

'Agent Ridley,' Pascal said to Anita. 'You drive. Mr Ross, we need to move fast. We're taking you to a hotel at the scene where you'll get a full briefing. And please note, your daughter is not in danger yet, but we need to move fast.' Pascal handed him the coffee. Drink this. It'll calm your nerves.

He absently took the Styrofoam cup and raised it to his mouth, his eyes starting to turn fearful. 'Just get going,' he said.

Anita burned rubber, scorching away from the curb, down towards the junction. Pascal put her cell to her ear and pretended to speak. 'Targets en-route, sir. ETA 2 minutes. Is she still safe?'

She felt Ross watching her as the car careened down the main drag toward the hotel, which was a block over. She nodded as if listening, then turned to him. 'She's okay for now.' The car drew up to the curb outside a small hotel. 'We're based here whilst this thing goes down,' she said. They got out the car and hustled him in, through the reception area, the desk clerk barely registering their presence, then up in the lift. Ross had finished the coffee, and looked slightly woozy. Pascal knew she needed to question him quick or they'd be wasting their time. She hustled the door open and pulled him into the room, pulling out a chair into which he sank.

He looked up at Pascal while Anita moved to a table on which sat a large camera which she now trained on Ross.

'Frank,' Pascal said familiarly. 'Your daughter Carmen is in no danger at all. We used that as a ruse to get you here because we need to talk to you confidentially, and without others knowing about it. Capiche?'

He looked at her wonderingly. 'Shit. What is going on? So, Carmen is safe?'

'Absolutely.'

'Then I can go, right?' he said, starting to rise.

'Wrong,' Pascal said, leveling the Glock at him. 'As I said, we want to talk to you.'

'About what?' he said, as his mind began to get a tenuous grip on the situation. 'I work in restaurant, for christsakes. What the fuck do the FBI want with me?'

'We want to talk to you about the killing of Vincent Fachetti. See, Frank, you were there, but you lied on oath about what you saw. We know what you saw, Frank. We've had Cimino and Lloyd DeMasi under surveillance for months, wire taps, the works, building a case that is massive, because its not just about conspiracy to murder across state lines, its also about massive bank fraud, interlinked with those murders. There's no more time, Frank, because Floyd Ritter's about to burn. We can protect you, Frank, but you only get one shot, and this is it. We need to get your side - the truth. This will be your one chance to save yourself. You don't talk, you'll never see Carmen again, outside of jail. But that'll be the least of your problems, because Tennessee is a death penalty state.'

Ross was now sweating heavily, but his face looked oddly calm and he had a half smile on his lips suggesting the drug was beginning to work, lowering his inhibitions. Pascal smiled down at Ross. 'So, Frank, we know you drove Fachetti to Harry's bar that night. We know Cimino was there as well. And we know Floyd Ritter turned up and he fought with Fachetti. This moved into the corridor leading off the bar to the rest-rooms. What happened in the corridor, Frank? Tell us in your own words, and you can fly out of here free as a bird.'

Frank smiled, his eyes bright and twinkly. In the background Anita began filming. He laughed. 'I don't think you're gonna like what I tell you?'he said.

'Try me, Frank. I just want the truth.'

'Okay, the knife,' he said. 'I didn't see where it came from. One minute it was in Vinnie's hand, then the nigger's, kinda back and forth. Don't know where it came from. I never see Vincent with it before.'

'What happened?'

'It was back and forth, like WWE, man,' he laughed. 'I saw Vincent get the neck cut. He was holding the knife then, slowly trying to push it into the nigger's gut, but he was straining to stop it. I think Ritter stamped on Vinnie's foot and he loosened the knife and it flew up and cut across his neck. Then they were at it again.'

'Could it have been Cimino's or Harry's knife?'

'Who knows. Could be. I said you wouldn't like it,' he said.

'What about the fatal stab to the heart?' Anita asked from behind the camera.

'I know I said in court I saw Ritter stab Vinnie in the heart, but I didn't,' he answered. 'I didn't see how or when he got that wound.'

'Come on, Frank,' Pascal said.

'Really,' he said. 'It all happened so fast. Vinnie staggered back against the wall, from the neck cut. I thought that might have been fatal. I heard the sound of the knife dropping on the floor - I don't know who dropped it - then Ritter turned and ran, and I followed him out to get an ambulance. Maybe Vinnie had the heart wound then, when he was sliding down the wall. I told Harry to get an ambulance and Cimino went out there. When I got back there about a minute later, Vinnie was dead. Lying on the floor, against the wall where he had sunk down, a blood stain still showing on the wall.'

'So, let me get this straight,' Pascal said, glancing at her watch. 'You lied in court about seeing Ritter produce the knife? And you lied about seeing Ritter deliver the fatal stab wound to Fachetti's heart?'

'Yes to both. I didn't see either.'

'And nor did you tell the court that Vincent was alive when you went in to call the ambulance?'

'Correct.'

'So, in fact, he must have been still alive when Cimino went out there?'

'I would say so, yes,' he said, his eyes fluttering.

Pascal knew he would fall into a deep sleep shortly, and should, when he awoke, not have a clear idea of what had taken place. That was one of the advantages of the drug. But it wouldn't wipe everything. He would remember some things, but not all. Pascal turned to Anita. 'Anything else?'

'Yeah,' she said, turning to Ross. 'Why d'you lie?'

'You ever met Cimino?' he asked.

'I reckon Cimino delivered the coup de grace,' Pascal murmured. 'Clearing up loose ends, and backing up the frame. But anyway, should have gone down as self-defense, at the least. There's no evidence it was Floyd's knife.'

She turned back to Ross, but he was now lying back snoring. 'We're done,' she said. 'Let's go.'

CHAPTER TWENTY-TWO

They sat around in hard-backed chairs in District Attorney Bill Monroe's big, airy office; Ned Peters, Jonas Calver and Anita Ritter.

'Folks, I've fit you in because you said it was urgent,' Monroe said. 'And with Floyd's date zooming up on us I gotta do all I can to make sure justice is done. My voters won't stand for nothing less.'

'Nice speech, Bill,' Peters said. 'But you can spare us the bullcrap.'

'Hey, Ned, there's no call for that kind of language,' Monroe said. 'Not with the little lady here,' he added, nodding at Anita.

'Perhaps I can cut this short,' Calver said. 'We're going to give you a sneak preview of something that'll likely be all over the media by sundown.'

'I'm listening, Mr Calver,' Monroe said, avuncular smile gone.

'Its a clip mailed to us last night, from an unknown source,' Calver said. He slid a tablet across the desk. 'I'm sure you'll recognize the state's star witness, Frank Ross, essentially recanting and admitting to perjury.'

Monroe watched the clip in silence, his face betraying nothing. 'Well now,' he said, when the tape had finished. 'You boys have certainly been busy, but I don't see anything here that's going to change the jury's verdict. It's still Floyd's knife, and Vincent Fachetti didn't stab himself in the heart.'

'So, let me get this straight,' Anita said. Calver put his hand on her arm but she shook it off. 'Your star witness now admits he can't say whose knife it was, and he didn't see the fatal stab wound. He lied. Not only that, another man, this Cimino, was there. And that means, what? Nothing?'

'That's right, Bill,' Peters chipped in. 'Ross now testifies Fachetti was alive when he ran out, but dead when he went back to find this Cimino fella standing over him. Bill, even if you don't buy Ritter as innocent, you gotta admit this would now go down as self-defense. No way is it a death penalty case.'

'Well now, Bill, that's a long leap you're making there. "Ross now testifies", you say? Well I ain't seen that,' he said. 'What I see is some uncorroborated tape of a guy you say is Frank Ross. You know something, folks?' he said, looking around at them. 'We had a little gathering the other day, folks supporting me, and we laid on a speech and some slides from our voter point man. He talked about fake news, and what you can now do on the net. Seems to me, just about anything is possible. You can't hardly believe your eyes anymore. So forgive me if I don't get all excited about this clip.'

'So, what are you going to do about it?' Calver asked.

'Nothing,' he replied. 'For now. You get a copy over to me, and my people will take a good hard look at it. Then we'll get back to you. In the meantime, Mr Calver,' he said with a knowing smile. 'You said the clip came from an unknown source. Well, you might like to tell that unknown source that releasing this clip to the media before we have had a chance to respond, is unlikely to help Floyd Ritter. In fact, I can tell you, that's a nailed down certainty.'

Calver stood up, stone faced. 'We'll get a copy of the clip over within the hour.'

A few moments later Monroe herded them out the door. When they had gone, he picked up his phone and asked his secretary to get him Cyrus Gillespie.

Mercy Reader rolled over and yawned. Inside she was bursting with happiness. She looked down at the girl sleeping beside her and wondered how someone so small and gentle could unlock her soul and passion in such a volcanic way. She studied the girl's black, almost purple skin, and gently kissed her cheek. The girl slept on untroubled. Mercy thought back over the last 18 hours or so, marveling at fate. Coming off a shift at Riverbend, despair and black depression had descended on her, the thought of Scooter turning up or being there, too much to bear. So instead of going home, she had stopped off at a local bar she had never been to before. It was a small place, a bit bohemian, more hippies and students than blue collar folk. Sitting in a corner with a beer, which soon stretched to four, her eyes had stared, unseeing at a wide screen TV on the wall that was showing old music videos from the seventies.

She hadn't seen the girl come in, oblivious to everything around her, just drinking the beer, which she wasn't really used to, hoping it would get rid of the fear in the pit of her stomach. But when the waitress had bought her fifth one over, the girl at the bar was looking at her and smiling. Mercy had instinctively turned around to see if there was someone behind her, but there wasn't, so Mercy had nodded her head at the stranger and looked away quickly, wondering whether it was a case of mistaken identity. But the girl was still watching her. It had set her to thinking back to the time when she had had a crush on a female friend in high school, years ago, which her mind had dismissed as harmless playacting. A lot later, after dead end relationships with guys who were either druggies, violent or obsessed with porn, had come marriage to another violent asshole. During this sojourn into suburbia, she was told she was unable to have kids which at the time she felt was a good thing, but later it had left her feeling crushed. Divorce had left her with just the little house and the clothes on her back, and then had come her ill advised fling with Scooter which had soon turned to nightmare. She smiled to herself. She was surely cursed in life.

'That's a pretty smile. Mind if I join you?'

The stranger was looking down at her. By then Mercy was well juiced. 'Why not,' she'd said.

Her name was Donna and she was a 37 year old librarian. Mercy had clicked with her straight away, drink and vulnerability helping things along. When Donna had asked her back to her apartment, Mercy hadn't hesitated, the thought of going home alone and finding Scooter there, too much to bear.

In the neat bedroom, Mercy couldn't help giggling when Donna had started kissing her. But then something had happened. After years of being sexually brutalized by guys, the thought had suddenly popped into her head, why not? So she had released herself to it, completely, and it had blown her mind.

Her mind cleared as she looked down at the sleeping girl and smiled just as the bedside alarm-clock exploded into sound. The LED said: 7.15 a m.

Outside, across the street in an unmarked car, Scooter sat and watched the apartment. His eyes were trance-like and he had a days growth of stubble on his chin. After twenty minutes, Mercy came out and got into a car that looked like a Uber, and left. Scooter pulled on some leather gloves, slowly humming to himself. He climbed out of the car and walked down the alleyway by the side of the apartment block, moving like a panther, all his senses heightened. He flexed his leather-clad fingers, and the easy smirker-smile started to re-assert itself on his face.

Calver watched from a short distance away as Anita spoke quietly to her father. Floyd was tearful, but managing not to cry outright. Calver turned away, not wanting to eavesdrop on the intimacy of their grief. He had told Anita on the way over that he wanted to give her a brief spell alone with her father before they got down to business. When he heard Floyd laugh a couple of minutes later, he looked up, surprised. Then Anita laughed too, and he took it as a sign to rejoin them.

'What you done to my boy, Jonas?' Floyd asked, half humorous, wiping his eyes.

Calver sighed. He'd hoped Anita would have explained the stand-off with Joel. 'Yeah. Me and Joel, we had a bit of a disagreement.'

Floyd's face looked pained.

'Daddy, you know Joel can be a headstrong jerk,' Anita said.

'I know, but I need you all pulling together, especially now.'

'Look,' Calver said. 'Its my fault. I should have kept my mouth shut. He's your son after all, and he only wants what's best for you.'

Floyd nodded. 'See, Jonas. I don't give a damn about the civil suit. Who pulled the plug, whatever. Let it lie. We got more important things to deal with. Mike Shapiro has done a good job for me, and so has Joel. Ned Peters is a drunk, and he let me down.'

Calver didn't say anything.

Floyd rubbed his face. He looked tired, eyes sunken, with shadows underneath. He said, 'Mike says you got some crazy notion about the clemency plea, putting stuff in about the bank. That right?'

'It's not crazy, pop,' Anita said. 'When's the last time a conventional plea for clemency worked in this state?'

Floyd smiled. 'You got something there girl.'

'Lets just try something different, Floyd, is all I'm saying,' Calver said. 'And I hear what you're saying about Ned Peters, but I'd like to keep him on board, because he's been a great help to me. You don't have to see him, and he's not going to make any waves with Mike Shapiro. He may have a drink problem, but he's a shit-hot attorney where it counts. Wisdom acquired from long experience, and we need all the help we can get. Besides,' Calver said, smiling. 'He's putting me up, and Anita and my investigator as well.'

Floyd looked at Anita. She nodded.

'Okay, but here's how I want it to be,' Floyd said. 'Joel's on a sulk for now, so I suggest you and Ned Peters get on with what you're doing, and leave Mike and Joel to handle the appeals. When Joel's calmed down, maybe you can patch things up. And Jonas?'

'Yeah.'

'I want to see a draft of this clemency plea before I sign off on it.'

'You got it.'

'So, it's like there'll be two teams, daddy?' Anita said. 'I can be the go-between.'

'Child, you know your brother,' Floyd said. 'He's just like his mother. Stubborn as a mule. Stay out of his hair until he calms down. I'll tell him Mike and him are in charge. I'm giving Jonas and Ned a chance to come up with the clemency plea because I don't want to turn them away when they've done so much work to help. I'll tell him I'll likely can what they do, and get Mike to do the final plea.'

A couple of minutes later they left the Riverbend facility.

As Anita drove the car she was silent, lost in thought. Calver looked across at her surreptitiously out of the corner of his eye.

She sensed his look. 'Its okay, Jonas. I'm alright, really.'

'I know, but its still a heart breaker, seeing your daddy like that.'

As she turned to reply, they both heard the loud, growling whoop of a police cruiser as it slotted in behind them, light flashing and swirling atop its roof.

'Shit,' Anita said.

Calver turned around in his seat to look back as Anita signaled and pulled into the side of the road. They were out in the middle of nowhere, flat fields either side, with little traffic. Calver watched as the cop clambered out of the vehicle. Even from a distance, he recognized the overdeveloped upper body and thin waist of Cyrus Gillespie.

Calver whispered as the cop approached, 'Its Gillespie. Looks like he was waiting for us. He'll bait you; do not rise or we're fucked. Sweet as pie, whatever it takes.'

Gillespie tapped the window. Anita sat for a moment, looking straight ahead, her eyes blank. Then she lowered the window.

'Keep your hands where I can see them. And let me see your driving license,' he said. He looked in across at the passenger seat as Anita slowly reached into her pocket. 'Morning, Mr. Calver,' he said, jaunty tone.

'Morning officer. Why d'you stop us?'

Gillespie ignored the question, leaning back as he studied the license. 'Step out of the car, please. Both of you,' he said softly, hand on his holstered gun.

'What is this?' Anita said, anger boiling up in her voice.

Calver grasped her wrist and squeezed it lightly. 'Do as he says,' he said.

'Smart boy, Calver,' Gillespie muttered and spat. 'I wont ask you again. Now move.'

They both got out of the vehicle.

'Turn around, both of you, lean up against the car and spread 'em.'

They did so.

Gillespie quickly and expertly frisked Calver. The sour smell of the man, a mixture of rancid animal sweat and the cheap cologne he'd sprayed over it, almost made Calver gag. 'Why d'you stop us, officer?' he tried again. 'What's your probable cause?'

'Your mighty mouthy, lawyer man, but this ain't New York,' he replied as he moved on to Anita. She was wearing a knee length blue skirt. He spat again. 'You never know what a nigger gal has in her panties until you check, right,' he said as he ran his hand up between her legs, roughly, making her yelp and swing around at the same time as Calver lifted his hands off the car and started to turn. Gillespie stepped back and pulled his gun. 'Now you all settle down, folks. We don't want anyone getting hurt.'

'Gillespie, you're storing yourself and the city of Nashville up one helluva lawsuit here,' Calver said. 'Lets all just walkaway from this.'

'Now, boy, you're beginning to rile me with your back talk. Against the car,' he said.

Calver heard the crunch of Gillespie's boots approaching. He felt movement and maybe heard the swish of the nightstick moving in the air before it hit. It came in sideways into his kidneys with huge force and a loud thwacking sound. Calver went down, moaning, pulling himself into a fetal position, arms and legs drawn in, as his body tried to cope with the pain. Gillespie knelt down beside him, pulling his wrists out and putting handcuffs on. 'Need to settle you down a spell boy.'

Gillespie hauled him up and walked him, hunched over, to the police cruiser. 'You sit here real quiet, boy, lessen you want me to soften you up some more. Cyrus is gonna have himself some fine black pussy before he takes you in. Don't go away,' he said.

Calver watched Gillespie walk back towards Anita, pain and fear flooding his senses. A half strangled sob escaped his lips. He nursed the dull throbbing pain in his kidneys as he watched Gillespie, who stood just behind Anita, talking to her. Calver tried to order his thoughts. What the fuck could he do? He had to try and stop this; help Anita. He was an attorney for Christs sake. Think. And think down the line as well. He moved his cuffed hands to his pocket, and felt the reassuring contours of his smart phone. He dug it out. He looked up. Gillespie had moved Anita so she now stood facing the boot of the hire car, Gillespie behind her, in front of Calver in the police cruiser.

Calver raised the phone up and quickly texted Ned Peters a message marked urgent, hoping the guy wasn't on a bender. Then Calver raised the phone so it showed just above the dash, and began filming.

Gillespie now had Anita bent over the boot, and was holding his gun to the back of her head. Calver watched as Gillespie moved his other hand to rip her thin blouse away, and then her bra. He moved his hand again to between her legs and forced it up, hunching the girl further over the boot, rolling her skirt up around her waist. As Gillespie started to tug her panties away, Anita looked around and her eyes met Calver's. It was a thousand yard stare full of grief and misery, but no fear. Calver's breath caught in his throat, desperation flooding his mind. He looked down at the cuffs, cursing, then his eyes saw the keys still hanging in the ignition. He moved instinctively, scrabbling across the central console into the driver seat, turning the key, the engine firing first time. As Gillespie turned, surprised, Calver slammed the car forward.

Anita rolled onto the boot swinging her legs up out of the way as Gillespie dived to the side. Calver applied the brakes at the last moment, so the car merely shunted the vehicle in front. At the same time Gillespie, now standing in a crouch to the side of the vehicle, fired his weapon. Calver's window disintegrated as the bullet whistled past his head. He immediately put his hands out of the window.

Gillespie straightened up out of the crouch, smiling. 'Attempted murder of a police officer. That'll look good on your resume, counselor,' he said. He nodded at Anita. 'Get in the car, sweetheart. We're going downtown.'

Five minutes later, Gillespie had Calver seated in the back of the car and Anita in the passenger seat. As the vehicle moved, Gillespie checked in with his radio, receiving messages that had come in in the last hour or so. Anita sat hunched over in the front seat, not speaking. Calver eased his smart phone out of his pocket again, keeping his head straight as if he were a broken man, just watching the scenery flash by. Gillespie intermittently, as he spoke on the radio, flicked his eyes onto the mirror, monitoring his prisoner.

Calver slowly and laboriously, trying to avoid looking down in his lap, typed another message to Ned Peters, this time accompanied by the video clip, assuming the camera had worked and caught anything. He pressed send, not holding out much hope that Ned Peters would even pick it up, or be able to do much if he did.

Calver settled back in his seat just as Gillespie finished speaking on the radio. The car surged forward and the siren began to wail. Gillespie grinned, half turning back over the seat to look at Calver. 'I told you and Peters to back off, but you didn't listen. Now you're gonna pay for it. You're going to gaol, Calver. Meantime, I'm gonna get this baby-girl in a cell where I can have some real fun, then I'm gonna watch her daddy fry.'

Anita lashed out her fist at Gillespie but he was waiting for it, grabbing her hand in mid air and laughing. 'Settle down, girl. That's another slap you just earned yourself.'

Calver felt his smart-phone vibrating in his pocket but didn't dare remove it.

For another twenty five minutes they traveled in silence, then they were pulling into a Nashville PD station. As the car slid into a parking space, the radio squawked, Gillespie grabbing the handset to his mouth and acknowledging. The announcers voice came over the radio: 'Chief, you oughtta know, we got a pushy journalist here, Kelly Phillips from the Tennessean, and attorney Ned Peters, plus a guy from NAACP.'

Gillespie slowly turned in his seat to look at Calver. 'Yeah. What the fuck do they want?' he asked, his face reddening with anger.

'To speak to you. They saying they have evidence of an illegal stop and search with no probable cause, sexual assault and breach of civil rights. And boss…'

'What?'

'They say they're gonna publish what they've got unless you immediately produce Jonas Calver and Anita Ritter, unharmed and explain why they've been brought in?'

Calver kept his face completely passive and immobile, repressing the urge to smile.

'Chief?' the announcer pressed.

'What?' Gillespie spat out.

'The mayor and the DA also want to speak to you.'

Gillespie violently smashed the radio back into its holder, terminating the call. He sat motionless, looking out at the wall fronting the parking space. 'You been filming with your phone, Calver? Clever. You sent them a clip?'

Calver stayed silent. Gillespie turned around in his seat, avuncular smile back in place. 'Seems like a stand-off, counselor. How about we both just walk away from this misunderstanding?'

'You must be fucking—' Anita started to say.

'I think that's a good idea,' Calver calmly interrupted her, reaching his cuffed hands up and putting them on her shoulder to calm her.

'You kill the story right here and now. I don't press any charges. We both go home to fight another day?'

'Sounds like a plan,' Calver said. Anita started to say something, but Calver squeezed her shoulder, cutting her off.

Gillespie held Calver's eyes for a moment, calculating. 'Most you could have got, is me with the girl, but I hadn't even started,' he said. 'You try and push it, I'll say I had to subdue you and was carrying out an internal search of the girl, and she was playing up. Yeah, you can pick holes in it, but I reckon it would hold.'

Calver nodded, then held his hands out. Gillespie smiled and removed the cuffs.

As they got out the car and began to walk away, Gillespie called after them, 'and don't forget folks, you still got an invite to Floyd's execution party. Have a nice day.'

CHAPTER TWENTY-THREE

Mercy finished her shift at Riverbend a half hour early, thanks to cover from a colleague who owed her. She skipped out to her car, still thinking about Donna and the sudden turn her life had taken. She'd go straight over there now and surprise her, stop on the way and get some roses and a bottle.

A half hour later she arrived outside the apartment block and parked up on the street. It was late afternoon and quiet. Donna had said she only worked mornings so she should be home. Mercy made her way up the staircase humming quietly to herself. Coming up the hall to the door, it was slightly ajar. Cocking her head to one side, frowning and gently pushing the door, it swung open revealing the dimly lit interior. 'Donna,' she murmured, then repeated louder. The lounge looked just the same, dusty, quiet and undisturbed, the drapes still drawn. Something didn't feel right though. Moving to the bedroom and pushing the door open, she froze, her mind unable to quite comprehend the tableaux revealed, her fist involuntarily jabbing into her mouth to stifle the scream that ricocheted up her throat.

Donna's dead glassy eyes stared back at her, but that was about the only thing recognizable. Mercy began to hyperventilate. There was so much blood she wasn't at first able to work out what she was looking at, but the horrific imagery slowly began to register. Donna had been roped naked to the bed, each arm secured to a bed -post. She had been stabbed multiple times in the chest and her throat had been cut.

As Mercy stood by the bed, she felt her phone vibrating. Like an automaton she absently connected, moving the phone to her ear by reflex, her eyes locked on Donna.

First she heard laughter that sounded familiar, then Scooter's voice. 'Your ex-girlfriend was sure a wild one, Mercy,' he chuckled. 'Didn't I tell you, when you're my women, you're my woman. That's it.'

Mercy was numb, empty, in lock-down shock, her mind unable to formulate a reply.

'What's the matter, girl? Cat got your tongue?' Scooter said, jeering tone. 'Don't you like Scooter's handiwork?'

'You need help, Scooter,' she whispered.

He laughed. 'Make sure you're home tonight, Mercy.'

'Yes, Scooter,' she replied like an automaton, her voice dead.

'That's my girl. You better phone 911,' he said, his voice back to normal. 'Make sure you don't mention my name.'

'Yes, Scooter.'

Across the road from the apartment block, in a pay-phone, Scooter replaced the receiver. He took off his blood spattered leather gloves and rubbed the stubble on his chin, his smile now virtually fixed in a permanent rictus. He took out a small silver vial from his pocket and ran a thick line of white powder onto the back of his wrist, then hoovered it up into his left nostril with a snort like a horse. He raised his head and watched Mercy as she left the apartment and walked to her car. It was time for him to leave before his brother officers descended on the place. He slipped out of the booth and made his way down an alley to the stolen car he had used for transport.

When Mercy got back to her car, for a long while she just sat there, looking out of the window but not seeing anything. She knew she was meant to call the cops, but she couldn't concentrate. All she could think of was Donna. Donna kissing her, smoothing her hair, making her feel complete, just for once in her entire life. And now Donna was gone. Mercy began to shake as the delayed tears came. She hugged herself and let the emotion rage and wash over her, then just sat, empty of all thought. The phone began to vibrate in her pocket again - let it ring forever. As she moved her eyes up, something in the well of the car caught her attention. It was the scrap of paper the girl in the breakfast diner had given her.

Her mind vaguely discerned a simple choice: either phone the number, or end it all. Just start the engine and drive the car into a brick wall. No more Scooter. No more pain. An image of her mother popped into her head. Her life had been one of beaten down drudgery, her soul eaten away until there was nothing left. And now she would be the same. Scooter would kill her as he had killed Donna. Smiling through her tears, she remembered a rare one-to-one with her mother when she had still had some life in her. Mercy had failed an early school exam and her mother had mentioned a simple dictum of Winston Churchill: "Never give up." But her mother had given up. She reached down and retrieved the scrap of paper, smoothing it out so she could read the number.

She sighed, sniffed and wiped a sleeve across her nose, then dug out her cell and phoned the number.

Pascal was sat across a table from Dalton McHenry, or Fingers, as he liked to be known. The guy had acquired another gaudy red bandanna which was now tied rakishly round his head. They were both studying the screen of his tablet.

'So, there's three currently incarcerated, one on death row with Floyd Ritter,' he said, pulling up a list on screen with brief bios for each. 'Why you want to know about these blanket head camel jockey's anyway? Islamic terrorism is so yesterday.'

'You know, back in the day, in the UK, that was my specialism; Islamic terrorism,' she said.

Fingers turned to her, checking her expression, to see if she was sending him up. She held his gaze.

They were sat in a Hookah bar in mid-town, Nashville and Fingers was imbibing iced blueberry spearmint smoke, whilst Pascal had a glass of wine. The place was small, dark and intimate, with spindly teak furniture, assorted rugs on the floor, and a bright big screen TV on a wall showing Turkish music videos. There were a fair number of people there, but Pascal and Fingers were holed up in the corner.

'Who's the death row guy, what was his affiliation, and when's he due?'

'Man, you don't want much for your buck, do you?'

'Stop complaining, Finger's. You know you love it.'

He drew in a large lungful of the exotically flavored smoke, savoring it, his eyes bright, hands silently working the tablet keys. 'Name's Abdul Rahman. Been in jail 4 years, for killing 5 people, including a cop. Nice. He'd sworn allegiance to Islamic State, or Daesh as the natives call it. Real head-banger. US born as well, if you can believe that. Didn't recognize the court. Tried to preach to the jury until the judge essentially muzzled him. He's probably got some way to go with the appeals process before he gets a date.'

Pascal nodded. 'Can you access details of his recent visitors?'

A few moments later, he said, 'Apart from his attorney, looks like he's only ever had one other visitor. A John Irving.'

'Can you get anything on him?' she asked, as her phone began vibrating on the tabletop.

There was no caller ID. She grabbed it up, connecting. 'Yes?' she said.

There was almost silence, but she could just hear quiet breathing in the background.

'You, you gave me your number,' the caller murmured, almost too quiet to hear. 'Said I should call you, and you would help me.'

Pascal's mind was blank, the line silent. Then the caller said, quickly, 'sorry, my mistake. I thought—'

'Mercy!' Pascal exclaimed, her memory finally kicking in. 'Wait. Don't hang up. I will help you. Where are you?'

'In my car. I can't go home,' she sobbed. 'He'll be there. He's just killed. He's, he's killed my friend…' Her voice tailed off.

'Come here, now,' Pascal said, giving her the address. 'I'm going to help you.'

CHAPTER TWENTY-FOUR

Calver was back at the house, in the kitchen, sitting at the table with Ned Peters. A call with Mike Shapiro was on the speaker-phone.

'I hate to be the bringer of bad news, Calver,' Shapiro said, his voice sounding tinny and small as it emanated from the speaker. 'Tennessee Court of Criminal Appeals have just refused to grant a stay. They said they were, and I quote, "far from satisfied that there was anything material for a new jury to look at." So, no reason to send it back to the trial court for another crack at it. Sorry old buddy.'

'You tell Floyd?'

'Yep. Just left him in fact. He's taking it as well as can be expected.'

'What now?'

'Well, we'll take a shot at the Supreme Court, but we're running out of road. And that brings us nicely to this crazy clemency plea idea you got. Floyd told me about your visit and what was discussed.'

'Yeah, and what did he tell you?' Calver asked, interested to see whether Floyd had stuck to his word.

'He told me he was giving you a shot at coming up with the plea to the Governor, but that Joel and I would stay in charge. I hate to say it, Calver,' Shapiro said, and Calver could tell he was far from hating it.

'He's just humoring you. And that old drunk, Peters. But I'll tell you. We don't have time for this.'

'Hey, less of the old drunk,' Peters chirped up. 'I was addressing the Tennessee appeals court when you were still in diapers, counselor.'

'Sorry, Ned. Didn't know you were there. No offense intended..'

'None taken.'

'Look, Calver,' Shapiro came back, determination in his voice. 'I get the impression Floyd's not going to go with whatever you come up with anyway, so why waste our most precious commodity: time. Let me and Joel do the plea. I know the Governor, you don't. That might count for something, because I'll tell you, he's old school. He won't react well to some wise-ass out of state attorney talking about the wrongdoing of Wall Street banks that happened more than a decade ago. I mean, come on? This is Floyd's life at stake here. Can we afford time for an experiment?'

Calver knew he didn't like Shapiro, and he didn't trust him, but what the guy said was persuasive. 'I hear you,' he said. 'But we're going ahead. Nothing to stop you doing a plea as well, then Floyd can decide.'

'Fine,' Shapiro said abruptly, cutting the connection.

Peters and Calver looked at each other. 'Not a happy bunny, I think,' Calver said.

'Yeah, and I'm guessing Floyd ain't too happy either,' Ned said. 'But, serious question, how is the plea going? You started it?'

'Yeah,' Calver said. 'Come and have a look, and tell me if I'm going in the right direction.'

He led Ned into the living room and the old desk-top Dell that sat on an Oak table in the corner. He pressed the tab bar. 'Sit down.'

Ned slid into the seat as the document materialized on the screen. It was in draft letter form:

To The Honorable Randall Lee

Governor of the State of Tennessee

Nashville State Capitol

Application for Executive Clemency on Behalf of Floyd Ritter

Dear Governor Lee,

We beg you to spare the life of Floyd Ritter.

You alone have the power to commute Floyd's sentence of death. We believe, respectfully, that the exceptional circumstances set out below warrant the exercise of your constitutional powers.

<u>The Law of Clemency</u>

The words of Article 3, Section 6 of the 1796 constitution of Tennessee remain unchanged in over two hundred and twenty years. They provide that the Governor of Tennessee, "shall have the power to grant reprieves and pardons."

While judicial review of a death sentence is bound by the facts in a legal record, crucially, "the Governor may review a request for commutation without being bound by such limitations." Workman v State, 22 S.W. 3d 807, 808-09 (Tenn. 2000. "Executive clemency operates outside the letter of the law. The executive clemency process is a vehicle for mercy." Workman, 22 S.W. 3d at 812 (Drowota, J. Concurring. In short, the Governor of Tennessee is vested with "the power to extend mercy, wherever he thinks it is deserved." Herrera, 506

U.S. at 867 (quoting 4 W Blackstone, Commentaries, 397).

Our appeal for clemency is asking you to do just that; exercise your judgment and discretion, unconstrained by strict legal considerations, but tempered with mercy. Forgiveness and redemption are fundamental principles of our Christian beliefs, held dear by many Tennesseans. We ask you to hold those fundamental principles in the forefront of your mind as you consider this question of the fate of Floyd Ritter: life, or death?

Floyd Ritter: the man

Floyd was born in Tennessee in *[note: fill in bio detail including marriage to Mary, move to Baltimore, children, career etc.]*

Floyd Ritter and his case - a parable for modern America

The facts of Floyd's case are simple, but the background to it is not. Since his arrest, Floyd has consistently denied killing Vincent Fachetti. The great 2008 financial crash may seem a strange place to start in a clemency plea, but we feel it is the right place to start in Floyd's case. Floyd and his wife Mary were hardworking aspirational Americans who did all the right things. They worked hard, paid their taxes, educated their kids, and like all hardworking parents wanted a better life for their children than they or their parents had had. They were, like millions before them, following the much vaunted and fabled "American Dream" where seemingly anything was possible, where you could reach for the stars and fulfill your dreams. And part of that dream was to own their own home, and in 2006 they got their chance. A broker, through and recommended by their local church, offered to arrange a low installment paying mortgage on a fine wooden frame town house in Baltimore. Floyd's small landscaping business was growing and flourishing, and Mary was moving up the career ladder as a valued and effective teacher, and so they felt confident in making this financial commitment.

For a while life was good for Floyd and his family as their dream steadily turned into reality. They moved into their new house and made it into a real family home. But then it all started to go wrong, to unravel. Their mortgage, along with millions of others, went sour when initially low teaser monthly installment rates soared, leaving homeowners unable to pay them. What followed was financial Armageddon with foreclosures on an industrial scale, a collapse in house prices, bankruptcies and a monumental crash. Millions of Americans were suddenly made destitute because of the rotten corruption at the heart of Wall Street. It was a corruption that crept out from the center and flowed down the tentacles out into all the states and counties in the land, stretching right down and starting, in the case of housing, with the broker.

In Floyd's case her name was Rita. The year she wrote Floyd and Mary's mortgage, she pulled down $800,000 in brokerage fees, and got free holidays to places like Aspen and Hawaii. But Floyd's mortgage should not have been sub-prime, because Floyd and Mary had A1 credit scores, but Rita falsified them, and so was able to sell Floyd and Mary a mortgage paying a much higher interest rate than they should have been given. But Rita and her many cohorts were not just falsifying good credit records into bad ones to jack up their commissions, they were also using the same fraudulent process to sell mortgages to people who had no credit record at all, people who had zero ability to service a long term debt. And up the chain from Rita the corruption and criminal dishonesty continued when these sub-prime mortgages were packaged up into exotically named special investment vehicles and sold on to gullible investors, who were then scalped as well by their own banks, who told them these were dead cert, gold-plated investments. In Floyd's case the bank at the top of the chain was M. J. Greenberg, subsequently bailed out and merged into what is now, Greenberg Metro Bank, still run by the same individual, Lloyd De Masi.

Floyd and Mary were victims of all of this. As the great recession hit, they lost their home, and Floyd's landscaping business went under. Mary could only get part-time work. When Floyd and Mary discovered what had been done to them by the corrupt predators of Wall Street, they decided, like many others, to sue, and so they did.

Mary and Floyd's lawsuit named a number of defendants, including Metro Bank and Lloyd DeMasi. And Mary and Floyd were tenacious; they endured, despite repeated threats against them. It has been said by commentators that Lloyd DeMasi has a philosophy that requires that he must win at all costs, in everything, and in this case it came down to Floyd and Mary's lawsuit, which they would not agree to settle or discontinue, as all the other litigants had. Floyd and Mary's refusal to bend to De Masi's will enraged him, because he knew that a big trial would re-ignite the scandal surrounding his bank, at a time when he were desperately seeking new investors. This, ultimately, is what led to the killing of Vincent Fachetti.

The Tennessee Court of Criminal Appeals has declined to grant a stay of execution to Floyd based on new evidence proffered to them by

Floyd's defense team, but this does not preclude us from using this evidential material in this plea for clemency. The evidence shows:

1. Since the 2008 financial crash, Lloyd DeMasi (LDM) and Greenberg Metro Bank (GMB) have built up a shadow or ghost organization within GMB. It comprises two strands; a financial arm of elite, exceptional financial operators who are versed and indoctrinated with the GMB philosophy (a kind of second rate Ayn Rand Objectivism), and who are expected to move on eventually, at the highest level, through the revolving door in Washington, but also at a lower level, throughout the financial ecosystem. They are supported by a second strand of people, who it is believed are better suited to security work and who make up a kind of protection squad. There is of course nothing illegal in these activities, on their face, but then again, as set out at the beginning of this plea, you are not restricted to legalities.

2. This protection squad, as we shall refer to it, is led my a man named Cimino, the *de facto* head of GMB security.

3. We believe Cimino was responsible for the death of a GMB employee, Melissa McCarthy, currently recorded as a suicide (overdose of narcotics). We have asked NYPD and the District Attorney to re-investigate this case, and we await their response. McCarthy was in this protection squad but had threatened to disclose information about it. This is a bold allegation which we are prepared to defend, vigorously, if those identified wish to challenge us in a courtroom. Furthermore, we highlight here (*add HTML link*) a clip we have posted as exhibit FR2, depicting a conversation between Cimino and Grace Van Zim, a senior executive of GMB and aide de camp to LDM, recorded at his Hampton's mansion.

4.   Earlier we averted to the civil lawsuit, instigated by Floyd and Mary, against GMB and LDM. Initially this was a kind of class action where they clubbed together with others, but eventually Floyd and Mary stood alone, because they would not settle. Mary was the prime mover in this litigation, and Floyd took a back seat. Throughout they were subjected to phone calls and intimidation, some of which is on record as reported to Baltimore PD. (See exhibit FR7).

5. In September 2012 Floyd and Mary came to Tennessee to visit their folks who still reside there. During that visit, Vincent Fachetti, the man Floyd is accused of murdering, came to where they were staying and threatened them, again, to drop the lawsuit. Floyd did not take it seriously, and told Fachetti to get off the property.

6. Seven days later Mary was involved in a serious car crash when her vehicle plowed into a large lorry exiting a junction. It is estimated she was traveling at 60 mph at the point of impact. Mary was an exceptionally careful driver who had never had an accident or been charged with traffic violations. She was airlifted to hospital, in a coma, and later Floyd took, on medical advice, the very difficult decision to turn off her life support. In all such serious vehicle accidents the site should be locked down for detailed investigation of the causes of the accident and to decide whether and where any criminal or civil liability might lie. This was not done in Mary's case. First, there was inexplicable delay in getting first medical responders in attendance. Second, the vehicle was prematurely removed from the site and then crushed within 24 hours of the accident. Third, the original accident report is missing, replaced by what we believe is a false one.

7. We can now reveal that the brake lines of Mary's car had been cut,

just prior to the accident. We highlight here (*add HTML link*) a clip we have posted as exhibit FR4, made by Jethro Tucker, a worker at the breakers yard where Mary's vehicle was taken after the accident. We have pixelated out law enforcement individuals from the clip, as our focus here is Floyd only, and others will need to consider their role in all of this at another time. The clip is detailed and clearly shows the crudely severed brake lines. The individual shown and heard in the clip is Cimino, *de facto* security boss of GMB. We believe the clip requires no explanation from us as to what it depicts, but we will emphasize one point: it clearly evidences a tight nexus between Cimino and Lloyd de Masi, and for the first time unmasks Greenberg Metro Bank's Chief Executive as the prime mover in conspiracy to commit murder.

8.   When Floyd had some control over his grief, he went looking for Vincent Fachetti, believing him responsible for his wife's death. He found him in Harry's Bar, Nashville. There was a confrontation, a physical fight. Fachetti ran into the corridor that led to the rest-rooms, at the back of the bar. The only known witness still living, who testified at the trial to what went on in that corridor, is Frank Ross.

9.   We can now reveal that Cimino was also present in Harry's bar during the confrontation. We highlight here (*add HTML link*) a clip we have posted as exhibit FR5. It is new testimony from Frank Ross, whereby he recants his original courtroom testimony, and provides a completely different description of what took place in the corridor. Now he does not know whose knife it was; now he confirms he did not see Floyd deliver the fatal stab-wound; now he suggests that any physical actions of Floyd were in self-defense; now he says he was not present when Fachetti died, but someone else was : Cimino.

10. As corroboration for Frank Ross's new found candor, we highlight here (*add HTML link*) a clip we have posted as exhibit FR9. It is testimony from a new witness who was present in Harry's bar that night, Velda Collins. She also places Cimino in Harry's bar that night.

11. Both witnesses confirm, and independently corroborate each other, that Cimino was the only person in the corridor when Fachetti died. Floyd had already left the bar minutes earlier.

12. Finally, we would make the point that it is not the intention or purpose of this plea to convict others for the death of Vincent Fachetti, but to throw light on what really happened that night, and to persuade you that there is very serious doubt as to whether Floyd killed Fachetti - he has been steadfast in his denial throughout. We would remind you that the knife involved in the confrontation between Floyd and Fachetti, has never been linked to Floyd, other than by the now recanted and discredited testimony of Frank Ross.

Since being incarcerated, Floyd Ritter has been a model prisoner *(insert more detail here)*. I have got to know him well. When he talks about the bank and De Masi and what was done to his family and how he responded, he has an interesting take on it all. He recalls the notorious New York subway killings of four black youths by Bernhard Goetz in 1984. Despite being a black man, Floyd identifies with Bernie Goetz who became something of a folk hero to some, in fighting a crime epidemic that the police seemed unwilling or scared to confront. Floyd, despite denying the killing of Vincent Fachetti, draws parallels between himself and Bernie, in fighting injustice when those charged with enforcing the rules will not do their jobs. The great financial recession of 2008 was caused by men at the top like Lloyd de Masi. It started with simple corruption and dishonest financial trickery that ran from the top to the bottom. When it all unraveled and we discovered what had been done to us, were the perpetrators punished for their wrongdoing? No. They were rewarded with billions of dollars of taxpayers bailout money, courtesy of the actions of the revolving door fraternity that ebbs and flows between Washington and Wall Street, something that even now De Masi is planning to ramp up and exploit further, via his secret army. Floyd and Mary tried to redress this, to get some justice via their lawsuit. They still believed in the American dream, that wrongdoing would be punished and they would be compensated, but that was not to be. At each stage they were thwarted and threatened, and eventually De Masi moved to a different level of criminality to stop the lawsuit: murder.

De Masi clearly wants the state of Tennessee to finish the job he started, and execute Floyd Ritter. Why else would Cimino currently be residing in Tennessee?

Final plea for mercy, redemption etc….

Ned Peters finished reading the on-screen draft, his expression thoughtful. Calver watched him anxiously.

'Not bad,' Peters finally said, rubbing his chin. 'For an amateur. Its got potential, but it needs some polishing. I like it.'

'Good,' Calver said, relieved.

'You get me half a glass of Wild Turkey, boy, and I'll get straight to work on it. See if'n I can't finesse this into something special.'

Calver went to get the bottle. He guessed it was going to be a long night

CHAPTER TWENTY-FIVE

By the time Mercy arrived at the Hookah bar, Fingers had left. She looked like a refugee from a war zone, face pale and eyes sunken and red from crying. She seemed like she was on the edge, at the end of her tether to reality, like some of the PTSD cases Pascal had seen. Over a fraught and emotional hour, Pascal managed to extract all the salient facts. When Mercy had finished speaking she sat quiet, the retelling seeming to leave her purged and calm.

'Did you call the cops, Mercy, like he told you to?' Pascal asked her gently.

She looked startled. 'No. No, I didn't. I forgot.'

'Good. We'll think about calling them in a minute. Did you notice a public phone booth outside the apartment?'

'No,' she replied absently, looking puzzled. 'Why?'

'Because he must have been watching the apartment when you went in. He didn't phone you from his mobile, did he?'

Pascal watched her eyes change as she processed the information. 'No. And yes,' she said, her eyes focusing. 'I'm sure there was a phone booth on the corner.'

'See, he wouldn't use his own phone, and he probably wore gloves in the booth.'

Mercy nodded, looking thoughtful, color slowly returning to her face. 'Look, you've been really nice and all, but seriously, what can you do against him?'

Pascal reached across the table and took Mercy's hands, looking into her eyes. 'People like Scooter can't be threatened, or warned off. It just doesn't work.'

'So, how can he be stopped?'

'Kill him is the simple answer, because people like him never stop. That's the only permanent solution, although there are maybe other options, short of killing him'

'You're serious, aren't you?' Mercy said, wonder in her voice.

'Absolutely.'

Mercy smiled gently, and her eyes softened. 'Why are you trying to help me? You hardly know me?'

'Lets just say I have a soft spot for the underdog, the friendless who have nowhere to go,' Pascal said, her eyes going smoky and distant. 'You know, when I was little more than a teenager, I killed my step-father. Went to jail. They thought it was manslaughter, so it was only a few years.'

Mercy raised her eyes. Pascal's were ice cold and steady. Mercy shivered and laughed uncertainly.

'You said Scooter will be at yours tonight?

'Yes.'

Pascal checked her watch.

'What about calling the police about Donna?' Mercy said. 'I, it feels bad just leaving her like that, lying there…....'

'If we leave it a bit longer, is it likely anyone else will go there and find her?'

'I don't know. See, I'd only just met her, was getting to know her. From talking, I'd guess she was quite solitary, and I know her family live way up north somewhere, so I guess its possible no one would find her for a while.'

Pascal nodded, thinking about Donna's wounds as described by Mercy. 'Does Scooter have a knife?' she asked.

'Yeah. Big old thing he's always playing with. Sometimes wears it in a sheaf, hidden inside his trousers.'

'How long to get to your place?'

'Ten, fifteen minutes.'

'What time would he normally show up?'

'Anytime. Varies. He likes to try and catch me unawares, but generally its later, ten, or after.'

Pascal checked her watch again. 'Good few hours yet.'

'What are you thinking?'

'Where's your car?'

'Outside. Why?'

'I need to take a look at it.' She got up from the table. 'Come on.'

Outside in the parking lot, Pascal spent five minutes searching around the car, while Mercy stood and watched with a puzzled frown. 'What you looking for?' she asked.

'This,' Pascal said, scrambling up from underneath the rear of the car. 'Its a transponder.' She held out her open palm, so Mercy could see the tiny device. 'Scooter's been tracking you. Give me your phone.'

'Why, what for?'

'Because five will get you ten, its bugged, or tagged as well.'

'Jesus and Mary,' Mercy said, fascinated, grief forgotten for a moment. She passed over her phone.

'Mercy, I've got some things I need to take care,' Pascal said. 'I'll take your car, because Scooter may try and find you, and you take mine. Just drive around if you like or go somewhere Scooter doesn't know about, but keep undercover. We meet back here at 6, change cars, and I'll follow you home, so I can get in place before he turns up.'

'What then?'

'We wait. And Mercy. Relax,' she said with a smile. 'I'll take your phone as well, and you can have this burner for essential calls.'

Pascal passed her the phone and they hugged, then parted.

Thirty minutes later Pascal sat in a gay bar on Church Street. The place was awash with neon light, predominantly purple, but other bright colors - greens, yellows and oranges - jostling to catch the eye. Long cylindrical lamps hung from the ceiling in a row over the bar which ran the length of the rectangular shaped room. Opposite the bar were booths, other side of a walkway. Across from Pascal, sitting in one of the booths, was Christoff Wisliceny, colored light continuously moving across his face as he talked, giving him a strange otherworldly appearance.

'I got your text and did some digging,' he said.

'Why the fuck do we always have to meet in places like this, Christoff?' she asked, looking around.

He ignored her moaning. He believed she was bisexual, so guessed the fuss was an act. 'This man, John Irving, who's been visiting Abdul Rahman in Riverbend?' he said

'Yeah,' Pascal said, immediately alert.

'Its a false name, and he's actually British. Possibly here illegally.'

'Tell me more.'

'There isn't much, and I had to call in some pretty hefty favors to get what there is,' he said with a reproving glance.

She smiled and raised her hand for the barman. 'Lighten up, Christoff and let me replenish your glass. That 12 year old malt taste good?'

'It passes muster,' he muttered. 'Okay, this man Irving, as far as we can ascertain, he's been here around 10 years. Converted to Islam over here, and is a stalwart at the Islamic Center Mosque here in Nashville. Obviously when Abdul Rahman was taken down and convicted, Homeland Security and the FBI were all over his associates, including Irving, but that's long passed now, and they obviously didn't find anything.'

'So what's he do now, and why is he still visiting?'

'Good question. I don't know is the answer. He runs a small construction firm that's probably a front for some type of criminal activity. The guy is bright, but also tough. He was in the UK army for a while.'

'He doesn't exactly fit the profile, does he?' Pascal said. 'Key question though. Do you think there is any kind of functional cell here, behind him and Rahman?'

'Courtney, you know from your time in MI5 in London, its very difficult to know. But, if the US intelligence community are not interested, it suggests the answer is no.'

'Yeah, Christoff, but what about the visits?' she said, her eyes going smokey and far away. 'What about the visits, huh?'

Christoff took a shot of scotch, his eyes following a trim young man as he traipsed past. 'I agree that's an anomaly. These people are not usually personally loyal to each other, the cause is all. So, yes, it raises a question.'

Christoff rubbed his face, then fixed Pascal with a sharp look. 'You know, Courtney, I know you better than most, and I have a terrible suspicion building in me that you are thinking of doing something beyond stupid. Something beyond the exploits of comic super-hero's? I hope you're not, because it can't be done. And yeah, you can relax, because I'm not going to ask.'

'Good. Then you won't have to worry, will you?'

He smiled. 'In case you're interested, I've got the guy's cell number.' He passed her a note.

She got up. 'Thanks Christoff.' She nodded.

He watched her walk away, a slow smile spreading across his face. Still, maybe he was wrong, maybe she wasn't barking mad. He sipped his malt.

Back in Mercy's car, Pascal dug out a fresh burner from her bag and powered it up. She looked at the cell number Christoff had given her, keyed it in and opened the text message function. She sat for two minutes, weighing things. Fact is there was no time left for fancy cover stories. If she was going to get any help with what she believed she was going to have to do, she would have to go in headfirst and upfront.

There was no time to finesse it. She typed in text:

"What do John Dillinger, the Anglin brothers and Frank Abagnale all have in common, John? Maybe we can help each other? I'm a friend of the cause. I'll call you tomorrow at 10 am."

She pressed send, then switched the burner off, put it back in her bag, and started the engine. Maybe she wouldn't have to do anything, in the end, but it was better to be prepared if things were going to go to hell. Still, at least things were starting to move. Time to deal with Scooter. She checked her watch. Mercy would be waiting for her. She edged out into the traffic, her body and mind starting to morph into operational mode where everything seemed brighter, her perceptions clearer; adrenaline in her system started to twitch and jitter.

As she pulled into the parking lot, she could see Mercy, looking forlorn, biting her lip, leaning up against the car. As Pascal got out, Mercy rushed over and hugged her. Pascal could feel her shaking. 'Its okay, Mercy. I'm here.' But the girl clung to her. Pascal let it play out for a moment, then gently held her away. 'Come on. You drive. I'll follow.'

When they arrived the small frame house was shrouded in darkness. They sat watching for a few minutes. It was a quiet neighborhood. They moved onto the porch, Mercy digging keys out of her bag. As she raised the key to the lock, Pascal grasped her wrist, putting a finger to her lips, listening.

'His cars not here,' Mercy whispered, looking around.

Pascal nodded. 'If he's tracking your car, he'll know you've arrived.' She took the key from Mercy and gently opened the door. 'I'll go first,' she said, moving slowly into the darkened hallway. Mercy followed, flicking on the light behind her. Pascal tiptoed along the hall, to the door leading into the living room, Mercy just behind her. Pascal opened the door and stepped through, Mercy following. As Mercy flicked the lights on, Pascal heard the unmistakable click of a handgun being cocked, then Mercy screamed, shut-off almost instantly by her hand going to her mouth.

He was sitting in a chair in the corner of the room, gun leveled at them, lazy confident smile on his face. 'Well now, looky here. Scooter's bagged hisself a threesome,' he said. 'You a dyke as well?' he asked, studying Pascal. 'You look like one. Watched you today in that queer cesspool bar on Church Street.'

She couldn't help the frown creasing her face. She must be getting old. He'd used the transponder, then tailed her and she hadn't noticed a damn thing. She glanced at the gun. It looked like a Glock 17, and it had a silencer. He'd come prepared.

His smiled widened. 'Scooter ain't quite as stupid as some folks think. So who are you? Saw you in the breakfast diner, didn't I?'

'I'm just a friend of Mercy's. Why don't you just let us go?'

'Uh huh,' he shook his head. 'Mercy, go get me a beer from the fridge. Don't try anything, less you want me to blow your girlfriend's kneecaps out.'

'Scooter—'

'Git,' he barked. 'Less you want some of Scooter's night stick. Hell, I'm beginning to think you like it,' he chuckled.

Mercy moved warily away toward the kitchen, watching Scooter all the time.

'I ran a vehicle check on that fudge packer you met in the bar,' he said, his eyes appraising her slowly, his expression coldly calculating.

Pascal shrugged casually, but underneath she had a bad feeling. The guy was far from stupid, and worse, he was deadly careful. Used the good ol' boy routine as clever cover for a pretty sharp mind. 'He's just a friend, like Mercy,' she said.

'I don't think so. He's tagged to the UK's Consulate in New York, so he's gotta be a spy. So what does that make you, stuck out here in Nashville? Can't figure it.'

Mercy returned with a can of beer that she handed to Scooter. He took it, then roughly pulled her down so she was sitting at his feet, looking up at Pascal. Scooter lifted up the gun again and leveled it at her. 'Carefully empty your pockets, and chuck your wallet over here. Then turn around, with your back to us, and get down on your knees,' he said.

Pascal slowly removed her wallet and threw it over, her mind calculating options, none of which seemed good, not whilst the gun remained unwaveringly trained on her.

'Take the rope out of my bag, Mercy, and tie her hands,' Scooter said as he pulled out Pascal's ID and studied it. 'Courtney Pascal, huh?'

'Scooter, she's just friend,' Mercy said. 'Just let her go. She doesn't know nothing. I'll stay, and, and we can do whatever you want. You know I'll never turn on you.'

'Oh, baby, I ain't even started yet,' he said. 'Tie her hands so I can see. And, Mercy. Why ain't you called the cops like I asked you to, about your little friend?'

'Shit, Scooter. You are one tough hombre when you're holding a gun,' Pascal said. 'But then most psychiatrists would say, based on what you did to Donna, that you're essentially afraid of women. I mean come on, Scooter. That was pure rage. What did she do? Laugh at your dick? You see, I have a theory about guys like you. You hate women and you hate gays as well. Women scare you with their vagina's and their breasts, but on the other side, you really hate gays as well, because deep down, you know you are one.' She looked over her shoulder at him, and laughed.

She was surprised at how quickly he moved. She felt the cold gun barrel on the back of her head, and heard the click. She closed her eyes, tensed and waited for Armageddon, but it didn't come.

'One more smart word, bitch, and I'll blow your fucking head off,' he said.

She could hear the tension in his voice, and knew she'd hit a nerve, but if she pushed too far, she wouldn't get out alive. She exhaled her held breath slowly, relaxing.

He moved back to the chair. He hadn't tested the ropes around her wrists. A tiny victory achieved by diverting his attention. It gave her a slight lift. She tested the rope, exploring the knot and tension with her fingertips. With time she might be able to undo the knots. She glanced back over her shoulder.

Scooter rubbed his crotch and winked at her. He turned to Mercy. 'Sweetheart, me and you is going to have us a session, and when I've finished, you're gonna phone the cops and tell them about your friend Donna like I asked you to. When that's done, I'll deal with your new friend here, but first she can go down in the basement.'

Scooter came over and pulled Pascal to her feet. He dragged her into the hall, to the door to the basement, which was under the stair case. It had a mortice deadlock, a Yale lock and a bolt, all looking new, as did the door. Pascals heart sank.

Scooter opened the door. Steps disappeared down into the murk. He gave her a violent push and she tumbled down the stairs, the light extinguishing as the door slammed shut above her. The sound of locks and bolts being turned echoed as her body came to a halt at the bottom of the stairs, moans escaping her lips as knocks to her knee and shoulder sent sharp pains through her.

Lying there, acclimatizing and listening, just the night sounds of a silent town-house basement, the odd creak of wood, water in a pipe, distant hum of central heating or air-conditioning. Rolling onto her knees and climbing to her feet, her mind whirring away. Had there been a light switch outside on the wall? Maybe it was inside. Clambering back up the staircase to the top, then using her nose, she felt slowly around where you would expect a light switch to be. Nothing.

Back down the stairs she began a slow traversing of the floor space, mapping out in her head the geography and placement of any items or furniture. After fifteen minutes of bumping into things and painfully stubbing her foot, a rough idea of the space lay out in her head. Then the muffled screaming began. It sounded like a dog or an owl to start with because at first it was intermittent, but then it became persistent. Not loud enough to rouse neighbors; her mouth was probably gagged in some way, but loud enough for Pascal to know exactly where it was coming from and why. Mustn't think about it or it would destroy her ability to function. And time was short, because as soon as Scooter finished whatever he was doing, he would come for her with the gun, and there was only one way that was going to end.

As those thoughts flashed through her mind, she toyed with the knot that bound her wrists, gently pulling it back and forth, loosening it, whilst her mind tried to picture the space around her. It was a small low ceilinged room, with a workbench along one wall, and what felt like a large rectangular freezer unit, along the opposite wall. She moved to it, lifting the lid, hoping it might have a light inside. It didn't. Looking up, there was a weak glow filtering down from a crack near the low ceiling. It was strange as the crack ran vertical, not horizontal. She clambered onto the freezer unit for a closer look.

It was a storm double door that obviously opened outward, hopefully into the side yard. Pushing up against it with her forehead, it wouldn't open, but there was some give. Trying again, this time ramming her head up against the doors - they felt rickety; maybe they'd break open if enough force could be deployed, but with her hands tied, it wasn't going to happen. She smashed her head against the doors in frustration, then sat down on top of the freezer, wanting to scream, while her fingertips continued to work on the knots, and now there was a little more play.

This time when the scream came, it was bloodcurdling and loud, ending abruptly. Maybe the neighbors would hear it, but even if they did, it would probably be dismissed as kids involved in horseplay. But it had had a kind of finality about it that worried Pascal, but no time to speculate. Maybe Mercy's ordeal was over for now, but that meant Scooter would be along soon. As that thought went through her mind she felt the knot start to unravel. Her fingers went feverish, scrabbling against the clock, but her actions were pulling it tight again, the opposite of what was needed. Stopping and drawing a deep breath, and starting again, this time lightly pulling and teasing the knot, this time it suddenly unraveled fast, and then it was open.

She chucked the rope on the floor, then as an afterthought, opened the freezer and felt around through the packets and freezing cold items, until she found something substantial. It felt like a leg of lamb. Up onto the freezer and swinging the joint up with all her force, the storm doors burst open with that first swing and street light flooded in on her. Breathing deeply for a second, then her arms were automatically hauling herself up, eyes peeking along the rim, then her body was sliding out, flattening herself against the wall.

The street seemed calm and quiet. Moving along the wall to the living room window, the drapes were pulled, but there was a small gap at the side where the curtain had snagged against an ornament on the sill, allowing her to see in. She could make out Mercy's inert form, lying on the couch face down, but with her head turned to the side on a pillow. Her eyes were closed, but her chest moved evenly up and down. Pascal leaned back against the wall and rubbed her face, relief surging through her. Then Scooter came into her sight line, entering from the kitchen, can of beer in his hand. But in his other hand he held a large hunting knife. Where was the Glock, she wondered?

Moving down the side of the house, there must be a back door somewhere; every house had one, didn't they? And then there it was in front of her. Up onto the stoop looking in, the door led into the lighted kitchen. Gently trying the handle, the door opened and she moved silently inside to the sound of Scooter's voice. He must be on the phone to someone. Peering around the door jamb, he was sat in the armchair with his back to her and phone to his ear, facing the couch on which Mercy lay. The gun was lying on the arm of the chair. Looking down she realised she was still carrying the frozen joint of meat. It would do.

She moved silently into the room in towards the back of his chair. At the last moment Scooter sensed something and began to turn towards her, his hand going for the gun, but it was too late, as the frozen meat smashed into his neck and lower head. He grunted and sprawled side-wise out of the chair into a heap on the floor, out cold. Pascal ran to Mercy, rolling her onto her back, cradling her head. Her eyes fluttered open, slowly focusing. 'You're late,' she whispered with a weak smile.

They both turned as Scooter groaned and slowly began to move. Pascal retrieved the gun while Mercy moved into a sitting position. Her right eye was black and there was a little blood dripping from her nose which she wiped with her sleeve.

'You got any masking or duct tape?' Pascal asked.

'In the kitchen, first drawer on the right.'

Pascal handed her the gun. 'If he moves, blow his fucking head off.'

'Pleasure,' she nodded.

Pascal got the tape and manhandled a groggy Scooter into the armchair. The tape was wound around his neck and the back of the chair, around and around, and the same with his wrists to the arms of the chair, and finally his ankles to each chair leg. She got some rubber gloves and picked up Scooter's knife, examining it closely, testing the blade. It had been sharpened and honed to a high degree. She used it to cut away his trousers and underpants, pulling the material away so he was naked around the crotch. He had left a half full beer can which she took a sip of before pouring what was left over Scooters head.

He spluttered and his eyes came open. He lifted his head, slowly taking in his surroundings, blinking, his eyes moving around. He tried to flail against the tape, but was barely able to move. After a moment, he seemed to relax back against the chair. 'You're both dead,' he said casually, his good ol' boy smile back in place.

'Not this time, Scooter,' Pascal said, matching his smile. 'But before we do anything final, I just wanted to ask you, nicely.'

'What?'

'Are you prepared to just walk away? Leave Mercy alone? Never contact her again, leave her out of Donna's murder investigation?'

'Nope. She's mine, until I say she's not,' he said, his eyes going cold. 'And you, whoever you are, maybe you need a lesson about the way things work out here. I'm the law, and we just about do what we please in this state. You just got to be connected, and I am. So if you got some dumb idea of trying to threaten me with Donna's murder, forget it. Go on, call the cops, give them the knife you're holding. I'll still walk. And then I'll come looking for you, and Mercy. How you doing, Baby?' he said, nodding at her.

'It's true, Courtney,' Mercy said, resignedly.

'You see. She knows,' he said, chuckling. 'So why don't you set me free, and maybe I won't hurt you too much.'

'You know, Scooter,' Pascal said. 'I knew you'd answer like that, but I wanted to hear it. At least you're honest. But even if you had agreed to walk away, you wouldn't be able to, because you're a born stalker, and they don't give up. Less you kill them.'

He laughed again. 'Go ahead. I ain't scared.'

'No, I guess you're not.'

'Okay, so let me go,' he said, smiling.

'Courtney,' Mercy said softly. 'Why don't you go. Leave us. I was never going to get away from him. Its like my fate is written in the stars, to be killed by another wife-beater, just like my mother. We can't fight him. You tried to help me, and I thank you for that. But you can get away, out of the state. So go, now.'

'That's good advice, little lady,' Scooter said, his confidence roaring back.

Pascal pursed her lips, pretending to think about it. She stood up, looking at Scooter, then she reached down and cut the tape around his ankles. 'Move your legs together,' she said.

He did so. She taped them.

'What are you doing?' he asked.

'I need you secured, so I can get away,' she said. She cut one of his wrists free. 'When I cut the other one, move your hands together, so I can tape them' She nodded at Mercy. 'Hold the gun on him.'

Scooter smirked. 'Okay, but you don't need to do all this. I'll let you go. Just let me free.'

'I don't think so.' She taped his wrists together, then cut the tape around his neck. 'Lie down on the floor, Scooter, face down. I don't want you coming after me, until I get a head start.'

He looked at her for a moment, shrugged and knelt down, rolling onto his front.

'Good,' Pascal said. She straddled his butt, pushing his shirt up and holding the knife over the middle of his back.

He looked over his shoulder. 'What is this?'

'I lied,' she said bringing the knife down hard into his spinal column, twisting it at the last moment as the tip went in.

There was a cracking sound and Scooter screamed. A moment later he soiled himself and urinated.

Pascal said, 'I'm guessing you're going to need a wheel chair for the rest of your life, Scooter, and that may slow you down some.'

He groaned, still conscious. Pascal clambered off his back, glancing at Mercy whose mouth hung open, a puzzled look on her face as she tried to work out what had just happened. Mercy got up and walked over to Scooter, pushing him lightly with her toe, then harder, rolling him over with her foot, so he was lying on his back looking up at her. He gurgled in the back of his throat as if he couldn't speak, and for the first time Mercy saw something in his eyes she had never seen before: fear.

Pascal said, 'If I had told you what I was going to do, Mercy, you would have stopped me?'

'Maybe.'

'That's why I didn't. See, I'm not emotional about anything, least of all a cockroach like Scooter. It had to be done, and no half measures would have worked. This completely removes him from your life as a problem, crucially, without killing him. It also protects other women. And let me ask you something. If you could go back and do the same thing to the guy who killed your mother, wouldn't you do it?'

Mercy didn't say anything. Instead she looked down at the broken body lying on the floor, her face expressionless. 'How's it feel, Scooter?' she asked, a grim smile on her face. 'You could have just walked away, but you couldn't do that, could you? You just couldn't leave me be. You took away a shining light, Donna. Murdered for nothing, just because she was my friend.'

Mercy seemed to shake herself. She turned to Pascal and said, 'I guess I shouldn't be happy over such a thing, but I think I am.'

'Good. He deserved it. And he'd never have stopped. This way he will.'

'What now?'

Pascal riffled through Scooter's jacket and pulled out a jangling bunch of keys. 'I'm going to dump him at Donna's place with the knife, and I'll need your help. If we roll him up in the carpet we can carry him there like that.'

They both crouched down by Scooter, who was softly moaning, and began rolling him up.

It took around two hours to get the body into Scooter's car, drive over in a convoy, set Scooter up with the knife at the scene, then get back to Mercy's place. Half way back, Pascal stopped at a public phone booth and phoned the cops, handkerchief over the mouthpiece, and told them to go to Donna's apartment, sounds of a disturbance.

Back at Mercy's, Pascal told her what to say when the police arrived, that she had just met Donna, had spent the night with her and left. Also tell them that Scooter had been stalking her, and tell them about his threats, but nothing else. Then just stick to that story whatever they said or did. In all probability they would find a way of absolving Scooter, but he would be out the force and unable to threaten her again, and would probably be in hospital for months.

Mercy took Pascal's hand, and looked into her eyes. 'I don't know how I will ever be able to repay you for what you've done for me.'

Pascal squeezed her hand back. 'That's kind of you, Mercy. But its not necessary. Getting a psychopath like Scooter off the street is a public service.'

'Well, if you ever want anything, you ask, yeah?'

'Okay,' Pascal said, getting to her feet. 'Now I gotta go.' She grabbed her bag and left, leaving Mercy sitting on the couch smiling to herself.

CHAPTER TWENTY-SIX

Calver sat at the desk carefully reading through the document on screen. Ned Peters sat to one side, a double-barreled shotgun across his knee. He was painstakingly oiling its stock, stopping now and again to look up to see how far Calver had got with reading the finalized clemency petition.

At last Calver finished and looked up. 'Its excellent, Ned,' he said. 'You've tightened it up and finessed the language so it sounds Tennessean. It reads better, much better than my version.'

'I don't know about that,' Ned replied, but Calver could tell he was pleased with his words. 'But its nice sometimes to get some praise, especially from another lawyer. So, now what?'

'Get it approved by Floyd and straight out to the Governor.'

'You know,' Ned said. 'You shouldn't get your hopes up, Jonas.'

'I know, but we gotta keep trying. I'm going straight down to Riverbend,' he said, hitting the print button on the computer.

Pascal checked her watch: 10 am. She lifted the burner to her ear and pressed the call button. She listened to the burring sound as she looked out at the screen of trees around the house. There was a click as the phone connected, and then a voice. 'Yes?' Clipped, military style.

'I texted you yesterday, so I'm sure you recognize the number. I'd like to meet and talk.'

'Who are you, and what do you want?' he asked, softly, the hard tone receding into blandness.

'Lets meet and I can tell you.'

'I don't know you?'

'Well, how will you get to know me if we don't meet? Look, we can help each other. Tell you what. I can transfer you 500 bucks of Bitcoin. You hold it; meet me; if its a blow-out. You keep it. So what d'you say?'

'How d'you know I got a Bitcoin wallet?'

'I checked you out. Now, we got a deal, or what?'

Silence. Then a click as he rang off.

'Fuck!' Pascal said, rousing Anita who had been dozing on the couch.

'No go?' Fingers asked, lounging on the edge of a chair, his bright red bandanna giving color to the room.

'No,' she said. Then, 'wait,' as she grabbed up the burner as a text message came in. 'He's sent the bitcoin address, saying pay it and he'll call back.'

Fingers smiled. 'How do I know he's not just gonna walk away with all my moolah?' he asked.

'He's intrigued. He'll take the bait, trust me. And if he don't, I'm good for it.'

Fingers nodded, took the burner and copied in the bitcoin address into his hand-held, and pressed pay. 'Done,' he said.

They waited. A few moments later the phone buzzed again.

'Come to my office in two hours,' he said, and gave her the address. 'Come alone. You will be searched. I will give you fifteen minutes.'

Pascal confirmed she'd be there.

Irving Construction occupied a corner lot downtown. It was a warehouse containing building materials, with a small office tacked on the side. The car park out front was empty apart from a black SUV, and a white van with the company logo on the side. Pascal pulled in beside it, got out and strolled over to the office doors and into a small reception area. It was manned by a single brown-skinned girl wearing a green headscarf, sitting in front of a screen. She looked up reluctantly. 'Yes?'

'Mornin'. I've come to see John Irving,' Pascal said.

As she spoke a door to her left opened and a man came out. He was medium height, compact, and moved lithely, his gray eyes scanning Pascal as she approached. She knew he was mid-forties, but he looked younger, dressed in chino's and a white shirt. He nodded and said, 'come through.'

His office was small and utilitarian; couple of green filing cabinets, no pictures, a large calender on the wall behind him, desk had just a telephone and an open laptop he had been working on. He patted her down without speaking, then gestured for her to take a seat. He sat across from her.

'So who are you, and what do you want?' he said, holding up his watch. 'You got fifteen minutes.'

'Let me ask you something first. Why d'you agree to meet? Okay, you're holding five hundred bucks, but I'm guessing my text message interested you. You worked out what Dillinger and the others had in common.'

'Twelve minutes,' he said. 'They all broke out of jail. So what? Again, who are you and what do you want?'

'My name is Courtney Pascal, and I'm ex-British intelligence, MI5 in fact. Specialized in counter-terrorism at one time, before they chopped me off at the knees and threw me out the service. Been over here a while working cases for a New York attorney.'

'And?' he said, his face betraying nothing.

Pascal sighed. The guy was turning out to be a harder nut to crack than she'd anticipated. Trouble was they'd run out of time, so she had to throw caution to the winds, go for broke and fuck the consequences. She took a breath, thinking for moment how absurd what she was about to say was going to sound. 'I'm working on the Floyd Ritter death penalty case. I'm wondering about the feasibility of springing him if everything goes wrong on the appeal side. But I need help, an organization behind me, and I thought that Abdul Rahman might have what I need. We go in together. Two birds with one stone,' she said.

He laughed. 'You're fucking crazy, lady,' he said, but his eyes were saying something different; it wasn't clear what.

Pascal shrugged. 'It can be done. And if it is, you get a massive media plug for the cause. What's the downside, especially as you guys apparently don't mind dying?'

He laughed again, but with less enthusiasm. 'Just to humor you for a moment,' he said. 'What exactly would you be bringing to the party? I mean, why would I need you if I was contemplating such a stupid and dangerous idea?'

'I have access to the Tennessee Corrections Department mainframe, huge experience in the logistics necessary to carry out such an operation, plus extensive contacts in the legal, government and intelligence communities. That's just for starters,' Pascal said. She watched for a moment as he digested it. She checked her watch. The fifteen minutes were up. She got up. 'I have no doubt you need to think about this,' she said, knowing he would not be the person to make any decisions, if there was a cell behind him. 'And I'm sure you would also wish to check me out. But, time is running out. I will call you tomorrow at 10 am. If its a no go, you keep the money and we forget we ever had this conversation.'

She nodded, turned and left. He watched her go with a bemused expression on his face, his eyes slowly turning thoughtful. He rubbed his chin, leaned over and grabbed the phone.

They were in Ned Peters living room chewing the fat. Around the room sat Ned, in a rocking-chair in the corner, Anita on the couch, while Calver and Kelly Phillips, journalist from the Tennessean, sat at the desk. Displayed on the desk-top screen was the finished Clemency Plea that Kelly had just finished reading.

'Wow!' she said. 'That's sure different.'

'Yeah, and Daddy loves it,' Anita said. 'He didn't want another, "Oh, please help me, mastuh, you gotta spare me cause my life's been so hard," bullshit'.

'So he wants it to go in?' Ned asked from the corner.

'He does,' Calver said. 'And he's happy not to wait for Shapiro.

"Just stick it in now", he said.'

'So what are we waiting for?' Anita asked. 'Lets shove it to the Governor.'

'Okay, we can do that right now by email, with a hard copy in the post,' Calver said. 'But I've asked Kelly here because I want to coordinate how we release it to the media, and which media. You got any thoughts on that, Kelly? So we can get maximum impact, try and put pressure on the Governor?'

'Lets get it to folks in the Occupy Movement,' Anita said. 'I still got some contacts. And like the yellow jacket French folk, the gilets jaunes'

'That's good, Anita,' Kelly said. 'Although not sure the story will have much traction internationally, but we can try. What the hell.' She turned to Calver. 'I say, get it in to the governor now. I'll run it today as an exclusive, and then I can feed it out to the big boys around the country. Meantime, Anita can do the same with alternative media online, and go to her contacts in the protest movement.'

Calver nodded. 'Sounds like a plan. Lets get to it.'

In the diner downtown where they'd first met, Fingers and Pascal were catching up. Pascal was on the phone, talking to Mercy. The police had just left her home, having taken a full statement. She sounded worn out, but relieved.

'How were the cops? How they treat you?' Pascal asked her.

'They were okay. Don't think the detective assigned knew Scooter, and I don't think they'd got there head around what they found at the apartment yet. But I suppose that will come.'

'Yeah, look, best to talk face to face.'

'I agree, and that's why I phoned. I've taken the day off work, and I'd really like to thank you properly, for what you've done. So, I was wondering if you'd come for dinner tonight?'

Pascal thought for a moment. Too early for the cops to be thinking about tapping phones or surveillance, if they were going to go down that route, so probably okay for now. 'That would be nice, Mercy. What time d'you want me there?'

'Say, seven?'

'See you then, ciao.'

She looked up to find Fingers watching her. This afternoon he was sporting a blue bandanna with white spots.

'What?'

'I saw the news, and the pictures,' he said. 'That scary traffic cop found at the scene of a gruesome murder, and apparently they're saying the guys gonna be a paraplegic?'

'And?' Pascal said, feigning puzzlement. 'Sounds like fate caught up with him. Listen, Fingers, how you getting on with getting into that mainframe?'

'Change the subject, why don't you,' he said. 'Okay, maybe its better you don't tell me nothing, or you might have to kill me, right?' He laughed. She didn't. 'Okay, lighten up. On the mainframe, it's no problema, man. I spent the last few days running queries to identify the structure of their database and searching for sensitive, personally identifiable information within their system,' he said, leaning forward, his eyes lighting up as he got into the technical detail. 'Once I'd accessed files of interest, I stored the stolen information in temporary output files, compressed and divided the files, and ultimately I've been able to download and exfiltrate the data from their network to my anonymous computer.'

Pascal nodded. 'Impressive. Not sure what it means, but do they know what you've been doing? Can they track it, or you?'

'What, you think I'm some kind of dummy?' he said. 'To obfuscate my location I routed all the traffic through 14 servers located in 5 different countries, used encrypted communication channels within their network to blend in with normal network activity, and deleted compressed files and wiped log files on a daily basis to completely eliminate records of my activity.'

Pascal stifled a grin. 'I hesitate to ask such a question after all that, but, are you in?' she said.

'What d'you think I was just telling you? Yes, I'm in.' He looked down at his phone on the table as it buzzed once. He checked the screen, reading something.

Pascal, looking out the window with a faraway look in her eyes, said, 'Fingers, you're pretty amazing with all that computer internet encryption jazz, so I've got a question for you. Something I been thinking about for a while.'

'Shoot.'

'Could you hack into the bank, thats GMB's bank accounts, and those of the CEO de Masi?'

Finger's frowned. 'Be tough. I could try. See, main street banks are crap, like the Federal government, but investment banks have some of the best encryption and defense systems in the world. I'll see what I can do.'

'Good. You mentioned the federal government being not so hot on security. Could you hack into like for Food Stamps or similar. See, in the UK, social security is often paid direct to the receivers bank account. I'm wondering if we could maybe hack in, and find out all those bank accounts?'

Fingers watched her for a moment, his eyes going wide. 'If you're thinking what I think you're thinking, you are fucking stone crazy.'

'I know, but can you do it?'

He blew out some air. 'I'll give it a try, but I'm not going back to jail.'

'No one's asking you to. Why d'you keep looking at your phone?'

He picked it up and looked closer. 'Because I just got my money back.'

'What d'you mean?'

'My 500 bucks of Bitcoin has just been returned.'

As he finished speaking the burner in Pascals bag began to buzz. She grabbed it out, checked the number, and connected. 'Mr Irving? I was going to call you.'

'Come to my warehouse tonight at 7 and we'll talk,' he said.

'I have a dinner date. Make it 6 and we're on?'

Silence, then, '6, it is.' The phone clicked off.

Pascal texted Mercy to say she would be a little late for dinner. She told Fingers to keep working and that they'd meet up the next day, then she left.

On arrival Irving patted her down again and then led her into the warehouse. It was filled with building materials, bricks, slabs of concrete, timber, some on pallets, other smaller items stored on shelving that ran in rows over a large part of the interior. At the side a bench, presumably where orders were taken; a couple of chairs had been pulled up to it. Irving gestured to them and they each took one.

'I checked you out,' he said.

'And?'

'On such a cursory examination, you look solid, but we're still looking.'

'We?'

'Yeah. We need to get something straight here. If we're going to talk seriously, you don't need to know shit about me, or who I may be talking to. And remember, Rahman has a long way to go before he gets anywhere near the death house. This is not urgent for us, but if you have some ideas and contacts, assets, then we might be interested.'

'Fair enough,' Pascal said. He was right. She was at their mercy in terms of time, so they could afford to be cagey and drive a hard bargain, but what choice did she have? If things went bad, she had to be ready. That meant keeping all options open and running.

'Another warning,' he said. 'I'm British and I read about you, couple years back saving the Queen in that bombing thing. We know you were in British Intelligence and I'm sure you still have contacts which is a plus and a minus. If you think you can parlay this into something you can trade with them, forget it. We'd take you out like swatting a fly.'

'Understood. I have no such intentions, and what could I give them anyway? But let me ask you something, or a couple things really. Can you get access to explosives, firearms - heavy duty - maybe helicopters, drones. And have you ever considered trying to spring him yourself?'

Irving got up and walked over to a pallet of timber. He ran his hand along the newly planed surface, lifting his finger to examine the dust. He turned back. 'The answers yes to both. On the ordnance side, yes, if its justified and required by the plan. And yes, of course we looked at ways Rahman might be set free.'

'Did you work up any kind of viable plan?'

'We kicked some ideas around. Trouble is, you need some kind of edge to have any chance of succeeding. I reckon chances are probably 70/30 against. And in Ritter's case, the clocks just about run down, so security will be even tighter.'

Pascal smiled. 'So, if its a suicide mission, presumably its right up your boys' street?' she said.

He also smiled, thinly. 'I sense a residual animus festering within you, to us and our cause.'

'I don't agree with killing innocent people,' she said. 'And that's another thing, if we join forces, there will be no killing.'

'In an ideal world, yes, but no plan survives first contact with the enemy. Earlier, I mentioned needing to have an edge to have any chance of succeeding. Do you have one?'

It was Pascal's turn to get up and wander around. She lifted a breeze block and hefted it, wondering what to tell the guy. Key, get him on board so he'd commit right now, and they could start detailed planning. 'I believe so. I can access the Tennessee Corrections

Department mainframe hub. That means we can send messages, corrupt instructions, control rota's, lock-downs and a load of other things I haven't even thought about.'

'I don't think that's enough on its own. It only needs a human to override anything you might do remotely.'

'That maybe so. But I have an ace in the hole. Someone on the inside.'

He looked up and met Pascal's eyes. 'Now, you have my interest,' he said. He reached under the bench and pulled out a lap-top and a cheap burner-phone that looked new.

They spoke for around 90 minutes.

It was 8.15 pm when Pascal knocked on Mercy's door. She'd spent fifteen minutes casing the joint, checking for surveillance. It looked clean.

After hugging Pascal, Mercy handed her a bottle of beer and led her into the living room where a table had been set. Pascal breathed in deeply, smelling the aroma seeping from the kitchen. 'Smells good,' she said.

'Fried chicken in a Cayenne paste, recipe handed down by my momma. You sit and I'll bring it in.'

As they ate, the conversation was sparse and they avoided talking about Scooter or the police. Mercy talked some more about herself, but then started asking questions about Pascal which caused her to clam up and start trying to move the conversation onto other topics. As the meal finished they moved to the couch and settled down.

'Any more from the police?' Pascal asked.

'They want me to go downtown tomorrow for some more questions, but other than that, nothing. I'm a bit surprised really,' she said, her face looking anxious. 'I mean Donna's murder has been all over the media. From the leaks quoted, story is, Scooter was called to the house, found an intruder who attacked him and then fled the scene?'

Pascal got up and went over to the mantelpiece to look at a framed photograph of a fresh faced middle aged woman with a passing resemblance to Mercy.

'My Mom,' she said.

Looks nice,' Pascal murmured.

'She was, but weak like me, especially when it came to men. Courtney, why d'you think Scooter hasn't tried to name you? The leak in the media is saying the intruder was male?'

'I don't know,' she replied, sitting down next to Mercy. 'I'm guessing he's got some kind of plan in play. Don't forget, he's got to avoid getting nailed for the murder, and that's not easy even with the police on his side, so he's got to be very careful about what he says. He may think involving me, although easy, is really not the best play, because if push came to shove, I could tell them exactly what happened, with timings and evidence. Big risk, and he's not a stupid guy.'

Mercy leaned her head back against the rest. She was sipping red wine from a glass and her eyes had turned pensive. 'Courtney, I know what you want,' she said tentatively, turning to look into Pascal's eyes. 'You don't have to lie about who you are, or your past. You've set me free, and I owe you plenty. You asked whether I would want to go back and do what you did to Scooter, to the guy killed my mother? Well, the answers, yes, in spades. You did what had to be done. Any way you cut it, I owe you, big time. What's it worth to get your life back and be freed from constant, grinding terror? Everything.'

Pascal held her eyes, at a loss how to react. She felt a little bit dirty, as she had done before on occasion when she had to use people. 'I don't know how to answer you, Mercy,' she said quietly. 'I'm not good with people. I'm a loner, some say asocial, even a sociopath, so its hard for me to feel too much guilt when I do bad things. How do you know about me? What do you know?'

Mercy leaned over and embraced Pascal, kissing her gently on the lips. 'Hush. Believe it or not, I know how to use google, and talk to people and put two and two together. And there's quite a lot about you from the UK, about saving the Queen from a bomb plot. Clue, you have worked extensively for a British attorney, Jonas Calver, who now practices in New York, and you still work for him on occasion. You're currently working for him on the Floyd Ritter death row case. I work for the correctional facility at Riverbend that holds him and are shortly due to carry out his execution. How am I doing so far?' she asked gently.

Pascal looked forlorn, a bit like a child caught out misbehaving. Mercy giggled. 'It's okay, Courtney. I don't bite. But I would like to know what you would like me to do for you, and if I do something, will I go to prison? Lose my great new life before its even started?'

Pascal's hard eyes went soft. Mercy watched, then leaned over and kissed her again, gently moving her lips over Pascal's face. Pascal did not resist.

<h1 style="text-align:center">CHAPTER TWENTY-SEVEN</h1>

As Mercy slowly awoke, early morning sunlight dappled across her face through the curtains fluttering in the bedroom window. She smiled as she turned on her side, then blinked as she took in the sight of Pascal sitting by the side of the bed, fully dressed.

'Good morning,' Pascal said. 'You were sleeping so peacefully, I didn't want to wake you.'

'You have to go?' Mercy asked.

'Yes, I'm afraid so. Look,' Pascal said, her face brightening. 'Put on a gown. I'll make us some coffee as we need to talk.'

A few minutes later they sat at the kitchen table, each with a mug, Mercy looking down into hers, deep in thought.

'Mercy, you mustn't get too attached to me,' Pascal said. She reached across the table and took Mercy's chin in her hand, lifting her face. 'There's a whole world out there, and no Scooter to bird-dog you. You're free. But right now, I need your help.'

Mercy nodded. 'So this was what? A one-night stand?'

'I don't know.' Pascal sighed. 'Look, when I came here last night I had no intention that we should….That things should happen the way they did, but they did, and it was wonderful. I told you before, I'm not good at this.'

'No, you're really not, are you.' Mercy got up, went around and hugged Pascal and kissed her on the lips, then went back and sat down.

'What was that for?' Pascal asked.

'Because for all your hard talk, underneath you're really just a sweet and vulnerable idiot. So, now, what do you want to talk about?'

'Well, firstly, from now on, we must not contact each other, other than by pre-agreed means. Thats not just because of Riverside, its also because the police may start watching you, tapping your phone, if they don't believe your story about Donna. I don't think they will, but they might. Get a cheap burner and only use to communicate with me, and only when its urgent.'

'Check,' Mercy said, smiling.

'This isn't a joke, Mercy.'

'I love it when you get angry. Your eyes go real cold and scary.'

'Mercy, you really need to take this seriously.'

'Okay, okay,' she said, putting on a mock serious expression.

'In fact, you mentioned scary. Well, I'll tell you scary. A guy named Cimino. Its unlikely you'll have any contact with him, but if he does turn up, be very careful. Don't believe any story he tells you and get away from him as soon as you can. You're life may depend on it.'

Pascal's words seemed to be getting through to Mercy. She nodded, looking somber. 'I understand. So I'll know, what does this guy look like.'

Pascal described Cimino. 'Before I go,' she added, 'I'd like you to run over everything you can tell me about Riverside. Internal procedures, layouts, manning levels, the works. I don't know yet if we're even going to try anything, so this may all be just a lot of hot air, but I need to know. And, lastly, have you met Floyd Ritter?'

'Yeah, I have. Quite a few times. He's a sweet guy, and I never had any problem with him. One of those who doesn't deserve to die, compared to some of the monsters they've got in there. But its the system.'

For the next hour or so Mercy talked. Pascal listened intently, occasionally asking questions. When they finished, Pascal left, but not before an emotional Mercy had clung to her, lingeringly kissing her, begging her to be careful. Pascal had slowly extracted herself from the embrace and told Mercy to take care as well, and be very careful. Then she left.

Lloyd de Masi stood at the grand windows of his office, looking down on Wall Street, phone held tightly to his ear as he spoke to his attorney. Grace Van Zim sat behind him, other side of his desk, staring at his tensed and hunched back as he spoke into the phone with barely restrained fury. At the side of the desk one of the screens carried CNN live, and half Van Zim's attention was on the evolving story of Floyd Ritter's Clemency Plea and the explosive allegations contained in it that the News outfit were covering in gory detail.

'Marty, you better fucking do something,' de Masi said into the phone. 'Or you're fucking history. Know what I can see from my window, huh? Fucking protesters with banners and placards. And you can bet there'll more. What you gonna do? This, this fucking Calver? What's he untouchable? He can spread a load of false stories about me, and the bank, accusing us of God knows what, murder, whatever, and we just gotta take it? Fucking do something, and get back to me within the hour,' he snapped, his last words delivered almost in a scream as he clicked the phone off and turned back to Grace.

'Boss, they're being very careful to say the allegations are uncorroborated at this stage?' Van Zim said

'What? That's meant to make me feel good? Where's Cimino?'

'Tennessee.'

'Its the girl, Pascal,' he said, almost to himself. 'She's the one producing all this shit. Should have dealt with her before. Mistake to let it run. We need to take her out, permanently, now. Get onto Cimino. No,' he said holding his hand up, thinking. 'No, wait. Get Cimino up here to report to me and I'll brief him direct. I'm moving out to the Hampton's while this shit blows over, so send him out there.'

'Boss,' Van Zim said, acknowledging the order. 'I'll call him now.'

de Masi looked back out of the window. 'If that crowd gets any bigger, get onto NYPD and tell them to clear them out. Also, beef up our security force, here and especially out at the Hampton's.'

'I'm on it, boss,' she said, getting to her feet and scurrying away.

Down on Wall Street Anita stood in a smallish group of protesters that seemed to be getting bigger all the time. Maybe it was only in dribs and drabs, a single person here, then a couple, then maybe a group of three, but it was growing. Anita felt exhilarated. At last she was doing something positive for her father. Standing up and telling the whole world about his plight - and they were starting to listen. She looked up at the gleaming skyscrapers around her, monuments to greed, built on the suffering of the downtrodden, for the benefit of the few.

She looked over at one of the placards and smiled again as she read the legend, printed in huge red letters as if written in blood: "Free Innocent Floyd Ritter." Another, "Tear down the walls of Capitalism." "Down with Banksters." "Gaol them All."

Her phone buzzed and she clapped it to her ear. It was one of her friends from the old Occupy outfit, now living in Tennessee, whom she'd spoken to before she left for New York. 'Wow, Anita,' the girl said. 'I'm watching your Wall Street protest on the news here. Its awesome.'

'Thanks Maria. Its really building. I never expected to get this many folks.'

'Say, we were thinking down here, in the group. Should we go out and protest at Riverside Corrections, like you on Wall Street?'

Anita turned it over in her mind. Maybe she better run it past Calver, but then time was slipping. 'Yeah, go for it,' she said. 'But only if you can get a reasonable number. Couple of stragglers with a foghorn and a tatty poster won't cut it down there. We need numbers.'

'Got it. I'll get back to you. Meantime, give them hell, Anita,' she said ringing off.

As she put her phone back and looked up, a microphone was shoved in her face. It was a TV news reporter with a guy behind her running the camera. The woman was tall and willowy with blonde hair and a hatchet face. She thrust the microphone forward some more, invading Anita's personal space. 'I believe you are Floyd Ritter's daughter?' she said.

'That's right. Names Anita,' she replied coolly

'Well, Anita, tell us why you're here, disrupting the business of

Wall Street.'

'Read the posters,' she replied. 'For too long the Banksters have got away with corruptly stealing our money, even whilst they drown in free money from the never still printing presses of the Federal Reserve. Even that's not enough for some of them. I watched Lloyd de Masi come to work this morning. He's the mighty CEO of Greenberg Metro bank. He's up there now,' she said, pointing up at the building. 'Probably watching us. De Masi and his goon, Cimino, destroyed my family, murdered my mother and framed my father. Unlike Maximus in the great movie, Gladiator, I doubt that I will get justice. That's why we're here, though. My father, Floyd Ritter, is on death row in Tennessee, about to be executed by the state for a crime he didn't commit. But now we know who did commit it, and yet still my father must die. Do you think that's right?'

'Well, the evidence in your fathers clemency plea has yet to be corroborated, and earlier the Supreme court of Tennessee rejected your appeal for a new trial based on new evidence?' the reporter replied.

'They didn't even look at it. The Tennessean law enforcement and justice system is as corrupt as that in Washington and Wall Street. My father never had a chance against that.'

'So what's your answer, Anita? Chaos?' the reporter asked.

'You still don't get it, do you?' Anita said. 'The judicial murder of my father is just one small part of the problem. If things don't change, at some point, the people in this country will rise up and reach for the pitchforks, as other peoples have done in earlier times. The Russian and the Chinese peoples in the last century had revolutions, and what was the first thing they did? That's right. They killed all the landlords. In our modern world it will be the rentiers, the billionaires sucking up all the pennies from the honest toil of all the people in this land, who are then left with just the scraps to live on. I believe that rentier class should be very scared for the future.'

As she finished speaking the sound of a police siren could be heard in the distance. Up ahead the flashing blue light of a squad car and then a massing group of police officers could be seen advancing towards them. A fellow protester whispered to her, 'you're the spokesperson, so we need to get you out of here. We can regroup in the park and then come back when they've gone.'

'Okay,' Anita said reluctantly. As she moved, the line of police began to advance on the crowd in a menacing fashion.

Later that day a sizable troop of removal vans and trucks could be seen meandering up the private road to Lloyd de Masi's Hampton's mansion, as his people moved his operation from Wall Street. Later still, mid-afternoon, Floyd himself flew in by helicopter, landing on the lush green grass just outside the front door. After jumping out and running in a crouch under the swinging rotor blades, he entered the house, moving straight up the wide sweeping staircase to his private office. He made himself a large brandy and then called in his guy running security at the mansion. As he waited, he watched the latest news on the Wall Street protest, and then came Anita Ritter's interview down on the street, recorded earlier in the day.

He watched incredulous as the girl looked right into the camera and called him a murderer. He coughed into his Brandy, his hands clenching and un-clenching as the rage rippled through him. Then the security guy was there, standing in front of him, waiting for instructions.

De Masi came out of his rage. He looked at the guy. 'Okay, you've seen the news. We got a war on, and we gotta protect ourselves. I want security beefed up tenfold, you got that?'

'Yes sir, I'll got on it straight away.'

'I want razor wire, dogs, cameras and guns. Regular patrols all over. The grounds, the house, outbuildings, everything. Comprende?'

'Yes sir.'

'And I want new, huge signs put up, saying this is Private Property and that trespassers will be shot, and I mean that, soldier. I want your boys to have shoot to kill orders. Any blow-back, I will back them 100%. If those protesters turn up here, I want us to give them a welcome they'll never forget, you got that?'

'Sir, yes sir,' the ex-marine shouted like he was back in Iraq, big smile on his face. Now maybe they'd get some excitement, rather then walking around like they were park rangers.

'Good,' De Masi said. 'Dismissed. Send Cimino in.'

De Masi sipped more Brandy as Cimino entered and took a seat across from him.

'We shoulda burned them all, Cimino,' de Masi said. 'The Ritter girl, Calver the lawyer, and most of all, Pascal.'

'I agree, boss, but we are where we are.'

'Okay, well do you know where she is right now?'

'No, we weren't tracking her. As we discussed before, we were just going to watch while the clock ran down until they fry the nigger. But, I can find her in about five minutes if we need to, with the help of

Gillespie the cop.'

De Masi leaned back in his recliner, sipping his drink. His head hurt and his mind was spinning. He needed this all to end so he could get back to making money. He looked up. 'Question, Cimino: is there any chance whatsoever that the Governor will grant clemency, or the court grant a last minute appeal?'

'My sources say no. None.'

De Masi nodded. 'But what if this protest goes national in a big way? Might that sway them?'

'I don't think so, boss,' Cimino said. 'I don't think it will matter. See, they're real insular down there. Lots of inbreeding. Maybe that's why they're all so fucking dumb. But it also means they don't like folks outside trying to tell them what to do. No, the nigger will fry. I'd bet a buck on it. Then again, you can't plan for the unexpected, something coming out of left-field.'

De Masi rubbed his face. 'I agree. Hunt her down and kill her.'

Cimino smiled for the first time. He languidly rose out of the chair and adjusted his suit so that it sat right. He looked down at de Masi. 'Relax, boss. That chick is history.'

CHAPTER TWENTY-EIGHT

Three hectic days had elapsed and Pascal again sat across from Christoff in the same bar, in fact in the same booth they had used before. She felt like she was re-living a recurring dream. Even the same colored lights seemed to play across his face as he sat there calmly listening to her. As she drew to a close, he tilted up his tablet and showed her the screen. 'Its the Tennessee Corrections Department's new Death Row Protocol for Riverbend,' he said. 'Hot off the press and quite a read at 90 pages.'

'As I'm a little pushed for time, just give me the skinny, will you?'

'Sure,' he said. 'So, the killing, or execution if you like, takes place around 7 p.m. Thursday. Its Tuesday night now, so you can follow the count-down. He will have been moved from his cell to the death watch area where he will be housed in a cell a few feet away from the execution chamber. Its under 24-hour surveillance. On the day of execution the prison staff test the closed circuit television and audio equipment used to broadcast the execution to witnesses in the prison. Make sure the crowd get glorious technicolor while munching on their Big Macs.

'While that's going on, other staff go to the secure storage facility to retrieve the LIC's, or lethal injection chemicals. These comprise three drugs: Midazolam, Vecuronium Bromide and Potassium Chloride.'

'What's the set-up there?' Pascal asked. 'Say, if the drugs don't work?'

'Never fear, my sweet,' Christoff said. 'They have plenty of back-up. The syringes are prepared one at a time, with a witness observing as they are filled. There must be enough drug to have two complete sets of nine syringes. The set they use is color coded red, with the back-up color coded blue.

'Okay, to get back to the procedure on the day, at 5 p.m. the state execution team arrives at the executioner waiting area, and their identities are to be known by the fewest number of staff necessary. At the same time, the official witnesses will be escorted through the formal prison checkpoint to a waiting area, where they will stay until its time to move to the execution viewing room.

'By this time, the guy tasked with monitoring and ensuring the anonymity of the execution team, the lethal injection recorder, will be in the execution chamber with an emergency medical technician. They check everything there, including making sure the phones work. Same time a member of the medical examiners staff and a doctor go to the capital punishment garage to await the death.'

'So what time does it kick off?'

'7 p.m. the extraction team goes to Floyd's death watch cell. Floyd will be dressed in a shirt, cotton trousers and either cotton socks or cloth house shoes. He must approach the door and have cuffs put on, then must move to the back of the cell and put his hands on the wall above his head. The team are prepared to use force here if there is a problem. Once out of his cell he is placed on a gurney, under restraint, and rolled into the execution chamber where the IV team establish an intravenous fluid line into both arms.

'The attorney generals rep and Floyd's attorney remain in the chamber until the IV's are secured and Floyd's hands taped, palms up, to the arms of the gurney. After that's done the victim's family and official witnesses are moved to the witness room, where the CCTV and audio systems are activated.'

'So what time does the party really start?' Pascal asked, checking her watch.

'Essentially, when they open the blinds at 7.10 p.m. revealing the execution chamber. Warden makes a last call to the Department of Correction Commissioner to make sure there has been no last minute stay or clemency. If that's a no, Floyd will be asked if he has any final words or statement to make. When that's done, they kill him.'

'Come on, Christoff, quit playing around,' she said. 'Take me through the injection routine.'

'Okay,' he said, thin smile. 'But this is thirsty work.'

She raised her hand to signal the barman for refills.

'Okay, so on the wardens direction, the executioner takes the first red syringe, containing Midazolam, and inserts it by twisting it into one of the IV extension lines. He or she will then exert slow steady pressure on the syringe plunger. Two syringes containing 100 cc of midazolam are dispensed into the arm, followed by a saline flush to clear the IV for the next drug.'

'What if there are problems, like there have been. Horror stories, when it doesn't work?' Pascal asked.

'You're right there. They've had some real humdinger fuck-ups, but that's where the back-up comes in. See, when they first start syringing, they have to check for swelling around the IV entry, or if there is resistance in the plunger. If so, they are directed to pull back on the plunger. And if the extension line doesn't fill up with blood as its supposed to, the executioner must stop using the line.'

'That's where the back-up comes in, right?'

'That's right. If red one fails, they restart the process using the IV line in the other arm, and the blue coded back-up syringes.

'After the midazolam has been administered, they must check if he's still conscious by brushing the back of a hand over Floyd's eyelashes, loudly calling his name twice and twisting his shoulder. If he's still responsive, they must administer the back-up syringes. If he is not responsive, they move onto the next stage which is administering the second two drugs.

'So, then, its basically rinse and repeat; two syringes of vercuronium bromide, to stop his lungs, followed by a saline flush; and two syringes of potassium chloride, to stop his heart.

'If all goes well, ha ha, five minutes later, the blinds are closed and the CCTV disengaged. A doctor will enter and examine the body and, nine out of ten times, declare death. The warden will then announce, "The sentence of Floyd Ritter has been carried out. Please exit."

'The witnesses will be escorted out of the prison while the medical examiners staff will remove the restraints and move the body into the vehicle located in the capital punishment garage, for onward transmission to any location where funeral arrangements have been put in place. And that, essentially, is that,' he said, concluding with a stiff shot of rum.

For a while Pascal sat silent, thinking. She began collecting up her stuff. 'Thanks for that, Christoff,' she said. 'One last thing. If you wanted to notify the FBI, or say, Homeland Security, about an imminent terrorist threat to Riverbend Correctional Facility, to cause maximum mayhem. How would you do it?'

This time it was Christoff who sat silent for a while, watching her through the constantly shifting light patterns, his thoughts far away. His eyes came back into focus and he smiled grimly. 'I'd anonymously tip-off Homeland Security, with some real, checkable meat, 10 minutes before it goes down,' he said. 'Then you could, if you were real crazy, pretend you were the FBI coming to the rescue.'

She smiled and clinked her empty glass against his. 'Who said I was crazy?' she said, getting to her feet and walking away. His mouth hung open for a beat, then he laughed.

The whole team had convened at Ned Peters place, and around the chaotic living room sat Calver, Anita, Pascal, Joel and Ned himself. It was dusk, a waning sun running its last light through the windows, and the conversation around the large room was muted.

'Are you okay, Anita? Calver said, looking over at her sitting in the corner, shadowed so you couldn't really see her face. 'You've been so quiet?'

'I guess I never really thought it would come to this. My daddy was so strong all his life. And now he's got, what?' she asked, lifting her arm and looking at her watch. 'Just 48 hours left on God's earth.'

'Hey, don't give up,' Ned said. 'We still got the Governor and the Federal appeals if he blows us out. And that protest thing has taken on a life of its own, little pockets all over the country.'

'That's right,' Calver said. 'And they're protesting in numbers outside Riverbend, and that's got to put extra pressure on the Governor.'

'You don't know this state,' Joel said. 'That banking crap in the clemency plea will have just put his back up.'

Calver's phone lit up before he could reply. It was a text message. He read the screen. 'It's from Shapiro,' he said. 'Governor is about to announce his response to the clemency plea.'

Joel picked up the TV remote from the coffee table and switched it on. He scrolled channels until he found a local news station. It had a picture of Floyd Ritter behind the newscaster as the audio filtered in.

"State Governor Randal Lee's office have just released their response to the clemency plea filed by Floyd Ritter's attorneys," the news reader said, looking down as she read the incoming report. "The statements says: 'The justice system has extensively reviewed Floyd Ritter's case over the course of a number of years, including recent additional reviews and rulings by the Tennessee Supreme Court. I must and will uphold the law. The recent protests and unrest we have seen around this state cannot change that, and they are not justified. Accordingly, the judgment and sentence stand, and I will not intervene in this case.'"

As the TV went blank and silent, Anita got up and went to the window. She stood with her back to the room, watching as the sun began to sink below the tree line. Pascal went over and embraced her.

'Its not over yet,' she said. 'You got to keep believing.'

'I told you,' Joel said, looking hard at Calver.

'You know, Joel,' Calver said. 'Ned's dug out the written notice of dismissal of the civil suit against the bank, and I guess you know who signed it?'

At the window Anita turned back to look at Joel.

He laughed, but it sounded false. He looked around the room, but his eyes kept moving back to Anita. 'Yeah, I signed off on it,' he said. 'So what? Daddy's attorneys said it was the right thing to do. And Daddy didn't know shit, not with his head up his ass. He didn't say it, but I know Daddy was scared they'd come after us again if we didn't stop the court case.' He looked at Anita, eyes full of pleading. 'You gotta believe me, sis.'

'What's the date of the notice of dismissal, Ned?' Pascal asked from the window.

Peters rummaged amongst some papers and held up a document which he peered at. '26th September,' he said

'What is this, some type of kangaroo court?' Joel said, anger rising in his voice.

'I don't like to snoop on people I consider friends,' Pascal said. 'Especially when they're going through a rough patch.' She took a sheet of paper out of her bag and walked over to the table and laid it down. 'Don't ask me how I got this, but its your bank statement, Joel, for September of that year. On the 20th you received payment of $50,000. Maybe you can explain where it came from and what it was for?'

'I don't have to explain anything to you people,' he said looking around at them with a show of bravado, but his eyes looked hunted.

'Yes, you do,' Anita said quietly. 'You owe it to me, but you also owe it to everyone else in this room. These people have put their asses on the line for our family. So spit it out, Joel. Or get the fuck out of here and don't come back.'

Joel turned slowly, panning the room, all eyes on him. He seemed to hesitate, breath catching in his throat, then he was moving to the sideboard and splashing Wild Turkey into a large tumbler and throwing it down his throat. He seemed hyper, walking to an empty chair and throwing himself into it. He leaned forwards, hands hanging down between his knees, eyes blank.

'They said it was for the best, for daddy,' he said, his voice a dull monotone. 'Shapiro came to me and laid it all out. We drop the civil suit against the bank quietly, no fuss. Its what Floyd wanted really, but he wouldn't say, specially to his own family. Shapiro said there was some bunce in it as well. He knew I was scraping by in New York, and it was just to tide me over, even a loan if I wanted.'

He looked up at Anita. 'I was desperate, sis. Daddy never gave me anything. It was always you he looked to. Always you. Anyway, I thought it was a one-off thing and it was for the best. We should just concentrate on getting Daddy free. But when Jonas and Courtney got involved in this, Shapiro started putting pressure on me, to spy on you. He said, if I didn't, he would tell you about the payment. It was that simple. I was trapped. I swear I did my best to try and cover, but I had to give them bits and pieces to be believable. I'm so sorry, sis.'

Ned was the first to break the silence, with a chuckle. 'Well, you ain't the first to fall for it. And I'm sure you won't be the last. But I don't think you done too much harm, son. And now its out in the open, we know where we stand.'

Joel looked towards Calver, hope in his expression.

Calver nodded. 'I think you and your sister have a lot to talk about, Joel, and maybe you should do it now.'

He got up out the chair. 'Sis?' he said, gesturing towards the kitchen.

She got up and went over to him. The slap seemed to come out of nowhere, Joel rocking back on his feet, hand up to his bleeding lip, shock in his eyes. After a moment, he said, 'I guess I deserved that.'

She glared at him a moment, then walked into the kitchen, Joel trailing behind her.

Pascal said, as the kitchen door closed behind them, 'is it true Floyd's chosen the electric chair, rather than lethal injection?'

'Yeah,' Ned replied. 'Trouble is, he's not eligible, because his so called crime was committed after 1999, so he's stuck with the lethal injection. Might give us a "cruel and unusual punishment," angle for appeal to the Supreme Court, though.'

'So what will be happening to Floyd right now?' Calver asked.

'Floyd will be in lock-down because its his final 72 hours, so they will have already moved him to a cell next to the execution chamber. And they'll have asked him what kind of a last meal he wants for his twenty bucks. I'd have me a nice big steak, I think.'

'What's the chances of the Federal court intervening now and granting a stay?' Pascal asked.

Calver looked at the kitchen door, making sure it was closed. 'Not far above zero, I'd guess,' he said. 'We'll chuck everything at them, but history's against us. We just need to keep on fighting.

Speaking of which,' he said, turning to Ned. 'Maybe we better hunker down and see what we can come up with?'

'I'll leave you to it, then,' Pascal said, shrugging into her jacket and taking out her car keys.

'Where you going?' Calver called after her.

'Later,' she replied as the door slammed behind her.

As that door closed, the kitchen door opened and Joel and Anita came back, Joel looking subdued, Anita grim faced. Calver quelled the question forming on his lips, figuring it was none of his business. Anita picked up the TV remote and switched it back on. 'So lets see how the Governors statement is going down,' she said, scrolling channels on the screen until she came to a news channel covering the story. As she upped the volume the correspondent was discussing the protest going on outside the Riverbend Correctional Facility, showing pictures of the large group of demonstrators there. There was also one protester supporting the execution, saying to camera, there would be many more as the clock wound down.

'Who's he kidding,' Anita said. 'I need to get down there.'

Then the camera was showing footage on Wall Street, outside Greenberg Metro bank, where numbers were continuing to swell, the narrator saying that anger and numbers were rising as a result of the governors decision to refuse clemency to Floyd Ritter. His voice then took on an urgency as he told his viewers they were cutting to their reporter outside Lloyd de Masi's Hampton's mansion:

......it looks like a stand-off between protesters and de Masi's security staff outside the mansion,' he reported as his cameraman was jostled, producing a shaky run of film.

Anita whistled. 'Wow. I never thought they'd get out there,' she said, her eyes shining.

'Unfortunately, local law enforcement will remove them,' Ned said. 'Those rich folks up there pay a lot for their policing, and they don't like the common peasants dirtying up their playground.'

'Ain't that the truth,' Calver said. He got up and went over to Anita. 'Look, we're working flat out on final appeals to the Supreme Court, but we gotta be realistic. So, we need to make arrangements for who is going to be there at Riverbend with Floyd as this goes down to the wire?'

'I know,' she said. 'Of course I'll be there with him for the final hours.'

'Shapiro says none of their staff need to go as attorney of record, so I'll be going along as well,' Calver said.

'Joel?' Ned asked.

'Yeah,' he said. 'I want to go, but I don't know if I can face it.'

'Where is Courtney?' Anita asked.

'Who knows,' Calver said wistfully.

They sat in Irving's warehouse again, at the same counter. 'Looks like we're on then,' he said, his eyes flat.

Pascal nodded. 'Did you get what I asked you for?'

'No problem,' he said reaching under the counter and lifting out an attache case. He opened it and removed a vial shaped like a test-tube, containing a liquid. 'What's it called it again?'

'Tetrodotoxin.'

'That's right. Kind of death drug, right?' he said, smiling now.

'Voodoo stuff. You want to fill me in on how you plan to use it?'

'Not necessary. Its just to assist me in getting my side to where we'll need to be. You concentrate on your side. I'm not asking you how you're doing it.'

'Fair enough.'

'What about the choppers?'

'Sorted. There's a charter outfit we're using, my backers are tight with. Got two birds for two days, and I got pilots for both.'

'Where are the choppers gonna be parked up?'

Irving gave her a location which she jotted down. She stood up to go. 'I said to you before, I don't want any killing.'

He nodded, smiling. 'My Jihadi brothers are ready to sacrifice all for the cause. We shall do all we can to avoid unnecessary bloodshed.'

Pascal knew that was pure bullshit, but she had to play along for now. 'If the Supreme Court grants a stay, I'm out and you can do what you want,' she said.

'We both know that's not going to happen.'

He was almost certainly right. She grabbed up her bag and left. She guessed it was going to be a long night.

CHAPTER TWENTY-NINE

It was mid-morning and they stood on a raised concrete walkway over a flat tiled area out of which water fountains erupted and children played. Cumberland Park was just up from the river and Mercy had suggested it because it would allow them to mingle with the crowds, if any one were watching. Pascal rested her arms on the raised edge of the walk-way and looked down on the gamboling kids, splashing around and shrieking at each other. Mercy stood next to her.

'We're just like a couple of proud mums looking down at our little darlings,' Mercy said, a tinge of sadness in her voice.

Pascal stole a sideways glance at her. Mercy looked tired. 'You okay?' Pascal asked her.

'So, so,' she said. 'You know, there's a strange atmosphere when we go into lock-down for an execution. Everyone on edge. And those folks outside protesting don't help. Gets like a circus.'

'Well, it'll soon be over.'

'Yeah, one way or the other,' Mercy said, turning slightly to look Pascal in the eye. 'My nerves are screaming and I'm on edge all the time. Keep expecting the cops to come and get me over Scooter, and waiting for you to tell me what you want me to do.'

Pascal reached over and put her hand over Mercy's, resting on the wall, squeezing it gently. 'Mercy, you don't have to help me. I can —'

'Yes, I do, and, and I want to.'

Pascal nodded, her emotions, always so repressed, for once blossomed out and felt mangled and alive. An unusual and unpleasant feeling for her. Inside she was conflicted, guilt over using Mercy, fighting desperation to try and save Floyd.

Mercy squeezed her hand back. 'What do you want me to do?'

Pascal took a breath. 'Can you get access to the LIC's?'

'The lethal injection chemicals?'

'Yeah.'

'Wow,' Mercy said, eyes going wide. Then she laughed lightly. 'Let me get my head around this.'

'Okay, but don't take too long.'

Mercy turned away from the water feature and rested her back against the wall, scanning the sky. The park was busy now. She stood impervious to the bustle around her. She turned and put her hands back on the wall. 'I think I can, yes,' she said.

'You know about the color codes?'

'Of course. Red's the primary, and blue is back-up.'

Pascal turned to look at Mercy, appraising her for a long moment. 'Okay, Mercy,' she said. 'The bag down by my feet is for you. Take it when you leave. If you can get access, tonight, during your shift, here's what I want you to do.'

Fifteen minutes later, Mercy picked up the bag and walked away, leaving Pascal leaning against the wall. Pascal remained there for another fifteen minutes before slowly making her way out of the park to retrieve her car.

As she drove away from the curb, across the street 100 meters down in an unmarked dark car sat Cimino and Gillespie. 'Want me to haul her in?' Gillespie asked

'No,' Cimino said. 'Follow her. Lets see where she goes. Its a shame you lost her in the park, Gillespie, because its obvious she was meeting someone.'

'Hey, no harm done,' Gillespie said with a pained expression. He brightened. 'We can take her down anytime you say. Got her wrapped up tighter than an Egyptian mummy.'

Cimino didn't answer. His words would be wasted on the stupid cop anyway. His mind wandered. The boss had said take her out, but Cimino was intrigued and wanted to discover what she was up to first, so it couldn't hurt to delay things a little. And besides, he was enjoying himself and wanted to savor the hunt.

It took Pascal 15 minutes to pick up the tail, dark car, three vehicles back, two occupants she couldn't identify from that distance. They must have followed from the park, but did they see her meeting Mercy? No way to know, but two in a car suggested not, as unlikely to have more than two bodies on a stakeout, and one would have tracked Mercy if they'd seen her, maybe. She approached traffic lights as they were changing, flooring the accelerator as they hit red, swerving right, horns blaring in her wake as she went through the junction, then taking another tight left, into narrow side streets where she geared up and hit 90, her engine revving and roaring as she shot down the narrow street, people jumping out of the way and shouting. Another tight right, into the curb and engine off. She watched her rear-view mirror, listening to the ticking of the metal as it cooled down.

After fifteen minutes she was sure she'd lost them. She dug out a burner from her bag and called Fingers for an update. She spoke with him for ten minutes, all the time watching her rear-view mirror. When the call finished, she realized she was intensely tired. She needed to get some sleep and recharge her batteries because of what was to come. Floyd would die tomorrow unless she could do something. She checked her watch. Just gone 2 p.m. It would be dangerous to go back to the shack if she was being searched for. She would find a cheap hotel and hole up until nightfall. She dug out her phone and checked for local places. Called one up and booked a night. It was five minutes away. She started the engine and slowly pulled away from the curb into the light afternoon traffic.

As Mercy walked away from the secure storage facility her heart was pounding and her breathing was ragged. She felt a mixture of euphoria and fear. What the hell had happened to her that she could do what she had just done? She guessed the answer was Courtney. The enigmatic and mysterious woman had turned her world upside down and made her feel alive again. Mercy quickened her step as her breathing began to come back to normal. Getting into the secure storage facility had not been difficult. She felt a little ashamed, but not much, and slightly amazed at how easy it had been. She told the guys on the security barriers that the warden had asked her to double check for him, as he didn't want anymore fuck-ups, and the guys had waved her through, simple as that, and in she had gone. Substitution had taken all of fifteen minutes, but now she had the incriminating chemicals in her bag. As she walked along the corridor she checked her watch; 3.10 a.m. It struck her that she was betraying colleagues, but she also knew there was a sizable proportion of staff who really liked Floyd Ritter, and many who didn't believe he deserved to die. The system sucked. How many rich white guys got executed for a knife fight killing? As these thoughts were passing through Mercy's head she rounded a corner and ran smack into her shift supervisor, Bob Krantz, a guy she really didn't like.

Bob was plump with a gleaming white domed head with a few straggles of lank black hair stuck down on it, and thick black framed glasses. He fancied himself as a bit of a lady-killer, and had come on to Mercy a couple of times without any success, and now he didn't like her. His eyes narrowed. 'What are you doing here, Reader?' he asked in his most officious tone, his suspicious eyes taking in the bag in her hand.

If she lied about the warden, he'd check, and she'd be history. And what about Courtney?

'What's in the bag, hon?' he asked. 'If its personal stuff, you know you shouldn't be carrying it around here. Lemme see what you got in there?' He reached for the bag.

Mercy felt she was going to faint, her heart banging even louder. In the background she heard steps approaching fast, and Bob's radio started squawking. Around the corner came an officer. 'Bob, you're needed,' he said, urgency in his voice. 'Attempted suicide, and he may not make it.'

Krantz watched her for a moment, conflicted, wanting to crush her under his heel, but knowing he needed to get to the suicide. 'I find you in an unauthorized area again, Reader, carrying personal stuff, I'll have your badge,' he said. 'Now get outta here.' He turned on his heel and followed the officer.

Mercy half collapsed against the wall, almost hyperventilating. She took a moment to steady her breathing then pushed herself off the wall and began moving. Her shift would be over soon, and she couldn't wait to get out. Her pace quickened.

Forty miles away Pascal shifted the weight on her aching knees. She was kneeling in a ditch and had been for over two hours, watching a silent and deserted airfield. There were a couple of light aircraft and two large hangers, all now shrouded in eerie silent moonlight. It was a little place out in the back of beyond, and she had had trouble finding it from the address Irving had given her. An hour earlier she had watched the two helicopters fly in. The pilots had moved them into one of the hangers, closed the doors, and left in a small white car.

Pascal checked her watch. 3.20 a.m. She was playing a hunch, but it looked like it was a bust. She stirred, ready to leave, but as she stood up, rubbing her aching knees, she heard the faint sound of approaching vehicles. She hunkered down again, retrieving her night vision binoculars. She watched as a two car convoy approached the hangers and parked up. Out of each car came two occupants. They made their way into the hanger containing the choppers, and closed the doors. One of the guys was Irving and she guessed the other three, all of middle eastern appearance, were likely to be his squad for the operation. Pascal reviewed the pictures she had taken, idly scrolling through the faces of the men.

She made herself as comfortable as she could and settled back to wait some more. After forty-five minutes the doors opened and the group departed. Pascal waited another fifteen minutes before rising from the ditch and moving around the perimeter until she came to the hanger containing the choppers. Other than the outer fencing around the airfield, there didn't appear to be any additional security; no CCTV or patrolling guards, and the hanger was not locked. She slipped inside. The lights were on; probably permanently. She studied the two choppers she had seen fly in earlier. There was a smaller blue Bell helicopter she knew she would be riding in, then the larger yellow chopper that looked like an air-sea rescue job, that Irving would be using.

Pascal knew little about helicopters and maybe her hunch was way off beam, but she figured it was better to be safe than sorry. She concentrated on the smaller Bell, starting outside, going over every inch, then moving inside. It took her an hour to find it. It looked like plastique, to be detonated by a radio signal, probably from a cellphone. It was taped into an almost impossible to get to alcove, that would not be looked at on a pre-flight check, and probably not even when the chopper was deep-cleaned. It took Pascal 30 more minutes to delicately remove it from its place, during which she carefully considered what to do with it.

Having weighed the odds and risks, she made a decision. Smiling grimly, she moved to the larger chopper to look for a suitable spot. Lifting up one of the floor plates there was a dark corner where she placed the device. Taking a last look around both choppers, then moving to the door, she checked her watch. It was almost 5 a.m. Within the next 15 hours, unless something happened, Floyd Ritter was going to die. And she needed some shuteye or she wasn't going to make it. She slipped outside and began moving fast, back towards her car, parked up about a mile away.

She came awake with a jolt, her eyes scanning the clock readout: 11.10 a.m. She knew she'd set the alarm for 9.30, but for some reason it hadn't gone off. The blinds were drawn tight and there was virtually no light seeping into the cheap hotel room, but she knew something was wrong. Something had woken her. Her hand moved under the sheet to the cable hand-switch for the bedside lamp. As she clicked it on, the blinds rattled up with a crack, flooding the room with sunlight. Standing beside the window, smiling, was Cimino, casually holding a gun in his hand. She blinked her eyes in the brightness, her mind blank for a moment.

'What's the matter, cupcake? You late for an appointment?' he said, eyebrow raised.

'What is this? What d'you want, Cimino?' she said, her mind grappling with fear and foreboding.

'Oh, just a little talk. Then I thought we might spend the day together, and maybe later, we can celebrate the death of the nigger. We could have a party. A farewell party. What d'you say?'

'I don't think so.'

'Okay. Well, the alternative is I place that soft pillow over your face and put a bullet through your head. How d'you like that?'

'How d'you like to kiss my ass? Is that how you did Mary Ritter and Vincent Fachetti? That's not working out so well for you, is it? And your friend Frank Ross sang like a canary.'

Cimino smiled. 'Yeah, and Frank Ross is wearing concrete boots lying at the bottom of the Cumberland River. And there's room for two down there. You got nothing, and it will pass, when you and the nigger are gone.'

'Fair enough,' Pascal said, trying to think of ways to push the guy, get an edge. But so far he was being real careful, eyes and gun unwavering. 'Look, mind if I get dressed, get some breakfast, coffee? Maybe you'd like some?'

'Sure, why not, since we're here. Put a wrap on, and call down, but don't try to fuck with me—'

'Yeah, I know. You'll blow my head off.'

'You got it.'

She retrieved her nightgown from the floor, wriggled into it and went to the phone. She ordered up a late breakfast of scrambled eggs and bacon, toast and marmalade, and a pot of coffee with two cups. 'You mind if I visit the bathroom? Come and watch me take a dump if you like. I've heard psycho's often get off on weird stuff like that; you know, toilet sex, golden showers. That float your boat, Cimino?' she asked with sweet smile.

Cimino smiled easily, completely relaxed, which irked her some, but she didn't let it show.

'Go ahead,' he said. 'I've checked out the bathroom, but leave the door open. Oh, and you mention sexual matters, well, I've got a real treat for you today. My good friend chief Gillespie is just dying to meet you. Like all peckerhead cops in this hellhole state, he has a kind of after hours private cops club where they all get together to have their fun, and guess what? You're going to be the big attraction today.'

He carried on smiling, watching her eyes, and she couldn't help the slightest of flickers passing through them before her self-control kicked in. But she knew he'd seen it.

'Go on now,' he said chidingly. 'You make yourself pretty for the boys.'

She moved into the cubicle. As she sat on the toilet seat she kept the fear at bay by trying to analyze her situation. The clock was now running down on speed. They'd be injecting Floyd in about 7 hours, and unless she could get out quick, it was over. Floyd would need the Supreme Court to do what they almost never did. She racked her brains. Her cellphones and gun were in the car, parked out on the street. She'd been so tired when she got back from the airfield she'd left her bag out there, almost sleepwalking to her room. It was a plus Cimino didn't have her phones, but having a spare gun around would have been nice. She washed her hands and face in cold water, trying to shock herself awake and into action, but it wasn't working. She'd just have to be hyper-awake, watching for that one tiny chance - and it would have to be a tiny chance with a guy like Cimino - and then take it. But would it come?

She moved back into the room to find Cimino eating some toast. 'Tuck in,' he said, gesturing at the table.

She sat down and began to eat. The scrambled eggs were cooked near perfect, not too runny, and the bacon was nice and juicy. The coffee was excellent too. She sipped some as Cimino's phone began playing an aria that sounded like Nessun dorma.

He grabbed the phone up. 'Yeah, boss,' he said. 'Got her here on ice. No problem.' He listened awhile, then began laughing, softly at first, but then it turned into something else, edging toward hysteria, his lips getting wet and spitty, but then just as he seemed to be going into meltdown, he managed to pull it back into something approximating normal laughter. He drew some deep breaths in. 'Consider it done,' he said, clipping the phone shut.

'That's some laugh you got there, Cimino,' she said. 'They call you laughing boy at school, when they bullied you?'

This time it was his eyes that showed a flicker and she knew she'd just hit a raw nerve. Time to double down. 'And opera as well?' she said. 'Puccini, no less. So, let's see; you're psychologically crippled from childhood trauma, and you like opera and killing people. That's a strange mix if I may say so, my friend.'

'Fuck you. Maybe you won't find it so funny when those rednecks cops are fucking you three ways to hell, before they cut your throat?' he said, his eyes simmering.

'My, such anger. And you won't be taking part? Women not your thing? What is it, little girls, or little boys? No, wait. Let me guess. Its corpses, isn't it,' she said smiling widely. 'Necrophilia. I should have guessed. I wonder if Frank Ross's ass got violated post-mortem? Be interesting to find—'

She didn't finish the sentence because Cimino crashed the gun down sideways into her head, knocking her cold.

CHAPTER THIRTY

They were in Ned's cosily chaotic front room again, the afternoon sunlight streaming in through the open windows. Calver was at the table, working on the ancient desk-top computer; Joel was slouched in an easy chair in the corner and Anita stood at the window looking out. Ned had gone out for his afternoon walk, and the only sound in the room came from Calver's chattering keyboard as his fingers worked on it.

'Where the hell is Courtney?' Anita asked the room in general.

Calver looked up. 'Boy, I've been asking that question for years. She goes AWOL sometimes, and then she'll turn up out of the blue. Don't worry.'

Anita frowned and checked her watch again. 'It's 2.30, Jonas,' she said. 'I guess we better get ready to ride out to Riverbend.'

Calver nodded and got to his feet.

'Sis?' Joel said.

She looked back at him, something in his voice cutting right through.

'I can't go with you,' he said, his voice shaky. 'I, I don't want to see daddy like this. I want to remember him how he was, with mom, when we was growing up. And,' he struggled. 'And I can't forgive myself for what I did.'

Anita walked slowly over to him, lent down and clumsily embraced him. He seemed stiff, but gradually relaxed into her arms. He shook as the tears came. Calver got up and quietly left the room.

'Its okay little brother,' she said, stroking his hair. 'I don't blame you for what you did, and I know daddy wouldn't. You see, it was always the bank, from day one, every bad thing that ever happened to us over the last ten years. In a way, we never had a chance.' She laughed bitterly. 'Look at this,' she said, holding up her tablet so he could see a headline and some text from the Tennessean. He raised his tear stained eyes. It read: "The Banksters weren't just crooks, they were also murderers. So alleges Floyd Ritter in his rejected clemency petition to Tennessee Governor……..".

'Too little too late,' she said sadly.

'You did something though, sis,' he said. 'You told the world, and you got folks protesting all over.'

'They won, though. In the end,' she said. She kissed the top of his head, got up and moved to the window. She looked back at him. 'I think daddy would want to see you, Joel. Really.'

'You think so?'

'I know so.'

He looked pleased but unsure. 'So, maybe I'll tag along. Or I'll sit and think, and come along later.'

'Daddy would like that.'

She left him looking bittersweet, half sad, half happy, as she went to get ready to go and see her father for what would almost certainly be the last time.

Pascal came awake slowly in pitch darkness, lying on her side, curled up. She tried to keep from groaning at the aching pain in the side of her head, and she could feel sticky, congealed blood that had run down onto her neck. Her hands were tied behind her back, and she could feel movement, wheels turning on a road. There was what felt like wool rubbing against her face which she guessed was a blindfold or hood of some kind. She lifted her her head, and it immediately came in contact with a barrier. She was in the boot of a car.

She relaxed back and began to feel around, trying to identify the exact parameters of the space, and if there was anything she could use. How long she had been under? It wouldn't have been an extended period, it never was, unless you slipped into a coma. What time was it? How long until they injected Floyd? The questions raced around her fevered brain with no answers. Her mind was blank. Fuck it. Just keep going. But then it hit her that Cimino would want to be sitting somewhere comfortable to watch real-time news of the execution, so maybe there was still time. She had to believe that. The vehicle begin to slow, her fingers still desperately working on the cords around her wrist.

John Irving sat in the dark gray SUV with blacked out windows as it ate up the miles. They would be at the airfield soon. He was pleased at how the pre-planning had gone, and indeed how easy it had all been. The previous night they had used their prodigious and inventive bomb making talents to great effect. Significant charges had been placed at a number of strategic spots around the perimeter of the Riverbend facility.

It would be quite a spectacle. They had used what they had left to wire up the girl's helicopter. He smiled. Her arrogance and disrespect to him would be repaid with interest.

He looked around at his four men, hardened Jihadi warriors ready to die for the cause. And their cause today was to get their martyr, Abdul Rahman, free. And if none of them made it, it wouldn't matter. Because it would still show their brothers and sisters around the world that their brand remained strong, that they could still mount a serious operation against the mighty US Satan, without fear. It would be an inspiration, whatever the outcome. Irving settled back in the car seat, his mind aglow with imagined headlines from around the world.

As Calver navigated the car through the final stages of the approach to Riverbend Correctional Facility, Anita sat quietly beside him, scrolling through images on her phone. But Calver could tell she wasn't seeing anything. Her mind was far away, and steeped in grief.

'D'you think Joel will come?' he muttered. 'I hope he does.'

'I don't know. I hope he does too, for daddy's sake.'

'Don't give up on your daddy yet, Anita. We're still waiting on the Supreme Court.'

She didn't say anything, which was retort enough. But now her eyes were directed out of the car windows, as they were beginning to come across people walking towards the gaol. It started with a trickle; a few, walking singly, then couples and small groups, some carrying placards. As Riverbend came into view Anita gasped at the size of the crowd already there, thronging all around the entrance and on the green area and stretching all around, a sea of faces, color, noise.

Calver smiled. 'My God, you see what you've done, Anita? I've never seen a crowd anything like this size for this kind of thing.'

She looked around at all the faces, a subdued smile on her face.

'Come on,' Calver said. 'Lets park up and meet them.'

As Calver maneuvered the car into the visitors parking area Anita was scrolling again at her phone, but this time she was seeing the pictures. 'Wow,' she said with pride. 'Its the same on Wall Street, and out at de Masi's Hampton's mansion.'

The vehicle was still for a moment and then she felt it shift up as someone climbed out, then a click and fresh air on her arms. Cimino's voice came in a harsh bark. 'Get out,' he said.

She lifted her legs over the back of the car and started to try and lever herself out, then felt his hand under armpit roughly hauling her out and onto her feet.

'It might help if you took the hood off, so I could see,' she said reasonably.

She felt a violent tug on her head and then she was blinking in the sunlight. They were parked in a back street, behind a row of what looked like commercial buildings with yards and refuse bins. There were a couple of empty Police squad cars parked in the road.

'Move,' Cimino said, gesturing towards a rear fire-door, in the back of one of the properties. Pascal cased the building as she approached. It was two stories' solid brick with all the windows covered over with dark gray painted panels.

Cimino opened the fire door and pushed her through into a short corridor that led to a single door with a keyboard panel by it. Cimino punched in a code, opened the door and pushed her inside.

As she stumbled in, her eyes adjusted to the low lights. They were in a largish room with a small bar at one end, a pool table and an old fashioned jukebox playing country music at low volume. There were three men, police officers, in uniform, but looking casual, like they were off duty. Two were playing pool and the other sat at the bar on a stool with a bottle of beer in front of him.

Cimino pushed her toward the guy at the bar. 'Gillespie,' he said with a nod.

Pascal appraised the guy, taking in the overdeveloped muscles on the shoulders and neck, almost bursting out of his uniform that was pulled tight across them. The head was small, age indeterminate. Elderly, no doubt, but very well preserved - botox, surgery and pills, together with an austere fitness regime, she guessed. His eyes were also small, and like those of a goat, empty, but the overall impression his face gave was one of merriment. Whatever he saw in some way amused him.

'So, this is the little lady caused all the trouble. The one you been looking high and low for, huh?' he said eying her up. He looked over at the two cops playing pool. 'Which of you young studs wants to break this fresh young thing in for me, huh?'

The two cops came over, laughing and joshing each other. They looked similar, like brothers, early thirties, receding hairlines, protruding teeth with smirky grins. 'These my nephews, Jessie and Robbie,' Gillespie said. 'Always keep it in the family I say, right guys?' he added.

They nodded, ogling Pascal, running their eyes up and down her.

Cimino said, 'turn the TV on will you, Gillespie. I want to see where they are with icing the nigger.'

'Sure thing,' he said picking up the remote from the bar and pressing a button, the screen on the wall coming alive with imagery. He handed the remote to Cimino who scrolled until he found a station showing pictures from outside Riverbend. He upped the audio.

For a moment all eyes were turned on the screen, surprise palpable at the size of the crowds of protesters

'Fucking pinko homosexual mongrels,' said one of the nephews. 'Burn em all.'

Pascal clocked the time shown in the bottom right hand corner of the TV screen. It was 4.30 p.m.

The first words Floyd said were, 'where's Joel?'

'He'll be along later, daddy,' Anita said quickly as she hugged him.

Floyd looked relaxed but his eyes had a weird, subtle kind of light in them.

Calver, to one side, watched them. For some unfathomable reason, seeing Anita embrace her father in such a way immediately reminded him of his first meeting with her in the snow all those months ago. And today she wore a white headband again, accentuating that memory - the girl with the halo. Calver shook his head, displacing the biblical memory. He moved to the side of the simple room to let Anita and her father have some intimate moments. He knew the next couple of hours were likely to be harrowing.

His mind wandered back to the pleasant gauntlet they had run, mingling with the crowds, as they had made their way to the Riverbend entrance. Security had moved the people some way back from the doors, behind barriers, but the crowd were still good natured. Many people stopped Anita to shake her hand and tell her they were with her and her father, and not to give up fighting. Away to the left had stood another much smaller group, possibly 20 people or so, with banners spitting hatred, exhorting the authorities to burn Floyd and all the other sinners of the world.

Once inside the building, Calver had made a last call to Shapiro who told him there was still no word from the Supreme Court and it would likely go down to the wire. He tried Pascal and the call went straight to voicemail. They had then been escorted through the elaborate security to the death watch area.

Calver turned back to watch father and daughter, now sitting, heads close, her arms around his shoulders, looking into his eyes, speaking quietly to him. Calver turned away again, his nerves jittering and jangling. He wondered whether he could bear the waiting, and what was to come after.

Cimino said, 'I'm going back to get her car. We don't want any loose ends. And Gillespie?'

'Yeah?' he nodded.

'Don't take any chances with her. She ain't quite as meek as she looks.'

'You hear that, boys?' Gillespie said, looking at his two nephews as Cimino walked away to the exit.

Jessie was tugging at Pascal's waistband. He looked up and said, 'what's that smell?'

Pascal smiled. 'Oh, I just shit my pants. I thought you boys might find it more romantic.'

Jessie jumped away from her as if he had been scalded, his expression a mixture of horror and disgust.

'Robbie,' Gillespie said, unperturbed. 'Haul her in the bathroom and clean her up, use the hose if you need to.'

Robbie grabbed her and pushed her towards a door. She let herself be led, hoping she'd get him on his own.

Inside, the room was small, a toilet, sink and a bath with a shower curtain across it. He ripped the curtain away and pushed her into the bath. 'Get naked,' he said.

'How can I with my hands tied?' she replied.

He watched her for a moment. 'Wait here,' he said, and went out. He came back with a knife, lent over and cut her wrist bindings. He put the knife in his belt and drew his gun, gesturing with it. 'Strip,' he said.

Pascal's eyes flashed across him, working the odds, weighing them against the running down clock. Not enough of an edge, yet; he'd almost certainly hit her if she tried for the gun in that small space. But now her hands were free.

'Move,' he said.

She watched him a moment longer, then moved her hands to her trouser fastenings, slowly undoing them. One thing she didn't suffer from was embarrassment about her naked body, and that was a significant advantage. Captors often stripped their victims to make them more vulnerable and less able to resist.

She stripped off her clothing, finally holding up her soiled pants to Robbie, hoping to further disgust him. He didn't rise to it, instead he gestured to the mobile shower head. Picking it up and turning it on, she adjusted the heat until it was right, then sprayed the nozzle over herself. For a mad moment she wondered whether to sing, then thought of Floyd, and the smile froze on her face.

When she was clean and dry, Robbie herded her back into the main room, a large towel draped around her.

Gillespie was still sat at the bar, beer bottle in his hand, Jessie occupying a seat alongside him. 'You prettied her up real well, Robbie.'

'Grab that towel off her,' Jessie said.

Robbie ripped the towel away. Pascal didn't flinch, just stood tall and relaxed, as if she were still clothed.

'She's one prideful bitch,' Robbie said. 'And she needs takin' down a peg or three. Get her on her on her knees, Jessie.'

'Hey, I'm first,' Jessie said, pushing Pascal down onto her knees. He began to unbuckle his belt.

'Go on, boy,' Robbie urged him. 'I'm next.'

Gillespie watched it all, eyes full of mirth.

Jessie let his trousers drop. He looked down at her. 'Open your mouth, bitch,' he said

She looked up at him. 'Sure, but you put anything in my mouth, boy, you're gonna lose it.' She held his eyes, her mouth widening into a smile.

She could see a flash of doubt.

'Roll her over,' Gillespie said calmly. He grinned. 'She ain't got no teeth in her ass.'

The boys giggled. They began manhandling her, and Pascal began to struggle, fight against them, looking for a chance. Gillespie took control again. 'Get her onto the pool table, on her front, then one can hold her down, and you can take turns.'

They began dragging her over to the pool table. If they got her subdued there, it was over, and Floyd would be gone. Her eyes desperately scanned around, looking for anything she could use, but now they had both arms pinned, and were relentlessly edging her toward the table. She could feel the edge of it now, pressing against her thigh, then they were heaving her up, grunting with the strain, then slamming her down onto the green baize. They rolled her onto her front, so her chest was over the table, and her feet still on the floor. Jessie bore down on both her hands he had gripped on her back, while Robbie was trying to pull her legs apart. He whooped as he jammed his fingers into her. 'Gonna ream this bitch out good, boy, and you is next,' he said.

Pascal couldn't move her hands, her eyes dazedly hunting for anything she might use, hope draining from her, but then she saw it, lying beside her on the baize; a pool cue. But her hands were held in a vice. She felt Robbie relax slightly as he got into position to thrust into her. An image of Floyd's face flashed into her mind. She let herself go completely limp for a fraction of a second, and then kicked up her heel with all the force she could muster; more by luck than aim, it caught Robbie in the balls. As he gasped, Jessie slightly relaxed his hold on her hands, enough to allow her to force her right one out to the cue, grasping and swinging it as she rolled. As Jessie leapt at her she jammed the cue tip into his right eye socket with all her strength, turning it as it went in a good four inches. He screamed, dropping to his knees, blood gushing from his eye socket. She rolled off the table and slipped behind Robbie, still crouching and nursing his crotch, and pulled the gun from his open holster, leveling it on Gillespie who still sat at the bar as if frozen.

Pascal approached him, watching the hand that was tentatively resting on his holster flap. 'Go on, pull it, fucker,' she said.

He held her eyes for a moment, tense. Maybe he aged as she watched him, because he looked old now. He seemed to relax back in his seat, moving his hand back away to the bar top and his bottle.

'Whatever happens, you don't get out of this,' he said. 'Its my people, and my state.'

'Wrong,' she said swinging the gun sideways with great force into his face.

It was unexpected and Gillespie took it full on, unprotected, his nose breaking and the force knocking him off the stool, sprawling onto the floor. She stooped down, grabbed his gun and walked over to Jessie who now lay still, probably dead. She got his gun as well, and moved onto Robbie, still moaning, lying in a fetal position holding his crotch. She pulled his hands behind his back and used his handcuffs, locking them securely. As she walked back past Jessie she pulled the pool cue out of his eye socket with an awful wet sucking sound.

Gillespie was now back on his stool, nursing his nose with a blood red handkerchief. Pascal's eyes flicked up to the TV screen, still on, showing a commercial. She looked over the rest of the bar. It was a homemade job like in someones front room; shelves, bottles of beer and whiskey, a few photographs of the guys in uniform. There was also a small plastic rectangular box containing Cd's. Curious, she pulled the box down, catching Gillespie's eyes unguarded for moment as she did so. She saw it for a second, something in the depths there, maybe fear, before the bland mirth descended on his face again.

The disks weren't Country and Western classics as she had expected. They looked blank and were in plastic cases with handwritten labels in felt tip. She read one: "Roasting da nigga schoolgirl," and guessed at the content. The others had similar titles; there were about twenty in all. She moved behind the bar, looking around underneath. Finding it, she looked up and around, studying the ceiling, locating the three cameras easily. She looked down at the small screen on the monitor behind the bar and saw herself, Gillespie and the two nephews; it was recording real-time.

'My, my, chief,' she said. 'Looks like we got us a whole mess of evidence here, enough to get you boys the needle.'

'Whatever you think you got, little lady,' he said, confidence back. 'It'll all disappear when we get free.'

She noticed his eyes flicking to the rear fire door, reminding her suddenly of the clock, Floyd and the fact that Cimino would be back anytime. She checked the TV screen: 4.50 p.m. Fuck. She needed to move. She ripped Gillespie's cuffs from his belt. 'Hands out, or your nose gets broke again.'

He smiled, holding them out. Cuffing him and herding him over to Robbie who was now standing, and pushing them both in the bathroom, she patted them down and removed their phones and wallets. Closing the door and running back, she dragged Jessie's body behind the pool table, then moving towards the bar she realized she was still naked and almost burst out laughing. As she draped a towel around herself, she heard the code being punched into the door locking system. Cimino was back.

CHAPTER THIRTY-ONE

Floyd and Anita had remained holding each other and talking quietly whilst Calver sat to one side reviewing paperwork on the case had brought along. They all looked up as the door opened and Joel appeared. He stood on the threshold looking unsure of himself, a tentative smile playing on his lips.

'Son,' Floyd said, rising to his feet, full of joy. 'You came.'

'Yes, daddy,' he said, moving to hug his father.

They held each other for a moment. Floyd held him away to look him up and down. He nodded. 'Sit with us, so we can talk. How you bin, Joel?'

He sat. 'I'm fine, Daddy. How are your holding up? You look good, man.'

'I'm good and strong, cause now I got both my wonderful kids here with me to face this thing down.'

Calver, at the side, tuned out, not wanting to eavesdrop on their intimate moments. His mind wandered. He had never witnessed an execution before and had never wanted to. Did anyone, he wondered. He remembered his conversation with Ned about the death penalty and the arguments he had deployed. In principle he had no objection to execution for the most heinous of crimes, if they could be sure of guilt, but often they couldn't, and the system on which such findings were made was deeply flawed. In the absence of a fair and effective system of finding guilt, the penalty phase of the system could never work effectively. And Floyd's case demonstrated all those faults. The system almost exclusively punished race and poverty. How many rich white guys ever got executed?

He looked down at the final appeal document and wondered when they'd get word from the Supreme Court. He knew there were instances where it came as they were literally inserting the needle. He hoped it wouldn't be that way. He checked his watch: 4.50 p.m. Couple of hours to go. He looked over at Floyd. They were in a huddle now, all three hugging each other and talking in hushed tones, but it didn't seem sad to Calver. The impression they gave was uplifting and one of hope. Floyd looked up and caught his eye.

'Come on over, Jonas,' he said. 'Come and talk with us.'

'Glad to,' he said rising to his feet and dragging a chair over.

The problem with the door was that it opened outward, so Pascal flattened herself against the wall, left side, on the basis Cimino's gaze would automatically move to the right as he came in, as that was where the bulk of the room lay. He came in quite fast and stopped two feet in which is when she loudly cocked the gun behind him. 'Hands up or I blow your head off,' she said.

He stayed tense, his eyes taking in the empty room. He started to turn.

'My fingers tightening on the trigger, asshole. I'll kill you easy as stepping on a cockroach.'

Cimino relaxed. Pascal moved carefully around to stand in front of him. 'Let me make it clear,' she said. 'I tell you to do something. You don't do it. I shoot you. Flesh wounds to start with. I'm guessing from what I know has been going on in here, the place is pretty much soundproofed, so no one is gonna hear.'

Cimino stared back at her, seemingly unconcerned. Even holding a gun on him it was going to be tricky restraining him. She moved back behind him and silently moved the gun barrel in close to the fleshy part of his upper thigh, and pulled the trigger.

Cimino went down groaning, both hands gripping his bleeding thigh. 'You fucking bitch,' he shouted, his breath haggard and labored. 'You're dead.'

'Man up, Cimino. It's only a flesh wound,' she said. She took out his gun and walked back, climbed up on the bar stool and sat looking down on him, toying with the gun.

Cimino started laughing, guffawing and wincing at the same time. He didn't go into melt down this time though. Maybe the pain was too much. 'You're too late, you fuck,' he spat. 'Niggers gonna fry, and then we're home free. And we'll get you, whatever you done. Where's Gillespie?'

'He's in the can with his nephews,' she said. 'You're right, though, Cimino. I guess you have won, you and de Masi. Its too late to stop Tennessee killing Floyd, but then if he did kill Vincent Fachetti, its surely right he should die, cause that's the law in this state.'

Cimino had managed to drag himself to the side of the space, and was now sat on the floor with his back against the wall, still nursing his thigh. 'You are one dumb broad,' he said, his teeth gritted against the pain as he massaged his leg. 'I offed Fachetti. It was me. And it was the perfect frame. I was on my cellphone with de Masi when I drilled the knife into Vincents heart. So they're gonna burn the wrong guy,' he said, and began to laugh again.

Pascal scanned the camera's, hoping they were still running. 'You did kill him then, and on de Masi's orders?'

'Yeah. It was wild man,' he said with relish, as if he were reliving it. 'I had de Masi screaming down the phone that we mustn't miss the perfect opportunity to frame Ritter. You know how the guy talks a hundred to the dozen. Thought he was never gonna shut the fuck up. And I'm there holding Vincent up against the wall by the neck, with Vincent's own knife.' Cimino started to laugh again. 'He started pleading, telling me what great friends we were. I said no we ain't, and drilled the fucker through the heart.'

Pascal checked the clock. 5.15 p.m. She used the final pair of cuffs on Cimino's hands.

He looked up at her. 'Get me a scotch will you?'

She went behind the bar, stooped down and pressed the off switch on the camera system, ejected the disk and put it in the plastic case with the other CD's. She grabbed a bottle of scotch and took it over to Cimino. He thirstily took a long shot, holding the bottle two handed, coughing and spluttering, but looking better when he focused again on Pascal. 'Join me in celebrating the imminent death of Floyd Ritter,' he said holding the bottle up again.

'He ain't dead yet,' she said, and smiled.

For the first time, Cimino's tough guy expression faltered. He checked his watch. He shook his head. 'You're too late,' he said, but there was doubt in his eyes.

'We'll see.'

She collected up all their guns and phones, chucked them in a bag with the CD's. The only exit was the rear door, presumably to keep the place secret and secure from prying eyes. She leveled the gun on Cimino. 'Give me the door code.' He did so. She went out and reprogrammed it to permanent lock. She didn't know how long it would hold them when they got their heads together but there was no time left to worry. She ran to her car, chucking the bag in the back, starting the ignition and burning rubber off the curb, scorching her way back into the traffic, speed dialing Fingers as she drove.

A corrections officer appeared in the doorway. It was time. He had given them a heads-up 30 minutes earlier, so they knew it was coming. Floyd, Anita and Joel stood, their arms across each others shoulders, in a tight bunching, heads bowed. They were murmuring to each other. Calver lent against the wall off to the side. He felt emotionally drained. Joel was weeping openly, but Anita seemed strangely calm. Floyd still looked relaxed, maybe holding himself together for his children. Calver couldn't help admiring the guy's dignity and courage. So much had been done to him, so much injustice. His livelihood and family destroyed, taken away from him, his wife murdered, and him now to die for a killing he didn't commit. And yet he stood tall, refusing to be cowed by it, drawing immense strength from his family and his faith.

Anita stepped back as her father hugged Joel for a moment. 'Go on, son,' Floyd said gently, untangling Joel's arms. 'Go with your sister.

I ain't afraid. I'm going to be with my Mary again, and we'll be happy like we used to be. You know, me and your mother, we was always so proud of you kids.'

Anita's breath caught in her throat, and she couldn't hold back the tears. They ran down her face. She stepped forward and kissed her fathers cheek.

'We need to go now folks,' the corrections officer said. 'I'm sorry.'

'That's no problem,' Floyd said. He held his hand out to Calver.

Calver stepped forward awkwardly with his hand out, then dropped it and threw his arms around Floyd and hugged him close. 'We still waiting on the Supreme Court, Floyd,' Calver muttered.

Floyd nodded. 'Don't worry, Jonas. I know you and Ned, and all the team did your best. I'm calm now, and ready. You take care of yourself.'

They stepped apart and Calver moved to the door where Joel and Anita stood. The guard moved them out and handed them over to be escorted to the waiting area.

In the cell, as Floyd heard their departing steps, he broke down. Not through fear, but in grief that he would never see his children again.

Pascal turned her car into the rest-stop area by the side of the road. Fingers was already there sitting in a beat up old orange Volkswagen Beetle. He sauntered over and climbed into the seat next to her. She was typing on a lap-top open on her knees. She didn't look up. 'I'm finishing a statement I been working on for a while which I'm going to email to you. I want you to print it off and mail it tonight with these,' she said, indicating the plastic box of Cd's.

'Mail it where?' he asked.

'FBI, with copies of just the covering letter to, the office of the President, L.A. Times, New York Times and the Washington Post.'

'Wow. What's it say?'

'You'll find out, as I don't have time to tell you. Essentially it's a potted history of what GM Bank and Lloyd de Masi did to Floyd Ritter, and the evidence. Its also got some detail about corrupt cops and murder in Tennessee, and a run-down of what I intend to do at Riverbend and why. And my acceptance of all responsibility for whatever goes down.'

'Shit. Okay,' Finger's said. 'What else?'

'Well, before you mail the physical disc's to the FBI, so they can check they're genuine, I want you to copy them onto your computer. This one' she said holding it up. 'Is the important one, because it contains Cimino's confession. Then I want you to email copies of the letter, together with a digital copy of this tape, to CNN, Fox news and MSNBC. Send it at exactly 7.30 p.m. Say its from the people carrying out the assault on Riverbend. You got that?'

'Absolutely.'

'Good. You bring what I asked you for?'

'Sure, he said, unrolling a large black sign with "FBI" stenciled in huge white letters on it. 'I brought two, like you asked.

'Thanks a bunch, Fingers. You clear on what I want you to do on the comms side, and when?'

'Absolutely. Disrupt Riverbend communications at 7.15 p.m. if I can, same time as anonymous tip to Homeland Security with the details you gave me about a terrorist attack.'

'In the tip you need to say you've given the same information to the FBI, but we're not going to do give it to them. You understand?

'Sure I do,' he said. 'We done? Where you going now?'

'You don't need to know.' She pressed send on the laptop and closed it, leaned over and opened the door for Fingers.

'You sure you don't want me to tag along?'

'Thanks for the offer, Fingers, but you done enough for me, man. Beyond the call of duty.'

'Okay,' he said. He picked up the Cd box and scrambled out of the car. He banged the top as she gunned the engine, and watched as she slid back out into the traffic. He watched her accelerate away.

It took her twenty minutes to get to the airfield. Again, it appeared deserted, apart from a gray SUV standing forlornly by the hanger. Pascal parked up and went inside. They were huddled in the corner talking in hushed tones which abruptly stopped when she sauntered over. John Irving, dressed in faded fatigues, rose to greet her.

'I wont introduce you to my men, other than your pilot,' he said. 'He's in the chopper' He took her arm and led her over to the smaller helicopter. 'This is Akim,' he said nodding at a slight young brown-skinned man who sat at the controls. The man nodded at Pascal and smiled.

Pascal unrolled one of the FBI signs and held it out to the pilot. 'Akim, would you mind affixing these to the side of the chopper?'

'No problem, ma'am,' he said, jumping down and taking the signs.

'Come,' Irving said, checking his watch 'A final run through.'

They moved over to a table at the side where there were some maps and a lap-top. They sat and began talking, occasionally leaning over the maps to make a point.

The room was small with chairs laid out in short rows in front of a large screen with a thick black curtain running across it. There were under a dozen people there, including Calver, Anita and Joel. Calver recognized a couple of journalists, including Kelly Phillips, who nodded at him. He also recognized Fachetti's widow, Carla, dressed in black, sitting quietly in the front row. Calver took his seat in the back row, next to Anita.

As they sat without speaking a corrections officer approached them. 'Mr Calver, d'you have a moment?'

'Sure,' he said, surprised. He got up and followed the man out.

'Sir, the warden has asked me to confirm that we just heard from the Supreme Court. They have declined to grant a stay. Said they could find no compelling reasons to stop the execution. I'm sorry, sir.'

'Thanks for telling me. Does Floyd know?'

'Yes, he's been told, and, and he's okay with it.'

'Thanks'

'No problem. If you'd like to go back in,' he said, looking at his watch. 'Its about to start.'

The helicopters flew low in a convoy of two as the sky began to pinken and drift into sunset. The larger chopper carrying Irving and his three men was followed by the smaller bird carrying Pascal and her pilot, Akim. Pascal checked her watch. It was 7.01p.m. She watched as the larger chopper began to pull away while Akim veered off to the right, and then they were flying solo. Pascal smiled as she watched the scenery; it would have been fun if she had been on her way to do something carefree and normal.

The already pent-up tension in the room spiked with a muted gasp as the black curtains drew back to reveal Floyd Ritter on a gurney. It was raised slightly upward so that he was facing the audience. He looked calm and rested and his eyes were clear. He was dressed in white garb and his bare arms were secured face up to the sides of the gurney, and IV lines ran into each arm. The audio boomed in the room as Floyd was asked whether he had any final words to say.

Calver felt and heard Joel, sitting beside him, quietly begin to weep .

Floyd cleared his throat. 'Just want to say to Carla Fachetti, I am sorry for your loss. I did fight with your husband, but I didn't kill him,' he said. 'Cimino, acting for Lloyd de Masi of GM Bank, killed Vincent. We have produced evidence of this, and more will come out, but it will be too late to save me.'

He paused to take a breath. 'I have tried to live a good life, and hope I have. I'd like to thank the Riverbend staff here who are only doing their job, and they have been good and kind to me. Its the system that sucks, not them. Also thanks to my lawyers, Jonas, Ned and Mike, who all tried their best. Lastly, to my wonderful children, Anita and Joel, I love you. Stay strong, always. Hope to meet you in the next world, but in a long, long time.'

He nodded to the officer.

Calver put his arm around Anita and held her as they watched the officer take a red syringe and screw it into the IV line. He then began to slowly push down on the plunger.

Joel began to quietly recite the 23rd Psalm. 'The Lord is my shepherd…..

Pascal was curious about Akim. She looked at him now, dressed in the FBI rig that Anita had worn when they'd hustled Frank Ross. Pascal was similarly attired. She pushed the black baseball cap back on her head and said through her face mike, 'you're a good pilot, Akim. How long you been flying?'

His face lit up. 'Four years and I love it.'

'Your friends didn't seem very, err, how can I put it? Friendly, to you?'

He looked at her, his face darkening. 'I made a silly mistake a while back. Went AWOL over a girl and they don't seem the forgiving kind.'

'Well, I'm glad you're my pilot today, because this ain't going to be no picnic. We need to go in fast and hard, and get out quick, if we can. We may not be coming back.'

'Good,' he said with a cheeky smile, 'because I'm up for a rumble.'

Pascal checked her watch. It was 7.15 p.m.

Calver could no longer watch, instead he looked down at the floor between his knees. The first injection seemed to have been successful, as Floyd's eyes had closed and he was unresponsive to his name being called, or having his shoulder twisted. Calver felt empty and sad, unwilling to continue watching the process as it slowly stripped Floyd of his dignity. If there were to be death throes, Calver didn't want to watch them. He wondered on the etiquette and whether he could just get up and walk out, but he didn't want to leave Anita, who continued to cling tightly to his hand, her eyes riveted on her father.

As those thoughts assailed Calver he heard a loud bang, muffled, but sounding like an explosion, and then another, louder and nearer. People started moving in their seats, looking around, wondering what was happening. The door to the room opened and a corrections officer entered at the same time as the black curtains swung back across the screen, hiding the execution chamber from view.

'Folks, we need to get you out of here fast,' he said. 'Somethings going on and we're not sure what, but your safety is our main concern. So I need you to move. Now.'

'What about my father?' Anita shouted. 'What's going on?'

'Ma'am, you need to move, or we shall have to use force.'

'I'm not leaving my—'

Her words were drowned out by another much larger explosion. Calver began dragging Anita along as they all began moving out of the viewing room.

As Pascal's chopper swooped low over the protesting crowds, she saw up ahead orange flame and blasts as Irving's strategically placed perimeter charges went off, then larger explosions from his men on the ground within the complex. Irving's helicopter had landed one minute earlier, and they should have blown the entrance to the execution chamber and released smoke grenades, and then moved on to their primary target of Rahman, still housed on death row.

'Put us down there,' Pascal shouted, pointing at an area near the execution chamber and the capital punishment garage, now swirling with smoke. She could see a few corrections officers milling around down there pointing up at her chopper, hopefully at the large FBI signs on the side.

Akim expertly brought them down in a swirl of dust, Pascal already jumping from the cockpit, her phony FBI badge held up. She ducked and ran to them, shouting, 'FBI agent Carrie Madison, sir. This is a terrorist attack to try and free Abdul Rahman on death row. We only just got word and I was closest. Reinforcements are on the way, including Homeland Security, and they'll be here any minute. You need to lock-down and concentrate your men on that death row inmate. I have been tasked with safeguarding the execution process around Floyd Ritter, given the national interest in the case. Where is he? Is the sentence completed?'

'I'll take you ma'am,' one of the officers said. Another was shouting into a radio, relaying what Pascal had told him, telling them to go to death row and try and contain it.

Another large explosion went off close by. The officer ducked and almost looked like he was about to run for cover. Pascal shook him. 'Come on, man,' she shouted in his face. It seemed to calm him and he began leading her again. As they entered the garage a man in a white coat and one guard stood around the gurney on which the body lay.

Floyd looked dead.

Pascal shouted, waving her badge. 'I have instructions to airlift the body to a safe location whilst this terrorist attack is contained and subdued.'

Both men looked frightened and cowed, grateful for any kind of authority. 'You,' she said to the guard. 'Wheel the gurney to the chopper now and get the body on board. Where's the warden?'

The doctor said, nervously, 'I haven't yet certified death, ma'am, but in the circumstances I guess……' His words tailed off and he looked around wildly.

Pascal looked in his eyes, seeing only confusion and fear. She shook the man and said, 'we'll take it from here, doctor.' He stepped back and she began hurriedly wheeling the gurney along with the guard. As they moved they began to hear automatic rounds and could see fire was burning around the death row building.

As they reached the chopper, Akim leaned down and hauled the body into the rear of the cockpit.

Pascal jumped aboard and shouted down to the guard, 'reinforcements here any second.' He gave her a kind of salute. She shouted at Akim, 'get us outta here.'

As they began to lift up, she saw up ahead the larger chopper also hovering just above the ground with Irving's team manhandling a prisoner on board whilst smoke and gunfire swirled all around against the backdrop of major buildings alight with savagely burning fires. Pascal was surprised and impressed Irving had got the guy out so quick. As they began moving she watched the larger chopper lift up and follow, starting to draw in beside them as they approached the perimeter of the Riverbend complex. As they drew alongside, very close, Irving was at the window, smiling, holding up a cellphone.

Pascal smiled back and gave him a thumbs-up, whilst shouting to Akim to get away from them. As Akim started to veer off, Irving theatrically pressed a button on his phone, gesturing at Pascal.

Inside the larger chopper, as Irving lifted his finger off the button, he heard a large double beep coming from underneath his feet. The triumphant smile on his face dropped a notch as his mind started to process the information. His smile froze, his eyes widening, as the truth suddenly dawned on him and he began making a mad scramble to get out of his seat as the chopper incinerated in a giant fireball.

It rocked the smaller craft making it swing wildly in the air. As they came out of it, now racing across the countryside, Pascal shouted, 'that was meant for us. I switched it last night.'

Akim looked at her in amazement, but she could tell he believed her.

'Where to now, boss?' he asked. 'I guess I owe you.'

'I guess you do. Back to base. We can use their SUV.'

'What about him?' Akim asked, gesturing at the body behind them.

She had completely forgotten Floyd. She scrambled into the back, her fingers reaching to his neck for a pulse. He felt very cold.

CHAPTER THIRTY-TWO

After a number of unsuccessful attempts by Calver to get something out of the stone-faced guard standing by the door, the group were finally released at 8.15 p.m. They were escorted to the exit by a harassed and close-mouthed corrections officer who would only say that the warden was about to give a press conference and they were welcome to watch it. They moved out onto a green area with many arc lights, cameras, journalists, protesters and a large contingent of law enforcement, kitted out in paramilitary gear. Smoke still swirled around, but all the fires had been put out.

The heavily sweating warden stood in front of a hastily placed lectern, senior officers and an FBI man standing either side of him. He coughed and looked around at the assembled sea of faces.

'This evening this correction facility was subject to a terrorist attack of unmitigated ferocity,' he said. 'Their purpose; to free convicted terrorist and cop killer, Abdul Rahman. They did not succeed. The helicopter carrying him exploded just beyond the perimeter. Thankfully there have been no civilian deaths and equally important, none of my staff were killed in the attack, although two are seriously injured and receiving medical attention. Now, while all this was taking place, we carried on with our business, and I can confirm that Floyd

Ritter's death sentence was successfully carried out tonight here at Riverside.'

There were sounds in the crowd of discontent and anger. Scowls and shouts. He paused and looked them over before continuing. 'The situation surrounding the events that occurred tonight is still developing and we are trying to get a complete picture of what took place. I will take a few questions, but please bear in mind we do not have all the facts at this time. To my right is FBI local bureau chief, Richard Donner who will hopefully answer the questions I can't answer.'

Kelly Philip's, standing beside Calver, was the first into the fray. She jumped forward. 'Kelly Phillips, the Tennessean.'

'Go ahead, Kelly,' the warden said, recognizing her.

'Sir, I was an official witness to Floyd Ritter's execution. But, we didn't witness confirmation, or certification of his death because you pulled the plug when the bombs went off. Can you confirm Floyd Ritter is dead and tell us where the body is?'

'I believe so,' he answered, then cut her off when she tried to come back, by pointing at another journalist. 'Yes?' he said.

It was a glamorous blonde with a cameraman by her side. 'Carla Dupont, CNN,' she said. 'Sir, we're getting reports of a communication from the person claiming responsibility for the attack. They say it's purpose was to free Floyd Ritter because he's innocent, and they have provided categorical evidence of this with a confession from the real killer. Seems the terrorist angle may have been some kind of diversion. There were two helicopters in the attack, weren't there? What's happened to the other one, and where is Floyd Ritter's body?'

The warden looked shaken. He mopped his brow with a small

white cloth. 'Chief?' he said, nodding at the FBI man.

He stepped forward, an African American, 6' 4", exuding authority. 'We are getting similar reports which we are in the process of checking, and until that's done we'll keep an open mind. Early indications are that the larger helicopter, carrying the bulk of the terrorist group, along with Abdul Rahman, exploded in mid-air, and that its likely that this was due to a bomb on board.'

The crowd erupted with more questions shouted at the podium, but CNN had kept the microphone. 'So, chief, where is Floyd Ritter, and who exactly is on that second helicopter, and where is it going?'

'Those are the questions we are attempting to determine.'

Anita was staring at Calver. 'Courtney,' she whispered.

Calver's expression was one of wondering bafflement, as if he were trying to work through a puzzle. Before he could respond, a clean-cut guy in a suit appeared alongside them.

'Sir, FBI,' he said, flashing a shield. 'Agent Dalmus. We need to speak to you, Ms Ritter and Joel Ritter, urgently about what has happened here tonight. Please accompany me. In the circumstances we are authorized to use force if need be.'

Calver sighed. 'That won't be necessary,' he said. 'Lead on.'

It was dark as the helicopter sped on, all its lights switched off. In the back Pascal was trying to wake Floyd, but he was unresponsive. She held a torch over his face, rolling back his eyelid; the pupils did not seem to react to the light at all, a bad sign she knew. She held her fingers on his neck and thought she could feel a very faint and slow pulse. But she couldn't be sure.

'We're coming in now,' Akim said through her ear-piece.

She sat frozen. What should she do? Her plan never extended to more than getting Floyd out. Was he alive, or was he already dead, or was he fading away? Drop him outside a hospital? She felt the helicopters feet softly make contact and settle, Akim killing the engine, the blades slowing and then coming to a stop.

He leaned over his seat, looking back at her sitting forlorn beside the prone body, her face a mask of indecision and doubt.

'He alive? What now?' he asked.

'I don't know.'

Akim watched her for a moment, moonlight seeping into the cabin, catching her face in a slant of faded white. 'How d'you know about the bomb?' he asked as he scrambled over the seat into the back.

'I guessed Irving was going to betray me. Breaking Rahman out would be a huge propaganda coup, and he wouldn't want Ritter clouding things,' she said, watching Akim as he examined Ritter.

'But how d'you know?' he persisted, rolling back Ritter's eyelids, his other hand feeling for a pulse.

'I didn't. I did something I've done all my life. I played a hunch. Went out the night before, checked the choppers and found the bomb.'

'And no qualms about blowing them all to hell?' he asked, looking up at her from the body.

'None. Those motherfuckers would have gone on killing innocent people. Rahman was their poster boy.'

Akim smiled. 'I'm not sad they're gone. I don't think I was cut out to be a terrorist, but you are one cold-hearted lady.'

'What?' she said, catching his look as he removed his fingers from Floyd's neck.

'He's one sick puppy,' he said. 'He ain't gonna make it. That pulse is just about gone, getting slower and fainter with every beat.'

'You know medicine?' she asked.

'Not much. I was training to be a nurse, but didn't get far.'

'We could dump him at a hospital?' she said.

'Not in the state of Tennessee. They'd just finish the job,' he said. He sat back on his haunches, looking pensive. 'I guess. I guess I owe you, you know. You saved my life.' He rubbed his face, thinking. 'I wouldn't want to get her in any trouble, but my cousin, Samira, is a doctor. She might help us.'

'Why the fuck didn't you say, Akim?' She said. 'What are we waiting for. Go check the SUV. Keys should be in the ignition.'

He looked at her for a long moment, wishing he hadn't mentioned his cousin. He shrugged and began moving.

Five minutes later they were on the road, Pascal driving and Akim in the back, juggling phoning his cousin and nursing Floyd's body that already seemed like a corpse.

'I told you,' Calver said, drumming his fingers on the desk. 'I don't know anything about this.'

'We don't believe you,' agent Dalmus said. 'So lets go through it again.'

They had been at it for 45 minutes already, round and round. Calver assumed Anita and Joel were probably being subjected to the same thing in adjoining cells. Dalmus was persistent but remained courteous.

Calver patiently started again. 'I was here to witness Floyd Ritter's execution as one of his attorneys. Supreme Court had declined to grant a stay and we were watching the execution when the bombs started going off. You say Courtney Pascal was responsible and you can't find her or Floyd Ritter. Well, tough luck. Its nothing to do with me, although I'll grant you she worked for me on the case. Now, I'm guessing, being the FBI, you already know a hell of a lot about her. If she's responsible for what happened here, she simply would not have involved me in it, or anything criminal, because I'm a lawyer, and it would likely destroy me. She just doesn't work like that.'

Dalmus smiled for the first time, light in his eyes. 'But you know it was her, don't you?'

'I don't speculate, Dalmus, but if I was a betting man, well…'

'So where would she take him?'

'Forgive me, agent Dalmus, but why do you assume he was still alive? I think they'd given him the fatal dose. He was gone.'

'We think she somehow managed to switch the lethal chemicals.'

'You're fucking kidding me,' Calver said, unable to stop himself from smiling. 'Wow. That is something, shit. Even for her.'

Dalmus wasn't amused. 'We'll get her,' he said. 'Its only a matter of time. Then she'll go to jail forever, and if Ritter's still alive, they'll just re-execute him.' Now Dalmus laughed. 'We got APB's all over, eyes in the sky, everywhere, most wanted TV campaign. She can't hide, not if he's as sick as we think he is. Maybe even dead. We'll get her.'

'Well, good luck with that,' Calver said. 'Can I go now?'

'No, you can't, but I will authorize a coffee break,' Dalmus said, getting up and going to the door.

It was a small white frame house in a largish plot of land in a row of similar properties. Pascal coasted quietly to the curb in front of it and turned the engine off. There was a light on, on the porch, but otherwise the property was in darkness.

'She here? What did she say?' Pascal asked. As she spoke she saw in her wing mirror a police car enter the top of the road, behind them. 'Get down,' she hissed.

She heard him moving in the back, banging and cursing in whispers. She held her breath, listening as the car slowly approached. It seemed like it had stopped, but then she realized it was still moving. It slowed to a halt beside the SUV. Pascal saw a torch beam play across the interior above her. She could hear the crackle of static and their radio through their open window. She felt as if she would scream as the tension drew out. Then the car began to move on slowly, then it was in front and she moved up in her seat watching the red tail lights flicker as it proceeded to the end of the road and turned into the highway. She let out a deep breath. 'Can we park round back, Akim?'

He said yes and directed her down an adjacent lane. Two minutes later they stood on the porch, holding Floyd upright. Pascal felt ridiculous, as if she were in some kind of ludicrous avant-garde surrealist play.

The door opened; a young brown face. 'Akim, I told you not to come,' she said through the gap in the door.

'We got nowhere else to go, cousin.'

'You're all over the media, everyone looking. I can't be involved,' she said. 'I'm sorry.' She started closing the door.

'So much for the Hippocratic oath, eh Samira,' Pascal said. 'This guy may already be dead. State have tried their best to kill him for something he didn't do. You want to help them, or try and save his life? Come on, Akim, lets go,' she said turning away.

'Wait,' Samira said, the door swinging open. Her eyes ran over Floyd. She rolled his eyelid up. 'Get him inside, in the living room, on the couch,' she said, her voice full of anxiety.

They moved him in, down a short corridor, to the living room, where they laid him down.

'What has he ingested,' she asked as she began running her fingers over his chest, under the white cloth top he still wore.

Pascal said. 'I'm not exactly sure. But I would say, certainly, midazolam, and possibly vercuronium bromide, and Tetrodotoxin,'

'Great. And you want me to save him? How?'

'Just try,' Pascal said.

The door buzzer went off like a grenade. They stood frozen. Samira was first to react. 'Akim, get him down in the basement. I'll get the door. Go.'

Pascal was beginning to like the calm young woman. Looked like competence and courage ran in the family. They quickly carried Floyd to the door under the stairs, then down into the basement.

It was kitted out like a home office. They laid Floyd's body on the table, then sat silent, listening to what was happening above.

Ten minutes later Samira appeared, coming down the stairs. She had a tray on which were some small vials, a syringe, and bandages. 'It was the local police, looking for Akim. I said I hadn't seen you. They seemed to believe me, but who knows.'

'Thanks, Samira,' they both said in unison.

She looked at them daggers. 'Right, I have work to do,' she said moving over to Floyd.'

Pascal noticing the TV in the corner, said, 'mind if we watch the news? I'd like to find out what the hell has been happening?'

'Be my guest,' she said. 'But I don't think you'll like it.'

Pascal grabbed the remote and switched on the set. The channel she chose was showing extracts from the warden's earlier press conference. Pascal and Akim watched the screen as Samira worked on Floyd. The channel then moved to a live feed interview with the FBI chief from the press conference. Behind him were blow-up pictures of Pascal and Akim, then footage of Floyd Ritter. It also showed old film of Abdul Rahman and John Irving. The camera panned back to the FBI chief speaking:

"These two individuals, Courtney Pascal and Akim Mohamed, are armed and dangerous and should not be approached. If they are sighted, call the number shown below immediately. It is believed these two fugitives are still in the greater Nashville area, and we can assure the public that we are closing in and will have them shortly."

The film clip moved to the news anchor asking a question, "and where is Floyd Ritter? Was he executed?"

"We are unable to say at this stage, but the likelihood is he is dead."

"And chief, what about the terrorist angle? From social media feeds we are learning that some Americans believe what happened to

Rahman and his crew was a good thing. And that this lady is some type of Robin Hood figure who freed an innocent man about to be killed by the state, and took out a whole team of murderous terrorists?"

The FBI man looked uncomfortable. "The Bureau does not concur with that view. These people are dangerous felons. They will be apprehended."

"Dead or alive, Chief?"

"Preferably alive, of course, but if they make the mistake of resisting, we cannot be held responsible for their personal safety."

The anchor tilted her head as if listening to something. "Chief, I'm going to cut in here and go over to our reporter outside Lloyd de Masi's Hampton's mansion for another breaking news story that is linked to this jailbreak."

The picture switched to a harassed looking reporter standing outside the mansion. There seemed to be crowds all around, some carrying pitchforks, although perhaps as symbols rather than weapons. The reporter spoke to camera: "Carrie, we have been here all evening monitoring things and the crowds have just got bigger and bigger. The police are keeping a low profile so far. We are told Lloyd De Masi and his personal assistant, Grace Van Zim have barricaded themselves in his office and are refusing to come out until the crowd is cleared. It appears their personal security people have baled out. I spoke twenty minutes ago to the protesters leader Josh Rollins, and this is what he said."

The face of an angry young man with beard and glasses appeared speaking to camera. "We've all seen the CNN footage of de Masi's henchman confessing to a conspiracy to murder Vincent Fachetti, the crime that Floyd Ritter was wrongly convicted of. We want Floyd acquitted and pardoned, even if its posthumous, and we want Greenberg Metro Bank and Lloyd de Masi indicted for conspiracy to murder. Then we'll disperse, otherwise we'll get him ourselves. The Banks and their corrupt and crooked CEO's have been allowed to run riot, rape, pillage, and even kill, with impunity. Indeed they have been rewarded for it to the tune of billions of dollars. Well, we are saying: enough. It stops, right here, right now."

Pascal and Akim stood dazed as they watched the screen. They both glanced up as Samira joined them, a wan, tired smile on her face. 'I've done all I can for him,' she said. 'Now we'll see. I have managed to stabilize his pulse and breathing, but they are still erratic and at a very low rate. We can only watch and wait. I believe he will either pull through or not make it and we shall know by morning.'

Pascal went over to Floyd. He lay, still looking like a corpse, but she could discern a light lifting and falling of his chest. Perhaps he looked peaceful rather than dead. 'I'll take first watch,' she said. 'Why don't you two get some sleep?'

Samira and Akim nodded and went up the stairs. Pascal guessed they had a lot to talk about.

It was 4 a.m. when the FBI finally released Calver, Anita and Joel. They climbed into the car with Agent Dalmus's words ringing in their ears, that they were still under suspicion. They were not to go anywhere without checking in, and the FBI would want to speak to them again. If Pascal contacted them and they didn't report it, they would become accessories. Calver couldn't summon the energy to argue with him, he just wanted to get some sleep.

As he drove through the early morning landscape it felt surreal. Anita voiced their thoughts. 'So where the hell is Courtney? And where's my dad?'

'I'm pretty sure we're going to find out, maybe sooner than you think,' he said.

Pascal could feel the hand on her shoulder, shaking her, so she turned her head and it was John Irving with half his face missing, one red eye glaring at her, full of accusation. She snapped her eyes open to see Samira's smiling face hovering above her with a cup of steaming coffee.

'Wake up, Courtney. Its gone 11,' she said.

'What the..' Pascal said as she scrambled upright on the living room couch. 'Why didn't you wake me? Is Floyd okay? Did he make it?

'Calm down. Floyd is fine. He's sitting up drinking coffee, much like you,' she said.

Pascal relaxed a bit and reached for the cup. 'Thanks, Samira. What's happening?'

'I woke you partly because we're expecting an announcement from the FBI any minute,' she said. She gestured at the TV and upped the volume.

There was a lectern with a mike and a crowd of reporters sitting in chairs facing it. The FBI chief with his retinue filed in and he stepped up to the mike:

"Good morning ladies and gentlemen. I'm here to update you on the search for Courtney Pascal, Akim Mohamed and Floyd Ritter. I hope shortly to be in a position to announce that they have been taken into safe custody. Earlier today our office received the original tape that has been watched so many times on our major news channels. That footage was from a copy, but we have now had time to analyze the original tape, and our experts agree it is genuine. Earlier this morning our agents arrested Antonio Cimino and Tennessee police chief Cyrus Gillespie and others, at an after-hours police club in Nashville. Furthermore, in consultation with the Justice department and the Office of The President, we are to give serious consideration to the dropping of all charges against Floyd Ritter and the granting of a formal acquittal or pardon. Not only that, a warrant has been issued for the arrest of the Greenberg Metro Bank CEO, Lloyd de Masi, and his associates. Corporate manslaughter charges may also follow. Agents are currently on site negotiating the withdrawal of protesters and the orderly and safe arrest of those persons. "

As Pascal watched, they heard a voice outside, coming through a loud hailer. 'This is the FBI. You are surrounded. Come out with your hands up. You have 1 minute before we come in.'

Above they heard the sound of a helicopter, then sirens. Pascal pulled a curtain aside and peeked out. The street was barricaded with law enforcement vehicles and she could see throngs of black clad agents with guns.

She stood up as Akim joined them. She looked at the cousins and smiled. 'Come on. Lets go,' she said. She moved to the door, pulled it open and stepped out with her hands up.

Epilogue

They sat around the large circular dining table; Calver, Pascal, Floyd, Joel and Anita Ritter, Mercy and Fingers. They had finished their meal and were all slightly juiced on the restaurants house red. It was a celebratory meal. Floyd was a free man and De Masi and Cimino had been indicted for murder.

'So tell us the truth, Courtney,' Anita said. 'Were you really going to raid GMB's bank accounts and pay all that money out to food stamp recipients?'

'You bet. If boy wonder here had hacked it like I asked,' she said looking pointedly at Fingers.

'Hey, man. You didn't give me nearly enough time,' he said. 'Anyway, GMB is history. Gonna be broken up. And no bail outs this time.'

Pascal looked across the table at Mercy who had been quiet most of the evening. 'Penny for your thoughts, Mercy?' she said.

'Oh, I been thinking about leaving Riverbend,' she said quietly, as if still wrestling with some indefinable issue.

'Good idea,' Calver said. 'You've been exonerated of any wrongdoing, but maybe thats just for the media, while they're watching, if you know what I mean.'

'I agree,' Anita said. 'But what you gonna do?'

'I been thinking I'd like to set up some type of charity or support unit to help abused women.'

'Good idea,' Pascal said. 'You'd be ace at it. Go for it girl.'

'You know,' Floyd said. 'I may be getting some serious money rolling in soon from the compensation cases Jonas and Ned are working on. And I might just stay here in Tennessee now. I was born here and I got to say, I've kind of got to like it again. Anyway, Mercy, I got a similar kind of idea. Set up an outfit to help death row prisoners. Maybe we could get together, see what happens?'

'Cool,' Fingers said. 'Maybe you got room for a wunderkind hacker in there somewhere?'

'Yeah, but you gotta stop wearing those bandannas,' Mercy said with a giggle.

THE END